ALSO BY TATE JAMES

MADISON KATE
Hate
Liar
Fake
Kate

HADES
7th Circle
Anarchy
Club 22
Timber

FAKE

TATE JAMES

Bloom books

Copyright © 2020, 2024 by Tate James
Cover and internal design © 2024 by Sourcebooks
Cover design by Antoaneta Georgieva/Sourcebooks
Cover images © Getty Images, Marilyn Nieves/Getty Images, Michael Dunning/Getty Images

Published by Bloom Books, an imprint of Sourcebooks
P.O. Box 4410, Naperville, Illinois 60567-4410
(630) 961-3900
sourcebooks.com

Originally self-published in 2020 by Tate James.

Cataloging-in-Publication data is on file with the Library of Congress.

Printed and bound in the United States of America.
PAH 10 9 8 7 6 5 4 3 2

To making smart choices and owning our own bullshit.

CHAPTER 1

Archer

"Congratulations, *Mrs. D'Ath*. Welcome to the family."

My brother's words hung in the air like a death knell. Damn, they were exactly that because there was no way in hell she would forgive me for this.

I couldn't look at her. My head refused to turn and see what was sure to be horror and betrayal passing over her beautiful face. I didn't need to. Not when Kody's tortured expression said it all as his gun arm lowered and his eyes pleaded with her.

She wasn't looking back at him, though. I knew her better than I knew myself some days. The staggering silence that followed Zane's words told me how she would react to this new development. She wouldn't yell or scream or punch me…no matter how much I hoped she would.

From the corner of my eye, I caught her stooping to swipe the folded papers off the step. She didn't look at them, just stuffed them into her back pocket and gave a short nod.

"Thank you for letting me know," she told my brother, and the ice in her voice was like a jagged blade straight through my heart.

Zane's brows shot up in surprise, his eyes shifting to meet mine once more. He didn't know her, though. He couldn't sense the cold, acidic fury coursing faster through her veins with every passing second. He hadn't witnessed her highs and lows, and he had no idea that this was worse than all of those lows combined.

I was fucked. Totally, completely, utterly fucked.

But I would still do it again. Given the same choice, offered the same opportunity to buy her, to own her and all her assets? Yeah, I'd do it again. In a fucking heartbeat.

"MK, it's not what it sounds like," Kody started to say, his voice threaded with panic and his gun at his side, forgotten, as he implored the girl he'd fallen in love with.

She wasn't listening. The second Zane had dropped his truth bomb, she'd shut us out. All of us… Because regardless of the fact that it was me who'd purchased her like a fucking prize cow at market, both Kody and Steele were complicit. They'd known all about it, about how deeply intertwined our lives now were, and they'd kept my secret.

In that light, their betrayal had to be so much more cutting. They'd made her care for them… They'd fallen for her in return. That, surely, was a bigger crime than what I'd done.

At least I've never fucked her.

Anger burned through me as I eyed my brother, ignoring everyone else for a minute. They'd directly violated the rules of our agreement, and crimes like that couldn't go unpunished. I'd proven my point to Zane over and over, but apparently all it took for him to forget those bloody lessons was a pair of great tits and some silken pink hair.

"Boss," Cass said quietly in his damaged voice, "we should go."

Smart move. Cass had known me since I was a kid; he'd been there as my grandfather put me through training. Hell, he'd been through it himself. He—even more so than Zane—understood what I was capable of. He'd sensed the shift in my mood and recognized the impending danger.

Zane gave me a small, cruel smirk, and a growl of anger burned through me. He claimed he was doing this for some debt he owed Kate's dead mother? I called bullshit. He was doing this to hurt me, and it was working. That motherfucker.

Cass and Zane climbed back onto their motorcycles, kicking the engines over. Kody shot me a confused look, and I knew exactly what he was asking me. Was I going to let them leave unharmed? Probably not. But it was more fun to leave the illusion of freedom, only to shoot out their tires right before they exited the property. Then? Well...then I daresay my big brother was well overdue for a lesson on exactly why I was a bigger, badder wolf in Shadow Grove than anyone else.

"Wait," Madison Kate shouted, her voice like a bucket of ice water over my bloodthirsty plans. She stepped over the bloody heart—the one stalker gift I was glad to see—and approached the two Reaper leaders. "I'm coming with you."

She didn't wait for permission, just climbed onto the back of Cass's bike like she fucking belonged there, linking her hands around his waist in a way that sparked my anger to murderous levels.

Cass was a fucking dead man.

"Hellcat, don't do this," Steele pleaded, his silent resolve cracking. "Don't fucking run from us. Please, baby, you need to hear us out."

For a moment, I thought he'd got through to her. Those violet-blue eyes of hers flickered with pain—and any emotion was better than the cool mask shuttering her true feelings away. But as quickly as it came, it shut back down. Her eyes flicked away from Steele like he no longer existed in her world.

"Go," she ordered Cass in a whip-crack voice. "There's nothing left for me here."

He was smarter than that, though—certainly smart enough that he hesitated and his brow creased ever so slightly with indecision.

"Boss?" he asked Zane, seeking direction.

"You can't be fucking serious!" Kody exploded, shaking his head in disbelief. "Arch, do something. You know you can."

Zane met my gaze, his lips curled in a smug grin of victory, and sour hatred filled my body. I wanted to kill him so fucking bad. The only reason he was still breathing was that he served a purpose in running the Reapers. That usefulness was fast running out.

"MK, come on," Steele tried again, taking two steps closer to where she perched on the back of Cass's motorcycle. "*Please*, trust us. Don't run."

"Archer!" Kody snapped. "Say something. Fucking anything."

But what the fuck could I say? Zane hadn't lied. He hadn't even misled her, although I had no idea what was in those papers, what proof he'd provided. But it didn't matter, did it? Money had changed hands, her piece-of-shit father had had his bad debts cleared and his life saved. All it'd cost him was his only child.

What a bargain.

When I said nothing, Kate's curiosity won out. I'd known it would. Her eyes met mine for one tense, soul-destroying moment. Her expression was shuttered, her pain and fury tucked carefully away behind a mask of indifference, but I knew it was there. She couldn't hide from me.

"Let her go," I finally said, holding her gaze and giving away nothing in my own. Two peas in a pod, we were. A match forged in the blood-drenched bowels of hell.

"What?" Kody exclaimed at the same time that Steele shouted a curse.

I let a small smile touch my lips because if there was one thing I was good at, it was getting under my wife's skin. All the better now that she knew the truth. We were married and had been for over a year.

Happy belated anniversary, babe.

"Let her go," I repeated, bleeding smug satisfaction into my smile and locking down all the howling pain inside me. "She knows she can't escape me forever."

This provoked a reaction from her, just as I'd expected. It was small, just a fractional lift of her brows, but the message she conveyed was clear.

Bring it on, motherfucker.

The roar of motorcycle engines filled the air as Zane and Cass took off, carrying my wife with them, and I did nothing to stop them. My vicious plans were abandoned as quickly as they'd been formed because there was no way I'd shoot out their tires when she was involved.

They knew it too, those bastards. Kate was their shield, and they'd keep her close to save themselves from my retaliation. That knowledge both infuriated me and eased my mind. As badly as I wanted to tear carnage through the Reapers for this breach of the rules, for this literal act of war against me...I couldn't. They'd keep her safe, guarded, protected, and that was something I'd failed miserably at recently.

Maybe she would be better off with Zane and his gang of criminal misfits, at least until we could neutralize the threats against her.

The three of us stood there in silence as the two bikes disappeared through the main gates of our estate; then Kody turned to me with an accusation clearly written all over his face.

I closed my eyes but didn't flinch. I knew what was coming well before his fist met my cheek, snapping my head back and making my ears ring.

I deserved that. And more.

"This is on you, Arch," he seethed, glaring daggers as I squinted back at him and dabbed my lip. He'd split it open, but I'd wager he wanted to do a whole lot worse. "This whole fucking mess could have been avoided if you'd been honest with her from day fucking one!"

5

I gave him a casual shrug, totally at odds with the screaming turmoil inside me. "Well, you know what they say about crying over spilled milk. She'll get over it."

This time I didn't see the punch coming—despite how badly I deserved it—because it came from Steele and was delivered solidly to my kidneys. He may not have any interest in fighting competitively, but he'd trained with Kody and me for years. That fucker could make a punch hurt.

"You fucked up, and you dragged us down with you," Steele growled, his fists clenched like he wanted to keep hitting me. "And you're not fooling fucking anyone with this blasé attitude, Arch. Just because you refused to fuck her doesn't mean you haven't fallen just as hard."

I grunted but couldn't force the denial past my lips. He was wrong, though. I'd kept her at arm's length because I'd known this day was coming. They should have done the same.

The two of them gave me disgusted, disappointed looks and stalked back into the mansion—my mansion—without another word. Understandable, considering there was literally nothing else to say. Nothing could take back what I'd done over a year earlier, and nothing could fix the betrayal and heartbreak Kate must be feeling now.

I sank down on the front steps, sitting my ass right beside the bloody lump of meat which had once sustained a rapist Wraith. Her stalker and I seemed to be more alike than I'd originally realized, considering I'd sent Kody out during the night to kill that piece of shit Wraith himself.

Scrubbing a hand over my scruffy stubble, I released a heavy sigh.

The cat was out of the bag, and now I needed to figure out where we went from here. Did I even really want to bring her home?

Of course, that wasn't even a question. Because deep down I

knew the answer. I'd known the answer to that underlying question for years, ever since I'd held the hand of a frightened eleven-year-old girl while she watched through the window as my father executed a man.

Did I regret my choices? Not a fucking chance. Owning her meant she was safe. She was free from servitude. But more important than anything else…it meant she was *mine*. And that was something she could never change.

CHAPTER 2

Madison Kate

Trepidation curled through my belly as Bree turned her car into the familiar driveway of Shadow Grove University. It'd been four weeks since that day on the front steps of Danvers Mansion—sorry, I meant *D'Ath* Mansion—and I was nowhere near ready to face my new reality yet.

But unfortunately for me, SGU wasn't going to go pushing the semester start date back so I could take a couple more mental health days hidden away in Bree's Aspen chalet, so here we were.

"I mean, they're probably not even going to be here," Bree offered with a hopeful shrug. "Didn't you say Steele was graduating after finals?"

I sighed heavily and stared out the window. It was still snowing, but it lacked the magic of Aspen. There was something about ski resorts that made them feel so totally removed from the rest of the world. They were quieter and cozier. It was so easy to forget all my real-life problems when, for four weeks in a row, all I needed to do was catch the first ski lift of the morning, then come back and drink mulled wine.

"I don't want to talk about them, Bree," I told her in a tired groan. We'd only returned from Aspen the day before and had spent the rest of the day and night decorating my new apartment. For some reason I'd gotten it into my head that my bedroom *needed* to be painted before I could settle in, so Bree had come over with wine and Chinese and we'd spent half the night playing interior decorator.

She bit her lip, shooting me a sheepish look as she stopped her car in a vacant spot some way from the campus buildings. We'd both overslept, so we were lucky to get a space at all.

"Right, of course," she said with a nod. "No more mentions of those-who-shall-not-be-named."

We piled out of her car and I shivered as the cold air bit through my sweater before I got a chance to pull my winter coat on. Bree checked her phone, smiling all girly, and I couldn't help smiling.

"Dallas?" I asked, and her cheeks flushed.

"Yup," she replied, all cagey and shit as she tucked her phone back in her bag. "Just wishing us luck for the first day back."

I laughed. "Uh-huh, sure he was. Pretty sure that wouldn't make you blush like that."

After everything that had gone down the night of Archer's fight, Bree and Dallas had been able to sort things out pretty quickly. Neither one of them had mentioned that weird interaction again—when Bree had thought Dallas was hitting on me—and they seemed totally smitten with each other. So I was happy for them.

He'd visited us once in Aspen, just after Christmas, but otherwise it'd been all hushed, late-night phone calls and dirty texts. It was cute as shit. It gave me hope that one day maybe I'd be able to move on from the three time bombs who'd detonated my heart and left it splattered all over the steps of the fake Danvers Mansion.

"So, do you know if Scott actually managed to transfer here?" Bree asked, linking arms with me as we made our way to the lecture halls. "He seemed pretty determined to make it happen." She waggled her brows at me, and I gave her a flat glare back.

"Stop it," I muttered, feeling my own cheeks heat. Except mine wasn't the fuzzy, loved-up glow that she got when Dallas dirty texted. Mine was embarrassment... I think. "He was just talking it up to try to get me to sleep with him."

Bree snorted a laugh. "No shit."

Scott was someone we'd met on a night out in an Aspen bar after a long day on the snow. He was a part-time snowboarding instructor and had been pretty forward about asking me out. I'd refused—thanks to my severely damaged trust in men and my shattered heart—and he'd become a pretty good friend to us in the weeks since. A flirty friend, for sure—he'd made no secret of the fact that he was attracted to me—but a friend nonetheless.

When it had come time for Bree and me to start packing up to return to Shadow Grove, Scott had declared he was transferring from Newton College. We'd all been decently drunk at the time, so we'd laughed it off. But the next day he'd left Aspen with a promise to see us on Monday morning.

"I mean, it'd be cool if he did," I added thoughtfully. "I could probably do with a few more friendly faces around here."

Bree scoffed. "Please. As if you need anyone else besides me. Come on, let's get inside and learn some shit." She cuddled into my side tighter, and we walked in sync into the main building, even while my nervous jitters increased with every step we took.

What were the odds of not seeing the guys at all? Bad, probably. The whole reason we'd left Shadow Grove and gone to Aspen was their relentless attempts to make me speak with them. Or Kody and Steele, anyway. I hadn't heard a damn thing from Archer himself. No calls, no texts, no showing up on Bree's doorstep uninvited...nothing.

Archer D'Ath.

My husband.

Just acknowledging that fact in my head turned my stomach and made my confident stride falter. The paperwork Zane had provided me with that day had been a copy of my marriage certificate. A marriage I hadn't even been present for. But as my consulted legal counsel had told me, good luck trying to prove that in court. It certainly looked like my signature on the certificate, and my father had signed off as my guardian. The documents had all been completed just before my eighteenth birthday, when I was still a minor.

The other document Zane had gifted me with was a bank statement showing multiple *enormous* payments made the same day that my marriage had been made official. I didn't have the stomach to dig any further into those accounts, but I could guess what they were. Archer had paid off all my father's bad debts in exchange for…*me*.

But why? That was what I couldn't understand. The amount of money he'd paid for my forced marriage was more than ten times what my inheritance was worth. So *why* pay it? He certainly hadn't bought me as a sex slave, like his great-grandfather had with Ana all those years ago. I'd basically begged him to fuck me, and he'd refused. So what the hell had he spent the money on?

Sure as hell couldn't have been my sparkling personality.

Unless this was all some elaborately sick mind game. Maybe that was why he'd been fine with his friends having their wicked ways with me, knowing that one day he could clamp a collar around my neck and yank the leash.

Fucking hell. I was giving myself a stomach ulcer just thinking about all the possibilities when I'd done such a good job putting it out of my mind in Aspen. I guess Scott had helped a bit with that. When he was around, he commanded so much attention, it was hard to think about anything else. Any*one* else.

Bree and I stepped through the doors into the building we both shared for this time slot, and she heaved a sigh. "I guess this is where

I leave you," she lamented. "You sure you don't want to switch to my nice, easy arts degree? Then I could move into your apartment and we could spend every waking minute together!" She beamed at me, and I rolled my eyes.

"We would kill each other in a week. Have fun, girl. I'll see you at lunch."

I left her and let myself into my first class of the day, hoping I wasn't too late. I whispered a quick apology to the professor on my way past, but she just arched a brow at me and continued talking. I quickly slid into the first empty seat I could see and hurried to pull my laptop out of my bag as silently as possible.

"Hey," the guy beside me whispered, and I did a double take when I realized who I'd sat down beside.

"Bark," I whispered back, "hey. Sorry, I wasn't even paying attention. How are you?"

He quirked a funny smile at me, then shifted his attention back to the projector screen that our professor was talking about. I thought for a moment he wasn't going to reply, so I opened my own laptop to take notes.

"I should ask you that," he murmured after a moment, giving me a sidelong look. "Last time I saw you, you were pretty out of it. Then there were ambulances, and someone said you'd overdosed on something?" His raised brow conveyed all of his questions around that, and I sighed.

"I'm fine," I replied, keeping it brief. "Someone spiked my drink." His eyes widened in shock, and I shook my head. "Like I said, Bark, I'm fine."

I shifted in my seat, making a clear point that I was interested in concentrating on the lecture and not in continuing our conversation. Bark let the subject drop, but I caught him stealing more than one curious glance at me throughout the class. When it was over, I grabbed my shit and bolted before he could ask me anything else.

Call me crazy, but I wasn't eager to stand around and chat about the most recent near-death experience I'd had. The fact that I'd had more than one was enough to keep me awake most nights as it was.

Bark called out after me, but I was already pushing through the door and hurrying down the corridor with my head down and my long, rose-colored hair creating a shield around my face.

Of course, that meant I didn't see where I was going until I'd run straight into someone's chest. Someone's hard, muscular chest. Someone's *very* familiar chest that smelled unmistakably of oak and subtle florals.

Ah, fuck.

Sucking in a sharp breath, I tossed my hair back and raised my chin to meet his eyes.

It was the meeting I'd been both dreaming about and dreading for four weeks and one I'd replayed in my mind over and over, testing out different insults and opening lines to craft the perfect encounter with my *husband*. Yet none of that could have prepared me for the staggering sense of pain, betrayal, and loss that tore through me on meeting his cold blue eyes in person.

Instantly I knew I wasn't ready for this confrontation. Not yet. Maybe not ever.

I tossed aside all those cutting one-liners I'd carefully prepared and simply skated my gaze away from his eyes like he was a total stranger.

"Excuse me," I said quietly, not giving in to the wild tundra of emotions churning within me and tearing strips out of my soul. "I wasn't watching where I was going."

I made to move around him like he meant exactly *nothing* to me, but he grabbed my wrist in a bruising grip before I could make it more than two steps. A sharp tug saw me turn back to face him, and his mask slipped a fraction, showing me a glimmer of guilt and regret.

Or maybe that was simply what I wanted to see because in a heartbeat it was gone again.

"Don't be childish, Princess Danvers," he told me in a cutting tone. One that made me want to grab his nuts in my hand and twist.

I arched a cool brow, refusing to let him under my skin. Not visibly anyway.

"Don't you mean, Princess *D'Ath*? Or would I be a queen?" I cocked my head to the side, meeting his eyes with my carefully practiced mask in place. We could have been discussing the price of postage for all the emotions I betrayed. Movement behind Archer caught my attention and my heart raced. Of course, the three of them were never far away from each other, but *fuck me*, I wasn't ready to face the trifecta of fake fucks all at once. Nowhere near ready.

Kody and Steele were heading our way, and I only had seconds to make my escape before I lost my shit in the middle of SGU and forced the dean to call in the coroner. Because no way were all three of them walking away from that conversation alive.

"Maddie, babe," a familiar voice greeted me a second before a strong arm was slung over my shoulders, "there you are. I was looking all over for you!" My new friend Scott grinned down at me with mischief sparkling in his hazel eyes. He knew all about Archer, Kody, and Steele. I'd spilled *everything* on New Year's Eve when I'd had way too many shots of peach schnapps and turned into weepy-drunk MK. So what exactly was he up to?

His gaze shifted from mine, and he frowned down at Archer's fingers around my wrist.

"Uh, bro, you got a good reason for grabbing my girl like that?" Scott raised a brow at Archer, seeming not even slightly intimidated by my surprise-husband's size and general air of danger.

Archer's lips twisted like he'd just tasted something sour. "Excuse me? Who the fuck are you?" He let go of my wrist, though, and I retracted it before he could change his mind. The fact that my arm happened to loop around Scott's waist was just a coincidence.

Scott gave Archer a quick up-and-down glance, then sneered like he was unimpressed. It was a hell of an act, and even I had to admit I was a bit impressed. I hadn't known he was such a good faker. Then again, that seemed to be a common theme around the men in my life, so why should I be so surprised?

"I'm her boyfriend. Who the fuck are *you*?".

Oh shit.

I'd had no idea that's how far he was going to take it. Had he forgotten to put his fucking brain in his head this morning? Anyone within a sixty-mile radius could see Archer wasn't the kind of guy you messed with, and the look on his face when Scott had said that...

"Madison Kate," Archer growled out from behind clenched teeth, "can I have a word with you? Alone."

Kody and Steele had reached us now, and I swallowed back a groan.

"No thanks," I replied to Archer, keeping my tone cool. I looked up at Scott and pasted a smile on my face. He'd already done the damage by declaring himself my boyfriend; there was no sense in ruining it now. "Come on, babe, you can walk me to psych."

Scott smiled down at me like I was his whole world. Like we were totally in love and my three violent, dangerous ex-*somethings* weren't standing mere feet away with murder painted across their features.

"It'd be my honor, beautiful girl."

We moved together, walking away from Archer, Steele, and Kody and letting the crowd of SGU students swallow us up. But just before we turned the corner, Scott paused and flashed a quick look over his shoulder. Then, before I could fully process what was happening, his lips were on mine in a kiss that acted like a bucket of ice water over my head.

He broke it off before I could shove him away, but the smile on his face was pure smug satisfaction. The way he shot another look in the direction we'd come said it all. He'd done that for the benefit of our audience… But holy shit, we needed to discuss some ground rules.

"Come on, Mads." He laughed, slinging his arm back around my shoulders again. "I told you everything would change this year. I've got your back, babe."

A chill trailed down my spine as I let him lead me in the vague direction of my next class. He had no idea what he'd stepped into blindly. If I didn't do something soon, I'd probably wake up tomorrow to find Scott's head delivered to my doorstep.

Except this time, it would likely be courtesy of my husband and his friends.

Fucking hell. So much for pretending they didn't exist.

CHAPTER 3

There was no time to speak with Scott about that kiss or his announcement that he was my boyfriend to three of—I was fast learning—the scariest motherfuckers in Shadow Grove.

Actually, I was just going to call it what it was. I didn't get a chance to talk to Scott about his *suicide attempt* in the halls of SGU this morning, but I made him promise not to do anything stupider before we could speak during my lunch break.

Of course, I should have known the guys wouldn't just leave it alone.

Five minutes into my third lecture of the day, the door slammed open, and I stifled a groan when I recognized the intruder. Clearly my professor did too, because he made no attempt to kick him out. Despite the fact that he most definitely wasn't a student in this class.

I scowled down at my laptop as he made his way across the room and stopped right beside the guy seated next to me.

"Move," Kody ordered the poor kid, who looked ready to faint as he scrambled to gather his shit up and flee to the back of the room. When the seat was vacant, Kody sat down and reclined like he owned the whole damn school.

Fuck. Maybe he did. I legitimately knew *nothing* about Kodiak

Jones, and suddenly I was questioning every small scrap of information he'd ever given me.

"Is that even your fucking name?" I asked him, letting my angry thoughts spill out before I could get a lid on them.

He turned to me with an arched brow. "Because Kodiak Jones is the kind of name I would pick as an alias?"

I shrugged, shifting my gaze back to the lecture screen. "Who knows? You've lied to me about everything else."

Kody was silent for a moment, and I could practically feel his frown. "Yeah, but I'd totally pick a cooler name. Like…"

I rolled my eyes, unable to help myself. "Like Max Steele?"

"I see your point. But I promise it's not a fake name."

"Because your promises are worth so fucking much," I replied in an acidic mutter. "What are you even doing here? You're not in this class."

He sat forward, leaning his elbows on the desk and staring at the side of my face. It was disconcerting, to say the least, and made it hard as fuck to keep my attention on the lesson and not look at him.

"But you are. So now I am too." His tone was so smug, I shot a sharp look at him, then instantly regretted my choice when his green eyes snared me. "I had a gap in my schedule and a burning desire to learn"—he trailed off, peering up at the projector screen before returning his gaze to my face—"sociological foundations. Really? Huh. Anyway. Here I am. Ready to learn."

I glowered at him, avoiding being caught by his hypnotic green eyes again. "Kody, I don't fucking want you here. Go away."

He just sat back, folding his arms over his chest. "Nah, I think I'll stay."

I sucked in a breath, counting to five in my head, then released it. He was trying to annoy me into talking to him, and so far it was working. Fucker.

Gritting my teeth, I turned my attention back to the lesson and tried my absolute best to ignore the fact that Kodiak fucking

Jones was sitting half a foot away from me. It wasn't easy. Especially when he shifted in his seat to stretch his arms over his head, making his shirt ride up and show off all those chiseled abs... Fucking hell.

"So, who's the dead man?" he asked after some ten or fifteen minutes of me pretending to ignore him yet focusing on him a hundred times harder than the lecture. I felt so freaking hurt and angry and betrayed by all three of them, but Kody made it *so* difficult to hold on to that.

I blinked a couple of times, focusing on what he'd said. "Huh?"

He arched a brow, leaning forward on the desktop again so that our faces were only inches apart. "The walking dead man." His voice was cold and lethal. Shit. "The one who deliberately kissed you in front of us this morning."

I groaned inwardly. Fucking Scott. I was kind of surprised Kody was here asking me about him rather than out in the woods somewhere burying his body in a shallow grave. I meant it as a joke, but a shiver ran through me at the edge of truth in that thought.

"Don't fucking touch him, Kody," I growled under my breath, giving up on taking notes from the projector screen and shifting in my seat to glare at him. "I mean it. You hurt him and I'll *never* speak to you again. Ever. Are we clear?"

He gave me a sidelong glance, running his thumb over his lower lip in a way that made me sigh in dread.

"Kody," I snapped, "are we fucking clear? Don't lay your damn hands on Scott or I'll castrate you."

His brow raised. "You'd have to touch my dick to do that... Now you're just giving me incentive."

My eyes narrowed with the promise of violence, and his grin spread wider.

"Okay, okay, I get it. From *this conversation* forward, we won't touch the walking dead man."

I scrubbed my hands over my face, the implication not lost on me. "Kody, what have you fucking done? If Scott's in the hospital or—"

Dead.

"He's not in the hospital, babe. Damn, we're not *that* bad. But I promise, I'll have words with the guys after class and let them know your little friend is off-limits for now."

These boys and their subtle edits of promises were going to be the death of me.

I blew out a long breath, picking my battles in order of urgency. "What did you do?"

A sly grin curled his lips. "Me? Nothing."

In other words, Archer or Steele was responsible. I'd put my money on Steele, considering how he'd escorted Bark to his car when they'd canceled my date with him. Fucking hell.

"Just…leave me alone, Kody," I muttered in a tired voice. "Pretend we never met or something. Act like you don't know me. It'd just be a hell of a lot easier for all of us."

He leaned closer, stroking my hair over my shoulder and making me shudder involuntarily. Kody playing with my hair was fast becoming one of my major turn-ons.

"I can't do that, MK," he whispered back, sounding broken and vulnerable for the first time in the whole time I'd known him.

A lump formed in my throat, and I needed to swallow before I could get words out. "Why not?"

Stupid me, I turned my face to meet his eyes and almost crumbled at the guilt and regret shining through his gaze.

"Because, babe," he replied, his whisper husky and raw, "no one can survive without their heart, and you're mine."

Fuck.

I tore my gaze away with almost physical pain, letting my hair drop like a curtain between us as I turned back to the lecture. Thank god for that too, as he wouldn't see the hot tear slip down my cheek at his words. Because if I really was his heart, how could he have betrayed me so badly?

Then again, I'd always known it was coming. Hadn't I?

Kody mercifully didn't say anything more, but he also didn't leave. For the rest of the class, he just sat silently beside me as I pretended to follow the lecture. My notes were probably total gibberish, but fuck it. When the lesson ended, I packed up my shit and bolted.

He let me.

It was actually surprising not to have him grab me or manhandle me or force me to talk to him the second we were out of class. But he did none of those things…probably because he knew his words had cracked my iron-clad exterior and taken root in my mind already.

Fucking hell. I could only hope he was joking about permanently signing up for that class, or this semester was going to be a thousand times harder than I'd mentally prepared for.

I ducked into a restroom, pulling my hidden phone out to text Bree. The "no phones on campus" rule was still enforced, but I'd grown accustomed to not being held accountable to rules while I was with the guys. Bree was just sneaky and handed in a fake phone at the gatehouse, like I was sure a heap of other students did. But I'd rather not flaunt it by texting in the corridors.

It was a simple "Meet me in the library" message, but when she didn't immediately reply, I anxiously tapped my phone against my lips, thinking.

I had no idea what class Scott might be in, and he wouldn't have disobeyed the no-phones rule. His older brother was a cop, so he was a total rule follower. I just hoped he was okay and Kody had been bullshitting me. Archer wouldn't have done anything. Why would he? For one thing, he wouldn't risk his UFC career by punching some random guy in public. For another, that bastard already thought he'd won. He *owned* me, so why would he care who kissed me?

Steele, though? Yeah, he might have.

One thing I'd learned with absolute certainty—those boys didn't fear repercussions. Not from law enforcement at any rate. It wouldn't shock me if they had the Shadow Grove Police Department on their payroll like actual gangsters. If that's what they were. Were they? Fuck, I had no idea. I was no closer to figuring the three of them out now than I'd been a month ago.

Secretive fucks. Well, not for long. I was going to pry them open like oysters, one way or another. I just had to figure out a way that wouldn't leave me broken and bleeding as a result.

"Shit," I breathed, tucking my phone back into my bag. I'd go to the library anyway and hope Bree got my message. There was no way I'd be able to concentrate on my next class anyway. Not with Kody dominating my fucking brain like he was.

I slipped back out of the bathroom, and my heart skipped when I spotted a familiar figure leaning against the wall opposite. The halls had cleared out somewhat as the new class time slot started, and there was really no way to hide.

But then again, who fucking cared for hiding?

His gray eyes met mine, his face cold and hard and his hood pulled up over freshly cropped hair, like he ever needed the added broodiness. The way he stared at me—guilty and remorseful and *accusing*—it was all too much to fucking deal with in the middle of SGU on my first day back. Nope. Just nope.

Decided, I shifted my gaze away from Steele's and started walking down the hall as though I hadn't even seen him there.

He didn't follow me, but I wasn't stupid enough to think that'd be the last of it.

They'd given me four weeks of space in Aspen, but now that I was back, they weren't content to sit back and stew any longer. This was always going to happen, and I'd known that. What we had together—Kody, Steele, and me—it was too fucking potent to just drop without a word. I knew it, but goddamn I wasn't ready to hash it all out. Not yet.

22

Sadly, Scott had forced the issue. There was no way on earth they'd just sit back and watch another guy lay his hands on me, place his lips on mine. Kody and Steele would be out for blood. Scott's…or mine.

At least Archer wouldn't get involved. Not until he received my divorce application anyway.

CHAPTER 4

Bree found me in our usual spot toward the back of the library about half an hour later. And she brought me a present.

"What the fuck were you thinking?" I all but screamed at Scott, then clapped a hand over my mouth to stifle my volume. No matter how cautious the staff were around me—thanks to my association with Archer and the guys—librarians were a whole other species. Those old birds weren't afraid of *anyone*, and I really didn't want to lose my nice, quiet thinking corner.

"Shh," he replied with a laugh. "It's a library, Maddie; keep your voice down."

I wrinkled my nose at his nickname for me. I didn't like it much, but I'd stupidly failed to correct him when he'd started using it. Now it was just too awkward.

Seething, I glared daggers until he lost the smile. The side of his face was puffy and purple and looked all kinds of painful. I bet he didn't even know how to defend himself properly in a fight, not that he'd stand a chance against *any* of the guys.

"What happened to your face, Scott?" I demanded, folding my arms over my chest as he and Bree sat down at my table. I knew full fucking well what had happened. His own recklessness. But I wanted to hear him admit he had been stupid.

His jaw clenched, though, and his eyes hardened with anger. I stifled a sigh. He hadn't even remotely learned his lesson.

"Scott..." I groaned, ruffling my hair with my fingers in frustration.

"I'm fine," he growled with an edge of anger. "I just tripped and face-planted into a wall."

I rolled my eyes. Fell into a wall. Like how Bark had fallen into his car door a few months ago? What a shocker.

"Dude," Bree commented with a snicker, "you forget to transfer your brain here with your body or something? Did you listen to *nothing* MK said about how dangerous those three are?"

Scott just scowled and folded his arms.

I drew a deep breath, thinking, then released it in a heavy sigh. "Okay, here's how it is. I'm not putting you in harm's way for my own revenge plans. You got off *fucking lucky* with that." I indicated his bruised face. "And I have no interest in being responsible for worse."

His brow dropped lower, and I didn't miss the way he flinched in pain when it pulled on his bruising. "Are you trying to say we can't be friends? Because that's bullshit, Maddie. They're fucking criminals and abusers, and you shouldn't let them get away with that shit. Babe, they lied to you for how long? And *used* you for sex all that time. They deserve to see you move on and be happy without them."

I flinched at his oversimplified version of events. It wasn't that cut-and-dried. They hadn't *used* me...no more than I had used them. I'd gone into those sexual relationships knowing full well they were hiding shit from me. I'd known all along that one day it'd all come crashing down around me and did it anyway. So no. They hadn't *used* me. But they had betrayed me and broken my heart. And that was a thousand times worse in my book.

"I didn't say we can't be friends, Scott," I replied, carefully calm so I didn't shatter into a million pieces all over the library floor.

"But you can't play this fake boyfriend card. It's going to get you killed."

His chin tilted with stubborn pride, and I groaned inwardly. He wasn't going to make this easy. "So what if it wasn't fake?" he pushed, a glimmer of excitement in his hazel eyes. "Be my girlfriend for real. You deserve someone who treats you better, Maddie."

Bree shifted in her seat and cringed when I shot her a glance. "This is awkward," she whispered. "I should really go and leave you to discuss this alone."

She didn't though.

I squeezed my eyes shut and rubbed my forehead. Like I seriously needed another pigheaded, stubborn-ass, prideful male in my life.

"Scott," I said finally, sighing for what seemed like the thousandth time. "No. I thought I was super clear about this when we met. I'm not interested in dating *anyone* right now. My life is way too complicated." *Not to mention I'm still legally married.*

Of course, I hadn't told him that part. Even when I'd been drunk and spilling my whole story, I couldn't voice that part out loud. That my father had sold me. That I'd been bought and paid for, property of Archer D'Ath.

Nope, even thinking it made me almost break out in hives. I'd just told him that they'd been hiding a life-changing secret and left it at that.

Scott wasn't backing down easily, though. "Maddie, I just want to be there for you," he said with a hurt frown. "You're so much better than those muscle-bound idiots. You need someone who respects you and worships you. I could be that guy."

Frustration took control of my tongue. "No, you can't."

Scott sat back, looking like I'd slapped him, and Bree let out a sound that seriously wasn't helping the situation.

"I just mean," I continued, trying to smooth over that clear

26

insult, "I don't want you getting hurt. Look what happened this morning, for fuck's sake! You got off easy too. I half expected to find you in the hospital when I heard they'd already gotten their hands on you." Scott opened his mouth to argue again, and I shook my head. "No, I'm serious, Scott. This is my mess to deal with. I don't want your life on my conscience just to make them jealous. Because that's all it'd be." I hammered that point home with a steady stare.

His frown deepened. "Well, that's not your choice, Maddie. If I want to do my part to help you make them pay, then that's *my* decision to make and my risk to take." He folded his arms again, and the look on his face was pure determination.

Fuck me.

I shot a glance at Bree, seeking help, but she just shrugged. "I say go for it," she offered with a smile. "You've warned him enough; if he still wants to stick his neck on the line to make your boys crazy with jealousy, then fucking let him."

I groaned. That *wasn't* what I'd been looking for from her. "Scott, they could literally kill you and clean it up so no one would ever know. This isn't some sort of game."

"And you've made this all perfectly clear, Maddie. I'm aware of the risks, and I still want to help. And who knows, maybe you'll realize I'm the right guy for you along the way." His smile was joking, but his eyes…not so much.

I shook my head. "This is a terrible idea."

Somehow, I convinced Bree and Scott to take lunch off campus with me, avoiding any more tense run-ins with the guys. After my last class of the day ended, I found all three of them lurking in the parking lot. Scott wouldn't finish for another hour, but thank fuck Bree was with me. She did exactly what I'd thought about doing a thousand times over the past four weeks.

27

"D'Ath," she snapped, storming up to him where he lazed against the side of his car. I wasn't dumb enough to think it a coincidence that he'd ended up parked right beside Bree. Not when he had his own reserved space directly in front of the main building.

Archer cocked a brow at Bree, giving her a dismissive once-over. And then she punched him in the face.

It was utterly brilliant. He hadn't seen it coming, so he made no attempt to dodge the strike. Her balled fist hit him straight in the eye, but then it was Bree who howled in pain because my poor, foolish friend had *no* idea how to throw a punch.

"What the fuck, Brianna?" Archer roared, clapping a hand to his face and glaring with his other eye.

Bree was moaning and clutching her hand to her chest but gave it a break to glare back at him. "You know you deserve worse, Archer," she snarled back at him. "Be thankful it wasn't your balls."

Steele and Kody just stared, shocked and way too amused.

I mean, I understood. I was barely containing laughter myself.

"Come on, Bree," I said, giving up on concealing the laughter in my voice. "Let's go. I'll get you some ice for that hand at my place." I took the keys from her pocket and unlocked her car, holding the door open in a clear message to *hurry the fuck up.*

"Your place?" Kody repeated, his amusement dissolving with a frown.

I gritted my teeth and refused to answer him. Kody was too fucking good at sliding past my defenses. Too good at cracking my resolve to ice them all out of my life. Permanently.

"Bree," I said when my friend just gave me panicked-rabbit eyes and clutched her hand to her chest. "Come on, let's go."

She cringed. "I don't think I can drive, girl. My hand really hurts." Her voice was tight with pain, and as she spoke her eyes welled up with tears.

Fucking hell.

"You probably broke your thumb," Steele commented, casual

28

as all fuck. "That's what happens when you don't form your fist properly."

"Wh-what?" Bree's eyes widened farther, and her face went ashen.

Steele just shrugged. "Probably. You shouldn't be driving until you get it checked out, though."

"It's fine," I snapped, my irritation boiling over. Not at Bree—she'd only been sticking up for me like a legit badass. She just had no clue what she was doing, and now the guys were going to exploit her injury for their own gain. Typical. "I'll drive," I announced, indicating Bree's car again. "Just get in; I'll take you to a clinic to get checked out."

Everyone stared at me in alarm at that. Everyone, including Archer.

"You're not driving," Archer told me, his tone harsh and final. I knew why too, and fuck if I didn't agree. But my stubborn pride wouldn't budge to make room for my PTSD over and dislike of driving, so no. Fuck that.

"Yes, I am," I replied, cocking a brow at him. "Bree, let's go."

She shook her head, and my heart sank.

"I'm sorry, girl. But I know how you are about driving on the best of days, let alone when you're all... *you know*." She wrinkled her nose at me and shot a seriously unsubtle look toward the guys. I wanted to argue, but tears were trailing down her cheeks. The way she held her hand told me she was really in pain.

"Kody will drive Bree to the clinic and get her checked out," Archer announced, giving orders like I gave a shit about his opinions. Spoiler alert, I didn't. "And I—"

"Can go meet Jase like you're supposed to," Steele finished for him. "Come on, Hellcat. I'll drive you home." He plucked Bree's keys from my fingers, then tossed them to Kody and wrapped his fingers around my wrist. He had me halfway across the parking lot before I could even formulate a protest.

29

I dug my heels in, wrenching my wrist out of his hold. "Stop manhandling me," I snarled. "I don't need you to drive me. I can call an Uber."

Steele blew out a long breath like I was throwing a temper tantrum in public, then arched his pierced brow at me. "That's not an option, Hellcat. It's me or Arch, your choice."

I glanced over my shoulder to see Bree's car pulling out of the parking lot already with Kody behind the wheel. Archer still remained, though, leaning against the door of his black Viper, staring at Steele and me. What the fuck was *his* problem? Kody and Steele, I understood. They wanted to apologize and make amends—if such a thing were ever possible—but Archer? He wasn't sorry. I could see it in his cold blue eyes.

But still, there was no way I wanted to be stuck in his car's small interior alone with him, so I took the lesser of two evils and reluctantly followed Steele to his bike. Thank fuck he'd brought his bike and not one of their cars. At least this way he couldn't talk to me while we drove.

CHAPTER 5

I tried to hold myself aloof as I slid onto the back of Steele's motorcycle, but the second my thighs pressed against his and my fingers touched the leather of his jacket...I crumbled.

Steele kicked the engine over and smoothly cruised out of the SGU parking lot with my arms wrapping tighter around him by the second. I almost didn't even notice that though I'd given him no directions to my new apartment, he seemed to know exactly where to go.

I'd put my trust in him that he'd take me home and *not* to their house, and apparently, he was going to do the right thing. For once. He didn't try to talk to me as he drove, and he didn't comment on the way my body stayed glued to his back like a second skin. When he pulled up in front of my apartment building, I took a second to pull my shit back together, and he didn't rush me.

Nor did he push the advantage. He and Kody were basically opposite sides of the coin in their approach to my anger.

"Thanks for the ride," I muttered, releasing his leather jacket with physical effort before sliding off the bike. I started to walk away, but he snagged the sleeve of my sweater, halting my escape and pulling me around to face him.

I heaved a reluctant sigh, and he took his helmet off to meet my eyes with concern shining from his own gray gaze.

"Hellcat…" he started, sounding pained.

I held my hand up, silencing him. "Stop calling me that, Steele. That's a nickname for someone you care for. Someone you trust. I'm neither of those things to you, and you've made that abundantly clear." Fresh pain rippled through me at those words from my own lips, but fuck it. Wasn't that the truth?

Steele's brow creased, but he didn't argue with me. He knew he'd fucked up.

"Why here?" he asked instead, motioning to the apartment building behind me. It was a new build and considerably nicer than I'd have expected from a Reaper-owned property. Then again, maybe I'd been letting gang stereotypes get to me. "This isn't safe, MK."

My heart sank when he called me MK and not Hellcat, even though that's exactly what I'd just told him to do. Stupid heart didn't know what was good for it.

"I disagree," I replied, folding my arms defensively. "In fact, I'd say this is probably the safest place for me right now."

Steele's shoulders sagged. "You know that's not true. You're safe with *us*."

I scoffed. "Am I, though? Because I've nearly died three times under your watch." It was a low blow, and I knew it. The stricken look on Steele's face made me want to immediately take the words back, but I couldn't. I *wanted* him to hurt because I was still in agony from his betrayal.

Pursing my lips, I sucked in a strengthening breath. "Zane offered me a place of my own, and considering my *husband* isn't providing me access to my finances, I was left with few other choices."

Steele sighed and scrubbed a hand over his buzzed-short hair. "Yeah, I get it. Just be careful, okay? Zane and the Reapers, they don't care about you. Not like we do. They just see you as a means to an end. A bargaining chip."

I shrugged, bitterness rising in my throat. "I think I prefer being a bargaining chip to being a possession."

His jaw tightened and his hand balled into a fist, but he didn't disagree with me. No matter how much he clearly wanted to.

I turned to walk away again, needing to create some physical distance between us. The longer I stood there talking to him, the fresher the memories were becoming—and not the ones that would help me maintain my righteous outrage either. They were the memories of all the sweet things he'd done or said, of the gentle music he'd played while I slept in his bed, or of the way he'd worshipped my body.

"Madison Kate," he called out as my hand reached for the glass door to the foyer. I paused, turning slightly to look back at him, still straddling his black motorcycle. "I understand that you need time and space right now, but you need to know…I'm not giving up on us. Not now, not ever." My pulse raced and my chest tightened. "I know I fucked up, *we* fucked up. But we're not going anywhere, and we'll do whatever it takes to fix this."

Frustration reared its ugly head, and I let it. Better that than the alternatives. "You can't fix this, Steele." I flung my arms out wide, trying to encompass *everything* that was broken. "Sometimes you just need to write off the truck and start over."

"You're not a fucking truck, MK." Steele's eyes hardened to granite, his jaw clenching in anger at my shitty analogy. I turned my back on him, not wanting to continue this conversation in public…or at all.

His motorcycle roared to life as I let the foyer door swing shut behind me, and I stalked over to the elevators without glancing back. As much as I hated to admit it, he'd dented my armor. I needed a solid bitch session with Bree to hammer the dents out and prepare for another onslaught the next day.

I wasn't stupid enough to think they'd give up so easily, and a small—okay, not so small—part of me was glad for that. As angry as I was, as hurt and heartbroken as they'd made me, I hadn't magically lost those feelings that had been developing before the truth bomb dropped. I wasn't fucking over them.

Any of them.

The elevator doors slid open on my floor, and I found my new neighbor on his way out of his apartment.

"Hey, Cass," I greeted him, trying to wipe the torrent of emotions off my face. The Reapers weren't my friends, and I wasn't about to go giving them anything to use against me later. Well… anything more than they already knew.

The ink-covered man just scowled at me. Also known as his resting *fuck you* face. It was like a resting bitch face but seven hundred times more threatening and intimidating.

"You look angry," he commented in a growl like breaking rock.

I hitched a brow, faintly amused. "Yeah, you could call it that."

Cass continued staring at me while I fished my keys out of my bag and unlocked my door. When he didn't say anything more, I paused with my hand on the door frame and cocked my head to the side.

"Is there something you need to say?"

His frown dipped a fraction deeper, if that was possible. "You got shit to do right now?" he asked, surprising the hell out of me. I'd thought he was just going to comment on… I dunno. The weather?

"Um," I replied, thinking about my bitch session with Bree, which could definitely wait. "No, not really. Why?"

The scary-ass gangster dude just nodded his head like he'd made his mind up about something. "Grab a change of clothes," he instructed me. "You can vent some of that rage on a punching bag."

My brows shot up, and I quickly took in his workout clothes and the duffel bag slung over his shoulder. Clearly, I'd caught him on his way to the gym.

"Hurry up," he added as I stood there gawking. "I don't have all day."

Curiosity—as always—won out in my brain, and I hurried into my new apartment to get changed. I barely had anything of my own, having walked out of my father's mansion—or *Archer's* mansion—with nothing but the clothes on my back. I'd been keeping a ledger of what I owed Bree, despite her insistence that I didn't need to pay her back, just the same as I was keeping a ledger of what I owed Zane for giving me a place to live.

When I regained what was rightfully mine, I'd be able to pay them both back. With interest. But until then, I was very much their charity case.

"Ready," I announced, leaving my apartment once more. I found Cass leaning on the wall beside the elevators looking decidedly bored.

His dark eyes gave me a brief once-over, and then he jerked a quick nod. "Let's go."

The gym he took me to was within easy walking distance and one of the Reapers' businesses, judging by the way the girl at the reception desk greeted Cass. He led the way across the busy gym to where heavy punching bags hung from the ceiling and dropped his duffel to the floor.

"You ever take a boxing class or something before?" he asked me. They were the first words he'd said since we left the apartment building, and I was sort of getting used to his silence.

"Uh, no," I replied, shaking my head. "Kody and Steele had just started giving me some self-defense training right before I left, but that's about it."

Cass grunted. "Self-defense, huh?"

I shifted my feet, thinking about the extra tricks Steele had been teaching me—how to break someone's fingers without a weapon or how to make a grown man pass out with just a pinched nerve in his neck. "Yeah, mostly."

The scary-ass dude just gave me a blank look, like he didn't believe me, then unzipped his bag to pull out a pair of boxing gloves. "You look like you work out. You'll be fine."

I glanced down at the huge gloves in his hands, then wrinkled my nose. He seemed to notice the same thing as me and frowned.

"Wait here," he ordered, dropping his gloves back into the bag and stalking in the direction of the reception once more.

More than a few of the guys working out in the gym gave me suspicious looks—some of them were even openly hostile—but I knew they wouldn't do shit when I was there under Cass's protection. I did, however, make a mental note to never come to the gym without him. Something told me more than a few Reapers begrudged my presence in their territory.

"Here," Cass grunted, returning with a pair of hot-pink boxing gloves in his hands, the tags still attached. He worked silently, taping my hands like I'd seen the guys do a hundred times, then helping me put the gloves on.

He showed me a couple of very basic moves, then pointed to a sandbag and instructed me to *do my worst*.

I was a bit sheepish at first, but when Cass rolled his eyes at me and suggested I picture Archer's face, things changed.

When Cass came back over to me some time later, I was sweaty and puffing and my arms were like jelly…but fucking hell, I felt better for it.

We didn't speak—shocker—as he helped me unwrap my hands and tucked the pink gloves into his duffel bag. He didn't offer to let me use the locker rooms at the gym, and I didn't ask. We just walked back to the apartment building as we were and silently made our way back up to our shared floor.

"Hey, Cass," I said as I reached my door and he continued along to his, "can we do that again sometime? I think I needed it."

He twitched a brow at me. "No shit." His mouth tightened, and then he gave a short nod. "Sure. I'll train you. But don't ever go to that gym without me. Lots of Reapers would love to try to send a message to your boys through you."

I scowled. "Not *my* boys."

Cass made a noise that I thought *might* be a laugh. "Sure thing, kid."

Yeah. I wasn't buying my bullshit either.

CHAPTER 6

The next week passed fairly uneventfully. Of course, Kody wasn't joking about transferring to my sociological foundations class, so I had to deal with him again on Thursday, and Steele had taken to just being freaking *everywhere*, so I couldn't get him out of my head.

One small mercy: I hadn't seen Archer again. Not once.

That should have made me happy, but come Friday, I found myself hitting the punching bag ten times harder than usual as I worked through all the complicated emotions his absence had caused me.

Cass hadn't been "training" me like Kody did with his clients. He mostly just gave me pointers or corrections, then let me vent all my frustration by belting the sandbag. The few instructions he did offer me, though, were incredibly helpful.

"You ever train anyone else?" I asked him on our way back to our apartment building after our session. "You're good at it."

Cass quirked a scarred brow at me. "A few."

He didn't elaborate, so I didn't push for answers. I'd never seen him speak to anyone other than me while we were there; he mostly just did his own thing while keeping an eye on me. So I could assume he wasn't *currently* training anyone else.

Outside our building, a familiar white convertible was parked with my perky, brunette friend leaning against the door.

"MK, babe! We're late. Did you forget?" Bree raised a brow at my appearance, all sweaty and exhausted, then eyed Cass with leering suspicion.

"Cut it out," Cass growled. "I don't fuck children." He stomped off inside, and I rolled my eyes.

"Seriously, Bree? We clearly just came from the gym. Not to mention he's probably got a good fifteen years on us." I glared at her, and she just shrugged.

"No judgments here," she replied with a grin. "He's hot. I'd do him…if I wasn't already taken."

I sighed, parking my hands on my hips. "Dinner and movies in Rainybanks. I had forgotten, sorry." How I'd managed that, I had no idea. Bree had literally reminded me less than three hours ago when she dropped me home from school. "Give me like five minutes to change."

My friend wrinkled her nose. "Maybe take ten. It's supposed to be a double date; you could put in, like, a fraction of effort."

I groaned heading into my building and pushed the call button for the elevators. "It's not a fucking double *date*, Bree. It can't be when Scott and I *aren't dating*."

Stepping into the elevator with me, she snorted a laugh. "Okay, sure, how's that denial going for you, MK? Because you're literally the only person who believes you're not dating. He's been all freaking over you this week."

Irritation welled up in me, and all the work I'd just done on the punching bag flew out the window. Scott *had* been acting like we were a couple all week, but I'd also been letting him. I'd thought he understood it was only in public and only for the sake of Kody and Steele…and Archer. But she was right. Scott *wasn't* getting the message.

"I'll have a chat with him tonight," I muttered as I unlocked my apartment and let her inside. "Kody said he'd hold off the dogs for now, but I think we both know that will have an expiration date."

"So what?" Bree shrugged. "You warned him. I warned him. Fucking *Steele* warned him when he slammed his face into a wall on day one. If he wants to stick his neck on the line over some misguided hope that you'll wake up tomorrow and realize he's your soul mate, let him. You need people on your team, MK. No matter what their reasons are."

"Disagree," I called out as I headed through to my bedroom to find some clothes. "I don't want to lead him on, Bree. He's been a good friend to us so far, but I get the feeling he could turn into a nasty enemy."

Bree wandered into my room and flopped down on the bed. "True. Okay fine, tone down the sexy tonight, and I'll make plenty of pointed comments about what great *friends* you are. There's no reason for him to be all handsy unless one of your guys is around."

I rolled my eyes at her calling them *my* guys…but I also couldn't stop the flutter of possession in my gut. Yeah, I was mad as hell, but they were still *mine* to punish.

Agreeing, I grabbed all my fresh clothes and took a lightning-fast shower to rinse off the sweat from my boxing session with Cass. I put minimal effort into my makeup—I would have skipped it completely, but in the back of my mind, there was that possibility that one of the guys would see me. They did have a talent for showing up wherever I was.

Once I was dressed, Bree and I headed out of the building only to run into Zane and another guy on their way in.

"Madison Kate," Archer's brother greeted me with a predatory smile. "You look nice. Hot date with the preppy kid, huh?"

My brows shot up. "You been watching me, Zane?"

His grin spread wider. "Of course. I keep eyes on all my assets."

A chill ran through me. That's exactly how he saw me, and I shouldn't forget it. I was an asset, a valuable one—right now—but nothing more. While I was under the Reapers' protection, I needed to get used to that mentality because I sure as shit wasn't one of them and Zane's sense of duty to his dead lover's daughter only extended so far.

"Well, then. Yes," I replied with a tight smile.

Zane shifted his attention to Bree. "And your Wraith boyfriend too?"

Bree's face froze like a deer in headlights. If deer had perfect eyebrows, of course.

"Um," she replied, "yup. That a problem, D'Ath?" Her words were coated in enough attitude that even I gave her a double take. Where had all this spunk suddenly come from?

Zane stared at her for a tense moment, and the guy with him shifted uncomfortably, like he expected the worst. But then the Reapers' leader tossed his head back and laughed.

"I like you, Brianna Graves. You ever get bored of that punk, Moore, you'd have fun with the Reapers." Zane shot my bestie a dangerous wink and carried on into the building with his companion. He paused before the door swung shut, though, and called out to me.

"Careful with the preppy kid, Madison Kate. His brother is on the wrong side of the coin."

I sighed as Bree unlocked her car, and we climbed in. Of course, Scott's older brother couldn't just be a nice, boring Shadow Grove officer. Zane'd just implied he was under the pay of *someone*, and I'd guess it was the Wraiths, based on the distasteful look Zane had given me as he said that.

"Well," Bree commented, turning her engine on and giving me a wide grin. "That was interesting."

My jaw dropped. "No way. Bree. Seriously? He was fucking my *mom*. Don't tell me you're interested!"

She cackled with laughter. "Oh my god, MK, you're too easy to stir up. Of *course* I'm not. Me and Dallas have a good thing going right now." She was quiet for a minute while she drove us out of the Reapers' neighborhood and headed in the direction of Scott's place. "But you have to admit, he's hella fine for an old guy. Some lucky bitch needs to nail him and Cass both. Together." She made a growling sound, like a horny cat, and I couldn't stop the laughter.

I was at least eighty percent sure she was fucking with me.

"Oh my fucking hell, Bree." I groaned when my chuckles subsided. "Just concentrate on driving. Dallas would have a shit fit if he knew you were fantasizing about Zane and Cass."

Bree snickered. "True. But you have to admit...those D'Ath genes are something fucking *else*."

I sighed because she was right. As much of an infuriating bastard as Archer was, I couldn't deny my raw attraction. That—of everything—had never been an issue between us. We'd always had that magnetic connection, even way back on Riot Night.

Funnily enough, that was a week before we'd been married. I'd just never known about it.

I pointedly changed the subject to something that hurt my brain considerably less than a certain D'Ath fuck who held my fate and fortune in his tight grip.

Rocket science.

If only I knew the first thing about it, I had no doubt it'd be a welcome brain vacation from Archer's mind games. Instead, I settled on asking Bree how her first week back at SGU had been. Changing the subject to anything that invited Bree to talk about herself? Always a guaranteed way to give myself a break from talking for a bit.

I loved my friend. I really, truly did. But damn, she loved the sound of her own voice.

By the time we'd pulled up in front of Scott's house, I'd totally pushed aside all the crap on my plate and was focused on having a nice night out with friends.

Emphasis on the *friends* part.

"Hey, gorgeous," Scott greeted me as he slid into Bree's backseat. He'd been waiting outside for us when we pulled up, and I got the feeling he deliberately didn't want us meeting his brother. "And, Bree. Hey, Bree, babe."

Bree snorted and rolled her eyes as she pulled away from the curb. "Nice afterthought, Scottie. How's your first week at SGU gone? Bet it's been interesting, seeing as you're fake dating the most talked-about girl on campus."

Scott sat back in the middle seat and grinned. "Who says we're fake dating?" he replied, shooting me a wink, and I barely suppressed a frustrated eye roll.

"I do," I replied, keeping my voice hard.

He gave me an easy smile back, unruffled by my rejection. "I know, Maddie. I was just teasing. So what movie are we seeing, again?"

The rest of the drive to Rainybanks, we chatted about movies and actors. I'd insisted we go to the next town over in an attempt to avoid running into anyone we knew or sparking any gang drama between the Reapers, Wraiths, and…whatever the fuck Archer and his boys were involved in.

Dallas was already waiting for us at the burger bar we'd chosen for dinner and greeted both Bree and me with huge hugs. Okay, a bit more than a hug for Bree. But generally, they were careful not to flaunt their couple-ness around me, which I secretly appreciated. Not that I had a problem with them being together, but no one liked being a third wheel when their friends got hooked up. Especially while experiencing some serious heartbreak.

Overall, things went pretty well, though. Scott and Dallas got along great, and it really did feel like just four friends hanging out. After burgers, we all headed over to the theater and grabbed tickets to the latest action movie. I hesitated a moment before agreeing to that genre, but when the other options were annoy-ingly cheesy rom-coms or family movies? No brainer.

It wasn't until about halfway through the movie that everything went to shit.

Then it just got steadily worse from there.

So much for a relaxing night out with friends.

CHAPTER 7

As I removed Scott's hand from my leg for about the eighth time, I lost my temper. Bree and Dallas were all snuggled up in the dark while we watched the movie, and apparently Scott was taking that as a sign to try to push the fake-dating angle a bit harder.

I wasn't in the fucking mood.

Grabbing my bag from the ground, I stood to leave, and he grabbed my wrist to stop me.

"Where are you going?" he asked me in a whisper, looking confused.

I stared back at him a moment before deciding that he really had no idea why I was leaving. He genuinely didn't understand that I wasn't interested and no amount of flirting and casual touches was going to change that fact.

"Bathroom," I lied, giving him a tight smile. "Back soon." Because the middle of a theater while a movie was on simply wasn't the place for an argument with Scott.

Tugging my wrist free of his grip, I hurried out without sparing my friends another glance. Bree and Dallas probably hadn't even noticed me leave, considering they were locked in a heated make-out session. So much for toning down the couple-ness. Maybe that was only when the lights were on.

Stepping onto the sidewalk, I took a deep breath of cool night air and blew it out in a long, exhausted sigh. Being friends with Scott was supposed to be a break from all the overbearing-asshole drama that Archer, Kody, and Steele brought me. He was supposed to be a change of scenery. Instead, he was just making things harder. More complicated.

I didn't need that shit in my life.

"Maddie," Scott called out, making me flinch as I spun around to face him. Of course he'd followed me even though I'd said I was going to the bathroom. What the fuck, dude?

"Scott," I replied, feeling the weight of the damn world on my shoulders. "You followed me."

"Of course I did," he snapped with a deep frown creasing his brow. "You were acting all weird, and I got worried. Bree said you shouldn't be alone too."

I didn't even try to hide my eye roll. Fuck's sake. Bree and I were going to have some serious words on what was acceptable friend behavior.

"Maddie, what's going on?" Scott pushed. "You seem really tense. I thought we were having a fun night… Weren't we?"

I arched a brow. Yep, evidently we were going to deal with this right here on the sidewalk. Fuck it. Rip the Band-Aid off. "Uh, yeah, we were. Until you forgot the fact that we're not *actually* dating and kept trying to push things further under the cover of darkness in there. What the fuck is going on, Scott? I have made it so freaking clear. We're not dating. I'm not interested in you like that."

He took a step back like I'd just physically struck him.

I instantly felt like an overreacting shithead.

"Wow, Maddie," he said after a moment, blinking like he was in shock. "I don't even know what to say. I wasn't *trying*

46

anything... I just thought... I don't know. You give me these mixed signals..." He trailed off with an uncomfortable shrug, but it just sparked my anger.

Fuck that gaslighting bullshit. I'd been clear from the get-go.

"What part of me removing your hand from my leg is confusing, Scott? What about that tells you that I want you to try again? I'm not playing some hard-to-get bullshit here, dude. I just don't want to fuck you. Okay?" I felt the stab of my own words and knew they were cutting him deeper. But fucking hell, man. Get a damn clue.

Anger flashed across his face. I geared up for a fight, but it was gone again in a second with a sheepish expression replacing it. "I'm sorry, Maddie. Really. I didn't mean to make you uncomfortable. Can we stay friends? I really like hanging out with you and Bree, and I don't want my stupid crush to ruin our friendship."

I raked my fingers through my hair, blowing out a breath and letting my irritation subside somewhat. Maybe I was overreacting a bit. Everything going on with my stalker, the guys, my *marriage*... it had me way on edge, and I was snapping at dumb shit.

"Yeah, all good, Scott," I said with a weak smile. "Just friends, okay? I'm not interested in getting involved with anyone right now."

He nodded quickly. "Totally understand. I'm sorry I kept pushing things; I really value your friendship, Maddie."

It was a bit much, but Scott was an intense kind of guy.

"Get down!" someone shouted just a split second before a hard body barreled into me and tackled me to the pavement. The crack of a gunshot rang out as my hip hit the hard concrete and a sharp pain shot through it. I tensed in preparation for my head to hit as well, but it didn't happen. Whoever had dove into me rolled, protecting my skull from what would surely have been a nasty bump.

I had no time to react as screams rang out and reality sunk in. Someone had just shot at me.

47

Strong arms banded around me as the person who'd just saved my ass started to pick me up, and I struggled violently. How the fuck did I know this wasn't another kidnapping attempt?

"Babe, it's me," Kody barked, holding me tighter as he found his feet and started running with me in his arms. "We need to get out of here."

Gunfire sounded behind us, back in the direction of the movie theater, and I craned my neck to see what the hell was going on. The huge glass window at the foyer of the theater—the one Scott and I had just been standing in front of—was shattered, probably where the bullet had hit. Innocent bystanders, normal people out for a movie or a walk or whatever, were scattered around on their bellies, crawling for shelter. The only people still standing were Steele, his gun aimed across the street and up into the building opposite as he shot back at my attacker...and Archer. He wasn't shooting; he just stood there like the force of his glare could kill the attackers and repel bullets away from his flesh.

Psychotic fuck.

"Get her out of here!" he roared to Kody, but his cold, blue eyes met mine.

Kody didn't reply, though; he was already approaching his royal-blue Maserati and clicking the doors open with his key fob. Seconds later I was dropped in the passenger seat, and the door slammed before I could form any kind of protest.

"Wait, Kody!" I shouted as he rounded the car to his side and slid into the driver's seat. I reached for the door handle to let myself out, but it was locked. What the fuck? Had he child-locked the doors? "Kody, I need to find Scott! Was he hit? What about Bree and Dallas? They were inside!"

"Archer's got it," he replied, gunning his engine and peeling out of the parking space without even waiting for me to buckle my seat belt. I scrambled to do so—my fear of car crashes had only gotten worse after the Halloween incident—then wrapped my

arms around myself. I was shaking, trembling all over as the adrenaline drained out of my body.

"Did someone just fucking shoot at me?" I asked in a shaking
voice. Maybe I'd jumped to conclusions. Maybe it was a coincidence. Maybe…

Kody shot me a quick look before turning his attention back
to the road as he sped us out of Rainybanks. "Yes."

My breath escaped in a whoosh. "Why?"

Kody's hands tightened on the steering wheel, his knuckles
turning white. "You didn't seriously think the threat was over just
because you moved out, did you?"

I jerked, stunned by the simmering anger behind his words.
"No, of course not," I snapped back, feeling…stupid as fuck. Wow.
I kind of had dismissed the threats on my life. Nothing had happened since that day before Christmas. Since my stalker had almost
killed me, then murdered Drew and that Wraith—a guy whose
name I still didn't even know.

"Why were you there?" I asked instead, not comfortable leaving the silence hanging between us. I was too on edge. Too fucking
keyed up and *scared*. "Were you guys following me?"

He snorted a humorless laugh. "Of course we were, MK."

I scowled. "Why?"

"Because people are trying to kill you!" he shouted, slamming
his hand against the steering wheel in fury and frustration.

I bit my lip to silence all of the dumb responses I wanted to give
him. I already knew *why* they cared if I was killed—I just didn't
want to admit that I did.

"Where are we going?" I asked instead when the silence became
too much to handle. "I'm not going back to your house."

Kody made an annoyed sort of grunt. "Technically it's *your*
house. The deed is in your name."

I whipped my head around, giving him a sharp look. "What?"

He shrugged. "Well, half yours."

My stomach sank. "I see." If it was *half* mine, then it didn't take an astrophysicist to work out who the other half belonged to. Apparently my secret husband had been more than happy to forge my signature long before I'd even known him. Or maybe that kind of contract only needed one party to sign? How the fuck would I know?

Come to think of it, maybe silence was better than talking after all. Biting at the edge of my nail, I turned my gaze out the window and tried to pretend I was anywhere else. Any*one* else. Because I was neck deep in drama and quickly drowning.

Kody didn't say anything more, but he also didn't return to the mansion we'd all been sharing until so recently. He drove straight to my new apartment, deep within Reaper territory in the former West Shadow Grove, then parked in a vacant parking space across the street.

"Thanks," I muttered when he released my door so I could get out, "for saving my ass back there." I started to walk away, crossing the street to my apartment block, but Kody followed.

He gave me a small frown when I glanced over at him. "You don't honestly think I'll just drop you off and leave, do you?" I raised my brows, and he shook his head in disbelief. "Have we even goddamn met? Fucking hell, MK."

I didn't argue with him because he was right. There was no way in hell he was just dropping me at the door and driving away with a wave and a honk. Not when someone had tried to shoot me in public not even an hour ago. And really, I wouldn't want him to.

We waited for the elevator in silence, and when it arrived, a couple of Reaper kids stepped out, only to do a double take when they saw Kody standing there.

"Whoa, yo, bro...you lost?" one of them asked him with a slight smirk on his face.

Kody just glared death, and the other kid—who looked slightly closer to my age—whacked his friend in the arm.

"Shut up, fuckhead." Then he gave Kody and me a small nod. "No disrespect and shit, yeah? He's new."

Kody didn't even reply to them, and the older kid dragged the mouthy one out of the apartment building like their tails were on fire.

"What was that all about?" I murmured as we stepped into the elevator and I pressed the button for my floor. "I vaguely remember some Reapers treating you the same way the night of Archer's fight." The night I'd almost died of a deadly fentanyl dose.

Kody arched a brow at me, looking next-level sexy and dangerous. Fucking hell.

"What was what about?"

I glared. "Seriously? You're gonna play dumb on this?"

The corners of his mouth twitched, and I could tell he was fighting a smile. Bastard.

"There's nothing to play dumb about, babe," he replied as we reached my floor and the doors slid open. He indicated I exit ahead of him, but his sharp gaze swept the corridor ahead of us to make sure it was clear of threats. "I doubt I've ever met those two in my life."

I stomped over to my door and unlocked it. Thankfully, I'd kept hold of my bag through everything in Rainybanks, so I wasn't replacing yet another phone and there was no need to bang on Cass's door for my spare key. Not that he was likely to be home at eleven thirty on a Friday night.

"I swear to fuck, Kodiak Jones," I snapped, pushing the door open and stepping back for him to enter, "if you lie to me one more time, I'll stab you myself. I've had enough bullshit to last me a damn lifetime. Either start coming clean or get the fuck out."

I stayed there in the doorway, leaning my shoulder against the jamb while Kody pulled a gun from his waistband and swept through my whole apartment. He flipped lights on and checked the closets, under the bed, behind the curtains—the whole deal—before putting his weapon away and returning to me.

"I'm not lying, babe," he told me with a small frown. "I don't

51

know those punks. Arch, Steele, and I, we broke ties with Zane and the Reapers about three years ago." He paused, his jaw tight, and I knew there was more to the story. Zane D'Ath didn't just let people leave his gang because they wanted to. The Reapers—just like the Wraiths—were life gangs. Once you were in, the only way out was in a body bag.

"But..." Kody continued, and I nodded in satisfaction. Smart boy. I closed my front door and tossed my keys onto the little table that I'd designated my key place.

"Maybe they heard some rumors about things from the past," he offered, mimicking my movements as I sank down onto the couch.

I shifted, turning slightly to face him. Despite all my anger and heartbreak, he was still Kody. I knew him. I cared about him. And yeah, I wanted to forgive him. Deep down...*really* fucking deep down, I wanted all the bullshit between us to go away so we could go back to being whatever the fuck we'd been. Before the murders. Before the information bombs. Before the betrayals...

But that wasn't possible. We couldn't turn back time, and no one I knew had invented a selective-memory erasing tool. So we either needed to move forward...or walk away.

I hadn't totally decided which of those options would hurt me less. For now, I just wanted to understand him better. I needed to know what made Kodiak Jones tick and why he'd chosen to keep such a monumental, life-altering secret from me, despite the fact that he'd known it would totally crush me.

"Tell me something real," I whispered, meeting his gaze as I rested my cheek on the back of the couch. "Something truthful."

He exhaled heavily, ruffling the top of his bleached hair with his fingers. The pink from my prank had faded almost completely out, and I found myself itching to trick him again.

"You want to know how we broke away from the Reapers," he said. It was a statement, not a question, but I nodded anyway.

52

"This isn't totally my story to tell," he started, but before I could interrupt with a snappy insult, he kept going. "But Arch and Steele can just kiss my ass if they have an issue with it. I told Arch I was done keeping secrets from you, and I meant it."

Ugh. Kody always knew the right things to say to hit me straight in the heart.

"So tell me," I gently prompted when the silence stretched between us. I pulled my knees up on the couch, getting comfortable as I settled in to listen.

He cast a sheepish look at me, his eyes tight with tension. "I'm trying to work out how to phrase it so you don't think the worst of us. Any of us. We've all done shit..."

"Like purchased underage girls and forced them into marriage without their knowledge?" I filled in the blank when he trailed off, and his shoulders slumped in defeat. "I'm teasing," I murmured, "but seriously, I feel like it can't be much worse than human trafficking. Right?"

Kody's answering smile was sad and tortured, and cold dread pooled in my belly.

"There's always something worse, babe. Always."

CHAPTER 8

"So I guess I should just tell you," Kody said after nearly a full minute of silence during which the tension kept building inside me. I was trying really hard not to speak, not to push him any harder…but it wasn't easy. I wanted to know all of it—the good, the bad, the awful. If there was going to be *any* chance of reconciliation between us, I needed to know it all.

He ran his hand through his hair again, then dropped his head back on the couch, looking up at my ceiling. "We never wanted to be in a gang. The three of us, I mean. None of us wanted to be like Zane and Damien. We didn't want to spend our lives committing crimes and using blackmail and brute force to remain free of incarceration. It just never sat right, you know?"

He flicked a glance at me, and I nodded. I could safely say that lifestyle had never appealed to me either. It was why Dallas and I had fallen out. But then I was a rich white girl, so I couldn't go judging others for their choices made in moments of desperation.

"Well, we didn't really get a choice. Arch… Damien tattooed him with the Reaper before he could even read. A mark of ownership more than anything." Kody cringed, then shot me an apologetic look. "Sorry, I'm getting off the point, and I'll feel like a total prick if I tell you their stories. Those ones aren't mine to tell, but this one sort of is." He cleared his throat, thinking. "Okay, so, we knew no one just left the Reapers, not once they were blooded in. It just doesn't happen. The Shadow Grove gangs are old-school. Lifers. We knew if we wanted to get free of that whole lifestyle, we needed something big, something bloody, and something that would last well past our departure."

"Or otherwise they'd just hunt you down and kill you later," I mused aloud, nodding. "Yeah, that makes sense. It explains the terrified look some of the younger Reapers get when they look at you guys."

Kody wrinkled his nose. "Yeah. We sort of left a reputation behind, which...I wanna say it snowballed into something bigger than it should be, but it hasn't. If anything, the effect has dulled over time. Soon enough, some punk-ass bastards will try to prove a point and take shots at us, and we'll have to...you know. Remind them why we're not to be messed with."

I drew in a deep breath and let it out slowly. I knew they'd done some bad shit in the past. I knew it just as surely as I'd known they were all hiding secrets that would bite me in the ass. So why pretend it's all such a shock?

One of the many mysteries of Madison Kate Danvers, I guessed. I apparently liked to blow shit up.

"I think I need a drink," I admitted. "You want one?"

How had I gone from wishing I'd never met Kodiak fucking Jones to offering him a beverage as we chatted on my couch? God only knew. I was okay with it, though. I'd probably do just about anything he wanted if it meant I finally got some real, honest answers.

"Sure," he replied as I hunted in my fridge and pulled out a couple of strawberry-and-pear ciders. I popped the tops off and returned to the couch, handing one to Kody.

He peered at the label and wrinkled his nose, looking horrified. "MK...what the fuck is this?"

"Delicious, that's what it is. Quit complaining and continue with your story." I took a long sip of my drink and licked my lips. "Mm, tasty."

Kody's gaze locked on my mouth, and he made a sound of frustration. "Keep doing that and I'll never finish this damn story, babe."

I bit back a laugh. "Sorry. Keep going."

He took a sip of his drink, then made a face like it wasn't as bad as he'd assumed before letting out a sigh. "Okay, so, I won't go into details, or we will be sitting here talking for the next three days. Arch told you a bit about his grandfather's training camps, right?" I nodded. "Well, they gave us all the skills we needed to act when we saw an opportunity. We discovered that the Tri-State Timberwolves were planning a hostile takeover of Shadow Grove."

I gasped. The Tri-State Timberwolves used to be one of America's most feared criminal organizations. They were brutal and bloodthirsty—totally devoid of humanity or mercy. They were also basically extinct. The scattered remains of the formerly powerful gang were nothing more than an annoyance to their home base of Tri-State.

"Right. I take it you've heard of them?" Kody arched a brow at me.

"Who hasn't? The Tri-State Massacre was all over the news for *months*. It was one of the worst gang killings in history." The pieces clicked together in my head as I said this, and my brows shot up in shock. "Wait. You mean…? No way. There were more than a hundred deaths that day. That's not even possible… Is it?"

Kody just took a gulp of his cider and shrugged. "Phillip's training taught us every useful skill he'd gained in his forty years as a black-ops agent and then more that he'd developed himself as he slowly lost his grip on reality. You'd be amazed what we're capable of, babe."

No shit.

"So…you killed them all." It wasn't a question anymore. "How'd that free you from the Reapers? And the Wraiths for that matter? Archer, all of you, seem to have both Shadow Grove gangs kind of shitting their pants when you're around."

Kody's lips curled in a grin at that description. "Well, that's the part that we needed to think long-term on. It's not enough to just strike out in a power move and make everyone scared as shit. Those kinds of threats wear off over time, and idiots—especially gangster idiots—will dismiss the rumors as exactly that. Rumors. So we needed to ensure we had both Zane's and Charon's balls firmly in our grip, you know?"

I wrinkled my nose. "Horrible metaphor but yeah, I get you. So what are you holding over them? How does it relate to the Timberwolves?"

"We hit the Shadow Grove gangs where it hurt the most. By cutting the Tri-State Timberwolves off at the knees, we were able to make some lucrative deals. We gained control of several of their businesses—legal and illegal. We cut off trade with the Shadow Grove underworld until they agreed to our terms." A small, satisfied smile ghosted his lips, like he was still proud of what they'd achieved. Fair enough too.

I nodded slowly, understanding the implications of their very strategic move. "You held them ransom for their own revenue streams. So the Reapers and Wraiths now only operate because the three of you allow them to?"

"In a simplified explanation, yes. We also have a few insurance policies in place to remove the temptation to just kill the three of us and take our assets for themselves." He took another long sip of his strawberry-and-pear cider and gave me an approving nod. "This is actually pretty tasty."

"Told you," I muttered.

We were silent for a long time while I processed all this new information. None of it changed the way I felt about the three of them—deep down, below my rage, betrayal and anger still stung—but it explained a lot. The idea that they'd been the ones who'd carried out the Tri-State Massacre was staggering and a little unbelievable. But I also didn't think Kody would lie about something like that. He clearly carried some measure of guilt about it, and that only endeared him to me.

He'd made some hard choices to change the path of his future, and while he'd probably do it again if needed, he wasn't gloating. He wasn't proud of the lives they'd taken in the process.

"Fucking hell, Kody," I said after the silence stretched with tension. "I guessed you guys had done *something*. But that's…a whole lot more."

"I know," he replied with a grimace. "I just wanted to give you the truth. It's the least I could do, considering everything."

Everything. In other words, considering the fact that his friend had bought me and married me without my knowledge, then he and Steele hadn't breathed a fucking word of warning to me. They'd just let me tumble down the rabbit hole of their dark and dangerous world and smiled the whole time.

But that wasn't totally fair.

"These people trying to kill me," I said, licking my lips. "Do they have anything to do with you guys? With what you did?"

Kody shook his head. "No. Or…not so far as we can tell. The attack on Riot Night, that was intended for you, and it was well before you became involved with all our shit. So far as we've been able to work out, it has to do with your inheritance from your mom."

I frowned, biting the edge of my thumbnail. It was a bad habit I'd recently developed. "Yeah, there's something weird about that too—"

The shrill sound of Kody's cell phone cut me off, and he gave me an apologetic look before fishing it out of his jeans. He took a look at the display and frowned.

"Take it," I told him, sure I knew who was calling. "I need to know that Bree, Dallas, and Scott are okay."

He quirked a quick look at me, then hit Answer on his screen before bringing the phone to his ear. The first thing out of his mouth was a relay of my concerns, and a moment later he gave me a nod and thumbs-up to indicate that my friends were all okay.

I let out a sigh of relief, then went back to my kitchen to grab us more drinks. I didn't need to sit there and listen in on his conversation with Archer, not after Kody had made it perfectly clear he'd answer any question I had. Better than that, he'd answer honestly, provided it was his story to tell.

Deciding to show him some small measure of trust—and desperately hoping it wouldn't bite me in the ass again—I dropped our fresh drinks back on the coffee table, then left him to his call while I went for a shower.

I kept my shower pretty quick because the last thing I needed after being shot at was more time alone with my thoughts. All that proved to me was how deluded I was in trying to cut the guys out completely. They were too heavily involved in everything right now, and my own problems—like my stalker and the people trying to kill me—weren't going to magically disappear just because I'd moved out of the mansion.

Fuck me, sometimes my own anger seriously blinded me to the bigger picture. Not that I'd be washing away all our issues like water under a bridge, oh hell no. But I'd be a fucking moron not to use them for what they were good at.

Them, the Reapers...all of them.

I'd use them to reclaim my inheritance, my life, and my freedom. Then, if anything was left in the bloody aftermath, I'd consider reconciliation.

Stepping out of the water, I roughly dried myself off, then tucked the towel around my body. I bypassed the clean clothes I'd brought into the bathroom with me and made my way back through to the living room where Kody still sat on the couch with his phone to his ear.

His glittering green eyes met my gaze as I stepped closer. Curiosity and suspicion vied for supremacy across his face, and I gave him a sly smile in return.

"Yeah," he was saying into his phone, "I think that's probably for the best too." His eyes didn't leave mine for even a second as Archer replied to him, and he mumbled an agreement.

I dropped my towel.

CHAPTER 9

"I've gotta go," Kody told Archer, hanging up his call and tossing the phone onto the table without even waiting for a reply. His brows hitched as he stared at me. At *all* of me. "Part of me knows this is a trap," he admitted, his eyes narrowing even as he ran his thumb across his lower lip and his gaze heated.

"So?" I replied, taking a few steps closer until I was standing between his spread legs. I slid my palms up my torso, cupping my own breasts and squeezing lightly. "You have a problem with being used, Kodiak Jones?"

His hooded gaze followed my hands, hungry with desire. "If it means being used by you, Madison Kate? I have no objections."

He reached out with both hands, grabbing my waist and lifting me to straddle his lap. The moment my weight was situated across him, his hands were in my hair, his strong fingers massaging the back of my head as he brought our lips together in a burst of passion.

"Holy fuck," he groaned when my hands found the hem of his shirt and slipped beneath the fabric. "MK, baby, you have no idea…" He trailed off as his lips met mine once more. This time his kiss was more demanding and needy. Our tongues met in a tangle of desire, and his hands held me firm against him like he was afraid I was messing with him…that maybe I'd get up and laugh, leaving him with aching balls and bruised lips as I took my own ass back to my bedroom to finish off with a vibrator.

I won't lie—the thought crossed my mind.

But then that'd just be denying myself something I badly craved. And I wasn't about masochism. So yeah, I'd see this through. I'd fuck Kody until I had cleared him from my damn mind—at least temporarily—then tomorrow I'd start working out how to get my shit back from Archer.

Who knew, maybe Kody could be convinced to play double agent for me.

Kody pulled back from our kiss, his hand cupping my face as his eyes drilled into mine. "You're plotting," he murmured. "I can practically feel the gears working in your mind."

"So?" I challenged him again. "Is that a problem for you?" I wasn't going to play around pretending like I wasn't. My heart couldn't handle being duplicitous like that, not when I still held real feelings for him. Better that he know from the get-go this was sex and *nothing more.*

"Baby girl," he breathed, his eyes imploring me. "Put it aside for tonight. Please."

Something in his tone made me pause. "Why should I?"

"Put it aside for tonight. Let me show you how much I've missed you…how much I've regretted hurting you every damn second that you've been gone. Then tomorrow I'll plot with you. I'll do everything in my power to help you."

I considered his words, running my tongue over my lower lip as I thought. "Why would you do that? You've always been clear where your loyalty lies. Always."

Kody looked pained, his palms stroking down my body until he grasped my naked hips, tight, like he never wanted to let go. "Do you remember what I said to you that night when we fucked in the kitchen?" I frowned, thinking, but he filled in the gap for me. "I told you that I *knew* we'd spend the rest of our lives apologizing to you. I knew it then and I know it now. So let this be the first of my never-ending apologies to you, Madison Kate. I'm so incredibly sorry."

His voice was hoarse and heartfelt, and it struck a chord deep within me where my fragile, fractured heart lay surrounded in barbed wire and razor blades.

I sucked in a breath, but it caught on the hard lump of emotions sitting in my throat. Fuck.

"We're not okay, Kody," I told him, even as I stripped his shirt off and tossed it aside. "We're really fucking far from okay. I don't even remotely forgive you for keeping such a monumental secret from me." My fingertips trailed down his chest to his belt, directly under my naked core.

He nodded, still holding my gaze captive. "I understand all of that."

I narrowed my eyes at him, suspicious, but I didn't stop unbuckling his belt and popping the fly on his jeans. He was so hard beneath the thick fabric it was almost entertaining.

"But...?" I sensed there was more to his statement. Call it Kody intuition.

"But I want the opportunity to get there one day. Even if it takes years, I want to do everything I can to fix what's broken here." His voice carried total sincerity, and fucking hell...I believed him.

I bit my lip, thinking on his words as I loosened his pants and freed his huge erection, then palmed it, making him suck in a sharp breath.

"What about Archer and Steele? I thought you three were the inseparable fucking brotherhood. Tighter than blood. Does this come with a caveat that I need to soften toward them too? Hidden clauses that exempt them from making apologies of their own?" I stroked my hand down his length, reveling in the way his abs clenched and his breath quickened.

"Fuck no," Kody replied on a heavy exhale. "No way. They made their own fucking mess; they can clean it up themselves." His fingers tightened on my hips, and I lifted up slightly, just enough that he could wiggle his pants down and kick them off his feet, along with his boots.

One of his hands left my hip, coming back up to cup my face in a grip that was just a fraction tighter than a loving gesture. Just a step toward dominating. He brought my lips back to his, kissing me deeply like he could push all his apologies into that one kiss.

He couldn't. But damn, it was a good start.

I continued kissing him, but I also reached between us and brought his cock to my core. Fuck foreplay, I needed to feel him deep inside me more than I needed to breathe. Our kiss broke off as I rocked my hips, groaning as he penetrated me, then shuddering as he pushed up, entering me deeper.

"They may be my brothers," Kody told me in a husky whisper as he thrust into me with toe-curling patience. His one hand gripped my hip tight, preventing me from rushing the process, and it was driving me insane. "But you're my girl. I had no idea what that meant to me before. I do now. I won't fuck it up again, babe."

Words failed me as he thrust the rest of the way in, filling me in the most perfect way and making my breathing quicken. He held us there for an extended moment, his tight grip on my face bringing my eyes back to his and locking our gazes together.

He always could read me like an open book, so I wondered what he saw in that moment. Whatever it was, it spurred him into action. Our lips met in a crash, his tongue invading my mouth with assertive dominance, and his fingers massaged my hip as he encouraged me to move on him.

Like I needed encouragement.

Small moans and whimpers escaped my throat without permission as I set a rhythm on him, feeling the delicious, decadent slide and scrape of his huge cock within me. I was an aching, needy mess after almost a month away from him and Steele. I could easily have come within those first few minutes.

But I gritted my teeth and pushed it off. Now that Kody had said literally the exact right things to melt my icy exterior, I wanted to enjoy fucking him. It was no longer me using his fantastic dick to scratch an itch... This was a step toward a new future for us. Even if I wasn't ready to admit that to him, I knew it was true.

Kody's hands found my breasts, palming them and squeezing. His fingers toyed with my nipples in a way that made me gasp and arch into his touch, which just provided access to my neck for him to bite.

"Fuck," I gasped as he nipped me hard enough to leave a mark—probably—and his fingers pinched my nipples. I loved that slight edge of pain, and I could already feel the evidence of it slick between us. I rolled my hips, relishing every inch of him inside me. "Kody..." I trailed off with a moan because I was quickly losing myself in his touch.

He was so fucking right; plotting could wait till the morning. This...*being* in the moment with him, it was so much better than the functional fuck I had intended.

"You're so close," he murmured, kissing up the side of my neck and nipping my earlobe between his teeth. "I can feel you clenching around me. It's fucking hypnotic." I let out a small, frustrated groan, and he chuckled. "Come for me, baby girl. I want you to come while you ride my dick."

My breath caught, and I moaned when his hands left my breasts. But he was just shifting his grip back to my hips. I fucking loved when they held me like that. Like I was totally under their control.

"Come on, babe. Scream for me." He gripped my hips tight, holding me immobile so he could take over. His hips thrust up into me over and over until I came to pieces with a drawn-out cry.

Fucking hell...he hadn't even touched my clit and I was a drenched, trembling mess.

His thrusts slowed, pausing when he was fully seated in me, and he grabbed my face for another bruising, possessive kiss. "Fucking beautiful," he breathed, his green eyes meeting my gaze from under heavy lids. "I need something from you, baby girl."

I blinked a couple of times, trying to clear the orgasm haze even as I writhed on his cock. He was so hard, so big, it was like he prolonged my climax just by staying inside me. "What?"

A devilish grin curved his lips, and his reply came in a dark, hedonistic whisper. "I need to taste you."

I gave a small whimper, but the next second I was flat on my back on the couch, my legs hooked over Kody's shoulders as his mouth met my pussy. I bucked against him, protesting the loss of his dick from my core, but he quickly replaced it with his fingers. Not the same, but it'd do when paired with the way his tongue worked me over.

A breathy stream of curses fell from my lips as he sucked, nipped, and licked, while his hand fucked me into a serious state of euphoria that I never ever wanted to return from. I was still recovering from my first orgasm, so it only took a few moments before I was screaming and clawing at his short hair.

Holy *shit*.

"Kody," I said, panting, "stop playing with me."

His face popped up from between my legs, slick with my arousal and a smug grin across his lips. Fucking shit, that was hot.

"Wouldn't dream of it, babe," he replied with a snicker as he kissed my lower belly and ran his tongue over my stabbing scar. They all paid such close attention to it whenever they saw it. I wondered if there was a level of guilt there that I'd been hurt under "their watch."

"So," I prompted with a feral kind of growl. "How do you want me?"

I was all boneless and euphoric from my double orgasms; if he'd told me he wanted to fuck me on a bed of hot coals, I would have been on board. Anything to get that third climax that I just knew was hiding over the horizon.

"Hmm." He swiped a hand over his face, his hungry gaze running over me. "Turn over."

I legitimately could not have turned over faster if I'd tried.

Kody shifted on the couch behind me as I pulled my knees up to raise my ass in the air, and I heard the jingle of metal.

"Do you trust me, babe?" he asked in a rough voice, then laughed. "I mean, stupid question. But *right now*, in this exact moment, do you trust me?"

My heart stuttered and raced. The obvious answer was no. Fuck no. I didn't trust *any* of them as far as I could throw them. Spoiler alert, I bet I couldn't even pick them up. But then...

"Yes," I breathed, contrary to all my better judgments screaming *no*. "Yes, I trust you, Kody."

Yeah. I was fucking doomed, and I knew it.

"Good," he replied. A moment later, he took my hand in his, bringing my arm back behind me and laying it across my lower back. Then he did the same to the other, crossing my wrists. A jolt of understanding—and excitement—ricocheted through me a moment before the leather of his belt kissed my flesh.

He tightened the loop with quick, practiced movements, then paused with one hand resting gently on my ass. "Is this okay, baby girl?"

I should say no. I should be totally horrified by the idea of being bound and helpless to a man who'd so thoroughly betrayed my trust not a month ago. But I wasn't.

"Yeah," I replied, and I doubted I'd ever uttered a more truthful word in my life. "Yes, fuck yes, Kody..."

"Good," he replied, sounding exactly as excited as I was feeling. His hands shifted back to my hips, finding his favorite position as he tugged my ass farther into the air and nudged my legs apart with his knees. "You like that, don't you?"

A low groan was all the response he got from me as I adjusted my weight on the couch. With my hands bound behind my back, I was left with my cheek buried in a cushion and my shoulder supporting my balance. Luckily, I was agile.

When he slowly entered me again, I moaned the whole time until he was fully seated.

He chuckled. It wasn't an amused sound; it was more of an evil-dictator kind of laugh. The sort of sound that conveyed how drunk on power he was and how badly he was planning on abusing that control. I was fucking *here* for it.

Kody's fingers looped through the belt binding my wrists, and his other hand grasped my hip tightly as he shifted his position slightly.

"Fucking hell, babe," he breathed with a throaty laugh. "This is not exactly how I expected the night to turn out."

I shifted my face, peering back at him from my supremely awkward position. "You complaining, Kodiak?"

"Fuck no," he replied, then proved his damn point over and over and *over*, fucking me hard enough that I briefly worried the couch might break. When his hand smacked across the round of my ass, I came screaming *again*, but this time he joined me. His fingers grasped at my hip, holding me firm against his pelvis as he finished inside me.

After he released my wrists, I had no energy left to move. We just lay there on the couch in a tangle of sweaty, sticky limbs as our chests heaved with exertion. My pussy throbbed and my butt cheek stung from the print of his hand, but it was a delicious sort of pain. My wrists were red, but I doubted it'd take long for that to fade.

Kody broke the silence first.

"Are we—"

"No," I cut him off, already sure what his question was simply based on his tone of voice. "No, we're still a really, *really* long way from being okay, Kody." I stood up and cringed when I felt the wetness of our combined orgasms slide down my thigh. "I'm taking another shower."

He let out a long breath as I swiped my towel from the ground. "Are you kicking me out?"

I paused at the edge of the room. That *had* been my plan—use him for sex, then throw him out on his ass with a few cruel words in a pathetic attempt to make him hurt even a fraction as badly as he'd hurt me.

"No," I replied, my voice soft. "Not right now."

Even without facing him fully, I saw some of the defeat leave his posture. "So you're giving me a chance at redemption, then?"

I groaned inwardly. This was a bad idea; I already knew it. And yet... "Don't fuck it up, Kody. There won't be another chance." I shot him a meaningful look, then continued through to the bathroom to shower again. Don't get me wrong, I *loved* fucking Kody and Steele without the thin barrier of a condom; there was something so totally raw and intimate and just plain dirty about it. But the cleanup was a pain in the ass.

In less than thirty seconds, Kody joined me under the water, and I grinned as he pushed me against the tile wall to fuck me again. He was clearly banking that all the endorphins from continual orgasms would keep me from changing my mind and throwing him out in the cold.

He was right.

Keep them coming, babe. Fuck yeah.

CHAPTER 10

I woke up the next morning to heavy knocking on my front door. Heavy enough that I worried whoever it was might break it down.

"What the fuck?" I mumbled in a sleepy, thoroughly fucked haze.

"I've got it," Kody whispered back, kissing my bare shoulder with hot lips. "Go back to sleep."

I didn't even think twice, dropping my head back into the pillows and yawning. It didn't even cross my mind that Kody was answering my front door in a telling state of undress.

Whoops.

"What the fuck?" a familiar voice roared shortly after the sound of my locks unbolting. "I told you to stand watch, not abuse the fucking situation!"

"She has a name, bro, and it's not *the fucking situation*." Kody was all smugness and gloating as he replied to Archer, and I smothered a laugh in my pillow. "Also, any abuse was totally consensual. In fact—"

"Kody!" I shouted, cutting him off. "That's enough."

The last thing I needed him to do was brag about how I'd *begged* him to smack my ass and tie me to the headboard just a few hours ago. In my defense, I'd lost track of how many times he'd made me come. So temporary insanity had to be excused.

The boys' voices dropped to lower tones, and I reluctantly dragged my ass out of bed. I didn't bother getting fully dressed—it was my apartment; why the fuck should I?—and instead just pulled a buttery-soft satin robe on over my bra and panties. I didn't even bother belting it.

In my living room, Archer and Kody were standing chest to chest with the air crackling between them like lightning. That, more than anything, proved to me how serious he'd been last night when he'd told me Archer could kiss his ass and fix his own damn mistakes.

Blame it on all the oxytocin flooding my system, but I was in the mood to mess with my archnemesis.

Strutting my shit over to the two of them, I couldn't help but notice the way Archer's gaze raked over my body. Not like he hadn't seen all of me before, right? Biting back my mean smirk, I let a pleasant and totally fake smile cross my lips instead.

"Good morning, Husband," I sang as I rose up on my tiptoes and pressed a lingering kiss to his stunned lips. "Did you have a nice night, sweetie? I know I did." I patted his cheek in a condescending way and winked.

The shock receded somewhat out of his expression, and his gaze darkened. "What are you fucking playing at, Princess Danvers?" His voice was ice-cold, and his eyes glittered with barely concealed anger.

I just clicked my tongue and gave him a smirk. "Now, now, darling. It's Princess D'Ath now. It's just what every little girl dreams of! Being married off by her father without her knowledge or consent." I sighed like a deliriously happy nitwit. "Thank goodness such an important decision was taken out of my silly hands. Whatever would I have done?"

With way too much swagger in my step, I turned and headed

over to my open-plan kitchen. I needed about sixteen gallons of coffee to keep up my sarcastic bullshit and not actually rip Archer's balls off with my bare hands. I was guessing by the way both he and Kody were watching me, they knew it too.

"What are you doing here, Sunshine?" I asked as I turned on my espresso machine and located a mug. "Last I checked, you weren't welcome in my apartment." I delivered this with a sickly-sweet smile and a flutter of eyelashes. He loved getting under my skin, and he thrived off my short temper. So he wasn't going to get it. I'd keep my cool and my placid bullshit smile if it fucking killed me. Because it'd kill him first.

"Last I checked, you had a new boyfriend," he sneered back at me, shooting Kody a glare. "One who is terribly concerned for your well-being after you were shot at last night."

A sharp jolt of guilt stabbed through me. Fuck. I hadn't even *tried* calling Scott or Bree to make sure they were okay. I'd just taken Kody's word for it and tossed all my problems out the fucking window.

I bit the inside of my cheek and kept my *Stepford Wives* smile in place. Fuck this bastard; he was trying to rile me up.

"Scott and I have an understanding," I replied, not even lying. We had an *understanding* that I wasn't interested in him, and therefore, I wasn't cheating on him. I could only hope Archer hadn't overheard that whole argument I'd had with Scott outside the theater.

His face twisted in disgust as he prowled closer to the kitchen. "What kind of guy willingly lets his girlfriend fuck other guys?"

My brows shot up, and I met his gaze directly without flinching. "I don't know, Archer. What kind of man lets his *wife* fuck his two best friends under the same damn roof as him?"

His lips parted to retort, but I snapped my fingers, cutting him off.

"Oh, duh, silly me. The kind of man who also never asked

his wife's consent to marry her." I pasted that stupid smile back on my face and flipped my sex hair like a twit. "Now, was there something you needed? Because I was really hoping to start my day with Kody's dick halfway down my throat, and you're sort of killing the vibe."

Kody spluttered a choking, laughing sound, then covered it with a fake coughing attack and indicated he was going to go and get dressed. After all, he was still in nothing but a pair of boxers.

A ripple of fury and frustration passed across Archer's face, and I checked a mental point in my favor. He really should leave now before I crushed him under my bare foot. After all, I needed to save the ace up my sleeve for another day when that plan was fully fleshed out.

"Actually, yes. Seeing as you're having so much fun playing the part of my doting spouse, we have somewhere to be. Put some clothes on; we're already late." He pulled his phone from his pocket, flicking through his notifications like he'd just dismissed me, and I seethed.

Fuck that for a joke. "No thanks."

His brows raised slowly, and his gaze swept up from his phone to meet my eyes. "I wasn't asking, *Wife*. Get dressed, or you can come like that. Makes no difference to me."

I let out a low, humorless laugh. "Or what? You going to force me, big man?"

Something dark and dangerous flickered through his gaze, and I couldn't fight the answering shiver that ran through me. Fuck.

"I could," he replied, his voice low and seductive. "Or I could just tell Steele to shoot the guy we caught last night. We've kept him alive in case you were interested in a chat, but I guess not." He gave a casual shrug and turned back to his phone, presumably to dial Steele.

Mother*fucker*. He had me, and he fucking knew it.

"Wait," I snapped, knowing full well I was playing right into his hands and unable to help it. "Fine. I'll go with you. But I swear to fuck, Archer D'Ath"—I came around the island to jab a finger in his chest—"if you're lying to me, I'll…" My words trailed off as he batted my hand away and trailed a fingertip down my chest, tracing the swell of my breast and making my heart pound.

"You'll *what*, darling? I hold all the chips. All of them. So start getting used to following orders; I won't tolerate these temper tantrums forever."

The words had barely left his mouth before my hand cracked across his face in a slap hard enough to leave an almost instant palm print.

"Spare me the alpha-male bullshit lines, Archer. I don't kneel for anyone." Then I let a mocking smile play out over my lips and arched my back so that my bra-covered breasts brushed the front of his shirt. "Unless I'm sucking cock. But you wouldn't know that… You never followed through." My lips were so close to his ear that I could have sucked on his lobe. But I didn't. I pushed off his chest and sashayed away, then tossed one last remark over my shoulder. "Maybe you could ask Steele? His dick is well acquainted with my mouth after all."

Back in my bedroom I found Kody sprawled out on my bed, stark naked, his hard cock in his hand and a sly grin on his face.

"Listening to you hand Archer his balls makes me so hot, babe," he confessed as he stroked himself with a sure hand. "Wanna see if we can make him break something?"

I snorted a sharp laugh, then glanced over my shoulder to where Archer stood in the middle of my living room like he had no fucking clue what to do next.

"Hell yes," I agreed. I kicked my bedroom door open wider, then climbed up on the bed without even bothering to take my underwear off. I just pushed it aside and sank down on Kody's cock with a long, *loud* moan.

74

Two seconds later the sound of breaking glass came from my living room, and I laughed into Kody's kiss.

Take that, Husband. *Piss me off again, I fucking dare you.*

Needless to say, whatever the fuck Archer thought we were late for, Kody and I ensured we were *very* late.

CHAPTER 11

Archer's guilt trip had sunk in enough that I called Bree on the drive to wherever the fuck we were going and double-checked that she was, in fact, okay. She assured me that she was. She and Dallas had still been inside the theater when it'd all happened, so they hadn't even known about the shooting until Archer had come to get them.

After hanging up with her, I dialed Scott and ignored the two sets of ears in the car that would undoubtedly be listening to every word of our conversation. The car was too quiet for them not to inevitably hear the other end, even though it wasn't on speaker.

"Maddie, baby!" he exclaimed on answering, and I cringed. "Are you okay? Why did it take you so long to call me back? I thought that meathead had kidnapped you!"

I gritted my teeth and bit back my desire to snap at him. But seriously, it was a bit melodramatic. He knew Kody was my ex, and he clearly hadn't been the one shooting.

"Sorry," I said back, instead of what I really wanted to say. "My phone got damaged." Total lie. "I just wanted to make sure you're okay. You didn't get hurt or anything?"

"No," he replied, sounding confused as fuck. "What? No, of course not. I tried to tell those idiots it was just a car backfiring or something. You didn't think it was a gunshot too, did you?"

I pulled the phone away from my ear, frowning at it like Scott had just started speaking Japanese. Kody met my gaze in the mirror, and I mouthed the word *backfire* at him.

He laughed.

Scott was still talking, though, so I put the phone back to my ear and pretended like I'd been listening to him all along.

"Uh-huh," I offered when he paused for a breath. "Hey, I have to go. I'll see you Monday, okay?"

"Wait!" he exclaimed before I could hang up. "Why Monday? What are you doing later? Maybe I could come over and watch a movie at your place, seeing as last night sort of got ruined by your exes."

Against my better judgment my gaze flicked back up to the mirror, and this time it was a pair of cold blue eyes that met mine. He gave a small shake of his head, and I breathed a sigh.

"Sorry, Scott," I found myself saying, "I'm busy. I've gotta go. Talk later."

I quickly hung up before he could push the issue any further and peered out the window. Archer had just parked outside a warehouse on the fringes of West Shadow Grove. It was familiar.

"Wait, isn't this where that Halloween party was held?" I frowned, unbuckling my seat belt and sliding out of the car as the boys both got out. "Why are we here?"

Kody wrinkled his nose, looking annoyed, but it was Archer who replied.

"You wanna talk to the guy who tried to kill you last night?" He cocked his head to the side, shoving his hands in his pockets.

I narrowed my eyes at him in suspicion. There were several other cars parked near us. Considerably more than I'd expect if there was a bloody, beaten man being held inside. "Yeah…"

A small, cold smile flashed over his lips. "Then you need to do something for me first."

Annoyance burned through my belly. "That wasn't the deal, Archer."

He just shrugged and started heading inside the warehouse. "It is now, Princess."

He disappeared into the warehouse, and I was left with the options of following or standing out in the cold indefinitely. I turned to Kody, like I expected him to provide me with answers, but he looked just as confused as I was feeling.

"If he's got something weird in there, I'll personally drive you home," he offered, "but that's Jase's car over there." He pointed to the silver BMW across the parking lot. "So I have to guess this is just work shit."

I scowled but let him lead the way into the warehouse.

"What's the fucking deal with Jase, anyway?" I muttered, walking close to him as slightly haunted memories flickered through my mind. The last time we'd come to this warehouse, it had been a makeshift Halloween party. Afterward I'd been pushed off the road, hunted, chased, and stabbed. Yeah, there weren't a hell of a lot of great memories inside this warehouse.

Except for making out with Kody.

"It's complicated," he replied, grimacing. "Wow, this place has taken shape."

I blinked at the artificial lighting of the interior and nodded my agreement. What had been a totally temporary, slapped-together bar a few months ago was now a permanent structure, and expensive, decorative chandeliers hung from the soaring rafters. Some construction was still in progress toward the far end, but the immediate area had been almost totally converted into an expensive, artistic night club.

"Oh good, you convinced her!" Nicky, the photographer from the guys' underwear shoot, called out and waved at me. She had a huge smile on her face and her camera clutched in her hand.

Suspicion quickly morphed into understanding when I took in the photo shoot setup, and I shifted my accusing glare to Archer.

"Convinced me of *what* exactly?" I demanded, folding my arms.

"The, uh," Nicky started to say, then gave Archer a quick look of confusion. "The photo shoot," she finished in an uncertain voice as she walked over to me. "Archer *didn't* discuss this with you?"

I shot the dickhead in question a sharp glare, and he just shrugged and gave me the kind of smirk that made me want to *kill* him.

"No, he didn't," I replied with a deep frown as I folded my arms over my chest. I shot a glare at Kody, but he looked just as surprised as me and shook his head.

"News to me too, babe," he added to clear up any possible accusations of a setup. "But I think I can guess." He ran a hand through his hair and looked around the room.

Whatever his guess was, he didn't say it before heading across the room to speak with Jase. He didn't need to.

"I'm so sorry," Nicky apologized, cringing. "I just assumed..." She indicated to Archer and back to me, and I sighed. It wasn't her fault that he was an overbearing son of a bitch with no concept of personal rights, liberties, or free will.

Gritting my teeth, I shifted my attention back to Nicky. "It's fine," I said, even though it really, really wasn't. "Why don't you explain super quickly whatever Archer was *supposed* to convince me about?"

She gave me an apologetic smile, then launched into a hurried explanation of how her client—the new owner of the bar we were standing in—had seen the images she'd posted before Christmas of Archer and me during the underwear shoot. The owner had gotten in touch and asked if Archer and I would do the advertising campaign for her new bar.

Apparently...Archer had accepted on both our behalf.

"That's…" I started to say, rubbing at my forehead in frustration. "Look, I really appreciate the offer and I'm flattered, but I'm not a model. I'm sure you have so many other girls who can do this with a whole bucketload more professionalism than I'd be bringing to the party."

"No, see, that's the problem," Nicky rushed to explain, holding her hand out as I took a step backward. "My client doesn't want any model. She wants *you*. Or you two." She sent a desperate kind of look to Archer, but I just shook my head.

"I don't know what to tell you," I replied, giving her an apologetic smile. "I'm not interested."

I'd made it all of two steps out the door when Archer grabbed my upper arm and jerked me to a stop. Anger flooded through me, and indecision over whether to go for his eyes or his balls was the only thing that made me pause.

It was all the hesitation he needed, though, his huge frame shadowing me close enough that I could feel his body heat radiating against my back.

"Here's how it's going to go, Princess," he told me in a low, menacing whisper. The words were delivered right into my ear, his lips brushing my skin as he spoke, and fuck my traitor body, I shivered. "You're going to come back into this bar *smiling*. You're going to get hair and makeup done, you'll wear whatever their designer wants you to wear, then you'll do *everything* Nicky asks."

I snorted with indignation. "In your fucking dreams, D'Ath."

His hand on my arm tightened, and his body pressed tighter against my back. "You don't even want to peek inside my dreams, Princess. It'd scar you for life."

I sneered, even though my back was to him. "You're right. It's probably full of bloody gang massacres and hostile business takeovers."

Archer stilled so much that I could have been leaning against a statue.

"So, Kody told you," he murmured after a moment. "It's a fucking miracle you still give me so much attitude, knowing what we're capable of. Doesn't matter. You'll do this, or you won't see a fucking hair of last night's shooter. I'll send the order to Steele to dispose of him *thoroughly*."

I snorted a sarcastic laugh, willing to call his bluff. "Or I can just call Steele myself and see whether he was serious about that apology he wanted to give me."

Archer's fingers tightened, and his teeth ground together. Yeah, he was losing the loyalty of his friends to me, and he fucking knew it.

"Okay then, how about this, darling?" he suggested with dripping sarcasm. "You do this photo shoot, or I call off Bree's security detail."

I froze. "What security detail?"

A low laugh shook his chest, and I leaned into him without really meaning to. "You didn't know? Your stalker sent a threat about her too. She's apparently a *bad friend* to you and deserves to be taught a lesson."

My blood ran cold. I could play with my own life, my own freedom. But I wouldn't risk Bree, and Archer fucking well knew it.

"Why do you even care about this photo shoot?" I demanded instead. "Like you don't have enough money already?"

He let out a short laugh. "This isn't about money, Madison Kate."

I rolled my eyes, even though he couldn't see it. "Sure it's not, Archer. Coming from you, who literally *bought me on the black market*, I doubt I'll ever believe anything is *not* about money."

"Well, this one isn't. The owner of this property is a good friend of mine, and I owe her a favor. Which means, *Wife*, that you owe her one by association." His voice was tainted with amusement, I was almost certain.

But still, I spluttered with indignation. "What? That's not a fucking thing." I struggled in his grip, trying to turn around and face him because the whole argument was getting stupid with him behind me. But he held firm and wouldn't let me move. Controlling motherfucker.

"Regardless, you do this, or I pull my guys from Bree immediately. What's it gonna be, Princess?" His tone was so fucking casual, like it wouldn't bother him in the least to leave Bree unprotected. We'd all seen what my stalker was capable of. He'd slit Drew's throat, then cut the heart out of her coconspirator. What would he do to Bree given half a chance?

With an enraged snarl, I wrenched my arm free of his grip and spun around in fury. "Fine," I snapped. "But you'll be paying for this bullshit later."

I stomped back toward the bar but heard him heave a sigh and mutter under his breath, "I already am."

CHAPTER 12

An hour later, my makeup had been professionally airbrushed on, my rose-pink hair swept up in a mass of perfect curls, and my outfit…seemed to be missing something.

"Where's the rest?" I asked the stylist.

We were set up in the women's bathroom, which was beautifully decorated with a chandelier and circular couch, makeup mirrors, low stools—even a couple of hair straighteners hardwired to the wall. All signs pointed to this being one of the most impressive new clubs in Shadow Grove.

The stylist, a twentysomething woman called Emma, laughed and wrinkled her nose. "You're so funny, MK," she replied, shaking her head. "You look spectacular. Here, these are the shoes." She held out a pair of deadly, black-patent-and-clear-acrylic Louboutins for me to put on, and I scowled.

"You're kidding. This is it?" I indicated the lingerie she'd dressed me in. It was all black, which I appreciated, but was little more than a corset with a tiny scrap of mesh covering my ass cheeks. Garters hooked to lace-top stockings, and with the high heels on… "Come on. This is a joke, right? Ha-ha, tell Archer he won this round."

Emma frowned, looking somewhat hurt. "You don't like it? That's Agent Provocateur... It's made of Chantilly lace."

Ugh, in other words the corset I wore cost more than the Louboutin shoes.

"It's gorgeous," I offered, "but I'm just confused. Why am I in lingerie for an advertising shoot for a club?"

Emma shrugged. "Because it's sexy as hell. Also, this will be a burlesque club when it opens, so ultra sexy was the briefing for the shoot."

I groaned inwardly. Of *fucking* course the briefing for the shoot was "ultra sexy" because god forbid it was Hazmat or some shit. Well, good luck getting Archer and me to reflect that vibe. Like I'd warned Nicky, I was no model. Nor was I an actress. So maybe she could make do with repulsed and resentful so long as we were both scantily clad?

Fuck. Was Archer going to be in underwear again?

"Come on, put the shoes on. We're already behind schedule." Emma prompted me, and I sighed as I sat down to do as I was told. She offered me a robe, but I waved her off. What was the point when I'd just take it off again? Besides, as much as I'd protested the skimpy outfit, Archer had seen me in a hell of a lot less on several occasions.

Nicky already had Archer set up in the lounge area, and I breathed a small sigh of relief to see he still wore pants. He wore no shirt and the fly was open on his pants, revealing some black underwear beneath, but...at least he wore pants. Small mercies.

He was sitting forward on a velvet armchair, a cut-crystal glass in his hand with amber liquor in it. His forearms rested on his knees as he stared down the camera lens like a fucking pro.

Damn him to hell. As badly as I wanted to sneer and make Zoolander jokes, he really was made for this shit. His myriad of tattoos drew the eye in a dangerous way, and I found myself tracing the black and gray ink far too carefully.

I could see why the owner of the bar wanted him. He was dark, dangerous, and next-level sexy as he took a sip of his drink, his cool blue eyes tracking the camera as Nicky clicked like crazy. She was talking constantly, giving him directions, correcting his face angles, telling him where to look and when to look back, but he was totally unfazed.

Maybe there was hope for him yet... Apparently he *could* listen to a woman when he needed to.

I took a couple of steps closer, feeling the pencil-thin stilettos sway my hips more than usual, and Archer's gaze snapped up to me from the camera.

Nicky snapped a handful more photos, but he wasn't concentrating anymore. His gaze was laser focused on me, raking over my whole body from head to toe like he was seeing me for the first time. Or seeing me with new eyes. It was unnerving as hell and made my step wobble slightly.

Suddenly, the intensity of Archer's gaze was all too much, and I cleared my throat to gain Nicky's attention.

"Did you need me somewhere?" I asked her in a tight voice, praying to all the fates she wouldn't decide she needed me in Archer's lap or something.

"Uh-huh, just a sec, hon," Nicky replied, still clicking away as Archer leaned forward to place his drink on the table, then sat back against the velvet armchair with his legs still spread and that *look* still on his face.

"What?" I snapped at him when it became too much for my nerves to handle. "Are you having a fucking stroke or something?" I parked my hands on my hips and fixed a combative glare onto my face. After *everything* he'd done, he didn't deserve to look at me like that. Like I was a woman he wanted to fuck the daylights out of. That was firmly off the table for Archer and me.

His lips curled in a ghost of a smile, and he swiped a hand across his face—seeming to hide his amusement—as his eyes shifted back to Nicky and her camera. He'd always had some decently long stubble, but he'd let it grow out enough that it could probably be classified as a short beard now. I hated beards on men. Or...I thought I did.

Fucking hell, maybe it was me who was having a stroke. Or certainly some sort of brain misfire. Because as much as I wanted to deny it, I was already imagining what his beard would feel like against my inner thighs.

Yeah, I needed some therapy or something.

"Okay, yes," Nicky said, lowering her camera and flashing me a bright smile. "Hot damn, you look incredible. Can I get you over here?" She indicated where she wanted me—thankfully not in Archer's lap—and I let my brain switch off a bit as she positioned us and went to work.

For the most part, I was able to ignore Archer. Or at least pretend he was someone else. Some random, faceless, nameless model who just happened to be in the same photo shoot...but then Nicky called out her next instruction.

"Excuse me?" I replied, blinking at her. Surely that had just been an echo of my own thoughts.

Nicky quirked a brow at me like she was trying not to laugh. She'd just set Archer up on a backless barstool in front of a cool light feature against a brick wall, and she wanted me to *sit on his lap*.

What the actual fuck?

My eyes narrowed, and my lips parted to tell her I was not okay with that—because my willpower only extended so far and I was all too aware it was possible to totally loathe someone and still fuck their brains out. But Archer gave me no choice in the matter.

His huge hands wrapped around my waist, and I let out a small squeak as he lifted me into his lap, my ass sideways.

"What the *fuck*?" I hissed at him, my teeth clenched to try to hide our animosity from Nicky and everyone else in the room. Most of them weren't paying close attention, thankfully, and I didn't actually give two shits if everyone knew I couldn't stand being within five hundred feet of Archer D'Ath. But I also didn't want anyone else—like Jase the creeper—sticking their nose into our fight.

He dropped one hand away from my waist, resting his wrist ever so casually on his thigh—the one I *wasn't* sitting on—and a small, mocking smile touched his lips. "Chill out, Madison Kate. It's just a photo shoot; I'm not going to go molesting you. I don't fuck unwilling chicks."

A snarl burned through me. "No, you just marry them while they're underage." My words were whispered, but the venom was clear.

Instead of releasing his hold on me, like I'd expected, his grip around my waist tightened, pulling me closer into his body. I wobbled, my arm shooting out in an instinctive reaction to save myself from falling to the floor.

"What is it that you're most upset about, Madison Kate?" Archer asked me in a dark murmur, his lips barely moving as he stared into my eyes. Somewhere in the background I could hear Nicky's camera clicking, but she'd stopped giving us directions. "Is it the fact that your father sold you? Or that I bought you? Or are you just pissed that I refused to fuck you when you were so clearly begging for it?"

Rage boiled within me, and I placed my hand against his chest, trying to shove him away—or me away from him, as it was—but his hand around my waist was tighter than the safety restraints on a roller coaster. Appropriate, given how I felt like I was on the most dangerous rusty, broken-down, old roller coaster imaginable when I was with Archer.

"Let go of me, Archer," I snarled, pushing against his chest to show I wasn't fucking around. My other hand was on his bare shoulder, my arm around the back of his neck, and I deliberately dug my fingernails in as I retracted that hand.

A deep, muscular shiver rippled down his back as my nails gouged red lines across his flesh, but still, he didn't shove me away. Quite the opposite. A small, frustrated groan left his lips a split second before his free hand clapped against my ass, lifting me, spinning me, and resetting me across his lap with one stocking-clad leg on either side of his hips and my pushed-up breasts close enough to his face that his beard brushed them.

"What the fuck are you—"

Boom. Hell froze over.

Or close enough. Archer's lips hit mine in a harsh, demanding kiss while his fingers tangled in my hair. My brain short-circuited, and for a second, I kissed him back. I'd lie about it later if anyone asked me, but I did. He had one hand in my hair, the strands so tightly wound around his fingers that I may as well have been a puppet under his control. His other hand was splayed across my lower back, but his touch was possessive and controlling, holding me tight against him as he kissed me senseless.

Not *totally* senseless, though.

With every scrap of willpower I possessed, I jerked my lips away from his, turning my face to the side as I fought to catch a breath. Everyone had to have seen that. Certainly Nicky had; she had her fucking camera on us.

"I thought you didn't fuck unwilling chicks," I snarled in a quiet voice, keeping my face turned away from Nicky's camera for fear of what she might capture there. It was bad enough that my pussy was throbbing where I was crushed against Archer's hardness and my whole body was lit up like I'd stuck my tongue in an electrical socket.

Archer let out an amused sound and ran his tongue over his lips but didn't release my hair. In fact, he used his grip there to turn my face enough that our gazes locked once more.

The corner of his mouth pulled up, and his cool blue eyes flashed with victory. "I don't."

I scowled. His implication was clear...that I *was* willing. Motherfucker.

With a furious, frustrated growl, I wrenched myself out of his grip and wobbled as my heels hit the floor once more. "You're barking up the wrong fucking tree, *Husband*," I hissed, reminding him—and me—of the honking big elephant in the room with us. "If you're looking for willing, then you'd be better off just fucking yourself. You've had plenty of practice with that lately, haven't you?"

His glare darkened, his amusement turning to a threatening scowl, but I'd run out of fucks to give. I'd also run right out of willpower and mental fortitude, and I badly didn't want to be one of those girls who lost all backbone the second her cunt got wet.

"Are we done?" I asked Nicky, spinning around and giving Archer my back. If he was wise, he'd use the cover to sort himself out. Otherwise this "ultra sexy" photo shoot was about to turn into soft-core porn.

Nicky's brows shot up, her camera held in one hand as she hesitated. "Uh...not really..." she started to say but quickly changed her mind. "Actually, come to think of it, I can work with what I've got."

I was halfway across the bar before she'd even finished talking. Kody was over near the main door talking to Jase, and when I stormed past him, he cut out of the conversation to follow me.

"What happened?" he asked in a worried voice as I shoved through the heavy doors and out into the frosty air outside.

"Seriously?" I demanded, whirling around to glare at him. The look on his face was pure confusion, though, and it only took me a second to realize he hadn't seen the kiss between Archer and me.

Kody's brow furrowed, and he shot a look back toward the warehouse bar we'd just left. "Do you need me to punch him again? I'm sure he deserves it."

I barked a sharp laugh and shook my head. My irritation flowed out with the crisp air I was inhaling. "Again? You've made a habit of punching him?"

Kody gave me a cocky grin, closing the gap between us. He draped his leather jacket over my trembling shoulders. "Baby girl. You shoulda seen the mess Steele and I left him in that week you took off to Aspen. Let's just say fight training stepped up a notch."

I grinned, letting all my anger and frustration at Archer fade away as Kody's hands slipped under his jacket and rested on my waist.

"Damn, I kinda wish I could have seen that," I muttered, picturing the boys smacking the shit out of Archer and him just fucking taking it because he *knew* he deserved it. Douchecanoe.

"Say the word, babe," Kody told me with total seriousness. "I'll happily reenact it for you. It's about damn time he woke the fuck up before we lose you for real."

My eyes narrowed as I glared back in the general direction of the bar. "To lose me, he'd first need to *have* me. Which he doesn't." My words were firm, but they lacked conviction.

Kody wasn't calling me on my denial bullshit though. "But... do I?"

Fucking Christ, he was all hopeful, pleading puppy-dog eyes. How the hell was it legal for a guy as hot as Kody to pull a move like that?

Linking my hands behind his neck, I tipped my head back to kiss him. Even with the stiletto heels on, there was a significant enough height difference that I still needed him to bend slightly. It was hot as hell.

"I'm still mad, Kody," I told him on a whisper after our kiss ended, "but yeah. You have me. Don't fuck it up again, or I'll castrate you with a pair of rusty scissors."

He groaned, pulling me closer and claiming my mouth in another kiss, this time loaded with naked desire and desperate craving.

"I fucking love when you get all stabby, babe," he told me in a rough whisper, dipping his head to claim my mouth in another searing kiss. The sort of kiss that could very easily lead into *more*... And given we were standing outside in a parking lot in the middle of the damn day while I shivered my ass off in lingerie, heels, and Kody's jacket? Maybe not the best time or place.

With a sigh, I took a small step back in an attempt to remind my body that we couldn't *actually* fuck while standing up in a public space. But movement caught my attention over Kody's shoulder, and my gaze shot to the front door of the warehouse-bar. It stood open now, and a shirtless, ink-covered, infuriating piece of shit stood there with a deep scowl on his face and his thick arms folded.

Something about him just made me *constantly* want to raise his blood pressure, and after that stunt he'd pulled in there, kissing me like that? Yeah, I wanted to poke the hornet's nest. With a flamethrower.

Dragging my tongue across my lower lip, I closed that small gap between Kody and me again, molding my body to his as I shot Archer a deliberate wink. I tipped my face back, seeking out Kody's lips again, but a slamming car door startled me.

"Maddie!" Scott's irate shout shocked through me, and I pulled back from Kody's embrace in confusion. "Are you okay? Hey, asshole, get your hands off my girl!" He grabbed Kody by his shirt, hauling him away from me in a move rough enough that it almost sent me sprawling onto my ass in the middle of the damn parking lot.

I kept my balance, though, which was more than I could say for Scott as he swung a terrible punch at Kody, missed, and pitched himself face forward into the gravel.

"Fuck's sake," I hissed under my breath.

Just what I needed. Another posturing fool acting like a goddamn caveman around me.

CHAPTER 13

Scott meant well, I knew he did. But his execution seriously lacked finesse. Picking a fight with a UFC trainer? Not his smartest move. Not by a long shot.

As he sprawled in the gravel, I sent a lightning-quick mental plea that he'd smarten the fuck up and recognize he was severely outmatched. But nope, he scrambled back up to his feet and launched back at Kody again, swinging his fists like he had a damn death wish.

Fucking idiot.

My lips parted to shout at him, to tell him to stop before he ended up learning exactly why Kody was training the hottest new face on the UFC circuit. But then something stopped me. I don't know what it was—maybe the fact that he'd shown up at this location totally uninvited like some kind of…

Shit.

Like some kind of stalker.

I stood there, frozen immobile as that thought took root in my mind. Kody must have taken my lack of protest as permission because a second later, the warm, wet spatter of blood from Scott's breaking nose hit me in the face.

Three seconds later, Scott was face down in the gravel. Blood flowed freely from his nose, and the muscles of his shoulder and neck strained painfully against Kody's arm bar.

"Maddie!" Scott shouted at me, and I swallowed a sigh. "Maddie, what the fuck? Are you going to just let him do this?"

Kody snorted a laugh, giving me a look that seemed to say, *What the fuck are you doing with this asshole?* Twisting Scott's hand until the weaker man screamed in pain, he ordered, "Quit calling her that. She hates being called that."

My brows shot up. How the fuck did he know that?

Regardless, I sighed and crouched down to look at Scott. I was still in my lingerie from the shoot, my designer shoes with their spiked heels wobbling slightly on the uneven ground. Thank fuck for Kody's jacket or I'd be turning hypothermic.

"Scott, what the hell are you even doing here?" I asked the more important question. Fuck the macho, posturing bullshit between boys. I wanted to shift the cold chill of fear chasing through me. "How'd you know where I was?"

Kody didn't let up, and Scott made a furious, pained sound. The crunch of boots on gravel alerted me to Archer joining the party, but I didn't acknowledge him.

"You told me," Scott replied, sounding all kinds of furious even through the blood of his broken nose. Or hell, maybe it wasn't broken. Maybe it was just badly bent. "On the phone earlier."

I frowned, meeting Kody's eyes. He'd heard my call with Scott, so he could verify. His head shake confirmed what I thought.

"No, I didn't." I was one hundred percent confident that I hadn't. The guys hadn't even told me where we were going while I was in the car and on the phone with Scott. So he was lying.

But why?

Scott didn't respond for a moment, and Archer's boot slowly came down on one of Scott's hands where it lay flat on the ground.

"How'd you know where to find her, Scottie?" Archer asked in

93

a dark growl. It was the type of voice that promised a long, drawn-out, and painful death if he didn't get the answers he wanted. It sent a hard shudder through me, and I bit my cheek to keep from showing my reaction.

Scott got a stubborn look in his eyes, and I lost my temper.

"Hey," I said, snapping my fingers in front of his face. "Answer the question. How'd you know where I was? Were you following me?"

Scott's eyes widened. "What? No! No, I wasn't... Ugh, I just didn't want to..." His words trailed off in a mumble, and Archer's boot ground his hand into the gravel, drawing a short scream of pain from Scott.

"Speak up," Archer ordered, and Kody snickered. Shithead.

"I didn't want to get Bree in trouble!" Scott shouted, looking up at me in accusation like it was somehow my fault he was admitting this.

My mood soured even further. "What the fuck is that supposed to mean, Scott? What does Bree have to do with anything?"

"Find My Phone," he blurted out when Kody tightened his grip on Scott's arm. "Your phone is still on Bree's account. I asked her to use Find My Phone and tell me where you were."

Chills raced down my spine, and I looked up to see what the guys' reaction was to that information. Kody was scowling. Archer just met my gaze with no expression, and that told me what I needed to know. It was up to me what we did from here.

I let out a long breath. "Scott, why would you do that?"

"I was worried," he replied quickly. "You sounded off on the phone, and I was worried about you. So I just asked Bree to track your phone and drove over to make sure you were okay. Clearly, I was right to be worried. What the fuck was this asshole doing with his hands all over you?"

The tension headache building behind my eyes was growing intense, and my temper was getting short. "Let him go," I told Kody, rising back to my feet with a heavy sigh. I pinched the bridge of my nose and took a couple of calming breaths as the guys *slowly* released my friend.

When Scott scrambled to his feet and made a threatening gesture toward Kody, I lost my temper.

"Scott, *stop.*" My voice was like a metal-tipped whip. "Just fucking *stop.*"

He did as I said, thank fuck. I doubted I could pull Kody off him a second time. Or Archer for that matter. No matter what our fucked-up baggage was, he was still protective as fuck. He wouldn't tolerate Scott's bullshit.

"Guys, can we have a minute?" I asked Kody because Archer was never going to listen. "I need to speak with Scott alone."

Neither one of the boys moved. Typical.

"Now!" I snapped, letting all my pent-up frustration and anger crack through my voice.

Kody nodded reluctantly, then gave Archer a shove in the chest to move him away from us. They didn't go far, but then again, I hadn't expected them to. Just far enough to give us the illusion of privacy.

"Maddie, babe," Scott said, reaching his hands out to me in a pleading gesture, "what the hell is going on? I thought you wanted to make them rue the day they crossed you?"

My lips twitched in a smile, despite the seriousness of the situation. Blood still dripped from Scott's face, but maybe his nose wasn't broken after all.

"Rue the day?" I repeated with a snicker. "What is this, *Pirates of the Caribbean?*"

Scott rolled his eyes with a wince. "No, that'd be making them walk the plank." He frowned, dabbing at his face with the hem of his shirt. "So, what gives? They hurt you, Maddie. They need to pay for that, and I don't think anything would hurt them more than seeing you move on." He reached out again, like he wanted to embrace me, and I dodged out of his reach.

Kody and Archer took a step toward us, but I held a hand up to stop them. I was fine, and they needed to quit treating me like I was breakable.

"Yes, they did hurt me," I replied, shifting my attention solely back to Scott, "but that's got nothing to do with you. The shit between me and them? It's between us. And how I choose to deal with it is entirely my call."

Scott's brow furrowed, and I could see the stubborn denial in his eyes. "But, Maddie, you don't have to do it alone. I want to help."

"And I appreciate that, Scott. But I don't need your help. I'm a big girl, and I'm perfectly capable of handling things myself. I told you last night I'm not interested in you as anything more than a friend. Pretending otherwise won't change that." I tried to keep my tone soft to take the sting from my words, but they hit home nonetheless.

His face turned hard, his eyes cold. "You told me you weren't interested in *anyone*, yet here you are dressed like that with *him* all over you." He cast a disgusted look at my lingerie, stockings, and heels combination—at least I had a jacket on—then shot a scathing glare in Kody's direction.

To Kody's credit, he didn't rise to the bait. He just grinned and waved like the sarcastic fuck he was.

I let out a frustrated sigh and ran my fingers through my pink curls. "Scott, I've made myself clear. Following me here, using Bree to track my location? It's creepy as fuck. I've got enough creepy in my life without you adding to it. So cut it the fuck out."

Scott's expression crumpled, and a pang of guilt hit me. He really did want to help, no matter how misguided he was. "I'm sorry, Maddie," he replied in a quiet voice, his gaze on the gravel at our feet. "I never meant to freak you out. I was just really worried about you, and Shane says these guys are involved in some really bad shit."

I frowned in confusion before remembering Shane was his

older brother, the one in SGPD and in Charon's pocket. Of course he'd say that.

"Listen, Scott, I'm fine. I know what I'm involved in"—now—"and I can handle it." Or…I fucking hoped I could. Either way, I wasn't getting Scott involved. "Maybe it wasn't such a good idea for you to transfer here."

I hadn't meant it as an insult, but the stricken look on Scott's face immediately told me he'd taken it as one. Fucking hell.

"Scott, I didn't mean—" I started to backpedal, but he wasn't interested.

"Forget it, Maddie." He brushed me off, stalking a few paces across the parking lot, then spinning around to glare at me once more. "I was just *worried*, but if this is the thanks I get, then I'll stop. When you show up on a morgue table because one of these fucking criminals chokes you a bit too hard during sex, then that's on you."

He stomped away dramatically, climbing into his car in a rage, but I didn't follow. His hypothetical was way too specific, and it was giving me the creeps again.

Could Scott be my stalker? My actual stalker?

Surely not. He was my friend, and he hadn't even been in Shadow Grove until a week ago. Not to mention he was way too young to have been stalking my mom.

I heaved a sigh. My paranoia was making me jump at shadows, but there was no chance for respite. I turned back to face the guys and spread my arms wide.

"Are we done here?" I asked in a sharp voice. "I'd like to question this fuck who shot at me now."

Kody frowned in concern as Scott's car screeched down the road, but Archer just gave me a feral, bloodthirsty smile.

"Your wish is my command, Wifey."

I snorted a surprised laugh and rolled my eyes. "If only that were true."

CHAPTER 14

Nicky managed to grab us for a few more shots before we got changed—but after letting me wipe the blood from my face—swearing that her client would be over the moon with the images she'd gotten. My irritation toward Archer had faded to make room for worry about Scott, so I just went with it.

It was a full hour later that we finally piled back into Archer's car and left the converted warehouse.

We drove in silence for some time, and then the strangest fucking thing happened.

"Thank you, Madison Kate," Archer muttered, shooting a quick look at me as his hands tightened on the steering wheel.

I was in the passenger seat beside him, so there was no way I could just pretend I hadn't heard him. Or rather, no polite way. Then again, I wasn't a polite girl, so I just flat-out ignored him and admired the passing scenery.

"Did you hear me?" Archer demanded after it became clear I wasn't going to reply.

Raising a brow, I turned back to him with a blank stare. "Did you say something?"

He shot me a confused glare. "Yes," he replied, vexed, "I said thank you."

I cocked my head to the side, frowning. "Sorry, what was that? I didn't quite hear you. Maybe you should speak up a little."

Kody snickered from the backseat, not even trying to hide it.

Archer's knuckles turned white on the steering wheel, and his jaw clenched hard enough that his teeth ground together.

"Don't fucking push it, Princess," he growled.

I scoffed and rolled my eyes, turning my face back to the window. Because seriously? *I* shouldn't push it? I wasn't the one in the shit here. That was all him. If anyone was pushing anything—

"I said thank you," Archer repeated, shocking the hell out of me. "That was a favor to a very important friend, so I appreciate you not being difficult about it."

My lips parted, but no sound came out. Holy shit, he'd just rendered me speechless. Was that... Had he just...

"Did you hit your fucking head or something?" I blurted out, frowning at him in suspicious confusion.

He shot me a quick look, flicking his eyes back to the road. "What? Why?"

I wrinkled my nose. "Well, you either took a head injury, or you've been body snatched. Either way, you're freaking me the fuck out. Stop it."

Archer shot me another quick look, this time with his brow furrowed in just as much confusion as I was feeling. Then, it was like the Matrix just kept fucking glitching.

He started laughing.

"What the fuck is happening right now?" I asked, shaking my head in disbelief as his broad shoulders shook with mirth.

Kody reached out and smacked him in the side of the head, cutting Archer's chuckles off quickly. "Quit it," Kody snapped. "You're freaking MK out. And me too, to be honest. Did you get laid last night or something?"

The amusement slipped from Archer's face like I'd imagined the whole thing, and he glared back at the road ahead of us.

99

"Or something," he grunted, his hands tightening on the steering wheel again. His sleeves were pushed up a bit, and I couldn't help staring at the way the muscles in his forearm flexed under his inked skin. Damn him for being so gorgeous. "I guess photo shoots just put me in a good mood."

I froze, carefully not looking at him. But I couldn't help the rush of warmth from remembering the way he'd kissed me during the photo shoot earlier.

Kody snorted a laugh. "Since fucking when? You hate doing that shit."

Archer didn't reply. He just reached out and turned the stereo on, cranking the volume up to end any conversation. But his whole vibe was different, and it was weirding me out big-time. More to the point, it was weirding me out that I'd only just noticed.

Had it just been because of that kiss during the photos? Or had he been acting strange this morning too?

Maybe this was just a new tactic in psychological warfare. Trying to throw me off my game. Well, tough shit. Nothing and no one would stand in my way now. I was getting my money *and* my name back, then running like hell.

"We're here," Archer commented a few minutes later, pulling to a stop outside a cabin in the woods on the outskirts of Shadow Grove.

I wish I were joking. A cabin in the woods. Like I hadn't lived my own slasher flicks enough lately.

"I swear to fucking god, Archer D'Ath," I said as we got out of the car, "if you've brought me here to slit my throat and bury me in a shallow grave, then think again. I'll more than happily drag you to hell along with me."

Archer just cocked a brow at me like I was fucking amusing or something, then stomped up the ancient wooden steps of the house. The whole veranda shook as he crossed it and threw the screen door open, and I frowned. Clearly, he wasn't worried about anyone knowing we were here.

"Babe," Kody commented, looping his arm around my waist and leading me in the direction Archer had disappeared. "Do you want me to accidentally kick him in the balls? It probably won't fix his weird mood, but it might make you feel warm and fuzzy inside."

I laughed but then decided I liked that idea.

"Yeah, actually that'd be great," I replied with an evil smirk. "I would have done it myself this morning if I'd thought I could land the kick without him dodging out of the way."

Kody paused, giving me an answering grin before kissing me quickly on the lips. "Consider it done, babe."

He linked our fingers together, pulling me into the house with him. Inside it looked just as abandoned and forgotten as it had from the outside. All the furniture looked ancient and wore a thick coating of dust.

I coughed, then covered my nose and mouth with my hand.

"I take it you guys don't come here often, then?" I asked in a dry tone, casting my eyes over every surface. All signs pointed to this being the start of the next installment of my slasher-film life. I'd put money on it that the original owner of the cabin was a skeleton stashed in the walls somewhere.

Kody shrugged. "Only when we need a place where no one will hear the screams." He took the creep factor out of his statement with a teasing wink, but I was also pretty sure he was serious. Why else were we here, after all?

Archer was in the middle of the living room shifting a coffee table. Then he rolled up the dusty, old rug and revealed a seriously high-tech trapdoor.

My brows rose as he crouched over it, opened a panel, and revealed a biometric scanner. He pressed his thumb to the scanner at the same time that Kody released my hand and crossed the dusty living room.

I watched the whole thing happen and still couldn't say for sure that Kody *hadn't* tripped on the rolled-up carpet. But the next thing I knew, Archer was rolling on the ground with his hands clasped between his legs and all kinds of inventive curses spewing from his mouth.

"Oh shit, sorry, bro," Kody apologized, sounding anything but. He pressed his own thumb to the scanner and hoisted the steel trapdoor open when it unlocked. Using the toe of his boot, he rolled Archer's groaning body out of the way and indicated I come over. "You ready, babe?"

I blinked at him, biting my cheek to keep from laughing at Archer. "This is where you keep your torture victims?"

I was mostly joking, but Kody just gave a shrug. "Gotta keep them somewhere. What better place?"

He nodded to the open trapdoor, where a ladder extended down into a fluorescent-lit space below. It was a wonder the light hadn't shown through the cracks of the floorboards…but then again, given the level of tech in the trapdoor, they'd probably thought of that.

"Steele's down there," Kody told me when I made no move to descend the ladder, "but I can go first if you want."

I gave the trapdoor a suspicious look, then—for some fucking reason—my gaze shifted to Archer, who was muttering curses and pushing himself up with a hand on the dust-covered sofa.

"Scared, Princess?" he sneered at me, and I scowled.

"What do you know," I commented to Kody in a voice dripping false sweetness. "Kicking him in the balls did reset his personality after all."

Flipping Archer off, I quickly descended the ladder into the artificially lit room below, only to find another locked door right in front of me.

"Can't be too careful when you're torturing and killing people, you know?" Kody said, stepping off the bottom rung of the ladder behind me, then pressing his thumb to another biometric scanner to open the next door.

I raised my brows, nodding as the door slid soundlessly open. "I guess not."

With Kody's hand resting on the small of my back, I drew in a deep breath and stepped into the next room. This one had less lighting, just one spotlight illuminating a chair in the middle of the room.

Or rather, the bloody, beaten man tied to the chair.

"Princess," Archer said behind me, his big dick energy just radiating all over my back, "meet Hank. Hank tried to kill you last night."

The man raised his head just enough to glare at me; then he spat a glob of blood at my feet.

"Finally," Hank grunted, "the bitch herself."

CHAPTER 15

Movement from the shadows startled me, but the solid fist that cracked across Hank's face brought a smile to my lips.

"Spit blood at her again and I'll rip your fucking toenails out," Steele promised the guy, then swept his sharp gaze over me like he was checking that none of the blood had touched me.

It was sweet, in a scary-ass killer kind of way, but still, I forced the smile off my face in favor of a hard glare. Just because Kody had softened my ire didn't mean that Steele automatically got a free pass. He had some serious groveling to do.

If he even wanted my forgiveness, that was.

"Hellc—MK." Steele's brow furrowed as he corrected himself mid-word. Logically I knew he was honoring my wishes by not using his adorable nickname for me…but a girl can have regrets, right? I liked him calling me Hellcat. "Are you okay? Were you hurt last night? Kody turned his fucking phone off and didn't send a full update like he was supposed to."

I flicked a glance at Kody, who just shrugged like he gave zero fucks. I mean…come to think of it, he gave plenty of fucks—that's why he hadn't answered his phone. But Steele probably didn't need to hear that part.

"I'm fine," I replied, but I was almost drowned out by Archer's scoff.

"Yeah, she's just fine," he muttered, snarky as fuck. "Kody gave her a full physical to make sure." The inflection in his tone made it abundantly clear what he meant, and Steele's frown deepened.

Hank started laughing. Apparently he was suicidal as fuck.

"Trouble in paradise, Maxy? Your buddy fucking your girl, eh? Shoulda just let me shoot the bitch and save you the trouble of doing it yourself."

Oh wow. He really did have a death wish.

Steele turned his back on me, leaning over Hank for a moment. There was a disturbing crunch; then Hank howled in agony as Steele straightened back up.

"Interrupt me again when I'm speaking to my girl, and I'll break the rest of them," he told their prisoner with a cold calm that gave me shivers. Looking past him, my eyes widened when I saw three of Hank's fingers on his right hand sticking up from the arm of the chair at an unnatural angle.

Wrinkling my nose, I clenched my teeth to keep from gagging. But seriously, broken fingers were all kinds of vomit-inducing. "Was that necessary?" I asked Steele instead.

"Yes," he replied, giving no further elaboration.

Now that I could take a better look at him, I found he was spattered all over in blood. Hank's blood, was my guess. It should have horrified me, but…it didn't. Not even a little bit. Just like the night of Bree's party when they'd beat the shit out of Zane's Reaper guy, the only identifiable emotion running through me was *excitement*.

Yeah, I was all kinds of fucked up. But so were these boys, so in some ways we were a match made in heaven. Or you know, the other place.

"S, where are we at on this prick?" Kody asked, moving farther into the room and flicking a light on over a table on the far wall. It was covered in tools. Tools that were smeared with blood. He picked up a pair of what looked like bolt cutters and slapped them against his palm menacingly. "We ready to make him sing?"

Steele gave a small snort of laughter before wiping the smile from his face with his hand. "No need," he replied. "Hank told us everything hours ago, didn't you?" He leaned over the bleeding, beaten man with a hand on either wrist. "Told us all about the hit out on MK and where to access the notice. Sang like a bird, right, Hank?"

"Fuck you," Hank spat back, his face twisted with pain and fury.

"Aw, no fun," Kody complained, pouting as he put the bolt cutters back on the bench.

Steele glared. "Like you haven't had enough fun."

There was a bite of anger to his tone that made my spine stiffen, but Kody—the fucking asshole—just gave a self-satisfied smirk and dragged his thumb over his lower lip. "I could always have more. How 'bout you, babe?" He waggled his eyebrows in my direction, and I groaned.

He would fast make me regret all that fun if he was going to rub Steele's face in it.

Hank guffawed, pulling all our attention as he bubbled blood from his lips. "Sounds like your girl's a bit of a whore, Maxy." He snickered, his beady eyes on Steele. He was poking a hornet's nest, and I frowned with confusion. Was he deliberately trying to make Steele kill him? Because he was going about it the right way.

This time when Steele's fist cracked across Hank's face, blood spurted from the mouthy prick and several teeth rattled across the concrete floor.

I gasped. "What the fuck, Steele?" I snapped, grabbing him by the arm and spinning him back to face me. He was as tense as a bow string, and his lips parted to argue with me, to defend his choice to smack the shit out of Hank. But I didn't much care. "You could have broken your fucking knuckles, you idiot," I scolded, taking his right hand in mine to check he hadn't done any damage.

After an entire week working out with Cass at the Reapers' gym, I was becoming more aware of things like that. Luckily, though, when I uncurled Steele's fist, I found he was wearing a glove of sorts. One with the fingers cut out and woven metal across the knuckles.

"I'm fine," he murmured under his breath, his tone losing that cold edge it'd had since I'd walked in. His hand turned over in mine, linking our fingers together briefly and squeezing. For a moment I almost forgot where we were. I almost forgot that there was a beaten, bloody killer strapped to the chair not five feet from me and that I was still staggeringly angry at Steele for keeping Archer's fucking secret.

I wanted to forgive him. I wanted to understand and let bygones be bygones. But my stubborn pride and betrayed trust wouldn't let me move on until he'd paid in some way. I unlinked our fingers and took a step away.

"We got all the information we need from Hank already, Princess," Archer said, dousing my weird mood with a bucket of irritation. "He's only still breathing for your benefit."

I shot Archer a small frown of confusion, but Hank started laughing again. Blood was pouring down his chin now from the teeth Steele had knocked out, but he didn't seem bothered. I supposed he was past that point by now.

"Isn't that cute, eh? Your boyfriends wanted you to see them kill a man. If that's not romance, I dunno what is." His lip curled in a blood-soaked sneer. "What's the reward for that these days? Blow jobs? Anal? I bet you're the kinda girl who loves a good gang bang, eh? Just like your mama."

I blinked at him, hardly believing what he'd just said. Cold fury built inside me like a tidal wave, but I gritted my teeth to hold it at bay.

"Do we need him alive for anything else?" I asked, keeping my eyes locked on Hank. "Or did you really just wait so I could see him die?"

"We thought you might appreciate seeing for yourself that there was one less threat on your life, Madison Kate," Archer snapped, sounding annoyed as hell at my question. He stalked over to the table where Kody stood and snatched something off it. "Recognize this?"

Archer tossed something at me, and I instinctively caught it. Cool metal touched my fingers, and my jaw dropped as I inspected what he'd thrown.

"This is…" I turned the folding knife over in my hands, then flicked the blade out to hold it to the light. It wasn't bloodred, like Archer's, but it was a deep enough orange that I could have easily mistaken it for red in dim lighting.

My gaze shot to Hank, accusing.

"You fucking stabbed me."

A blood-covered grin curved his lips. "Not as many times as I should have."

Fury raced through me, filling every inch of my body, and then…nothing. I went numb and emotionless. Or that's what I thought, until I found myself driving the orange blade deep into Hank's thigh.

I gasped in shock as hot blood coated my hand, and Hank let out a short scream of pain. It quickly faded to laughter, though, and I clenched my teeth.

Stabbing him back hadn't been a conscious thought, but now that I'd done it, I couldn't just run away like a scared bunny. And I sure as shit wasn't leaving the weapon sticking out of his leg like an invitation to try to fight back.

Nope, I tightened my jaw and wrenched the knife back out again, catching a spray of blood to the face in the process. Maybe I'd nicked an artery.

"Like mother like daughter, eh?" Hank taunted me as I took a shaking step away from him. "She loved the violence too. Turned her on."

Bile rose in my throat. "You don't know the first fucking thing about my mother," I told him in a hard voice. A flicker of pride warmed me at the strength in my voice. Not even the slightest quiver of fear or upset showed through, despite the tornado of emotions that was sweeping back into me. So much for that calm that had allowed me to stab a man.

"Can I kill him now?" Kody asked when Hank started a jarring mix of laughter and groaning. "He's just talking shit to try to get under MK's skin."

Steele scowled. "Fuck you. I've been the one down here with him all damn day; if anyone kills him, it's me."

Archer let out a heavy sigh from beside me, and for a second I thought he was irritated by their argument. But then he fucking joined in. "I'll kill him," he declared. "It's only fair, seeing as Madison Kate thought it was me who stabbed her."

Hank was still grinning at me while the boys debated who got to kill him, and I knew he had more poison to come. None of it would be helpful, though. None of it would give me any relevant clues on who was trying to kill me or who was stalking me. When Steele said they had all the information they needed, I believed him. He was thorough.

"All this blood and violence is making you wetter than a slut in summer, eh?" Hank taunted me in a low voice. The guys didn't even hear him as their argument escalated. Who knew they each had so many reasons why they should get to end this prick's life?

I heaved a sigh and gave Hank a bored look. "Slut-shaming insults are so passé, Hank. If you weren't about to die, I'd suggest you work on new material." Casting a glance at the guys, I found them still animatedly arguing their points, so I slipped past Kody and picked up the gun sitting between a mallet and a blowtorch.

It was heavier than I'd expected, but the weight of it in my hand didn't scare me. Quite the opposite. While I'd never learned to shoot, I had listened and paid attention. I knew Steele carried a Glock-19, and I'd bet it was already loaded.

Without giving myself a moment to second-guess what I was

doing, I closed the space between Hank and me. With the gun just an inch from the back of his head, I squeezed the trigger.

Bang.

Just like that.

Blood and chunks of Hank's head spattered the room, and the single gunshot echoed through the small space with deafening volume.

My hand remained steady as I lowered the weapon and carefully placed it back on the tool table.

The guys just stared at me, aghast but silent.

"Problem solved," I told them.

Clearing my throat, I carefully stepped past the bleeding mess that was Hank and made my way out of the room. I made it as far as the ladder before my hands started shaking.

One of the guys called something out after me, but I wasn't listening. By the time I'd clambered out of the trapdoor, my ears were ringing and my whole body trembling.

I'd just shot a guy.

I'd just killed someone in cold blood.

What the *fuck* had I been thinking?

When I stumbled out of the dust-filled cabin, my eyes were streaming and my stomach churning.

I'd shot someone. I was a fucking murderer.

Warm hands grabbed my upper arms as my knees buckled. Strong arms wrapped around me, saving me from crumpling into the dirt beside Archer's car.

I'd just killed a man, and now I was no better than the guys. Blood was on my hands now, and I could no longer turn my face away and feign innocence to the dark, violent world they were involved in.

Princess Danvers was long gone. If this didn't prove it, nothing would.

Maybe I was a D'Ath after all.

CHAPTER 16

Steele stood there with me for ages, just hugging me to his body and not speaking. He didn't whisper platitudes or reassurances. He just held me while I pressed my face to his chest and let the adrenaline, fear, and shock ebb from my bloodstream.

His embrace said more than any words ever could. It told me that no matter what else was going on, no matter how much unresolved bullshit there was between us, he was still there for me. When I needed him—and I did—he was there for me, unquestioningly.

When the trembles finally subsided, Steele silently coaxed me around the side of the cabin to where his car was parked. He popped the passenger door open for me, and I slid inside without a protest.

It wasn't until we'd driven away from the cabin—without Kody and Archer—that I looked over at Steele.

"Where are we going?" I asked him. My voice came out quiet and kind of hollow.

I'd just killed a man.

Steele looked back at me, holding my gaze longer than he should have, considering he was taking the mountain road much faster than the legal speed limit. That was something that should have frightened me, given my history with car crashes, but it didn't.

Was I broken?

"I'm taking you home, MK," he replied, shifting his gaze back to the road.

I frowned. "What about..." I trailed off, unable to finish that sentence out loud. I didn't need to, though. Steele knew where my head was.

"Kody and Archer can fucking clean up that mess. It's the least they can do after hogging all your time today while I was doing the dirty work."

It shouldn't have been funny, but a smile pulled at my lips anyway. He was just so fucking casual about torturing that guy... and about me killing him. Then again, after what Kody had told me about the Tri-State Timberwolves, I shouldn't be surprised. Steele was no stranger to violence and death. None of them were.

He drove with one hand, dropping his right hand to rest on his thigh, and I stared at the glove he still wore.

"That was smart thinking," I murmured, reaching out and taking his hand in mine. The glove was fastened with a Velcro strap around the wrist, and I peeled it open. Flakes of dried blood dusted the leg of my jeans as I tugged the glove from Steele's hand and inspected his skin for damage.

"Arch got them made for me years ago," he replied as I ran my thumbs over his knuckles, reassuring myself that he hadn't just fucked up his hands for the sake of getting *my* answers out of Hank. "After...after Rachel died, I did some dumb shit. Got into fights and messed up my hands a bit. Instead of sidelining me or trying to *fix* me, he just got those gloves made. They're like brass knuckles that also protect my hands. Win-win."

I released his hand somewhat reluctantly, turning my attention to the glove I'd stripped off him. The leather was soft, like it'd seen a lot of wear. Despite the violent purpose of the garment, I couldn't

112

help but love it. Not just because it kept Steele's hands safe but because Archer had done a thoughtful thing for his friend. Maybe he was only a massive cunt when I was around.

"Why did Hank have one of Phillip's knives?" I asked after a long silence. "I thought they were only given to people who earned them in his training program."

Steele glanced at me. "They were."

My brows hitched. "Hank was in his program?" Steele jerked a short nod. "But I thought... Actually, I have no idea what I thought. I guess I *assumed* Phillip's training was meant to help kids get out of the crime life. Not train them to be better criminals."

"It was," Steele replied. "But Phillip wasn't always operating with full mental capacities. And his idea of *saving* us was somewhat skewed. Loads of his trainees used what they learned to make a successful life of crime. Like Hank and Zane."

I nodded my understanding. "And like you three." I wasn't accusing them, just stating a fact. But Steele's hand tightened on the steering wheel anyway.

"Yes." He agreed, his voice clipped.

"How did he know my mother?" It was a question I didn't want to ask, but I knew the curiosity would eat away at me. "The way he spoke about her—"

"He was trying to piss you off," Steele said, his tone firm. "He likely met her once or twice with the Reapers, but that's it."

I frowned. "Hank was a Reaper?"

Why the fuck hadn't Zane said something? Did he know?

"No, he was just an associate. Hank was a freelancer, mostly hired muscle. Occasional hits. Very minor league." Steele sounded seriously unimpressed, and I agreed.

I sighed. "I suppose I should be grateful he was so minor league. Probably the only reason I'm not dead now."

"Or because you've got three of the best watching your back at all times," he muttered under his breath. I shot him a narrow-eyed look, and he just shrugged. "Hank being a shitty hit man helped too. I'm surprised he even passed Phillip's training at all."

I looked out the window, propping my face up on my hand, then cringing when I touched sticky blood on my forehead. I needed a shower so freaking bad, but I doubted I looked anywhere near as bad as Steele. He really should have worn black when torturing a guy.

"Are you hungry?" he asked some minutes later. I arched a brow at him, and he shrugged. "I've been dealing with Hank since about ten o'clock last night, and Archer didn't leave me any snacks. I'm fucking starving."

Now that he mentioned it…yeah, I was pretty damn hungry.

"There's a drive-through a couple blocks south of my apartment," I suggested. "I don't think we should try entering a restaurant looking like this."

Steele quirked a smile at me, his eyes taking in the blood spatter on my face and neck. "Fair point."

We didn't speak again as he drove us back into Shadow Grove, and that was perfectly fine by me. Steele never felt the need to fill silences with idle chatter, which only gave more gravity to his words when he did speak.

The girl at the drive-through gave us a bored look when we pulled up to the food window, which almost set me off laughing. Here we were, drenched in blood and gore ordering burgers and Cokes. She probably assumed it was fake.

Outside my building, Steele parked in a free space, and I clutched the warm bags of food to my chest as we made our way inside. I should have just thanked him for the ride home and told him to fuck off. But…my grudge could wait. We both needed to wash up and eat. And I needed to know what he'd learned from Hank.

The lobby was empty, luckily, but the same couldn't be said for my corridor. Just as we stepped out of the elevator, Cass's door opened. He and Zane stepped out, chatting, but their conversation cut short when they saw Steele and me.

A cruel sort of smile curved Zane's lips, and Cass just scowled.

"Well, well. Looks like you two have been up to mischief. Where was our invitation?" Zane was mocking, his gaze sharp, and I was starting to figure out why his brother disliked him so much. What the fuck had my mom been thinking?

Oh yeah—bad-boy syndrome. Something I was all too familiar with.

"Nothing to do with you, Zane," Steele replied before I could say anything. Not that I had any snappy comebacks to that.

I killed a man today.

"Are you okay, kid?" Cass asked me in that gravelly rumble of his. "Not your blood, I hope?"

I shook my head. "Definitely not mine."

"Good." He jerked a nod, then brushed past us to stab the elevator call button.

Zane stayed a moment longer, that devilish smile playing across his face as I fished out my keys and unlocked my apartment door. I owed Zane a lot and had every intention of paying him back. But I could smell a fight brewing between him and Steele, and I'd probably had enough violence for one day.

"Oh, while I remember"—Zane snapped his fingers like the thought had just occurred to him—"I set up that meeting you asked about, Madison Kate. She can see you Monday at ten if that works?"

I froze. My shoulders bunched, and I fixed a careful smile to my lips before I turned back to face him. "Yep, sounds great," I replied quickly. "Text me the address?"

Zane grinned, giving Steele a smug look. "Can do. You two have a good night, alright? And if you need any help on a cleanup—"

"We don't," Steele snapped, cutting him off. "It's handled."

Zane shrugged. "Always willing to help if you need it." His smile was that of a crocodile luring a goat closer to the water.

Steele scoffed. "I just fucking bet you are."

There was an awkward standoff then, with Steele and Zane staring at each other like they could win something by refusing to blink first.

Fucking children.

My stomach grumbled, so I pushed my front door open farther and stepped inside. "Thanks, Zane. I appreciate you setting that meeting up." I shifted my gaze to Steele. "You coming inside or what?"

His eyes narrowed at Zane in an unspoken warning; then he stepped inside my apartment and let me close the door behind him.

With the panel of wood separating us from Zane D'Ath, I let out a long breath before glaring at Steele.

"What the fuck was that all about?" I asked, making my way over to the kitchen and dropping our bags of food on the counter. "I thought you might stab him in the throat if he got any closer."

Steele grimaced. "Maybe." I rolled my eyes, and his lips quirked in a smile. "Just bad blood between us. He was being a shithead to try to get a rise out of me."

"Seems like it worked," I replied, folding my arms under my breasts.

Steele smirked. "Is he currently bleeding out in the hallway? No? Then not even close." He paused, his smirk melting into a concerned frown. "You know he's using you, right? They all are. Zane and the Reapers don't do anything out of the goodness of their hearts...because they don't *have* any goodness."

"You used to be a Reaper too," I reminded him, my voice soft as I braced my hands on the counter. I knew so little about his history with the Shadow Grove gangs. Why didn't I know more? Had I really been so dick drunk with Steele that I hadn't gotten to know him beyond what was right in front of me?

Then again, did his past really matter in the grand scheme of things? I knew who he was now...and I *liked* him. Even in spite of our current situation. Whatever had shaped him to be this person was interesting, but not a deal breaker. Was it?

"My point exactly," Steele replied, holding eye contact with me like he was daring me to flinch. He was totally full of shit, though.

I rolled my eyes. "Oh, you have no goodness, huh? Sure. And I'm a three-headed unicorn who shits rainbows and farts glitter." With a sigh, I shook my head. "I'm just going to wash my face, and then you can shower."

Making my way over to my bedroom and the attached bathroom, I tried really, *really* hard not to think about what had happened the last time Steele used my shower to rinse blood off his skin.

"I don't need to shower," he called after me as I ran my sink tap and inspected the mess coating the side of my face and neck. "Just toss me a washcloth or something."

I shook my head at my own reflection and destroyed one of my pristine white washcloths to wipe all of Hank's blood from my face. I hadn't been spattered by too much, but it still made my skin crawl nonetheless.

When I was satisfied that it was all gone, I rinsed out the cloth and dried my face before heading back out to the kitchen.

"Get in the damn shower, Max Steele," I ordered my guest in a hard voice. "You're not getting bits of Hank all over my sofa, and it's straight-up unsanitary to eat with blood under your nails. Go."

He gave me a narrow-eyed glare but must have decided it wasn't worth the argument because a moment later he sighed and started toward my bathroom.

"I don't have any spare clothes," he commented, pausing halfway there.

I bit my lip, swallowing back the totally inappropriate excitement at his comment. *Not* now, *MK.*

"I'm sure you'll survive," I replied in a dry tone, totally unable to meet his eyes for fear he'd spot my arousal from across the room. "There are plenty of towels, and I've got a robe hanging on the back of the door. Throw your clothes out, and I'll put them in the wash."

My gaze was on the decorative lamp in the corner of my living room, but I could still see Steele in my peripheral vision. So I saw the grin spread across his face at my suggestion.

"Throw my clothes out for you? Like you've never seen me naked before, MK." His tone was teasing, but his avoidance of *Hellcat* made my chest tighten. But that was only made worse by the fact that he proceeded to grip the bottom of his T-shirt and raise it.

I froze. I fucking froze.

My eyes were still on the lamp. Sort of. He knew I was watching him strip, though... *Oh for the love of god.*

His jeans hit the floor after his T-shirt, and I stopped breathing. It took every ounce of my willpower to turn my back on him and pretend I was totally unaffected by his nakedness.

I wasn't making a good show of it. As I reached for our bags of takeout, his hands came down on the counter to either side of me, caging me in.

"You're not uncomfortable seeing me naked, are you?" he teased, his voice a soft murmur in my ear, and I clenched my teeth to hide the shiver running through me.

I forced a laugh. "Of course not. Why would I be?"

Steele gave a low laugh. Not a single part of him touched me, yet I could feel him everywhere. It was intoxicating. I really was dick drunk on Max Steele.

"So how come you won't look at me?" he countered, amusement threading his voice. "Or are you worried it'll be too hard to keep your hands to yourself? And then where does that leave your feelings of anger and betrayal?" He no longer sounded teasing, just matter-of-fact, like he already knew that was exactly what I was thinking.

Gritting my teeth, I turned my head just far enough to see his bare arm all the way up to his tattoo-covered shoulder. "Go and shower, Steele. The food's getting cold."

He didn't immediately move, letting out a breath that bordered on a sigh, like he was disappointed I hadn't risen to his bait. When he finally shifted his hands from the countertop, it was to brush my hair away from the back of my neck.

"For what it's worth," he said quietly, all traces of teasing gone like they'd never existed, "I'm sorry. I'll probably be sorry for the rest of my life. But I'm not giving up on us, Hellcat. You mean too much to me now."

I didn't respond. I *couldn't*, even if I knew what to say. The lump in my throat was way too thick for words to make their way out.

Steele wasn't hanging around to hear my response—or lack thereof—and moments later I heard the click of the bathroom door closing and the shower turn on.

Only then did I release the breath I hadn't known I was holding. It whooshed out of me in a shudder, and the dampness of tears slicked my cheeks. I quickly swept them away with the palm of my hand, but nothing could shake the mess of anxiety Steele had managed to stir up inside me with those few words.

It was what I'd wanted to hear from him for over a month, wasn't it? So why the fuck couldn't I accept it?

It was too easy, that was why. They were just *words*. I needed more than a pretty apology to let go of the betrayal he'd dealt me in keeping Archer's secrets. Torturing Hank for information was a damn good start, though. Even with the massive chip on my shoulder, I couldn't deny that.

I guess I would just wait and see how forthcoming he wanted to be with that information now.

CHAPTER 17

After I got myself changed, I tossed Steele's blood-crusted clothes in my washing machine and reheated our food in the oven—because everyone knows it's the *only* way to reheat takeout. Microwaves just make it all soggy and gross.

"Can I eat now?" he asked, appearing around the corner with a waft of steam following him.

My mouth instantly went dry. He was fresh and clean, all traces of blood and gore gone from his skin, but he'd taken my suggestion of wearing my bathrobe seriously. The thin, navy blue satin was so tight across his shoulders and arms that I knew he'd stretched it out of shape already, but the way he'd belted it at the waist was all too precarious.

Fucking hell. I knew he didn't have any underwear underneath because Steele *never* wore underwear, and that thought alone had me biting the inside of my cheek.

"MK?" he prompted, raising his brows at me. A slight smile teased at his lips, though, and I felt my cheeks warm. Dammit. I'd been caught perving.

"Yup, sure can," I replied, clearing my throat as I turned away to collect our food and hand him a plate.

We took our food over to the sofa, and I flicked my TV on before starting my burger. It was just some reality TV show about glass blowing, but anything was better than having nothing to fill the awkward silence while we ate.

Steele seemed totally unconcerned with the tension in the room, though. He took his time finishing his food and seemed almost entertained by the glass-blowing competition on my huge flat-screen. When I finished, I placed my empty plate on the coffee table and shot him a serious look.

"So, are we going to talk about this or what?" I asked, despite the wave of anxiety washing through me.

Steele cocked his pierced brow at me and finished his mouthful before placing his plate on top of mine. "Okay, let's talk about it." His tone was calm and careful, and he ran a hand over his buzzed hair. "I didn't tell you about the marriage contract, and I should have. I had plenty of opportunities and I chose to keep my mouth shut every single time and I fucking shouldn't have. I know that *now*, but hindsight can't change the past. So, I'm sorry. It was the wrong choice, and I seriously wish I'd done things differently."

His gray eyes met mine, and I didn't for a second doubt the sincerity of his apology. But…

"That's…that's not what I meant," I replied in a choked whisper. "I meant the fact that I killed Hank."

Both his brows shot up, and his lips parted. "Oh. That."

I nodded. "That. But…yeah, I mean I guess we need to talk about all the other shit too."

Steele shifted on my sofa, turning to face me more but also letting my far-too-small-for-him robe part in an all-too-tempting kind of way. It took every shred of my willpower to keep my eyes on his face and not *anywhere else*.

"You're right; we should talk about Hank," he murmured, running his tongue over his lower lip and flashing me his piercing. "That was the first time you've killed someone, huh?"

My eyes widened, and I spluttered a sound of shock. "*First* time? Yeah, Max. I can't say I've been going around shooting people and keeping it quiet. You know I haven't ever..." I drew a deep breath, shaking my head in disbelief at my own actions. "I've never killed someone, no. I've never even shot a gun before at *anything*."

He reached out and took my hand in his, linking our fingers together loosely. "I know. Sorry, that was a dumb thing to say. But for what it's worth, you looked like a seasoned professional. Smart move shooting point-blank to eliminate the risk of missing."

I snorted a short laugh. "Like there were any other options in a room that small."

Steele quirked a half smile. "Trust me, before Kody learned to shoot, he'd have messed that shot up. Probably would have hit Archer in the foot again."

"Again?" I repeated. "Damn, I wish I could have seen the first time."

He shared a grin with me, then squeezed my fingers. "Are you okay? It's been so long since any of us had our first kill, I've become a bit desensitized to it all."

I took a moment to consider his question. Was I okay? The expected answer was no. No one should be okay after taking a person's life. Right? So why was I so calm?

"I think I am," I finally replied in a whisper. "Or maybe the reality of it hasn't quite set in yet. But I don't feel...*anything*. I'm not torn up with guilt or regret or fear. I'm just...I don't even know. Relieved? That's fucked up, isn't it? I should be feeling more."

Steele didn't immediately placate me. He released my fingers, then shifted closer on the couch and wrapped his arms around me in a tight hug. It was the gesture of comfort I hadn't even known I needed, and I clung on for dear life.

"Let's get something straight, beautiful," he murmured in my ear, his voice low and gruff. "There's no *right way* to deal with a situation like this. There're no rules around human emotions and instincts. If Hank dying by your hand makes you feel relieved, then that's pretty damn understandable. He tried to kill you twice and would have tried again if he'd been released. Maybe he would have succeeded next time."

A ripple of dread ran through me, and I tucked my face against Steele's neck. My arms were around his waist, and the sensation of his hard body encased in my satin robe was doing all sorts of confusing things to my head.

"I thought I had three of the best watching my back," I teased, trying to lighten the mood.

Steele's embrace tightened. "You do. But not even the best are infallible."

I knew what he was referring to. He was constantly beating himself up over my getting stabbed at The Laughing Clown. Hell, they all did, if I was being fair.

"Halloween night wasn't your fault," I told him, pulling away from his hug far enough to meet his eyes. "I was running away. You can't exactly keep me safe when I'm doing everything possible to get away from you."

His brow furrowed. "Is that what you're doing now too?"

I bit my lip, my stomach in a mess of knots. "No."

Tension drained out of Steele's rigid frame as the line between his eyes softened, and somehow that obvious relief reassured me I was making the right move.

"I'm not running away from you guys this time," I elaborated. "I just needed some time and space to get perspective and let my heart mend somewhat. The simple fact remains that someone has put a hit out on me, right?"

Steele nodded, confirming what I'd deduced from the Hank situation.

"Right, well, that's not going to just go away because I moved out. And there's still my stalker...even though he's been scary quiet recently. I'm nowhere near equipped enough to keep myself alive without help, and I'm smart enough to recognize that." I cleared my throat, collecting my thoughts.

"He hasn't been quiet," Steele informed me. "The Reapers must be running interference on your mail here, so he's been dropping it off at the house."

I grimaced, remembering Archer's comment about Bree being threatened. "Do I even want to know what he's sent?"

Steele shook his head. "I wouldn't." His embrace was looser, but his arms were still draped around my waist like he couldn't *not* touch me. Something I was all too comfortable with. "Why are you still here, MK? The Reapers only want to use you."

I shifted back slightly, running a hand through my hair. "They're doing a pretty good job of keeping me safe so far, aren't they? No stalker mail. No attacks when I've been here alone." I tilted my head to the side, giving him a considering look. "Besides, what are they gaining from helping me?"

Obviously something. I wasn't a total moron. I just wanted Steele to confirm my suspicions.

He gave a dry laugh. "Protection."

My brows shot up. "I thought you were going to say money."

Steele shook his head. "I'm sure Zane wouldn't turn down money too, but no. The spineless prick was getting paranoid Archer was going to make a move against the Reapers. He's been searching for leverage since the day we made our move and carved a piece out of his kingdom, and now he has it. You."

I shook my head, not understanding. "How does me being here keep him safe? Aren't the Reapers supposed to be scary motherfuckers?"

He grinned. "They are. But there's always someone scarier, and in this case it's us. So long as you're here, under the Reaper's *protection*, then they're safe."

I took a moment to let that information sink in. It lined up with what Kody'd told me about how they'd bought their freedom from the Reapers with the blood of the Tri-State Timberwolves. Zane must be seething about his little brother holding a position of power over him, so in return, he "helped" me out and I gave him exactly what he wanted. Leverage.

"Always someone scarier, huh?" I muttered, running a hand over my tired face. "So, who's scarier than you three? Or do I want to know?"

Steele gave a short laugh. "That's easy. There's only one person scarier than Archer in this part of the world, but I don't think you'll ever have to worry about him."

I squinted at him. "Let me guess. Hades?"

He gave me a nod of confirmation. "I'll introduce you some-time when everything is less...volatile. You two would probably get along great."

Needing to shake off some of the nervous energy coursing through me, I stood up from the couch and made my way back to the kitchen to grab us Cokes from the fridge. Then I ducked around the corner to my little laundry and tossed Steele's clothes in the dryer.

"So, will you tell me everything you got out of Hank?" I called out, trying to force my brain to focus on the more immediately important subject. "Or is that classified, and I'll have to play stupid mind games with Archer to learn anything valuable?" I returned to the couch and handed him a Coke can, then opened my own.

"Fuck that," he replied, cocking his pierced brow at me. "If Arch wanted to keep all the info classified, he should have fucking stayed and done the dirty work himself."

I grinned. Yeah, Archer had burned one too many bridges lately. Steele, like Kody, was firmly on Team MK these days.

"You were right that someone has put a hit out on you. There's a website, to put it simply, where jobs can be listed. It's very anon-ymous and highly illegal—of course—but that's where your hit is listed. Hank took the job, but when he doesn't make contact

125

within a set time frame, the job will be automatically relisted for someone else to take."

I let out a strangled sound, my chest tight. "So someone else will come after me then? Someone possibly better than Hank?"

Steele grimaced. "Yes. Until we can eliminate the source."

"You mean find out who wants me dead and kill them?"

"Exactly. It'd be pointless just trying to shut down the listing. The technology behind those sites has some of the best cyber-security in the world. No one other than the site creators them-selves could ever hack it. Besides, there'd be nothing stopping whoever is responsible from just listing it again elsewhere." He sipped his drink and settled back against the couch, his free arm extended along the back behind me, not quite touching but so *very* close.

I swallowed another mouthful of Coke and desperately tried to calm the shitstorm of emotions raging within me. Someone wanted me dead—enough that they were hiring professionals. But who? Why?

"Did he tell you how much money was on offer?" I asked. Why it mattered, I had no idea. Maybe I just wanted to understand what a person's life was worth.

Steele gave me a curious look. "I didn't ask, but I can find out from the listing."

I let out a long breath, letting it carry some of my anxiety with it. It would probably be a long freaking time before I could forget the fact that I'd killed someone. But…it didn't bother me as much as it should.

Steele was right. Hank would have killed me, just like the next guy would try. I didn't have to feel bad for putting my own life first.

"What else will you tell me?" I asked him in a tired voice, lean-ing my head on his arm along the back of the couch.

His fingers looped through a lock of my pink hair, and he tugged it gently. "Anything. Anything you want to know, I'll tell you. No more secrets, no more lies. I meant what I said earlier—I regret how everything went down, and I want to prove that to you."

I turned my face toward him, meeting his eyes. "Anything, huh? Will you tell me why Archer *bought* me? Why he kept it this huge secret and treated me like shit from the day we met? Why he fucking *married* me without my knowledge or consent?" Just asking those questions was raising my blood pressure again and getting me fired up.

"I could," Steele replied, his gaze steady. "But do you really want me to tell you? Or would you rather hear it from *him*?"

I held eye contact with him for a long time, wanting to kick back and accuse him of keeping Archer's secrets *again*. But I believed him. If I pushed, if I really wanted him to tell me everything, he would.

"Fucking hell," I groaned, rubbing my tired eyes and cursing out Archer in my brain. Steele knew me too damn well because I *did* want to hear it from the douche canoe himself. I wanted to hear his reasoning directly from his lips. And I wanted to punch him in the fucking teeth for it because *no* reason could justify what he'd done.

Steele just gave an understanding chuckle, tightening his arm around me to scoot us closer together once more. "Ask me something else," he urged in a heartfelt whisper, his lips brushing my neck and sending shivers of warmth through my whole body. "Anything else. Let me prove that I'm not hiding anything from you, Hellcat. Please?"

Fuck. I couldn't possibly hold my grudge against him much longer. He was beating down my defenses just as surely as Kody had the day before.

"Tell me…" I paused to think—something that was harder to do than it should have been, but what could I say? I wasn't dick drunk. I was just…Max Steele drunk. "Tell me something real.

Something true." *Tell me I'm not imagining this intense connection between us. Tell me you didn't lie to me for sex and nothing more. Tell me you care...*

He didn't immediately respond. His fingers threaded into my hair, tangling around the strands at the roots as he tipped my face back and locked eyes with me once more.

"The *truth*, Madison Kate," he murmured, "is that Riot Night wasn't the first time we met."

CHAPTER 18

Steele's words made my heart pound painfully hard, and my mouth went dry with dread.

"What did you just say?" I breathed.

The way his fingers were tangled in my hair, I couldn't run away. I couldn't even break eye contact with him. So I couldn't pretend not to see the raw emotion in his eyes as he spoke.

"Riot Night wasn't the first time we met, and it sure as hell wasn't the first time I started falling for you." His voice was rough, and it made my breath hitch as I tried to inhale deeply.

I shook my head—as much as I could in his grip—and frowned in confusion. "I don't understand. When have we met? Why wouldn't I remember that?"

His lopsided smile was gentle but pained. "It was about six months before your mom died. We think the trauma messed with your memory, or maybe something happened afterward when your dad kept sending you to therapy. Whatever it was, it seems like you've just *erased* these patches of time from your memory. But...I remember."

A hollow ache filled my chest, sorrow for those lost moments. I'd met Steele before? Why couldn't I remember that? I wanted to. So damn badly.

"Tell me everything," I whispered, desperate. "I want to know."

He studied me a moment longer, then released his grip on my hair like he'd reassured himself I wasn't going to flip my lid and kick him out in the street for withholding this information so long. But it wasn't his fault I couldn't remember, and I wasn't entitled to his memories.

"There's not a whole lot to tell," he admitted, trailing his fingers through my hair, then bringing his arms around my waist once more. We were facing one another on my couch, but we could have been on the freaking moon and I wouldn't have noticed, for how focused I was on his face. "Your dad had gone away on some business trip, and your mom decided she wanted to spend those three weeks with Zane. She didn't want your dad to find out, though, so instead of leaving you in the care of your housekeeper, she took you with her."

I frowned. "Took me with her *where*?"

Steele grimaced. "Reaper headquarters."

My brows shot up. That seemed like a really bad place to bring an eleven-year-old.

"Anyway, when Damien found you—this mouthy, fearless, little blond girl—hustling one of his guys at pool, he flipped out. He had some huge argument with Zane, and then next thing we knew, you were *ours*." I made a sound of surprise, and Steele quickly shook his head. "Not like that. We were your babysitters for three weeks."

"We?" I repeated, giving him a suspicious look.

He wrinkled his nose. "Yeah. Me and Arch. Kody was looking after his grandma at the time, down in Texas."

I blinked at him like an owl. He and Archer had *babysat* me for three weeks, and I had zero recollection.

Licking my lips, I searched for some kind of cohesive thought pattern within the scattered mess of info in my brain. "So...what happened?"

Steele shrugged. "Not much. Your mom told everyone she'd

taken you on vacation to see her parents, and then she and Zane shacked up for three weeks. You, me, and Arch just hung out and played a shitload of video games. We had fun." His expression was nostalgic but tainted with sadness.

I frowned. "But something happened, didn't it? Something that Archer has been hating me over for eight fucking years."

Steele parted his lips to answer, but my phone started ringing on the kitchen counter. I glanced over at it, scowling and mentally willing it to shut the fuck up.

"Whoever it is, they can call back," I grumbled. The ringing stopped, then immediately started up again.

I wanted to ignore it and hear the rest of Steele's story—*our* story—but a small thread of worry wove through me. What if it was important? Archer had said Bree was in danger.

"Fuck it," I hissed when my phone started ringing for the third time. I stood up and hurried over to answer it before the call could cut out again. I hesitated a second with my thumb over the green Answer Call button, noticing it was Scott. But why call three times in a row if it wasn't important?

"Scott, what's wrong?" I demanded, bringing the phone to my ear. Steele stood from the couch, flashing me a whole lot of leg from the split in my bathrobe as he crossed the room. I could barely even concentrate on Scott's reply as Steele leaned against the counter beside me.

"...on my way over," Scott was saying when I tuned back in.

I startled. "Wait, what? On your way here?"

"Yes, Maddie. That's what I just said. Are you even listening?" Scott made it sound like he was joking, but there was an edge of irritation to his voice.

I rolled my eyes and bit back a sigh. "Sorry, I was just...busy. Now isn't really a good time, Scott. I'll see you Monday, okay?" I made my way over to my closet-sized laundry while I spoke. Steele's clothes were dry, so I pulled them out.

"It's no trouble. I'm almost there. I grabbed your favorite ice cream too!" Scott sounded so enthusiastic, but I just wanted to tell him to fuck right off. Except…I'd made a promise to myself the day I arrived in Aspen that I'd make more of an effort with friends. I couldn't stay so damn isolated all the time, so involved with Archer and his boys. I needed my own support network, and Scott was a part of that.

Or he would be if he could get it through his thick skull that we would never be more than friends.

I stifled a sigh as I handed Steele his clothes, and he gave me a curious brow raise. As badly as I wanted to finish that conversation with him, it was probably for the best that we'd been interrupted. Every minute I spent with him, my resolve weakened, my anger faded, and my cursed forgiveness crept in. Besides, every time the secrets involved Archer, I really did want to hear it from him firsthand.

"Okay, sure," I found myself mumbling to Scott on the phone. "I'll see you soon, then." I ended the call and gave Steele a shrug. "You should probably go anyway, make sure Kody and Archer haven't been arrested with a dead body in the trunk of their car."

Steele quirked a grin, taking his clothes through to my bedroom to get dressed. "If they have, they can get themselves out of that mess faster than it'd take to call me for help. Shadow Grove cops aren't stupid; they know who really runs this town."

He dressed and came back out in seconds.

"Oh yeah?" I commented, regarding him with a shrewd look. "And I guess that's you three, then?"

Steele gave an easy shrug. "Us. Zane. Ferryman. Hades." He handed my robe back to me, and I curled my fingers around the warm satin. "Shadow Grove hasn't been ruled by the police department in a really long time, MK."

I bit the inside of my cheek, hating that we were back to "MK" again but too much of a stubborn asshole to admit it. Instead, I walked over to my front door and opened it for him.

"Will you be okay here alone?" he asked with a frown, tugging his boots back on. "I can come back later if you want."

Yes, please come back.

"I'll be fine," I told him, contradicting my own thoughts. "Scott and I had an argument earlier; he probably wants to make amends." Steele wanted to argue with me, I could see it all over his face. But he didn't. He just gave me a long look, then sighed and scrubbed a hand over his head. "All right, just...call if you need me. Okay? No matter what time."

I jerked a nod and he exited my apartment. He made it all of three strides down the corridor before my control snapped.

"Did you mean what you said?" I called after him, bracing my hand on the doorframe. He paused and turned back to face me, confused. "When you said you..." My voice threatened to dry up, so I swallowed heavily. Goddamn nerves. "When you said you haven't given up on *us*?"

You mean too much to me now. Those were his words, and they were echoing in my mind like a song stuck on repeat.

"Every damn word," Steele replied without hesitation. "I know that I fucked up, and I know that I hurt you, but I can't change the past. All I can do is change the choices I make in the future and hope that maybe one day it'll be enough to earn forgiveness." He quirked a smile. "I figure torturing a guy for seventeen hours is a good place to start."

I rolled my eyes and bit back a grin. "Yeah, I guess it is."

Steele came back to where I stood, reached out, and gently tucked a stray curl of pink hair behind my ear. "You're one of the best things in my life right now, MK. I'm not risking losing you again, okay?"

Stupid, lovesick butterflies took flight in my stomach, and I cursed every moronic one of them. Fucking butterflies never thought with their heads.

"Okay," I replied after a pause, "but on one condition." I bit

133

my lip, already kicking my own ass for being such a goddamn pushover.

Steele cocked his head to the side, silently questioning, and his fingers slid into the hair at the nape of my neck.

"Stop calling me MK," I whispered, my eyes locked on his pretty gray ones. There was a flicker of confusion in his gaze, then understanding and satisfaction.

His lips pulled up in a grin as he dipped his face to mine. "Anything you want, *Hellcat*."

Steele's kiss was the final nail in the coffin of my anger. Every press of his lips and swipe of his pierced tongue stripped my defenses away and touched my soul. I moaned as my body melted under his hands, and I probably would have dragged him right back into my apartment had we not been interrupted.

As it was, a pointed throat clearing made us reluctantly part.

"Maddie," Scott hissed, standing there in front of the elevator with a bag of ice cream tubs in his hand, his nose a painful shade of purple, and his cheeks flushed red with outrage. "What the fuck? I *thought* I was your boyfriend?" He gave Steele a deliberate look, like I was meant to still be keeping up the charade.

Yeah, that wasn't happening.

Steele just gave a smug laugh and pressed a very deliberate kiss to my lips before letting me go.

"Keep dreaming, champ," he told Scott, clapping him on the shoulder as he passed. "She was never yours."

The wink Steele shot me as he stepped into the elevator was pure sex, and I almost forgot Scott was standing there as I held Steele's gaze until the doors slid shut.

"Maddie," Scott snapped, looking all kinds of pissed off—something I seriously didn't have the patience for after the weekend I'd had so far.

I blew out an irritated sigh. "Scott, I thought you were coming over to make up for that creepy-ass shit you pulled this morning.

But if you're just here to act like a spurned lover, which you're *not*, then you can turn around and fuck right off. I'm not in the mood."

Whoops, there went my whole plan to make more friends.

Scott's face flashed with intense anger, but it was gone as soon as it'd come. Instead, he smoothed his features out to a calmer, more placating expression.

"I'm sorry," he replied in a careful tone. "I'm sorry. Really. I just...I know they really hurt you, and I'm worried. That's all." He took a couple of steps closer, but I blocked the doorway with my body, my hand still braced on the frame.

"Maybe it's not a good idea to hang out tonight," I told him with a frown. "I think I just need some time to myself."

Scott shook his head. "What? No, don't be silly. I brought ice cream." He held up the bag in his hand like that was somehow an access card to my apartment. Yeah, not today, buddy. Besides, I could see the label through the clear plastic bag—mint choc chip. Gross.

"Thank you. That was sweet." No pun intended. "But I really would prefer to just call it a night. We can hang out on Monday at school, okay?"

Scott tried to protest again, but I was already closing the door in his face. Not the politest I'd ever been, but also not the most *impolite*, so I should get points for that much.

He knocked on the door after I'd closed it, calling out my name. But I just flipped my locks and retreated back to my couch. The glass-blowing show was still on, and I quickly found myself way too engrossed in the god-awful potato sculpture one of the women was making.

Then again, art was so subjective. Just because it wasn't to my taste didn't mean others wouldn't love it like it was the next statue of *David*. Maybe. They *were* very realistic old potatoes made out of glass.

My phone rang again, and I missed seeing whether the potatoes won as I went to answer it.

"Hey, girl," I said, bringing the phone to my ear. "What's up?"

"Not much," Bree replied. "Just got home from a dinner date with Dallas. Did, uh, did something happen with Scott today?"

I froze, apprehension rippling through me. "Why do you ask?"

"I dunno," she replied with a laugh, "maybe the twelve missed calls I just had from him? I wanted to call you before I replied, though. Is he being a needy weirdo?"

I let out a long sigh as I took my phone back to the couch and flopped down. "Big-time. Hey, did you seriously use your phone tracker to tell him where I was today? That's not cool, Bree."

"What?" she shrieked, almost bursting my eardrum with her shrill volume. "No! Fuck no. No way. Is that what he said?"

I groaned and rubbed my eyes. "Yep."

Bree dissolved into curses. Creative curses. Dallas was really influencing her vocabulary.

"Do you want to come over?" I asked, cutting her off. "I could really do with an in-person bitch session if it's not too late?" I glanced at my phone and wrinkled my nose when I realized it was already after nine.

I half expected Bree to say no, but I should have known her better than that.

"Hell yes," she replied quickly. "I can be there in fifteen. Want me to bring wine?"

I grinned. "Please. And ice cream." Fucking Scott had given me a craving.

Bree laughed. "You bet, what flavor?"

"Anything but mint chocolate chip," I replied with a gagging noise.

"Well, duh," she replied with a snort. "Everyone knows you despise that toothpastey shit. I'll see you soon."

I ended the call and tossed my phone on the coffee table. I'd made the right call to send both Steele *and* Scott home. A girls' night with wine and ice cream was *exactly* what I needed to de-stress.

Hopefully.

CHAPTER 19

Bree knocked on my door halfway through the next round of the glass-blowing competition and promptly wrinkled her nose at my choice of entertainment.

"Taking up a new hobby, girl?" she teased, taking the other half of the couch and handing me a pint of cookie dough ice cream with a spoon.

I moaned in relief and eagerly pulled the top off it. "You're the best. And this show is weirdly addictive. Find something else, though." I tossed her the remote, and she started scrolling while I crammed my face with delicious ice cream.

She selected an equally trashy reality TV show about nail art, then muted the TV and turned to face me with a frown.

"All right, spill. What was that shit about Scott using my phone tracker? I can tell you, hand on heart, I haven't even spoken to him today. Whatever the fuck he said I did, he's a damn liar." She pressed her palm to her chest, and her expression was fierce. I didn't blame her; it was a pretty serious accusation from Scott.

I stared back at her as I finished my mouthful, then sighed heavily. "Yeah, I didn't think you would have. He showed up at this warehouse-bar-conversion thing where I had a photo shoot with Archer—"

"Wait, *what*?" Bree's voice rose to shrill levels. "Rewind. Wait, no, tell me about the Scott thing first, *then* rewind and fill me in on what the fuck you were doing with Archer."

I shot her a grin as I took the unopened wine from her bag and twisted the cap off. I took a gulp straight from the bottle before explaining further. The weekend had been a hell of a mess already; I deserved to drink wine without a glass.

"Okay, so Scott showed up at this photo shoot in the old West Shadow Grove warehouse district and started a fight with Kody." I cringed, remembering the pathetic punch Scott had tried to throw.

Bree sucked in a dramatic gasp. "He didn't. Is he brain dead? There was no way he could have won that!"

I snickered. "I know, girl. Trust me, he is the worse for wear now. Anyway, I asked him how the fuck he found me when even *I* hadn't known we were going there. He claimed he'd asked you to use your phone tracker."

"That mother*fucker*," Bree hissed. "I'm going to break his damn nose. Why the fuck would he say that? It's not true. You know that, right? I would never do that."

I hesitated only a fraction of a second before I nodded. "You'll have to get in line on breaking his nose, babe. Kody hit him pretty hard this morning. But yeah, I didn't think you'd do that. It didn't really ring true when he said it."

She frowned. "You hesitated. Did you... MK, I would never put you in danger deliberately. Is this because of what happened after Archer's fight?" Her voice was small, hurt, and I felt like an asshole for rehashing a closed argument. That night, when she'd thought Dallas was hitting on me and taken off, she'd had no way of knowing I'd been drugged. Afterward, the guys hadn't let anyone else into the hospital to see me, but Bree and I had worked it all out in Aspen. We were good.

"No, no way. I didn't seriously think you'd done anything. But... I dunno, girl. You've been a bit sketchy since I got back from Cambodia, haven't you? There was a moment when I wondered if maybe… I dunno." I bit my lip at the stricken look on her face, but the damage was done. It was a conversation we were way overdue for.

"I…" Bree started to protest, but before she even got any words out, her face crumpled and tears welled up. "I'm sorry," she sobbed, and I scrambled to put my ice cream and wine down so I could hug her.

"Bree, babe. What's going on with you? I feel like the worst kind of friend that it's taken this long for me to even ask." I tried to keep my voice calm and understanding, but she was freaking me out. What was she apologizing for?

She sobbed into my shoulder for a couple of minutes, and I just ran my hand over her hair in the only soothing gesture I knew. Emotions and comfort weren't exactly my forte.

"God, I'm so sorry, MK," she sniffled as she peeled her face away from my T-shirt and swiped at her eyes. "I'm sorry. I'm such a fucking mess right now, and I'm the one who's been a crappy friend. I just…" She trailed off into another round of crying, and I clambered off the couch to fetch her some tissues from the bathroom.

"Here," I said, sitting back down and passing her the tissue box. "Take your time, girl. You don't have to tell me if you don't want to; I just want you to know I'm here for you. Okay?"

Bree blew her nose and dried her eyes, then shook her head. "No, I need to tell you. I *want* to tell you. It just never really seemed like the right time, you know? You've got so much on your mind with the stalker and the *killers*, and then there's your whole marriage thing? You seriously have so many more important things…"

"Whoa, no. Bree, I'm *never* too busy to listen to your problems. I'm sorry I made you feel that way." Guilt gnawed at my stomach to see Bree's raw emotions. I really hadn't been available to her since I'd come back. I'd been so caught up in all my problems… Yeah, they were heavy problems, but that didn't excuse how I'd ignored her pain.

I reached out and snagged the bottle of wine again to hand it to Bree.

"Drink, then talk. I'm listening."

She took a couple of calming breaths, then did as I said. She took three long swallows of the wine, an Australian Riesling, and then handed me back the bottle.

"Okay. Fuck. Okay, here goes." She didn't meet my eyes, instead looking down at her hands. "So, right before you got back from Cambodia"—she paused, taking another breath for courage— "about three weeks before, I guess, I found out that I was pregnant."

My jaw hit the floor.

"What?" Shock froze my brain for a few seconds, and fresh tears trailed down Bree's face. "Are you still…" My eyes shot to her flat stomach, and I shook my head. "No, obviously not. Sorry, that was dumb. What happened? Was it…was it Dallas?"

Bree let out a bitter laugh. "I wish. No, it was just some guy that I'd been seeing. It was so fucking dumb; the whole relationship never should have happened. But he was so charming and sexy and…I dunno. It was dumb. When I told him, he totally flipped out and ended things."

That motherfucker.

"Bree, fuck. I'm so freaking sorry." Because what else could I say? I couldn't even imagine what she'd been going through when I blew back into her life with my petty revenge plots and boy problems.

She shrugged, sniffing. "It is what it is. He wanted me to get rid of it, and I panicked. I just…I did what he wanted because I thought we had a future together."

My heart constricted painfully for her. Whoever this guy was, I was going to fucking castrate him.

"Bree…" I clenched my jaw, swallowing the words of pity that had been about to spill out of my mouth. Bree deserved better than my pity; she deserved payback on that fucker. What kind of man got a girl pregnant, then emotionally manipulated her into an abortion, then still left her heartbroken and distraught? I knew that was what had happened; the pieces clicked together all too easily without her having to say it.

"Anyway, that was, like, almost six months ago," she continued, brushing aside all the pain with a watery smile. "And something good came from it all, so I can't be too down on life."

I quirked a knowing smile. "Dallas?"

She blushed and nodded. "He went with me to the clinic after David didn't show up for my appointment. I guess that's the other reason I've been acting so fucking weird around you."

I frowned, confused. "Because of Dallas? Why? We haven't spoken since…well, basically since he went to jail, like, four years ago. You knew that."

She sighed, grimacing. "Right, I did know that. But what *you* didn't know was that Dallas never went down for armed robbery. Or he did on paper, but he was nowhere near that convenience store. Your dad set him up as punishment for sleeping with you, like a warning to other Wraiths not to touch his property."

My jaw dropped for the second time. "What?" My exclamation was strangled and horrified. It struck a note of dread and recognition in me, though. Vaguely I recalled something my father had said over the phone, while speaking to Archer. Something about *handling the situation*. I'd been so caught up in my own shit, I'd totally forgotten about it until now.

She wrinkled her nose. "Yeah, it's fucked up. No joke. But Dallas never told you, right?" I shook my head. "And he never even *blamed* you for it. He was all forgiveness and…I dunno. I just got the feeling he was still crazy in love with you. So then when you showed up again, like, three weeks after we reconnected, I panicked a bit."

Understanding washed over me, tempered by shock from what she'd just told me. Holy *shit*. My dad was an actual, irredeemable cunt.

"You thought I was going to see Dallas again and fall madly back in love now that we're both all grown up?" I asked her, and she gave an uncomfortable shrug. "Probably didn't help that the first time I needed extra assistance in my revenge plan, I called him in. Fuck, I'm sorry, Bree. If I'd known—"

"But you didn't," she cut me off. "And that's on me for keeping it all secret. I'd developed this…I dunno, this fixation with how I equally wanted to *be* you and also wanted you to go back to Cambodia and leave us the fuck alone. I swear, it was a short-lived thing, and my therapist thinks it was just a messed-up way my brain was dealing with the guilt and grief and… I'm just really sorry, girl."

She inhaled and exhaled deeply, her shoulders rising and falling as she got her emotions under control. Another tissue took care of the fresh tears, and she blew her nose before continuing. "I never ever betrayed your safety, though. Not like Scott was implying. There were a couple of moments where I *so* badly wanted things to go back to the way they were, you know? Before Riot Night when we were just spoiled princesses with nothing more stressful in our lives than what nail polish to wear and how shitty the Shadow Prep boys were in bed."

Her insistence on throwing parties and going out for girls' nights suddenly made a whole lot more sense, and I fucking *got it*. At least once a day, I found myself nostalgic for when my life was a whole shitload less complicated—exactly what Bree was saying—so yeah, I fucking got it.

"I'm sorry it took me this long to realize you had bad shit going on, Bree," I said softly. "You can always talk to me, okay? Any fucking time. And if you need that normalcy, then let's just do this. We can have normal without risking my crazy stalker cutting out our hearts and dropping them off on the doorstep in a gift-wrapped box."

Bree cringed. "Geez, when you put it like that, I feel like an even bigger moron for wanting a *girls' night* without your shadows." I laughed, but she covered her face and groaned. "Okay, can we change the subject now? Can you please tell me about this photo shoot with *Archer*, of all people? I thought you'd declared holy war on those three?"

I laughed at that. "I have. Or I had. Ugh, Kody and Steele are impossible to stay truly mad at. But tell me something before all of that?"

She nodded quickly. "Anything."

"Are you okay now? Like, really okay? You said you have a therapist?" I eyed her carefully, searching her face for any signs of bullshit. I didn't want her just telling me what I wanted to hear.

But when she nodded, I believed her. "I am. I do have a therapist. Dallas talked me into going just after you got stabbed and I had a bit of a panic attack."

Guilt clawed at me again. It brought all new clarity to the way she'd defended the guys' bullshit moves to keep me safe.

"Well, I'm glad you have help. And that Dallas is being good to you. But if you ever need to talk…"

She smiled with a touch more warmth. "I know. I should have just told you sooner. Now *please* explain the Archer thing."

It was my turn to take a few long swallows from the wine while I gathered my thoughts. It was hard to believe it'd only been a little over twenty-four hours since Bree and I had been at the movies with Dallas and Scott. What a shitstorm we were living in.

"All right," I started, letting out a long breath. "So I'll start with how I ended up fucking Kody, and then I can tell you how I shot a guy today."

Bree's jaw dropped much like mine had at her revelations.

"Holy shit," she breathed, looking shocked as hell. "I knew you'd jump him first. I bet the sex was insane too."

My laughter this time was edging on hysterical, and she gave me a knowing grin.

"Tell me about all the orgasms first; *then* we can talk about shooting people. Goddamn, my best friend is a legit badass now." She muttered the last part, but her smile was proud. She wasn't horrified in the least, and I fucking loved that about Bree.

It felt all kinds of amazing to have my friend back, for real.

CHAPTER 20

Bree and I sat up talking for most of the night and fell asleep on the couch sometime just before dawn. Neither of us had anywhere we desperately needed to be the next day, though, so we didn't give two craps. All that mattered was that we'd reconnected *properly* for the first time since I'd been arrested on Riot Night.

At some point, when I hadn't been asleep anywhere *near* long enough, I woke up with a chill. Grumbling under my breath about sleep disruptions, I dragged a blanket out of the linen closet for Bree, then climbed into my bed to snuggle under blankets. I'd been tucked in for less than a minute, though, when my phone let out a shrill tone and just about made me pee myself in fright.

I dove across to where I'd left it plugged in beside the bed and hit the answer button before even checking the screen so it wouldn't wake Bree up.

"Hello?" I said in a hushed voice, blinking wine haze and sleep from my eyes. No one replied.

Confused, with my heart still pounding hard from the fright, I pulled the phone from my ear and peered at the caller ID.

"What the fuck?" I muttered, putting the phone back to my ear. "Bree? Why are you calling me from the living room?"

No answer, again. Maybe it was just a butt-dial while she was sleeping? But then...no, I could hear breathing. Heavy breathing but not the sort of someone sleeping.

Scrambling out of my blankets, I bit back a wave of apprehension.

"Bree, if this is your idea of a joke..." I started to say, opening my bedroom door and heading back through to where I'd left her asleep on my couch. "Then it's not fucking funny."

The heavy breathing continued in my ear, and when I rounded the corner of the couch, my mouth went dry. Bree was exactly where she'd been a few moments ago, tucked under the blanket I'd just placed on her and snoring softly. Fast asleep.

I swallowed heavily, frozen in place as I stared down at Bree's sleeping form, and the heavy breathing continued in my ear like it was mocking me.

"Who is this?" I whispered in a raspy voice. My eyes searched the room. Had someone broken in and taken Bree's phone? Was someone still here? "Who are you?"

No response.

"It's you, isn't it?" I asked after a moment when I spotted Bree's phone on the carpet beside the couch. I picked it up and held it in my hand, but the screen was dark. "You're my stalker. How'd you do this? Did you clone her sim card or something?"

No response but the breathing increased in speed, laboring quickly but heavily like he was actually getting off on my fear.

Anger swept through me. "You're a fucking psychopath," I hissed into the phone, my fingers clutching the device so hard it hurt.

I placed Bree's phone down on the coffee table and left her to sleep, taking my nightmares back into the bedroom with me. She didn't need to be dealing with this shit after everything she'd told me last night. Waking her up now wouldn't change anything anyway.

"You're sick. What did you hope to achieve by this call? Huh?

Just wanted to scare me? Well, bad news, fuckface. I'm not scared. I'm pissed off, and when I find you, you'll wish you'd never messed with Madison Kate Danvers. That's a fucking promise, you bastard."

I ended the call with trembling fingers, then sat there in the middle of my bed staring down at the screen for a long moment. I was a damn liar—I was *terrified*—but I'd be damned if I let him know that. That was what these predators fed off, wasn't it? The fear of their victims.

Small shivers coursed over my skin like I was ice-cold, and my teeth chattered. It wasn't a physical cold, though. It was just straight up panic.

My phone rang in my hands, and I stifled a scream as the screen lit up with Bree's name once more. This time I didn't mess around. I rejected the call and turned my ringer to silent. Still, I sat there and stared at the screen as it happened again, and again, and again. Countless times, my stalker tried to call me from Bree's number.

Eventually, I turned my phone off completely and placed it face down on my bedside table.

I was shit scared; I wasn't even going to pretend otherwise. But what the hell could I do at five thirty in the morning? I couldn't call anyone. What if he'd somehow tapped into my phone too? I didn't even know if that was possible, but I wasn't taking chances.

After I'd spent way too long staring at my ceiling and imagining all kinds of eyes in the shadows, I gave up on sleep. I needed to do *something* to work off all my anxious energy, and I was pretty sure the gym opened at five every day.

I quickly changed into workout clothes and tied on my sneakers, then scribbled Bree a note to let her know where I'd gone in case she woke up. Doubtful, as she could sleep through a nuclear bomb when she'd been drinking, but better safe than sorry.

Leaving my apartment, I hesitated halfway to the elevator. Cass had warned me not to go to the gym without him, and the idea of even stepping foot in the elevator on my own was giving me hives.

"Fuck it," I growled under my breath and changed direction to bang on my surly neighbor's door. He was probably asleep, but at least I could make him aware of where I was going...just in case something went wrong. I couldn't call Kody. What if *all* my calls went to my stalker? Then I would basically just be setting up a date to get kidnapped or killed. Nope, my phone wasn't safe at all.

I waited for a couple of moments, then decided he wasn't home. I'd made it two steps back toward the elevator when his door slammed open and a seriously pissed-off gangster appeared in the doorway.

"Kid," he growled. "What's wrong?"

My mouth opened, but no actual words came out. He was, for all appearances, totally naked with just a towel clutched to his junk, and ink covered almost every fucking inch of him. Bree was kind of right about Cass being hot as hell...for an old guy.

"Kid," he snapped. "You'd better have a really good reason for interrupting me right now."

"Um," I started, then flushed when I heard a woman's voice from farther inside his apartment. "Sorry, I shouldn't have knocked. I was just planning on going to the gym and wanted to, uh, clear it with you I guess."

Cass stared at me, totally impassive, and I *definitely* regretted not just going on my own.

"Wait here," he finally said. "One minute."

His door slammed in my face before I could protest. It reopened again less than a minute later, and Cass stepped out dressed in his own workout gear.

"You didn't have to come with me," I protested, feeling all kinds of awkward as a sultry, red-haired woman in a rumpled cock-tail dress followed him into the hallway. She glared absolute daggers at me, and I badly wanted no part of that poisonous energy.

"Yes, I did" was his only reply. He barely even acknowledged the woman as he stabbed the elevator call button, then stepped inside the box. "Come on, kid. Let's go. I've got shit to do today."

Uncomfortable as hell, I joined him and the redhead in the elevator and tried not to fidget with the tails of my braided hair while we descended to the foyer. Cass made no move to introduce me to his friend, and she was trying to skin me alive with the strength of her glare, which I pretended not to notice.

When we got to the lobby, the girl tried to pull Cass into an embrace, and he shook her off like she meant less than nothing to him. He hailed a passing taxi and all but shoved her inside, then slammed the door.

"Was that necessary?" I commented, watching the taxi drive away.

Cass just glared at me, and I found myself babbling. Better to pick apart his love life than talk about the reason I so badly needed to hit the punching bag at five thirty in the morning.

"Who is she, anyway? Girlfriend?" I fell into step with him as he strode down the block toward the gym. Or I had to take two or three steps to every one of his giant strides, but I kept up well.

He gave a grunt of disgust in reply. "Not even close, kid. She's no one."

My brows shot up. "Well, that's rude. She's clearly not *no one* if she was good enough to fuck."

Cass rolled his eyes. No shit. I counted that as a win for simply getting a human reaction out of him. "Okay, fine. She's a place-filler. Happy?"

Well, now I was even more intrigued. "A place-filler is hardly an improvement on *no one*, but I get the picture. So...what's the story, then?"

He levelled a glare at me, holding the front door to the gym open for me to enter. "No fucking story, kid. Let it drop."

I grinned. I'd spent enough time with Cass to know he wasn't going to hurt me over a bit of teasing banter. He *cared* about my safety in his own gangster sort of way, regardless of what Steele thought the Reapers' real motivations were.

"No way," I replied with a laugh. "Okay, if you won't tell me, I'll have to guess." I thought on it for a moment while we made our way across the mostly empty gym to the punching bags. "She's a place-filler…which means you're fucking her *instead* of the girl you really want to fuck. Ex-girlfriend? Ex-*wife*?"

Cass remained impassive, helping me tape my hands and get my gloves on while I waited for a response.

He must have realized I wasn't letting it drop too, because he let out an irritated sigh. "Not ex-anything. Just unavailable."

I pursed my lips, thinking. Then gasped. "Rival gang?" Cass's face flickered with something close to surprise, and I knew I'd hit the jackpot. "Damn, Cass. That's Shakespeare shit, right there. Which gang? Wraiths?"

"I'm not discussing this with you, kid. Hit the damn bag and vent whatever has you so squirrely at this time of morning." He pointed at the bag. "You know what to do."

He stomped away, ending our conversation, and I was left alone with my scattered thoughts once more. Damn it.

Breathing deeply, I took to the bag and tried to work out all the fear and paranoia from my stalker's latest game. It was so freaking hard, though, when I had no face to picture on the bag. So instead, I found myself pounding my gloves into the images of Hank and Archer. Always, always, I ended up venting my frustrations over *Archer D'Ath*.

He'd kissed me at the photo shoot…and I hadn't hated it.

What the fuck was wrong with me?

CHAPTER 21

Despite telling Scott I'd see him Monday morning, I decided to skip my morning classes. I didn't want to risk being late for the meeting Zane had set up for me, and if Archer caught wind of what that meeting was? Yeah, I could see some dire emergency suddenly stopping me from getting to it.

Bree had been horrified when I'd come home from the gym and told her what had happened with my stalker calls. She'd gone out straightaway and come back with a new sim card for each of us, prepaid ones that she'd loaded with more than enough credit to last us months.

"This way, if we're not on a plan, there's none of that phone-tracking bullshit," she'd told me. Smart girl.

I still didn't want to risk contacting *anyone* else, though. Not until I knew the call would actually go to the person intended and my stalker wouldn't intercept it. So I'd just have to tell the guys about it when I inevitably ran into one of them in person. If my stalker had cloned their numbers as well as Bree's, it wouldn't matter what number I called from; it wouldn't reach them.

"Do you want to take my car?" Bree asked on Monday morning when we were both getting ready for the day. She'd stayed with me the rest of the weekend and run interference when Scott turned up *again* wanting to hang out.

I wrinkled my nose. "No…not really. Thank you for offering, though."

She nodded with understanding as she curled her hair in my bathroom mirror. "All good, girl. Whenever you're ready." She wasn't being a bitch about my driving aversion, simply offering me easy opportunities to work through it. "Do you want me to come with you or anything? I don't mind cutting classes."

I smiled at her in the mirror as I swiped mascara over my lashes. "Nah, I'll be fine. Zane actually offered to drive me over there himself."

Her grin turned sly. "MK, you saucy minx. Adding the older brother to your harem too?"

I spluttered. "Oh, ew! No, Bree! Jesus, girl, he was fucking my mom. He was almost my stepdad. Gross. Also, he's just the lanky, sneaky version of Archer, and I've got more than enough D'Ath bullshit in my life right now."

She just rolled her eyes, teasing. "Okay fine, spoilsport. You've got a decent point there. Well, just stay safe, okay? With everything you've told me, it sounds like your life could be in even more danger now than before."

I grimaced. "Right, unless the next guy is as lousy a shot as Hank was."

"I'll keep all my fingers crossed for that scenario, girl," Bree replied in a dry tone. "Okay. I'd better get to school, then. You sure you're okay on your own?"

I nodded. "Trust me, I'm far from alone here. The Reapers aren't letting anyone get their paws on their human shield." I wasn't even bitter about it either. It was a mutually beneficial relationship—they remained safe from Archer's ire, and I got the resources I needed to rip up that bullshit marriage contract.

"All right, I trust you to make smart decisions, MK. Call me afterward, and I'll pick you up, okay? We can do lunch *without* that snake, Scott." She smacked me on the ass playfully on her way out of my bathroom, then called out, "See ya!" on her way out of my apartment.

Fucking Scott was turning into yet another complication that I didn't have the time or energy to deal with. Why the hell had he lied about how he'd found me on the weekend? What was he covering up?

The only logical conclusion Bree and I had come to was that he'd followed us when we left my apartment in the morning. Definite creeper behavior.

The only thing we needed to work out now was if he was a harmless creeper who just didn't understand correct etiquette for friendships...or one that was much more sinister. Like a stalker.

I took my time finishing getting ready, dressing in the most corporate clothing I had in my meager wardrobe: black pencil skirt, navy satin blouse, and black, stiletto heels. My makeup was flawless and my dusky-rose hair twisted into a neat chignon. I needed this meeting to go well because I had no plan B.

A knock sounded on my door right on time, and I opened it to find Zane standing there with another of his gangster dudes.

"Ho-ly shit, Madison Kate," the leader of the Reapers commented with an appreciative whistle. "Maybe my little brother was onto something by wife-ing your ass before anyone saw it on the market."

I curled my lip in disgust. "Don't be a sleazy old man, Zane. You were almost my daddy...and not in the sexy way."

Zane's companion snickered a laugh, and the Reaper leader himself just grinned broadly. "Sassy bitch, just like your mom. Come on, then." He stood back so I could lock my door, and then his buddy shadowed us out of the building.

"Madison Kate, this is Roach, by the way. He's gonna keep an eye on you this morning because I have some business to take care of downtown." Zane jerked his head to the shaved-head, tattoo-covered punk. Despite his hardcore gangster look, he didn't seem like a bad guy. He even offered his hand to me to shake.

"Worried about keeping your insurance policy safe, Zane?" I taunted him with a raised brow as Roach unlocked an old-school muscle car across the street.

The Reapers' leader just shrugged and lit up a cigarette. "Based on the amount of blood you and Steele were wearing the other night? I'd be stupid not to be concerned. You two were up to no good, and that shit has a way of blowing up if you're not watching out."

I couldn't disagree with that statement, so I just nodded and followed Roach into the car. Apparently Zane wasn't coming with us at all, because once I was strapped in, Roach pulled away from the curb.

We drove most of the way in silence. I was lost in my thoughts, and Roach seemed to have nothing to say beyond offering me a cigarette when he lit up. I declined. The Reapers laced their tobacco with weed, and I needed all my wits about me.

When he parked, I was surprised to see him get out of the car with me.

Roach just shrugged. "Boss says to keep eyes on you at all times."

Given what I now knew about the hit on me, I wasn't going to argue with that. Not that I believed I wasn't being watched by anyone else as well. One of the three boys would have eyes on me.

I couldn't wait to see what they'd do when they realized who I was meeting with.

Roach and I took the elevators all the way up to the thirty-fourth floor of the high-rise, earning all kinds of curious looks from smartly dressed corporates. I gave my name to the girl at the reception desk, and we were ushered through to a waiting area.

We'd only sat there a few minutes before an attractive,

middle-aged woman with auburn hair exited an office and approached us.

"Madison Kate?" she asked with a warm smile. I nodded, standing, and she held out her hand. "It's nice to meet you; I'm Demi."

I shook her offered hand. "Thank you for squeezing me in, Ms. Timber."

"This way." She invited me with her, indicating I follow her into the office. I shot Roach a warning look, telling him to stay put, but he seemed like he wanted to argue.

"She's perfectly safe with me, Roach," Demi told my bodyguard. "You can see her through the window, okay?"

The tough guy looked uncertain but didn't protest as I continued into the office and Demi closed the door behind us.

"Take a seat, Madison Kate," she offered, rounding her huge desk to sit down herself. "Now, why don't you start from the beginning. How does a smart, well-connected girl like you end up married to a D'Ath without knowing about it?"

I grimaced. "I wish I knew," I admitted. "But I guess the real question is, can you get me divorced?"

A sly smile crept across Demi's face. "Not annulled? You were underage; there's possible grounds."

I smiled back at her, letting all my spite and malice shine through. "Annulment sounds so very painless, don't you think? I want to hit Archer where it will hurt."

My new attorney gave an equally malicious laugh. "In his wallet? I like your style, Madison Kate. All right, let's get your name back and half the D'Ath fortune to boot."

CHAPTER 22

My meeting with divorce attorney Demi Timber lasted much longer than my allotted appointment time. After I discovered she had all kinds of ties to gang families and businesses herself, I found myself opening up to her about the whole sordid story.

By the time I left, we'd come to one conclusion: I needed to work out if my father had signed a prenuptial agreement along with my marriage contract.

As badly as she wanted to get on board with my rather simplistic plan to divorce Archer and take half his assets in the split, she had her doubts if it would be possible. Considering my father had *sold* me, not just married me off, she'd quite wisely pointed out that there would be a safety net in place for this exact situation.

A clause that might see me forfeiting my *entire* inheritance—however much that really was—in the event of me filing for divorce.

In short? It was too risky to prematurely serve Archer with divorce papers like I wanted to.

But it wasn't a totally wasted meeting. Demi was convinced there was more going on with my inheritance and my mother's family line than anyone was letting on. She'd also suggested—like

I'd already considered—that the hit was someone who'd financially benefit from my death.

Unfortunately—or fortunately, I guess—that wasn't Archer. He couldn't access my money until I turned twenty-one. So I had to be *alive* to turn twenty-one. That in and of itself shed some light into why he seemed so determined to keep me breathing.

It was stupid, I knew it was, but somehow the knowledge that he could be keeping me alive for a monetary payoff…it hurt. Way more than I was really willing to admit, even to myself.

"All good?" Roach asked as we made our way out of the lawyers' offices and rode the elevator back down to ground level.

I gave him a tight smile. "Maybe."

Demi had offered to do some digging into my inheritance and my mother's forged records for me. She seemed genuine about wanting to help, and right now I needed all the players on my team that were possible.

We stepped out of the building, and Roach froze dead in his tracks.

"Ah shit," he muttered. "Fuck." He gave me a conflicted look; then his gaze darted over my shoulder. Somehow, I already knew what had him cursing and looking a whole lot like he was thinking about running.

Straightening my spine, I turned around and leveled my best bitch glare at the raging ball of testosterone barreling down the sidewalk toward us. Me. Toward *me*, because he possibly hadn't even seen Roach standing there beside me.

"Darling, what a coincidence running into you here," I greeted him, my voice saccharine and my smile pasted on. "Did you also have a meeting booked with a divorce lawyer? This could be a bit awkward."

Archer just blinked at me, like I was confusing him, then shook his head dismissively. "Thanks, Roach, I'll take it from here." He didn't even look at the Reaper when he spoke, his eyes remaining locked with mine.

"Uh, come on, man. Zane gave me a job…" Roach sounded pained, but Archer clearly gave zero fucks about the repercussions he'd catch from Zane.

"Madison Kate, walk or be carried. Your choice." Archer was so matter-of-fact, like he didn't much care either way. But he wasn't fooling me. The vein in his temple was throbbing, and his tattooed fingers were flexing at his sides like he wanted to form fists.

I called his bluff.

"Carry me then, Sunshine. Because I'm not going anywhere willingly with you in this mood. Are you hitting the 'roids again, babe? You know that shrinks your dick even worse than usual."

I should have known better. By this stage, after putting up with Archer's bullshit for almost six months, I *really* should have known better.

He just shrugged, and the next thing I knew, my ass was in the air over his shoulder and my face had smacked into the back pocket of his jeans.

"Arch, dude. I can't just let you take her," Roach protested— weakly, I might add.

Archer clearly thought Roach was no threat because he just let out a laugh. "You gonna try to stop me, Roach? I'm not above shooting your knee out in broad daylight. Test me." His voice was cold and threatening, and to be honest, I didn't even remotely blame Roach for backing down.

Archer strode back down the sidewalk and dumped me unceremoniously into the passenger seat of his midnight-black Stingray. He must have had it repaired over the break because the last time I'd seen that car, there'd been a whole heap of damage to the left side from Steele's silver Challenger exploding right next to it.

I didn't bother trying to climb out and run when he slammed the door shut and casually moved around the hood to his side. It would be thoroughly pointless, and the only thing I'd gain from it would be a few dents to my dignity.

A few *more* dents, that was.

"Are we late for something?" I asked with heavy sarcasm when he gunned the engine and peeled out of the parking space. I quickly clicked my seat belt on because fuck dying thanks to his crazy-ass driving.

He didn't reply. He didn't even *look* at me. Just drove like… Okay, I had to be fair. He drove like a NASCAR racer or something. Steele had mentioned Archer was the one who drove well in real life, but I'd sort of figured that meant he could parallel park like a champ. Not *this*.

But still. With my history of car crashes, I found myself flinching every time he took a corner too fast or overtook someone on a dangerous stretch of road.

"Breathe, Kate," he muttered at some point on the outskirts of Shadow Grove when I almost had a heart attack thanks to the speed he was taking the turns. "I'm not going to crash. Just take a damn breath."

I was too freaked out to argue. I just did as I was told. In truth, I hadn't even realized I *wasn't* breathing until he'd pointed it out.

"Where are we going, Archer?" I asked in a shaking voice, attempting to distract myself from the vivid images of a thousand and one different crash scenarios playing through my mind.

He flicked a glance at me, his brow creased, but his speed eased off ever so slightly. "Shooting range," he replied in clipped tones. "It's time you learned to shoot properly."

Of all the things he could have said, I hadn't expected that. "Why?"

His fingers flexed on the steering wheel. "Because you shot someone over the weekend, and it was damn lucky you didn't accidentally shoot your own foot off. Had you *ever* fired a gun before?"

I frowned, irritated at his tone. He was acting like I was some kind of incompetent moron, when I'd quite deliberately fired from about two feet away so I *wouldn't* miss.

"Of course not," I snapped. "When the fuck would the Princess of Shadow Grove have learned to shoot?"

He gave me a glance, and his lips twitched. "Nice to know you're claiming that crown."

Annoyance simmered in my belly, and I scowled. "Shut up, asshole."

"Don't be like that, Princess. Open communication is such a key aspect to a successful marriage, after all." The grin he shot me was pure mockery, and I refrained from punching him in the throat. The second he stopped the car, though, he was going down.

I just shook my head and stared out the window at a total loss for words.

"You seem different," I commented after a few minutes of silence.

"How so?" he replied. He didn't even sound combative or suspicious. Just…curious. That was exactly what I'd meant.

I bit the inside of my lip, considering what the fuck I was going to say. "I don't know. You're just…" *Less angry, more relaxed. Less infuriating and more…tolerable?* "…different."

He shot me another quick glance but didn't say anything. We drove the rest of the way in total silence without even the distraction of music to detract from the tension filling the car and growing with every passing minute.

By the time he pulled to a stop in front of a shooting range set way up in the mountains behind Shadow Grove, I was practically clawing at my skin. It was safe to say I regretted commenting at all. Now that I'd pointed out how his attitude had changed, the tension between us was only getting worse.

I unbuckled my seat belt and climbed out of the car before he'd even shut off the engine, then hesitated in front of the entry doors to the range.

"Aren't you eager," Archer commented, pushing the door open and holding it for me to enter.

"Eager to get this over and done with," I snapped back at him. "I have better things to do with my day than suffer your infuriating presence, *Husband dearest.*"

He shot me a sharp glare as my heels clicked on the concrete floor of the shooting range's front shop. "Yeah? Like trying to apply for an annulment? Good fucking luck, Princess. I take my business arrangements seriously and would never leave a loose thread like that hanging out." His tone was pure arrogance, but his face flashed with anger. He was probably just pissed that I would even try to screw him over.

I said nothing back but silently thanked him for confirming my suspicion. An annulment would be a dead end. I knew it sounded too easy to work—regardless of legal grounds—and besides...I wanted to cut out a pound of D'Ath flesh when I regained my name.

The range seemed empty of other people, but the steady crack of gunshots clued me in to at least one other person there.

"Oh good, your instructor is here already," Archer commented, walking straight over to the door behind the cashier's desk and opening the lock with a combination code.

I gave him a narrow-eyed glare. For some reason, I'd assumed *he* was teaching me. Not that I was objecting to someone else, but...

"You must be a pretty lousy shot if you're outsourcing that task," I muttered, then mentally berated myself for saying that much. What was wrong with me that I was *disappointed*?

Archer just huffed a laugh, leading the way through a door where the gunshots grew louder with every step. "I can admit when someone has superior skills. Meet your teacher for the day."

The dude in a black hoodie with his back to us popped off a few more shots at his target, then placed his gun down and turned to grin at me. His gray eyes swept over me from head to toe, and heat flared in his gaze.

"Hellcat, that's an interesting outfit for a shooting lesson."

I rolled my eyes. "I wasn't exactly given a chance to change. Caveman here grabbed me off the street and tossed me in his car."

Steele shot Archer an accusing glare, but he just shrugged in response.

"I guess I forgot my manners when I found my *wife* coming out of a meeting with Demi Timber." His tone was edged with sarcasm and anger, and that fun little vein throbbed in his temple.

Aw yeah, someone's ego was bruised. *Suck it, bitch.*

Steele's brows shot up, and he gave me a curious look. "That's the meeting Zane set up for you?"

I jerked a nod. "Yep."

Steele's unreadable gaze passed between Archer and me a couple of times; then he shook his head and sighed. "All right, let's do this. Arch, fuck off and get us coffee."

I grinned at his casual dismissal of the big bad bastard, and Archer looked like he wanted to punch his friend in the face. Still, he didn't argue. With one last, all too lingering look at me, he stalked out of the gun range, letting the door slam closed heavily behind him.

Looking around, I didn't find Kody anywhere nearby, which seemed odd. I cocked a brow at Steele. "Where's the third stooge today?"

Steele flashed me a grin, stepping closer and placing his hands on my waist. "Getting us coffee. Proper coffee, not that sewer water Arch drinks."

I snickered. "Smart." Acting on instinct, I looped my arms around his neck and tugged the hood of his sweatshirt down. He wore a ball cap underneath, and it was an insanely sexy look on him. "So, you're going to teach me how to shoot, huh?"

A wicked smile crossed his lips. "I'm going to teach you all kinds of things, Hellcat. But we'll start with shooting today." His hands tightened on my waist, and his eyes burned with desire. "I can't wait to see you handling a gun in this outfit, by the way. Maybe I owe that surly bastard a thank you after all."

Desperately fighting the grin that wanted to plaster across my face like I was a lovesick moron, I forced myself to step out of his grip. "Well, let's do this, then. I'm excited to learn." I couldn't help myself—I shot him a suggestive look over my shoulder as I approached the area where he'd left his gun.

Steele let out a groan. "Torture," he muttered under his breath. "Pure fucking torture."

He wasn't joking either.

CHAPTER 23

The guys hadn't been messing around when they'd mentioned Steele's marksmanship skills. It was seriously scary how good he was. When he was moderately satisfied with my skills on the indoor range using his Glock, he took me outside to introduce me to long-range guns.

"Holy fucking shit," Kody declared when he arrived sometime later. "Did I bump my head on something? Because I'm pretty sure this is a scene right out of my dreams."

"I knew you dreamed about me," Steele replied, giving him a cocky smirk from where he lay beside me in the grass. We were both belly-down, my stiletto heels in the air as Steele talked me through the intricacies of sniper rifles and ranged shots, and his passion for the topic carried through in his every word.

Kody snorted a laugh and placed his tray of takeaway coffees down on the grass before stretching out on my other side. "Tell me this sexy-secretary-with-a-sniper-rifle look was deliberately planned to piss Archer off, because it's freaking gold," he commented with a broad grin.

"It wasn't, but I'll take the win if it's working," I replied, letting Steele take the rifle back out of my hands. He hadn't let me shoot it yet; I had just been learning how to use the scope.

Kody nodded. "Oh yeah, it's working. He's inside pretending not to watch from the window and generally being a sore loser. Did you seriously meet with Demi today, MK?"

Steele was packing up his guns, so I assumed we were done for the day and propped my head up on my hand to look at Kody.

"Yeah, of course. You guys know her?" Yeah, I was shifting the subject away from my possible divorce. Kody, Steele, and I... we were only just starting to rebuild the trust. I didn't need them giving me their opinions about this crap between Archer and me.

Kody nodded. "We know of her mostly. Never had need of that type of legal counsel myself, but she does give a lot of advice to and do odd jobs on the side for the Shadow Grove gangs."

"How come?" I asked, genuinely curious. She had struck me as a well-educated, successful lawyer. Why would she need to mess around with gangs and criminals?

"Demi Timber," Steele commented, locking up his long rifle case with a click, "is a *Timber*wolf."

My brows shot up and my mouth fell open. I scrambled up to sitting and stared hard at Steele to work out whether he was kidding.

"I thought they were extinct...so to speak." I searched my memory for what I knew of the Tri-State Timberwolf massacre, including what Kody had told me recently.

Kody shook his head. "Not exactly. That was what the media reported, but in reality they're just, I guess, under new management. Smarter management that understands being in the public eye only hinders their ability to get shit done."

That certainly gave some credibility to Demi's understanding of my unusual marriage circumstances and explained why she hadn't batted an eyelash at my rough-looking escort this morning.

"Here." Kody handed me a coffee in one of those fancy, stainless steel travel mugs. "I went all the way to Nadia's; that's what took me so long. You have no idea how bad the coffee has been in our house since you've been gone, babe."

I snickered, sipping my coffee. It was still warm, thanks to the insulated mug, and just as delicious as I remembered Nadia's coffee being. "I can imagine. How does he even drink that shit?"

My gaze wandered back to the main building, and a flicker of movement in the window confirmed what Kody had said about Archer watching us. Creep.

"Probably because it's as bitter and dark as his soul," Kody joked, and Steele snickered. I just rolled my eyes and took Steele's hand when he offered it to help me to my feet in my high-heeled shoes. I'd left them on because I loved the way he was looking at me today.

The three of us headed back inside, and Archer seemed totally uninterested as he slouched against the wall, texting someone on his phone.

"While I remember," I said to Kody and Steele, ignoring Archer right back, "I had an incident yesterday and had to get a new sim for my phone. So I dunno. You guys might want to get yours checked too."

All three guys stared at me, and the tension in the room all but crackled.

"Well, that explains why you didn't reply to my messages this morning," Kody muttered, folding his arms over his chest.

"An incident?" Steele repeated, ignoring Kody. "Explain that."

I shrugged and gave him an abridged version of my stalker's creepy calls from Bree's number.

"But she was there in the apartment with you?" Steele asked, and I nodded.

"Yeah, she was fast asleep and her phone was literally in my hand, so I know it wasn't her." I was quick to make that clear because I was sick of them casting suspicion on literally *everyone* in my life.

None of the three of them spoke for a long moment; then Archer hurled his phone at the wall in an explosion of anger. It smashed into pieces, scattering bits of glass and metal all over the floor. Just in case he hadn't killed it enough, he then stomped on the remains.

I gaped at him in shock, ready to yell at him about anger management issues, but then Kody and Steele pulled out their own phones and destroyed them under their boots.

"What the fuck, you guys?" I demanded. "You just needed a new sim card. That was way too dramatic."

Archer rolled his eyes and made a scoffing noise. "Don't be an airhead, Madison Kate. You're better than that." He held out his hand like he wanted my phone.

I scowled. "Fuck you, D'Ath. I replaced my sim already; you don't need to smash my phone like a 'roid-raging ape."

His teeth ground together hard enough for me to hear, and he grabbed my wrist. A sharp tug pulled me flush against his body, and he held me tight while his other hand fished in the pocket of my pencil skirt for where I'd stashed my phone.

"Arch, let her go," Steele snapped, his voice edged with warning.

"Gladly," Archer snarled, releasing my wrist with an abrupt shove. I stumbled back a couple of steps while he crushed my phone under foot. "Kody, sort out new phones. Take care of Bree's too."

Kody let out a heavy sigh, sweeping his hand through his blond hair. "Yeah, all right. Babe, you wanna ride back with me?"

I opened my mouth to reply, but *of course* Archer got there first.

"No, she's coming with me. We have some things to discuss in private." His tone was cold and dickish. Maybe I'd imagined his shift in his attitude after all because this was classic Archer D'Ath once more.

"Screw you, Sunshine," I sneered back at him.

He raised a brow at me. "Really? I told you before, I'm not interested. This is getting embarrassing now, Princess."

167

My face flushed as my anger reached new heights.

Kody just snorted a laugh, though, and shook his head. "Keep telling yourself that, Arch. Maybe one day you'll actually believe it."

Steele smirked. "It'll be the same day that pigs fly and Zane wears lingerie."

My anger quickly morphed into amusement. Especially when Archer's glower darkened. His friends were making fun of him.

"Uh-oh, looks like the tables have turned," I mocked him.

He just scowled back at me. "Regardless, Kody, go. Time is ticking."

Kody made a sound of agreement, then stepped between Archer and me, breaking our stare-down. "He's actually right. I need to sort out these phones quickly. If your stalker hacked Bree's, he could have done a hell of a lot more than just clone her number. I'll swing past later, okay?" He smacked a quick kiss on my lips before I could protest, then shot Steele a lightning-fast look that I imagined roughly translated to *keep an eye on our girl and don't let Archer fuck it all up again.*

Or maybe it was just a look. Who knew?

He took off out of the empty range, and I leveled my stare at Steele. "Explain?"

"If our phones were compromised, then there could have been any number of spyware modifications added. Shit that doesn't get removed with a sim card." Steele didn't seem *as* concerned as Archer, but he was definitely worried. "There's every chance you're right that he just cloned Bree's sim to freak you out, but it's better to be safe than sorry."

My lips parted, and understanding rippled through me... closely followed by embarrassment. I should have thought of that, but it hadn't even occurred to me.

"Oh," I replied, feeling totally stupid.

Steele gave me a gentle smile. "It's okay. You couldn't have known."

"She would have if it hadn't taken a day and a half to tell us about it," Archer said, waspish as all hell. "Come on, Princess. Time to go."

He grabbed my upper arm in a tight hold, basically dragging me with him as he strode outside again. I let out a squeak of protest, but it was all I could do to keep my balance and not land on my ass in the dirt. He was damn lucky my coffee cup had a lid, or it would have spilled and *then* I'd be forced to remove his skin with a potato peeler.

"Arch!" Steele barked from behind us. "Hands off. Don't make me smack some manners into you like Kody did the other week."

"You could fucking try," Archer muttered, but his grip on my arm eased off before he jerked the passenger door of his car open for me. "Get in, Madison Kate."

I folded my arms and glared back at him. "And if I don't?"

Something flickered across his face that was way too close to amusement for my liking. These boys had all too much fun throwing me around like a rag doll, so it really wasn't smart for me to challenge them. Then again, I had to get my kicks somewhere, right?

"Archer, lay off," Steele snapped coming across the parking lot toward us. "I can take her home when I've closed up here. You don't need to do this shit right now."

Archer didn't look over at his friend, his eyes locked on mine. "I disagree. My lovely wife and I are way overdue for this particular chat. Get in the damn car, Madison Kate."

"You don't have to," Steele told me, his tone calm but firm. "You can come with me."

But my curiosity was piqued. What did Archer want to discuss so badly that he was willing to be such an insufferable bastard about driving me home?

"It's fine," I told Steele with a small smile. "Archer won't hurt me, will you, Sunshine? After all, you need me alive for my twenty-first birthday or this whole sham marriage was for nothing, isn't that right?"

Archer just smiled. "Get in the car."

I rolled my eyes at his attitude but did what he wanted anyway.

Maybe I was being an idiot, but a small part of me just enjoyed antagonizing him. It was fun, simple as that. Obviously, it was likely to bite me in the ass sooner or later. But that was a risk I was willing to take over and over again.

"So?" I asked after placing my coffee in the cup holder and buckling my seat belt. "What vitally important discussion do we need to have? Is this the one where you confess you're secretly in love with me and everything you do is for my own safety?"

He cast a *what the fuck* kind of glare at me as he pulled out of the shooting range parking lot and accelerated onto the mountain road.

"Wait, no," I continued on, not bothering to wait for him to reply, "this is when you apologize profusely for ruining my whole fucking life and explain that this whole sour attitude you're rocking is the product of a chemical imbalance in your brain. Right?"

He snorted a laugh. A short one, don't get me wrong, but a laugh nonetheless. "Ruined your life? I seem to remember *saving* your life on several occasions."

I rolled my eyes, but he had a point. "Whatever."

"Tell me about your meeting this morning, Madison Kate." His question—or demand—wasn't what I'd expected, but I should have. Of course he wasn't just going to let that go so easily.

"Can't," I replied with a truckload of sass. "Attorney client confidentiality, you know?"

"That only applies for your attorney," he said, the irritation in his voice clearly conveying that didn't care for my games. Well, too bad.

"But does it?" I mused. "I might seek legal counsel on that."

"Princess, quit the bullshit. What did you discuss with Demi?"

I batted my lashes at him, knowing full fucking well he could see me even while his eyes seemed to be on the road ahead. "Why do you care, Sunshine? Are you gonna be a sad panda when I find a way to dissolve that bullshit marriage contract? Did you think this was all going to end in a fairy-tale happily ever after or some shit?" I scoffed. "Maybe you should look into spending some of that D'Ath fortune on a therapist, babe. You seriously need your head checked."

Archer's jaw clenched and his temple throbbed. "Don't be so fucking naive, Madison Kate. You're smarter than that."

I seethed. It drove me nuts when people suggested I was being intentionally dense, and he probably knew it.

A bitchy retort started to form in my mind, but it was gone again in a flash as Archer suddenly gunned the engine. I let out a small yelp of surprise, clutching my door handle for stability, and he shot me a quick look.

"Hold on," he said, rather unnecessarily. "We're being followed."

I spun around to look, and Archer hissed a curse at me.

"Get your head down," he snapped. "Quit giving them a fucking target in case they're planning to shoot at us."

I gaped at him in shock but did as I was told, slinking down in my seat a little more. I stayed like that for several minutes, eventually squeezing my eyes shut as Archer's driving grew increasingly hair-raising.

When I felt the car slowing, I peeled my eyelids open cautiously and glanced over at him.

"Lost them," he informed me with a quick glance. "You okay?"

I licked my lips several times to fix the serious case of dry mouth that had just hit me and nodded. "Do you care?" I replied, an edge of bitterness in my voice. I hadn't meant to say that out loud, but my filter grew faulty when I was scared.

Archer slowed his car and rolled to a stop directly in front of my apartment building, then speared me with a hard stare.

"Of course I care, Kate. Your safety is important to me." His voice was gentle, and it sent a shock wave of emotion rolling through me.

For a long, way too tense moment, we just sat there with our gazes locked and silence reigning supreme through the car. Archer was the first to look away, turning his gaze forward as he tightened his grip on the steering wheel.

"I need you alive for another two years and one month, or I don't get my payout." His tone was harsh, and it cut me as effectively as any blade.

I drew a sharp breath through my nose, then unbuckled my seat belt and popped my door open with sharp gestures.

"You're a piece of shit, you know that?" I asked him as I paused halfway out of the car. "It's no wonder you needed to buy a wife. No woman could possibly tolerate your damaged bullshit willingly."

He didn't answer. He didn't even look at me.

Shaking my head in disgust, I climbed out of his car and slammed the door behind me. I didn't pause and I sure as shit didn't look back at him as I stormed into my apartment building. His car remained in front of the glass doors, though, not leaving as I stepped into the elevator.

It wasn't until I got back into my apartment that my resolve cracked, and I looked out the window. Only then did the black Stingray pull away from the front of my building, like he wanted to be sure I'd made it safely inside.

The lengths he'd go to for that *payout* were impressive. Especially considering he had absolutely no need for my money.

Prick.

CHAPTER 24

True to his word, Kody arrived on my doorstep a couple of hours later while I was contemplating dinner.

"New phone," he announced when I answered my door, handing me a device identical to my old one.

I took it from him with a smile. "Thanks," I replied, standing back to let him in. "I hope you put this on Archer's credit card."

Kody smirked. "Of course. It's the least he could do."

I closed the door and wandered back over to my kitchen, where I'd been browsing through takeout menus that had been stuffed into my mailbox over the past week or so. "You want to stay for dinner? I was deciding between Chinese or Mexican."

"Damn, babe, who knew you were such a chef," Kody teased, taking the two top menu choices out of my hands and inspecting them. "Yum, tacos."

"Excellent choice," I murmured, taking the Chinese menu back and returning the losers to a drawer in my kitchen. "And don't be a hater just because I can't cook. I've had a personal chef my *entire* life. Even in Cambodia we had a cook."

He just dropped the Mexican menu onto the counter and placed his hands on either side of me, boxing me in. It was such an alpha-male, dominating move, and I secretly loved it. "I love everything about you, MK," he told me in a low voice, his body crowding me against the island and giving me vivid memories of the first time we'd fucked—in the middle of the night, on the kitchen counter.

"Mmm, nice save," I replied, tilting my face back to peer up at him as his hard length brushed against my lower belly. "But suddenly I get the feeling you're not all that hungry for takeout."

A wicked smile touched his lips. "See, babe? You totally get me. It's like we have a psychic connection, and I *love* that."

His kiss was gentle and unhurried, a sensual exploration of my mouth. My breath hitched, and my arms snaked around his neck, pulling him closer and silently pleading for more.

"As much as I want to take this further," he murmured against my lips, his body crushing me into the cupboards, "you should really order. Food around here always seems to take forever to arrive."

Instead of letting me go, he just reached out and snagged my new phone from where I'd left it and handed it to me. Then he proceeded to kiss my neck in teasing pecks while I dialed the restaurant and placed an order for us. Kody pointed to several items while I spoke to the girl on the other end, and I added them to my order.

"That's a shitload of food, Kodiak Jones," I commented when I ended the call.

He laughed lightly before claiming my lips in an intense kiss that stole my breath away and left my knees weak.

"I ordered for Steele too," he told me when our kiss ended. "Otherwise, he'll eat all of ours."

"He's coming over?" I tried to remember when, exactly, I'd invited both boys over for dinner. Then I remembered that they do whatever the hell they want, and right now...that was me. Or making amends with me at any rate.

Kody just gave an easy shrug, his hands slipping under my tank top and pushing it up to expose my midsection. "Probably. He mentioned yesterday that you guys talked things out…" He arched a brow at me, inviting me to elaborate on that statement.

I wrinkled my nose, thinking. "We did. He, like you, is extremely hard to stay mad at when he gives a genuine apology." I narrowed my eyes at him. "You're a little bit charming, you know that?"

Kody beamed. "I do my best for you, babe. Besides, we really *are* sorry for how everything went down."

I placed my phone back on the counter, then looped my arms around his neck, threading my fingers into the back of his hair. "He told me about some stuff from before my mom died."

Kody looked surprised. "He did?"

"Yeah," I replied, searching his emerald eyes. "Did I meet you back then too? I don't remember any of it. Steele said you weren't there, but…" I shrugged. It seemed weird not to ask, in case Steele was mistaken.

He shook his head. "No, I was in Texas looking after my grandma. By the time I got back, shit had already hit the fan, and you were just a ghost to both Steele and Arch." He paused, giving me a small smirk. "I wanted to meet you, though. Steele talked about you all the time, and I was jealous as hell. You sounded so cool."

I gave a little laugh. "Oh yeah? I guess I didn't leave such a good impression on Archer, then."

Kody grimaced. "I guess Steele didn't tell you all of it."

Anxiety turned my stomach. "No, we were interrupted. But it's fine. Archer can tell me his own shit when he's ready to pull that stick out of his ass. I've survived this long without those memories; I'm in no major hurry to uncover whatever I did to earn eight years of hatred from him."

"Fair enough," he replied. "But for the record, Arch doesn't hate you. Not even close."

I snorted a sarcastic laugh. "Agree to disagree, Kodiak. He's actually said it to me."

"Well, what can I tell you? He lied." His brow creased, and his thumb traced the scar on my stomach. "MK—"

A knock on my door cut off whatever he was about to say, and we both cast confused glances in the direction of the sound.

"I thought you said food was slow," I asked him, and he shrugged.

"It usually is. I once waited four hours for tacos, no joke. I mean, they were great tacos, but come on." He released me and made his way over to the door to answer it. It should have annoyed me that he was acting so at home in my apartment, but it didn't. I liked it.

"Not tacos!" Kody called out, swinging the door open farther, then sauntering back toward me.

"You ordered tacos?" Steele asked, walking through my door. He closed it behind him and made sure to flip my deadbolt. "Did you get enough for me?"

Kody shot me a smug grin, and I rolled my eyes.

"Yes, we did. Kody ordered for you, though, so blame him if it's not what you like." I moved over to my living area and sat on the couch, tucking my feet up under me. My lips were still warm and puffy from Kody's kisses, but I wasn't about to go initiating a threesome before my burrito arrived. So I needed some space.

"Here." Kody handed Steele a phone from his pocket. "Squeaky clean."

"Thanks, bro," Steele replied, turning it on and scrolling. "Aw, you saved all the important numbers for me too. You do care."

Their teasing banter continued until our food arrived, and then we turned on a movie while we ate. Bree texted me at some point between my burrito and the caramel apple empanadas, letting me know Kody had dropped her new phone off earlier and that she'd pick me up for school in the morning.

"Hey, did you get a new phone for Scott too?" I asked after replying to Bree's message. "Bree, Dallas, and Scott are the only people, other than you guys, that I ever talk to. And Zane, I guess."

It was on the tip of my tongue to tell them Scott's lie about how he'd likely followed us instead of using a phone tracker. But I knew it'd only make them suspicious, and I was pretty sure Scott was harmless.

Kody and Steele shot each other a glance, and Kody sighed. "I forgot about Zane. But yes, I got one for your creepy fake boyfriend. Just figured I can give it to him tomorrow and not make a special trip today."

"You gotta do Zane's too," Steele told him.

Kody groaned. "Do I have to? What do we care if MK's stalker is tapping his phone?"

"What if he talks to someone else about the security on this place or mentions booking her another meeting or something? If the stalker has Zane tapped, he could set her up and not even know it." Steele was all logic, but it churned my stomach. I hadn't thought any of that was even possible.

Kody let out a heavy sigh. "Fine, I'll do it tomorrow. Fucking Zane. Don't blame me if my fist slips and hits him in the face, though."

Steele gave him a wild sort of smirk. "Let it slip an extra time for me, would ya?"

"Actually, now that you mention Scott, MK," Kody said, turning his attention back to me with a serious expression. "Did you speak to Bree about that whole phone-tracking crap? That was some sketchy shit from her."

Dammit. I should've known he wouldn't forget.

"Bree didn't do anything," I told them with a sigh. I hated that they'd know Scott crossed a line, but I hated them suspecting Bree even more. "She's got a lot going on right now in her personal life, but she's not the shady fuck you guys think she is. Scott lied.

He never even spoke to her that day, let alone used her lost-phone tracker."

Steele shifted in his seat, running a hand over his face. "Hellcat, you know what that means, don't you?"

"Scott isn't my stalker," I replied, already knowing what he was trying to say. "He just isn't. Yeah, he's a bit needy and can't seem to take no for an answer, and his social skills are seriously lacking. But he wasn't even *in* Shadow Grove until recently, and he's way too young to have been my mom's stalker."

Steele and Kody exchanged a look, and I knew they disagreed with me.

"That's true," Kody offered, "but you can understand why we might keep an eye on him all the same."

I snorted a laugh. "Like you aren't already." I stifled a yawn and wiped my hands off on a napkin. Exhaustion was hitting me hard, and my eyes felt gritty and sore.

"We should go," Steele commented, clearly noticing my sleepiness. He whacked Kody in the leg as he said it, and Kody scowled.

"Or," the playful, blond asshole suggested, "you could go, and I could stay over to make sure MK stays safe tonight."

"Don't be an ass, Kody," Steele replied, standing and collecting up all our trash. "MK needs sleep, and that's the furthest thing from your mind right now."

I grinned because he was totally right. The sultry look Kody shot me confirmed it too. "Max is right," I said. "Besides, you two aren't totally off my shit list yet. We aren't just falling straight back into old habits like that." I snapped my fingers, and both guys looked resigned.

"Well, I'll just need to find some other bastard to torture for you, then," Steele suggested, and I grinned.

Kody frowned, thinking, then his brows shot up. "I let you use me for sex to piss off Arch," he pointed out, like that was a good enough reason to be forgiven.

I scoffed, laughing while collecting the last of our leftovers and following Steele over to the kitchen to dispose of everything.

"That must have been a real hardship for you, Kody," Steele commented with heavy sarcasm.

Kody laughed, wrapping his arms around me from behind as I rinsed the few plates we'd used. "I could show you what else is *hard*..." he murmured in my ear, and the suggestion was more difficult to turn down than I really wanted to admit.

"Go," I ordered them both in a firm voice before I could change my mind and strip them both naked. "I'll see you tomorrow before class, right?"

"You bet," Kody replied, kissing my neck before letting me go. "I'll text you later."

He headed out the door first; then Steele grabbed my face for a fast but bruising kiss. When he let me go, he gave me a wink.

"Lock the door, Hellcat," he murmured, then pulled it shut behind him.

I knew he'd wait to hear me close the bolts, so I quickly flipped them over. For a moment, I just leaned my forehead against the door while I caught my breath and let my racing pulse return to normal.

Fucking Steele; he knew I wouldn't be able to get that kiss out of my head for the rest of the night. Good thing I was plenty experienced with handling my own needs.

CHAPTER 25

The next few days passed in relative calm. No one tried to kill me, no one delivered creepy packages, and Scott was back to the guy I'd met in Aspen—normal, a little flirtatious, but thoroughly uncreepy. I appreciated the breathing space.

Kody and Steele had made it their mission to win me over—more than they already had—and were helping run interference with Archer for me.

Interference sometimes resulted in Archer taking a rough elbow or knee to the body, but that only endeared the guys to me further. It wasn't like Archer was any stranger to taking a hit, and for everything he'd put me through? Yeah, he could take a couple of friendly knocks.

After his snide comment about keeping me alive for a payout, I decided to quit pandering to his bullshit. I was sick of putting myself in a position where he could tear me down in a few callous words, so I was simply not risking it. All week, whenever he'd tried to corner me alone or asked the guys to fuck off so we could talk, I'd completely iced him out.

Fuck that noise. Until I heard back from Demi on how to end our sham marriage, I intended to pretend Archer D'Ath simply didn't exist.

Surprisingly, both Kody and Steele were giving me space. They met me every morning with coffee and snacks, and we spent lunch together, along with Bree and Scott, but they didn't insist on shadowing me home after classes were over.

On Thursday afternoon, after Kody had dragged me around the corner of the human sciences building and kissed me until my knees went weak, I slid into Bree's car with a dazed smile.

"So as much as I love having time with you again," she commented, giving me a knowing look as I ran my fingers through my tousled hair, "I'm surprised they aren't glued to your side twenty-four-seven. I'd have thought the moment you gave them an inch, they'd take a mile."

I ran my fingertip over my swollen lips. "Me too, girl. But I'm pleasantly surprised that hasn't been the case. Kody and Steele seem to be serious about winning my trust back."

Bree hummed a sound of amusement. "Like they haven't already."

I grinned. "Yeah, well, they don't need to know that. Gotta make them work a bit harder, you know?"

"Oh, I wasn't disagreeing. Just laughing. Anyway, are you working out with Cass again this afternoon?"

Hitting the gym in the afternoons with the big, tattooed, scary motherfucker had turned into a routine, so I nodded.

"Cool, I have my therapy session today, so I can't hang out," Bree told me, "but call me when you get home so I know you're still alive, okay?"

I grinned. "You sound like Steele now."

She batted her lashes at me. "Oh, I sound like I'm totally head over heels in love with you and willing to burn down the whole city to find who's trying to kill you?" She laughed. "Not totally wrong. I *do* love you, bitch. But I don't wanna fuck you. Big difference."

"Uh-huh, sure you don't," I teased. "I'd totally give Dallas some competition in bed."

She laughed again, shaking her head as she pulled up in front of my apartment building. Cass was already standing out front, chatting to a couple of younger Reapers, and I knew I needed to hurry the fuck up. Grumpy Cass was funny, but pissed-off Cass was scary, and he hated waiting for me.

"Hey, does Kody know you've been working out with Cass?" Bree asked as I unbuckled my seat belt and grabbed my bag.

Guilt washed through me. "Um…it hasn't really come up. He's been training Archer every day anyway, so…"

Bree arched her brows at me. "So…what? That's totally not an excuse for not telling him. You *know* he's gonna be hurt that you're training with the Reapers instead."

She was right, obviously. "I know, but there's something very soothing about training with tall, dark, and scary over there. It's *just* boxing and nothing sexual, you know?"

She nodded. "I get it. But considering everything you guys are doing to work on *trust* and *honesty*, I feel like you need to come to the party yourself. You can't just expect them to tell you all their secrets and become open books when you're keeping shit from them. Even something innocent like this."

I sighed. "I know. It's just weird going from wanting to feed them all to the sharks to whatever the fuck we are now."

Bree shot me a smirk. "You mean now that your *feelings* are involved rather than just your genitals?"

"I fucking wish our genitals were being involved more," I grumbled. "This whole *respecting my space* thing is slowly driving me insane. Other than those few quick make-out sessions between classes, it's—"

A sharp knock on the window interrupted what I was saying, and I was startled to find Cass scowling through the glass at me.

"Sorry," I yelped, popping my door open. "Catch you later, Bree!"

"Move it, kid. I've got places to be tonight." Cass rumbled the words after me as I hurried inside the building and stabbed at the elevator call button. I just needed to dump my bag and change; I could be back downstairs in five minutes, max. Still, I held two fingers up to Cass as I ducked into the elevator. Better to be optimistic.

Cass hadn't been kidding about needing to be elsewhere. He kept our session short—but intense—then briskly escorted me back to my apartment afterward.

"You know, everyone at the gym seems to know me now," I commented as I dug for my keys to unlock my door. "I would probably be fine going without you."

The big guy just gave me a flat stare. "No."

He waited, arms folded over his sweaty shirt while I unlocked my door and stepped inside. "I'm heading out for a meeting at Club 22," he told me in a low rumble. "You've got my number if you need me, but I've also got a couple of the new recruits on security downstairs."

I gave him a smile and wave, thanking him for the workout session before closing my door and locking it. In the last few days, Cass had taken to advising me when he was going to be out of the building. It made me suspicious that something had happened, maybe some stalker mail, but the inked-up Reaper had been tight-lipped when I'd asked.

Shrugging off the worry, I stripped down and showered, washing the sweat of my workout off and shampooing my hair.

As I stepped out of the bathroom, toweling my hair dry, I spotted my phone flashing with an incoming call on the bed where I'd left it.

There was a missed call from Archer—weird—but the incoming one was a whole lot more welcome.

"Hey," I answered, bringing the phone to my ear and tucking my towel tighter around my body. "If you're with my bad-tempered husband right now, do me a favor and punch him in the dick?"

Steele laughed. "I'm not, but I'll make sure to do that when I head back downstairs."

I bit back a sigh. The sound of his voice in my ear was doing all kinds of things to my body. Maybe it was because I'd just been talking to Bree about the lack of sex in my week or maybe it was because I was currently naked...but fucking hell.

"So, what are you doing, then?" I asked, tossing my hair towel onto a chair and climbing onto my bed. I hadn't intended for the question to sound so suggestive, but it definitely came out that way.

Steele must've heard it too, as he let out a soft chuckle. "Well, I *was* going to ask if you wanted to hear a new piece I'd been working on. But I get the feeling you have something else in mind."

I got comfy on my pillows, grinning up at the ceiling. "Maybe. But I want to hear what you're working on first. I haven't heard you play in way too long, Max Steele. I miss it." *I miss you...*

We'd made up, but things were far from back to normal. I wanted normal again...just without the lies and secrets. Was that so much to ask for?

He hummed a sound, like he was thinking. "All right, but first you have to tell me something." I heard the soft, slow chime of piano keys and knew he was running his fingers over them gently, thinking about what he was going to play.

"Anything," I replied. "No secrets anymore, right?"

He made another humming sound, then lightly depressed a couple more keys. "What are you wearing right now, Hellcat?" His voice was pure sex, and my nipples hardened against the rough towel.

"Why do you want to know? I thought you were going to play something for me," I replied with a soft laugh.

"I am," he answered, his tone edged with wickedness, "but I want to be able to picture you while you listen."

Excitement flipped my stomach over, and I tugged my towel loose. I wasn't worried about anyone telephoto-spying on me; I hadn't opened my heavy blackout curtains once since moving in.

"Right now?" I asked, licking my lips. "Absolutely nothing. You caught me just as I was getting out of the shower."

Silence. Then a rough inhalation, and I chuckled.

"I changed my mind," Steele said after a moment, and the soft chime of his piano keys slowly formed into a tune.

"You're not going to play for me?" I asked, somewhat disappointed.

His breathing was slightly rougher than it had been a few moments ago, and his fingers still toyed with the tune he'd started. "I am," he replied after a pause, "but I want you to play for me too."

It only took me a second to understand what he meant; then my whole body flushed with warmth.

"Max Steele," I gasped in feigned scandal, "are you asking me to masturbate over the phone for you?"

He let out a pained groan. "Yes, fuck yes. Unless you want to switch to video call?" The hopeful tone of his voice was almost enough to have me agreeing, but I'd need time to work out the best angles and… Nah, too hard.

"Video call next time." I compromised. "Now play me this damn piece while I imagine your fingers on me instead of your piano."

Steele let out another groan. "This was either the best idea ever or the worst. Fuck, okay, I'm putting you on speaker."

I grinned. "Fine, I'll stay quiet then."

"Don't you dare," he growled. "Arch and Kody are in the gym with music blasting, anyway. They won't hear anything."

It wasn't like I really cared if they did…but it was cute Steele thought to mention it.

Muffled sounds filled my ear as Steele switched to speaker-phone and probably placed his phone on the desk beside his key-board. Or maybe he'd propped it up on the music rack. Either way, there was only a short pause before he started playing.

My breath caught in my throat as the first haunting notes

traveled through the speaker to me, and I found myself totally transfixed by the beautiful, soulful melody Steele had composed.

"Hellcat, we had an agreement," he muttered some minutes later after I'd totally lost myself in his music, and my pulse raced once more.

I let out a low chuckle. "That we did."

Holding my phone to my ear with one hand, I cupped one of my breasts with the other. My nipples were already hard, and just a gentle roll of my fingers brought a moan to my lips.

"Shit," Steele breathed, but he didn't stop playing. "Describe it, baby. Tell me what you're doing…what you want *me* to be doing to you."

"Nah-ah," I replied with a laugh as I moved my hand lower and spread my legs open. "That wasn't part of the agreement." Not that there really was any agreement, but whatever. Playful banter didn't always need to be factual. "Just play for me and listen while I play for you."

Besides, I'd never been able to concentrate enough to dirty talk with any real success. It pulled me too far out of the moment, and right now, I wanted to be totally in the moment. It wasn't the first time I'd serviced myself while picturing Steele or Kody or both of them… I might also admit to Archer's face flashing across my mind in my darkest moments. But it was the first time Steele knew I was doing it and listening.

My fingers danced across my pussy, finding the slick wetness between my legs and dragging it up to coat my clit. Closing my eyes, it was easy to picture Steele's fingers on me. The way he manipulated the piano keys, the way I knew he could manipulate my body…

A breathy whimper pulled from my throat as I toyed with my clit, and Steele hit an out-of-place note, then swore.

"This was a terrible idea," he muttered, but there was an edge of laughter that brought a broad smile to my face. My cheeks were flushed with heat, my back arching off the bed, and my pussy throbbing with need.

"You're telling me," I replied on a moan. "I don't even have any of my vibrators here. You have no idea how badly I want something bigger than my fingers right now."

Steele's tune cut off abruptly with a crash of notes like he'd just smacked the keyboard. "Fuck it," he growled. "Switch to video. Please, Hellcat...I need to see your face when you come."

My phone bleeped in my ear, and I pulled it away to see the notification that Steele wanted to activate cameras. I bit my lip, smiling and feeling evil.

"Baby, come on. Please, hit accept." His voice was pure need, and I wasn't even going to pretend I didn't get off on the power of it.

Instead of doing what he wanted, I kept fingering myself, bringing my orgasm closer with every stroke and thrust.

"Hellcat, you're killing me," he groaned. "Please, beautiful. Please..."

I laughed a low, sex-filled sound, then hit accept on his request. His face filled my screen a moment later, and my grin spread wider.

"If you think I'm giving you any other angles, you're shit out of luck," I told him, then gasped as a ripple of pleasure lit up my lower belly. Fucking hell, I was so close.

Steele's eyes brightened with hunger as he drank in my features. I was flat on my back, my wet hair a mess around my head, and my eyelids heavy. It was kind of disconcerting to see myself in the little screen box, but also a bit of a turn-on knowing what he could see.

"This is the only angle I need, Hellcat," he murmured back, his tongue darting out to wet his lips. "You look like a freaking angel when you come."

I laughed. "Some angel."

Steele just shrugged, his gaze intense. "A fallen one, then. Either way, it's a biblical experience. Are you close?"

I pulled my fingers from my soaking core again and brought them back to my clit. "God, yes. Steele…" I uttered his name on a moan as I rubbed myself into climax, crying out as the waves of pleasure ripped through my whole body and my legs shook. It was all I could do not to drop my phone on my face, instead gripping it hard enough to leave dents in my palm.

It took several moments for my head to clear and my breathing to slow; then I was able to refocus on my phone.

"Was that what you wanted, Max?" I grinned at him, my whole body like liquid as I rolled over to my side. I held the phone on the pillow beside me, so it was like we were actually in bed together.

His brows were raised, his lips parted, and face flushed. "So much better," he replied in a mumble. "I need a cold shower or something."

"Or you could just come over and give me what I really want…" I bit my lip, the offer of hot sex unmistakable in my voice.

His brow creased and he gave a pained groan. "You have no idea how hard it's been to stay away this week, Hellcat."

I gave a shrug. "So don't."

He heaved a sigh. "I have to. For one thing, I want to start things over with you. Last time I went about everything wrong. I was selfish and secretive and didn't…I didn't do things the right way. There's so much more between us than just incredible sex, Hellcat…" His gaze was steady, locked on mine in an unflinching apology.

Emotions swirled in my chest, and I found myself without words for a moment. Was this Steele's way of telling me that he *cared* on an emotional level? That he…loved me?

"Steele—" Whatever I was about to say, I cut it short when all the lights in my apartment shut off.

"Hellcat?" he asked. "Did your lights just turn off on their own?"

I frowned, sitting up enough to check the lamp beside my bed. Nothing.

"Yeah, looks like the power cut out or something. I should check if the whole building is out or if it's just a fuse here." Heading back to my bathroom in the dark, I snagged my robe and pulled it on.

The light of my phone was still enough that Steele could just see me, and he let out a small laugh as I placed my phone down to belt the robe.

"That looks so much better on you than me," he commented, and I grinned.

"I dunno, babe," I replied, teasing, "you looked pretty hot in it."

"There was supposed to be a storm coming this weekend," Steele said, the clicking of keys telling me he was on his computer. "Maybe the wind knocked out your power." There was something in his voice, though, and he tossed the phone down on his bed while he pulled a shirt on.

"You don't think that's what it is, though," I observed. A trickle of fear ran through me.

Steele didn't immediately reply, his face grim as he left his bedroom. "I'm coming over," he said instead. "I'll be there in fifteen, or less if Arch drives."

Yep, now I was really worried. I made my way back out to my kitchen and tried the lights there. Nothing. The oven and microwave were dark too.

"It's probably just the storm coming through," I murmured, not even believing myself. "But yeah, I think maybe it's not the worst idea for you to come over."

Steele grunted a sound of agreement, his footsteps pounding as he ran down the stairs. "Stay on the phone with me, okay? I need to know you're safe. Just hang tight."

I wrapped my free arm around my middle, biting the edge of my lip in nervousness. "I should call Cass," I said, checking the time. He'd said he was going to Club Twenty-two, but it was for a meeting, not a night out. Maybe he'd be back already.

Steele's brow furrowed further. "I'd rather you stay on the line with me, babe."

I shrugged. "Yes, but you're fifteen minutes away at least. Cass might be just across the hall. I could go and knock, I guess?"

"No!" Steele's reply was a sharp yell. "No, don't unlock your door. Just... *Fuck*, just call me right back, okay?" I saw him burst through the door to the gym and caught a flash of Archer and Kody sparring on the padded mats.

"Yep, absolutely. I'm sure it'll be fine, though." I was reassuring him, but neither of us was buying it.

"Stay inside; keep your door locked. I'll be right there. Hellcat—" He broke off with a frustrated sound. "Fuck it. I love you. Stay safe."

The call ended before the shock of his words could fully sink in, and for way too long I just stood there staring at my blank screen like a stunned rabbit.

Maybe I'd heard him wrong? Maybe the panic of the situation was mixing with my post-orgasm euphoria, and I was imagining things? But nope. It had been a clear line, and I hadn't misheard him.

Steele had just said that he loved me.

CHAPTER 26

It took me another couple of moments to shake off my shocked haze; then I quickly searched my phone for Cass's number. He'd saved it for me earlier in the week when Zane had told him about the incident with Bree's number. I hadn't used it yet, but I was sure as hell glad I had it now.

It only rang a couple of times before he answered.

"Kid. What's happened?"

Thumping club music played in the background, and my stomach sank. He wasn't home in his apartment. Shit.

"Just a power outage," I told him, keeping my voice as calm as possible. The last thing the Reapers needed was their guest hostage getting all girly over a blackout. Besides, Club Twenty-two was even farther away than the guys' house, so it was pointless to worry Cass. "I was just checking if you were home or not."

"I'm leaving now," he told me. "I'll get the recruits to check the circuits. Stay put in your apartment, kid. Don't fucking leave."

He ended the call before I could assure him that I was no fucking idiot—I wasn't going anywhere.

So now I had all the big bads coming to my rescue. I just needed to stay alive until they got here.

In an attempt to distract myself from the anxiety churning my stomach, I went back through to my bedroom and pulled on some clothes. I hardly needed to be practically naked in nothing but a satin robe when Archer arrived, that was for sure.

A heavy knock sounded on my door, making me jump in fright, and I clapped a hand over my mouth to cover the little shriek that escaped.

My first reaction was that Steele must have gotten Archer to drive after all, but then… A quick glance of the time on my phone showed only five minutes had passed since my call to Steele had ended. Even with the way Archer drove, that'd be impressive.

Just in case, I grabbed my butterfly knife from my dresser and slipped it into my pocket.

Clutching my phone in my hand, I hurried back through my apartment to the front door and used the peephole to check who was there. Of course, with the power out to the whole building, there wasn't enough light to see who it was, just the shadowy shape of a man. Just one man, though, so it was unlikely to be Steele and the guys. I couldn't see Archer and Kody choosing to stay behind at the house. Not when Steele was clearly as worried as I was.

My visitor knocked again, and I clenched my jaw to control my fear.

I wanted to call out and ask who it was but swallowed the words before they left my lips. Better they think no one was home, even if it was one of the Reapers working security.

"Maddie?" the shadow man called out, and the fear drained out of me in a rush of relief. "Maddie, are you home? The power's out to the whole building."

No shit, Scott.

With one hand, I unlocked the door to let Scott in, but with the other I hit dial on Steele's number. As confident as I was that Scott was harmless, it didn't cost me anything to be cautious.

"Hey, are you okay?" my friend asked when I swung the door

open. "I thought I was going to get stuck in the foyer when the power went out." He gave a short laugh, moving past me into my apartment.

I quickly closed the door and locked it again, breathing deeply to try to calm my hammering pulse.

"I'm fine. What are you doing here, Scott? You scared the shit out of me." Folding my arms under my breasts, I gave him an accusing frown. My phone was still in my hand, tucked under my armpit. I didn't know why I felt like I needed to hide it from Scott, but I did.

"Me?" He sounded surprised, giving a weak laugh. "Damn, Maddie, here I was thinking you'd appreciate a knight in shining armor coming to your rescue." His tone was joking but there was something…off.

I took a small step backward. "Scott, *what* are you doing here?"

He frowned, seeming hurt by the suspicion in my voice. "Uh, I came by to study for my English lit paper. Remember? You said you were going to help me…" He held up his book bag to demonstrate his point, and the tension dropped from my shoulders.

"I did. Shit, I'm sorry, Scott. I totally forgot." Now that he mentioned it, I vaguely recalled agreeing to help him. He'd been talking about it at lunchtime, and when I said I could probably give him some pointers, he'd invited himself over.

I glanced at the screen of my phone and saw the call was still connected to Steele. I didn't end it, just slid my phone into the back pocket of my jeans.

"Well, I don't think I can be much help right now," I said, giving him an apologetic shrug. "I'm just waiting for Cass to get back and check the circuits. Probably just a blown fuse or something, but until he gets here it's, uh, all a bit dark."

"That's okay, Maddie. I don't mind." Scott beamed at me, but instead of leaving—which was what I'd been angling toward—he headed over to my kitchen and started hunting through my drawers, using the flashlight on his phone for light. "You should probably have a flashlight in here somewhere. Or candles at least."

I wrinkled my nose. "I don't have those things. Why would I have those things?"

Scott laughed, and it made me want to punch him in the teeth. "It was a fully furnished apartment when you moved in, right?"

I took a few steps closer, confused. "Yeah, so?"

"So you didn't need to buy silverware or plates or anything, right? The kitchen was fully stocked with stuff?" He raised a brow at me, and with the shadows cloaking him, it was kind of a scary image.

I nodded. "Yeah, it was."

"Right, well then, there will most likely be some emergency supplies." He continued hunting through my drawers and cabinets until he located what he was searching for. "Ta-da!" He popped up from the cabinet under my sink, brandishing a flashlight in one hand and a packet of tea-light candles in the other.

"Told you," he said, pure smug satisfaction. It only made me punchier.

I gave a small shrug. "Cool. Shows how often I've looked through those cabinets, I guess."

Scott just laughed. "Yeah, you're not exactly a domestic house-wife kinda girl, huh?" The way he said that like it was a personality failing made me seethe. He clicked the flashlight on, testing it, then gave me a cocky smile. "Shall we?"

I shook my head, confused as hell. "Shall we...what?"

"Go and check the circuits. They're pretty standard; we just find the fuse that tripped and flip it back on. Just like that, easily done. Or would you rather sit here and wait for Cass to get back like some kind of weak, whimpering damsel in distress?" He scoffed a bit, and my teeth ground together hard.

I was spared the need to respond, though, as my front door rattled with a series of hard knocks, and I spun around to answer it.

Scott rushed past me, though, shoving me away from the door

with his arm extended. "Stay back," he ordered me. "It could be anyone."

I rolled my eyes as he pressed his face to the peephole. "Or it could be Steele, who I was on the phone with when the power went out."

Scott shot me a frown, then nodded. "You're right. It is. Why were you on the phone with him?"

I ignored his question and pushed him out of the way so I could unlock the door again. The second it opened, Steele collected me up in his arms, hugging me to his body so hard it almost hurt.

"What the fuck were you thinking?" he hissed in my ear as his arms tightened around my middle even more. "Why did you open the door to him? What if *he* cut the power?"

"To what end?" I replied in a low voice. My lips were right by his ear, and there was no need to project our conversation for everyone to hear. "He's not my stalker; he's just a bit intense. Besides, I called you back, didn't I?"

Steele released me just far enough to grab my face between his hands. "And I appreciate that, Hellcat. But in future, call me *first* so I can tell you not to open the fucking door, okay?"

His gaze was intense, blazing with protectiveness and heat, and when he crashed his lips into mine, it was with a staggering ferocity. I kissed him back with equal vigor until Scott muttered something snarky under his breath.

Steele let me break away from his kiss but didn't let me go far. His hands shifted down to my waist and held me against his body when I turned around to face Scott. Only then did I realize Kody and Archer had both followed Steele into my apartment.

Kody was grinning broadly, but Archer looked like he wanted to stab someone in the head. Probably me.

"Well, thanks for coming by," Scott told the guys, "but I've got this handled." He waved his flashlight like that was the answer to the whole blackout.

Archer just scoffed and snatched the flashlight out of Scott's hand. "What the fuck are you doing here, Scottie? I thought we told you to back the fuck off."

"Calm the hell down," Scott sneered back. "I had arranged to come over and study with Maddie tonight."

"Seems awfully coincidental," Kody drawled, stalking closer to Scott, then circling around him like a predator. "You show up right after the power goes out."

Scott laughed like he thought Kody was joking, but it was an uneasy, nervous laugh. "What, you think I cut the power myself? For what, exactly?"

Archer shrugged with a fluid rolling of muscles that captured my attention way too effectively. Steele's fingers tightening against my belly snapped me out of it, though. Fuck Archer; I didn't need his damage in my life.

"You tell us, Scottie," Archer replied, oblivious to the way I'd just ogled him. "What would have happened if you'd convinced Madison Kate to go down to the basement with you?"

Scott gaped. "Are you serious right now? Maddie, is this for fucking real? What's going on here?"

I licked my lips, trying to work out what *was* going on. Could the guys be right about Scott's convenient timing?

"Kody, why don't you and Archer go check the circuits with Scott?" I suggested, trying to keep the whole situation from blowing up into a fight. "Cass should be back any minute now too. He said his guys would go check it out, but I guess they're slow."

Scott scowled at me, probably hurt that I hadn't jumped to his defense, but Kody smiled and clapped his hand down on Scott's shoulder.

"It'd be our pleasure, babe. Maybe Scottie boy can help us check for any signs of foul play down there." Kody's fingers tightened on Scott's shoulder, making my misguided friend flinch as he was shoved out of my apartment door.

Archer remained behind a moment longer, his ice-cold gaze sweeping over me once from head to toe. Whatever he'd been trying to talk to me about couldn't have been that important, though, because he gave a short nod to Steele, then followed Kody and Scott.

Alone, I turned around again in Steele's embrace. I reached up and cupped his face in my palms, just like he'd done to me before. "Max Steele," I murmured, my tone stern as I held his eyes. My heart was racing and my stomach a mess of nerves, but I couldn't hold my tongue any longer. "You told me you loved me."

A slow smile creased his face, and he pulled me closer, his hands gripping my ass. "I did." His lips brushed over mine, teasingly soft. "I do."

Ugh. Max freaking Steele was going to melt me into a sticky puddle of goo if he kept this up.

This time when his lips brushed mine, I took charge and kissed him with all the potent, scary fucking emotions he'd stirred up in me. I might still be too damaged to voice it aloud, but I knew it in my mind and in my heart—I loved him too.

CHAPTER 27

My plans to strip Steele naked and ride his dick like my own personal pony were thwarted by *another* knock on my door, and this time it set me into a nasty fucking mood.

"What the fuck now?" I snapped, throwing the door open.

Cass just raised one scarred eyebrow, then shot his gaze to Steele behind me. "I see you've got things handled, then?"

"Sorry," I apologized, my cheeks heating with embarrassment. Who knew I could be such a bitch when denied some good dick? "Um, yes."

"Cass." Steele greeted my unofficial watcher. "Arch and Kody are in the basement checking the circuits with Scott."

Cass grunted a sound. "Scott. There's something off with that kid."

I sighed and rolled my eyes. "Not you too. Sorry for calling you away from your meeting. I just freaked out a bit." I wasn't dismissing their concerns as much as I was making out. Scott *was* being a bit strange, but I firmly believed he was just a bit messed up, *not* a stalker. So the last thing I needed was for all the scary-ass motherfuckers in my life to decide Scott was a problem that needed *taking care of*.

"Good. Fear will keep you alive, kid." He smoothed a hand over his short beard and gave Steele a serious look. "I had Bones and Gregory watching the building. You see them on your way in?"

Steele placed a hand on my hip, possessive bastard. "The new kids? No, we didn't see anyone at all."

Cass nodded, expressionless as ever. "Can't get through to them. Something's going on."

As if on cue, Steele's phone chimed with a new message, and he pulled it from his pocket. "Fuck." He sighed. "Arch found your boys, Cass. Basement."

My brows shot up and my mouth went dry. Somehow, I didn't think he'd found them sleeping on the job or playing poker.

"Wait here, kid," Cass ordered me, then turned to stride toward the stairs.

I snorted a sound of disgust. "Fat fucking chance," I muttered, following as Steele moved out into the hallway to join Cass. Emergency lighting illuminated the common spaces, but it was dim at best.

Steele just shot me a knowing smirk, then pulled a gun from the back of his jeans and handed it to me. "Shoot first, ask questions later, gorgeous."

Cass gave my weapon a curious look as we caught up to him, but he didn't try to send me back into my corner. Instead, he gave an approving nod.

"'Bout fucking time you guys taught her to shoot," he grumbled to Steele as the three of us jogged down the nine flights of stairs—lit by minimal emergency lights—to the basement. "I was wondering if I'd have to do that as well."

"As well as what?" Steele asked with a hard edge to his voice.

Cass shot him a smug look. As smug as Cass—man of stone—was ever capable of. "I've been teaching the kid to throw a proper punch. Got a lot of aggression to work out, don't ya?" He cast a glance at me, and I just glowered back at him.

"Oh man," Steele replied on a short laugh. "Kody will kill you when he finds out."

Cass just grunted a slightly amused sound. "He can try. Let's not forget who taught that little asshole how to fight in the first damn place."

I was burning to know more about *that*, but I also recognized it was neither the time nor the place for get-to-know-you chats with Cass.

We descended the rest of the stairs in relative silence, and I was careful to keep my borrowed gun pointed to the floor. One shooting lesson did not make me an automatic badass, but I'd put up a good front if forced to.

When we got to the basement door, Cass and Steele worked together with practiced efficiency, and I was reminded that not so long ago, they'd been on the same side. Not a single word passed between them, but they seemed to understand each other perfectly.

I just hung back, staying out of their way. It seemed like the smartest course of action, considering I was the least capable of our little crew.

"Over here," Kody called out from the near pitch-blackness of the basement. Farther into the area, a flashlight flickered around the walls, and Steele pulled out his phone to use as a light for us.

When we drew closer, I saw what they'd meant about finding Cass's boys.

"Oh fuck," I breathed, swallowing heavily when my bare foot touched sticky, cooling blood. "Are they...?"

"Dead?" Archer finished for me, his voice a cold growl. "Very. Getting your throat slit is one of those things that are hard to survive."

I didn't have the energy to snap back at him. I just stared down at the two dead Reapers and the utterly massive amount of blood soaking this corner of the basement.

My stomach roiled with nausea, and I tried to take a deep breath to calm it down. All I inhaled, though, was the metallic, meaty smell of fresh blood. It made me gag.

"Are we clear down here?" Steele asked, and Archer grunted an affirmation.

"This the work of your stalker, then?" Cass asked, directing the question at me. It wasn't an accusation, just a question.

I pressed a hand to my mouth, trying hard not to breathe any deeper than necessary. "I have no idea," I whispered. "Maybe?"

"Unlikely," Archer offered. "There's no note. No dolls. No *gifts*. This was more likely an attempt to kill you, Princess."

Kody was messing around with the circuit breaker while Scott held the flashlight for him. A couple of moments later, there was a heavy *thunk*, and all the halogen lights throughout the basement flickered back to life.

"Bingo," Kody announced, closing the rusty metal door with a slam. "I knew those electrical skills would come in handy one day."

With the light from above illuminating the whole basement, there was no ignoring the two dead Reapers at our feet.

"What's the working theory?" Cass rumbled.

Scott looked so pale he was almost gray, and if the puddle of puke near the circuit box was any indication, he wasn't holding it together well at all.

"Good question," Archer replied, sounding sour as hell. "Why cut the power? How would that lure Madison Kate down here to be killed? Unless he had a surefire plan for that."

"Like a *friend* who wanted to fix the breaker?" Kody suggested, throwing Scott a deliberate side-eye.

Scott paled even further. "Whoa. No. This was... I had *nothing* to do with this. Besides, there must be loads of other residents in this building! How could anyone know who would come down to check on things?"

"Actually, there's not," Cass mused.

"He's right," Steele commented. "Only about thirty percent of the units are being rented right now. The rest are waiting on renovations after some serious water damage a few months ago. And the few residents who *do* live here were all at Reaper HQ tonight. That's why Cass left these two to keep watch."

Cass shot him a narrow-eyed glare. "Been keeping tabs on us, Steele?"

He scoffed. "Of course I have."

"Okay, so somehow tonight's bad guy knew that the building was basically empty, then cut the power to…what? I don't get it." I shook my head in confusion, running my fingers through my hair.

"Perimeter alarms," Cass muttered.

Archer sighed. "Cutting the power deactivated the perimeter alarms on Madison Kate's apartment. He wouldn't need to lure her out; he could just break in and kill her right there without alerting anyone."

I wrinkled my nose. "I dunno. That seems like a really weak plan. Why take off after killing these guys? Why even bother with the power at all?"

Kody just shrugged. "It's just a working theory, babe. We will keep investigating. What matters, though, is that he *did* take off and you're still alive. Right?" He gave me a smile that was probably meant to be encouraging, but I couldn't muster one up in reply. Not with two dead gangsters at my feet.

I heaved a sigh, shaking my head. "Well…now what?"

"Clean up," Cass answered with a grunt. "I'll contact Zane. He'll want to talk to you all."

Archer curled his lip in a sneer. "Zane can kiss my ass."

"Stop it," I snapped at him, balling my fist at my side in anger. "Stuff your ego and attitude back into a box, Archer. Zane lost two of his guys tonight because of *me*. You can fucking well put your personal bullshit aside and speak to him with civility for one goddamn night. Understood?"

Archer's eyes flickered with surprise, his brow twitching as he stared back at me, unblinking. No one else spoke, no doubt waiting to see how he was going to handle being told what to do.

I tensed my shoulders and stiffened my spine. If he wanted to fight me on this one, I wasn't backing down.

To my surprise, though, he just jerked a nod.

"Take Madison Kate back upstairs," he said to Kody and Steele, his voice totally devoid of emotion. "Cass and I can handle this mess."

Kody arched a questioning brow but didn't push the issue. Instead, he stepped over the puddle of blood and wrapped his arm around my shoulders. "Come on, babe."

I handed Steele's gun back to him and started to leave the basement when I heard Scott yelp in pain.

Spinning around, I found Archer's heavy hand clamped onto the back of my friend's neck. Scott's face was pure terror, his eyes pleading for me to save him.

"Run along, Princess," Archer called out. "Scottie is gonna stay here and help us. Aren't you?" He gave Scott a little shake, like a naughty puppy caught in its mother's mouth, and my friend gave a shuddering nod of agreement.

I breathed a sigh, too damn tired to try to mediate that mess.

"Leave it," Steele murmured. "Scott is being a shady bastard. Let Arch and Cass scare the daylights out of him a bit."

I shouldn't. I really shouldn't. But they were right. Scott *was* being shady, and it was starting to freak me out. If they could nip it now before things got out of hand, who was I to argue?

With a tired shrug, I continued out of the basement with Kody and Steele. We took the elevator back up to my apartment floor, but Kody paused when he reached my door.

"Is there any chance you guys forgot to close the door when you left?" he asked, turning to Steele and me with a worried look on his face.

Glancing past him, I saw what he was talking about. My apartment door stood an inch open, but I couldn't remember if that was from us or…not.

Steele scowled at the door, shaking his head. "I don't remember. I got Arch's text, and we hurried straight down. I thought we pulled it shut, but maybe it didn't close?" He looked to me for confirmation, but I had no clue either.

Kody pulled his gun out, and Steele did the same.

"Better safe than sorry, babe," Kody told me with a wink, then he and Steele made their way through my apartment, checking for any intruders. When they seemed satisfied no one was lurking in the shadows, they began walking the rooms more slowly. They scanned all the corners, ceilings, light fixtures…all with an app on their phones.

Cameras. They were searching for cameras or listening devices or something. Just the idea gave me chills.

"Clear," Steele announced, tucking his gun and phone away.

"Same," Kody said, reappearing from the bedroom looking considerably more at ease than he had a moment ago.

Closing and locking the front door, I let out a long breath. We probably had left it open, but knowing they'd made sure no one was lurking inside my apartment took a worry off my shoulders.

"So what do we do now?" I asked, rubbing at my arms. I wasn't cold, just stressed right the hell out.

Kody shrugged, pulling his phone out. "Just chill. I'll order pizzas. It'll take the guys a while to clean up downstairs, and Zane will come by at some stage."

I made my way over to the couch and sat down heavily. All these killers and stalkers and headstrong boys were aging me way too fast. I needed a break. Maybe a tropical island getaway where my only concern was applying enough sunscreen and ordering another piña colada.

Steele sat down beside me, flicked the TV on, and pulled me

into an embrace. I relaxed into his warmth, breathing deeply and letting his solid strength ground me.

Kody called in a pizza order—enough for all of us, including Cass, Zane, and Archer—then squeezed onto the other end of the couch. He lifted my feet, bringing them into his lap before giving a short laugh.

"What?" I mumbled, already half-asleep.

He slipped back off the couch again, returning a few moments later. "You have blood on your feet, babe," he told me. He proceeded to wash my feet with the warm washcloth he'd grabbed from the bathroom. When he was satisfied they were clean, he sat back down and brought my feet back to his lap.

"Action movie okay with you, Hellcat?" Steele asked, cycling through the options on Netflix.

I nodded because they could have put *Dora the Explorer* on and I wouldn't have noticed. Not when Kody was rubbing my feet like he was a professional masseur.

"Nice choice," Kody commented on whatever Steele had selected. "Charlize is a badass bitch in this one."

Yawning, I let my heavy lids fall shut as the boys discussed the movie. They could wake me up when pizza arrived or if Zane turned up. Until then, I was just going to rest my eyes a little.

There were two dead gangsters in the basement, and a killer had just tried to lure me out of my apartment to kill me. Yet somehow, snuggled up on my couch with both Kody and Steele, I could let it all go.

CHAPTER 28

I woke with a gasp, my heart pounding and fear coursing through my veins. Sitting up, I looked around in a panic, confused, until I recognized my own bedroom. My own bed.

The last thing I remembered was falling asleep on the couch while waiting for pizza. The guys must have relocated me rather than waking me up.

Blinking the sleep from my eyes, I swiped a hand over my face and climbed out of bed. My phone, connected to its charger on the bedside table, showed it was midmorning already. I must have really been exhausted.

Sounds of conversation filtered through from the living room, and I made my way out there to see who'd stayed over. I was only wearing my panties and long-sleeve top from the night before, so someone must have taken my jeans off for me.

"Good morning, gorgeous." Steele greeted me with a smile as I shuffled around the corner. He was in my kitchen, buttering toast. Where the hell had he found toast? Or butter? My fridge only contained takeout leftovers and drinks.

"Hey," I mumbled, then yawned. "What happened last night? I thought we had to do the whole thing with Zane."

Kody swooped in, wrapping me in a warm hug and kissing my hair. "We did. You didn't need to. I tucked you into bed before they arrived because you were way too peaceful to disturb."

Warm fuzzies made me smile, and I leaned my face back to kiss him on the lips. "Thanks, babe," I replied with a wink. "But I really can't miss any more of my classes this week. Can one of you give me a ride? I guess I already missed Bree."

"Of course," Kody said, and Steele nodded his agreement.

"She came by but we wanted to let you sleep." Steele leaned across the counter and handed me a slice of toast covered in raspberry jam. "We also grabbed you some groceries." That was delivered with a wink, and I rolled my eyes.

"I was surviving," I muttered but took a big bite of the toast anyway. "I'll take a shower and be ready in a few, okay?"

Taking my food with me, I hurried to my bathroom and cranked the shower on. It only took a few minutes for the water to heat, but it was enough time for me to finish my toast and tie my hair up in a bun to keep it dry.

I rushed through my shower, conscious of the time and how horribly I was falling behind in some of my classes. But when I turned the water off and stepped out of the steamy cubical, I froze.

"Guys!" I shouted, hearing the note of panic in my own voice.

Both of them appeared in the bathroom door in an instant, looking confused and worried. I pointed to the mirror.

The steam from my shower had fogged the glass over and revealed a message.

YOU'LL ALWAYS BE MINE.

It was written in that familiar, jagged script, and there was no doubt in my mind who'd left it there.

"Shit," Kody breathed. "I guess we were wrong after all. Last night was the stalker, not the killer." I nodded, having just come to the same conclusion.

"Unless they were both here," Steele mused, snapping a picture of the message, then grabbing one of my hand towels to wipe it off the mirror.

Kody gave him a thoughtful look as he grabbed a towel as well and handed it to me. "Killer tries to lure MK out with the power outage, and the stalker scares him off. Then...comes in here while the perimeter alarms are down and leaves a love note?"

Steele shrugged. "Maybe. It does seem to be his MO, doesn't it? Protecting Madison Kate while also doing everything possible to freak her out?"

Wrapping myself up in my towel, I shuddered. Moving past the boys, I headed to my closet to grab some fresh clothes.

"I don't get it," I grumbled as I hunted for my black skinny jeans. "I wish whoever was trying to kill me would just..." I trailed off with a frustrated growl as I found my jeans, then headed to my dresser for underwear.

"Just fuck off and leave you alone?" Kody finished for me, and I nodded with a weak smile.

"Pretty much," I agreed, sighing. Then I groaned. "Are you fucking kidding me?"

All of my underwear was gone. All of it. On the bottom of the empty drawer, one word was written in a dark substance that looked way too much like blood for my liking.

MINE.

Rage and frustration filled me, and I slammed the drawer shut again, despite the fact that Kody was still staring at the message.

"I don't have time for this shit," I muttered. I quickly dressed sans underwear and caught Steele's eye. "Maybe my stalker is doing you a favor today, Max."

He quirked a grin in response, but the lines of his face were tight with worry. Still, they didn't protest when I hurried them out of the apartment.

Steele drove, dropped Kody and me off at SGU, and said he'd call later. He didn't have any classes on a Friday, and I strongly suspected he was heading back to my apartment to do a more thorough search—a suspicion that was confirmed when I realized he had my keys.

"Come on, babe," Kody said, slinging his arm around my shoulders, then kissing my head. "Let's go learn some shit. Then maybe I can talk you into a lunchtime quickie." His grin was pure sex when I glanced up at him, but I just laughed and shook my head.

Don't get me wrong, I was crazy tempted. Hell, I almost wanted to blow off class altogether. But I knew I needed to catch up with Bree and Scott at lunch and make sure Scott's face was still in one piece.

"Okay, fine," Kody sighed. "How about I just talk you into moving home?"

We'd just reached the main building, and he let me go long enough to open the door for us. I leveled a glare at him as I passed through.

"Not fucking happening, Kodiak Jones." I was standing firm on that one.

He frowned but still tucked me back under his arm again. "I understand your reluctance, babe. But look what happened last night. You're a sitting duck there on your own, and what if—"

"Kody," I snapped. "No. I'm not moving back into *Archer's* house. Let it go."

He didn't want to. Not by a long shot. But he very wisely did as I asked and let the subject drop...for now.

Something had shifted with him, though, and throughout the whole of our sociological foundations lecture, he kept his hand on my leg. Whether he was tracing patterns on my jeans or just casually resting it there, it was like he just couldn't *not* touch me. Come to think of it, he'd been like that all morning.

"Hey, is everything okay?" I asked when our lecture ended and we packed up our things. "You seem… I dunno. Something's off."

Kody's eyes widened somewhat; then he shrugged. "I'm all good," he told me with a weak smile.

I gave him a narrow-eyed stare but let it drop. Maybe he was just shaken from last night, like I was. Regardless, he seemed to be getting something out of constantly touching me, and I liked it too.

"So I have to train Arch again this afternoon," Kody told me as we made our way through campus to the dining hall, where Bree and Scott were most likely already waiting. "Do you maybe want to come along? I kinda, uh, I'd really feel better if I could keep my eyes on you. You know?"

Yep, he was still freaking about the killer-stalker incident.

I stopped walking, turning to face him in the middle of the path we were on. "Kody, I'm fine. As far as attempts on my life go, that was a pretty mild one." I paused, remembering the two dead gangsters. "I mean, for me."

He frowned, worry etched all over his face. "Yeah, but it was a fucking creepy one. Cutting the power, killing the two Reapers watching the place, and leaving notes on the mirror? That's some fucked-up psychological shit. I'm concerned he's escalating and that sooner or later we won't get there fast enough."

I bit the corner of my lip, nodding. "That's fair. I'm not dismissing that at all. But this shit with Archer and me…it's too fucked up. I can't move back into his house while I'm trying to *separate* from him. And that's on top of the fact that I want to stab him in the fucking face with a rusty spoon every time he opens his mouth."

Kody's lips twitched into a grin. "Want me to kick him in the balls again?"

I laughed. "I'd never say no to an offer like that. But as for this afternoon, no. I have, uh, something that I do in the afternoons. Totally safe, I promise. I'm not putting myself in any stupid situations just to prove I'm a strong, independent woman."

He scowled, not distracted by my babble. "What is it?"

I cringed. Bree was right; I should have been up-front. "Uh, Cass...um, Cass is training me down at the Reaper gym."

Kody just stared at me. "Training you...how?"

I shrugged, wanting to change the subject so freaking badly. But I needed to offer the same transparency he and Steele were giving me. "Just boxing, mainly. He said it was a good outlet for my pent-up aggression."

Kody nodded slowly, then sighed and ran a hand through his hair. "Fair enough—he's right."

I blinked a couple of times, confused. "Wait, that's it?"

He tilted his head to the side. "That's what?"

"Uh, I dunno. I thought you'd be...angrier." I wrinkled my nose, baffled as all shit. "Or something."

His eyes flickered with something like amusement. "So why'd you do it if you thought I'd be angry?"

My lips parted, but no valid response formed. He kinda had a point there.

"Look, babe, I'm not going to give you grief over doing something that both helped you work through your feelings *and* gave you valuable physical combat skills. Would I have preferred you'd asked me to train you? Hell yes, of course. But I can't fault you for training with Cass. He's old, but he's still in pretty good shape." Kody's grin told me he was ripping on Cass for the fun of it. I'd gotten the impression not all of the Reapers were in my boys' bad books.

I rolled my eyes. "He's not old, Kody. He's probably only thirty-five or something."

Kody snickered a laugh. "Actually, thirty-three. His life experience is aging him faster."

211

I huffed a sigh. "Whatever. So you're not mad?"

He gave me a shrewd look. "Depends. If I'm mad, will you try to cheer me up?"

Typical Kodiak Jones.

Reaching up, I grabbed his face between my hands and planted his lips against mine. It was all the encouragement he needed, and his arms banded around my waist as his mouth devoured mine with fierce hunger. But as much as I wanted to take things further and *really* make sure I'd cheered him up, we were still standing in the middle of SGU campus with students all around.

"Later," I promised him in a husky whisper as we broke apart.

He gave a small groan and kissed me again. "I'll hold you to that, babe."

Interlinking our fingers, we continued on our way to the dining hall, smiling like dazed, loved-up idiots. Bree was bound to comment on it as soon as she saw us, but I couldn't care less.

Kody made me feel like the center of his whole universe, and it was totally addictive.

CHAPTER 29

When I met Cass for our workout that afternoon, he told me about new security measures that had been installed in the building during the day—upgraded alarm systems and a security guard in the foyer.

"Kid, I know shit is all messed up between you and Arch right now," Cass rumbled on our way back from the gym, "but it might not be a bad idea to move back there."

I stopped dead in my tracks. "What?"

Cass just gave me that face. The resting fuck-you face. "What?" he parroted, and I scowled at him.

"What fucking gives, Cass? I thought the Reapers needed me here as an insurance policy against Archer's celestial wrath." I parked my hands on my hips, my tone accusing.

He didn't blink. "The *Reapers* do. *I'm* telling you that it might not be the best idea for your own safety. Get it?" He gave me a pointed look, then continued walking.

I hurried to catch up, turning his advice over in my mind. If Cass was admitting that I wasn't entirely safe in the Reaper-owned building, then I needed to take that seriously.

But fucking hell, I couldn't go back to Archer's house. There had to be another option.

"Anyway, I'm supposed to be babysitting you tonight." Cass looked as excited about that as he would be about getting an enema.

I shook my head. "You don't need to. I'll be just fine with you across the hall." Besides, hopefully Kody would come over later, seeing as Steele was working on more security stuff and Archer was an insufferable prick.

Cass just shrugged. "Orders. No one wants to see you sliced and diced, kid."

"Well, agreed. But I also don't need you breathing down my neck while I'm studying. You're just across the hall, right? You can play babysitter from there." We'd just reached our floor, and I gave his apartment door a pointed look. "Last night was a fluke. I can't see anyone getting the jump on me when you're right there, can you?"

Cass ran his palm over his short beard like he was considering my point. Clearly, he wasn't looking forward to sitting on my couch all night while I wrote essays and watched reality TV.

"What about if I promise to text you every half hour so you know no one has jumped out of a closet and strangled me?" I was making light of the situation, but that was all too scary of a possibility these days.

He huffed a sigh. "Every five minutes."

I grinned, knowing I'd won. "Ten minutes."

"Fine," he grumbled. "But I'm sweeping your apartment first."

Not arguing with that requirement, I unlocked the door for him and waited while he checked every nook and cranny imaginable. Only when he was satisfied that no one was hiding and no cameras had been placed while we were gone did he return to the hallway.

"Clear," he informed me. "Every ten minutes, understood? If I don't hear from you, I'm breaking the fucking door down."

"Understood." I nodded firmly.

He squinted at me a moment, like he was trying to work out if I was up to no good, then finally turned to his own door.

"Think about moving back with your boys, all right?" Cass told me as he unlocked his own door, then stepped inside. "Make smart choices, kid."

That advice echoed around my head as I entered my apartment. Make smart choices. Had I been doing that thus far? Probably not. So yeah, Cass was right. I needed to start making the smart choices that would keep me *alive*.

Even if it meant accepting help from Archer goddamn D'Ath.

Tomorrow, though. Tonight Kody would come over and we could have one freaking night together without Archer listening and jerking off in his room next door. And then maybe I could let Kody think he'd talked me into moving back to the mansion. Maybe I could keep a few shreds of my dignity intact that way.

After I showered—and noticed that my bathroom mirror had been professionally cleaned—I got changed and went back to the living room to study and cook dinner. And by cook dinner, I absolutely meant order takeout from the local Chinese restaurant again.

For a couple of hours, I worked my way through my assignments, finally making a dent in the work I'd been letting slip. Every ten minutes on the dot, I sent Cass a thumbs-up emoji. He didn't reply to any of them, but the messages were marked as "seen," which was good enough. Meanwhile, I was growing increasingly impatient to hear from Kody. When I'd told him "later," I'd thought he understood that I wanted him to come over after his training session.

When I finished all the work that was due for my classes, my phone finally lit up with Kody's name.

"Hey, I thought you'd forgotten about me," I joked as I picked up the call.

"Never in a million years, babe," he replied. "We just finished, but I got a call from Jase. He needs me to go and talk about some investment shit for a line of sportswear we've been working on. Can we raincheck?"

Disappointment soured my gut, and I groaned. "Jase needs to see you at eight thirty on a Friday night? He's the worst kind of party pooper, I swear to god."

Kody laughed. "I know, I'm sorry. He made it sound really important. Cass is still there with you, right? He said he'd keep a lookout so Steele could work on some security measures."

"My big bad babysitter is keeping me safe, don't stress." I glanced at my phone, noting that I needed to send Cass another message in two minutes. "Call me when you're done. I want to hear all about this sportswear."

"You've got it. I'll come by in the morning, and we can do something fun, just the two of us." He sounded genuinely apologetic, and I actually looked forward to whatever he'd come up with in the morning. It sort of sounded like he wanted to take me on a *date*.

I sighed. "Fine. Good luck."

"Thanks, babe." He ended the call, and I tossed my phone on the couch, disappointed. But my night didn't need to hinge on my guys being free to hang out. I was a self-sufficient kind of woman, after all.

Picking my phone back up again, I sent my check-in message to Cass, then called Bree.

"Hey, girl!" she greeted on answering. "Dallas says hi too."

I caught the rumble of Dallas's voice saying, "Hey, Katie," in the background.

Dammit. There went that plan. "'Hi back' to Dallas."

"What's up?" Bree asked, her voice chirpy and enthusiastic.

"Nothing," I replied with a sigh. "Just seeing what you were up to, but I think I already have a fair idea." I gave her a chuckle, and she giggled back.

"Um, yeah. But I can ditch Dallas's ass if you need girl time. Want me to? I can be there in half an hour." She must have been at Dallas's house across the city.

I ran my fingers through my hair. "Nah, I'm fine. Enjoy your night, girl. Call me tomorrow."

"Okay." Bree sounded reluctant. "Are you sure? Dallas won't mind."

In the background, Dallas disagreed. I laughed. "Totally sure. I'm going to call it an early night instead."

Bree and I said our farewells, and then I ended the call.

I tapped my phone against my lips a couple of times, debating then dismissing the idea of calling Steele. I didn't want to distract him, and I knew he'd have called if he was done.

An early night sounded so much better than hours of endless trash TV, so I packed up my school materials and dropped my empty takeout boxes in the trash.

Heading into my bedroom, I texted Cass to let him know I was going to bed. He replied this time, telling me to check that my door alarm was set and the bolts secure. Pictures or it didn't happen.

I didn't even argue it with him, just did as he asked. Better safe than sorry, and what had he told me? Make good choices? Well, not pushing back on simple safety measures was probably on that list.

It wasn't until I was tucked up in bed and on the verge of sleep that a thought occurred to me. Steele was sorting out security? What security? Alarms were already in place, and there was a guard at the desk in the foyer. Besides, Steele's area of expertise was more hands-on than tech.

If he was working on my security, I'd bet money that there would be another body to be disposed of by morning.

That thought should have scared me. It should have made me fear for the mental stability of the boys I was involved with. But it didn't.

Instead, I fell asleep feeling safe and protected because Max Steele loved me and he wouldn't stop killing until the threats against me were eliminated. Of that, I was sure.

217

My phone vibrating and bleeping on the bedside table woke me some hours later, and I rubbed my groggy eyes. Squinting at the screen, I read Cass's name on the caller ID, and a harsh chill swept through me.

Just as I pressed answer call, a heavy knock pounded on my front door. I flinched but gritted my teeth and brought the phone to my ear. No doubt Cass was calling about whoever had come to visit.

"Kid," the grumpy gangster rumbled before I even said anything. "You're fine to answer the door. It's just Archer."

I stifled a groan. "Are you watching my door?" I asked instead of the curses I wanted to voice.

"Yes," Cass replied, his voice flat. Then he hung up.

Great.

With a sigh, I tossed my blankets off and climbed out of bed. It was just after midnight, so whatever Archer was here for, it must be important. I just wished it were Kody or Steele instead. At least I enjoyed their presence and wasn't even remotely stabby around them these days.

I took a quick look through the peephole, just to double-check, then unlocked all my new bolts and deactivated the door alarm.

"Darling." I greeted Archer with a saccharine smile as I swung the door open. "What an unwanted surprise. What do you want?"

His hands were braced on either side of the doorway, his face tilted toward the ground. At the sound of my voice, though, he lurched forward and probably would have crashed straight into me if I hadn't jumped out of the way. Instead, he just staggered into my apartment and went straight to the kitchen, yanking my fridge open with way too much force.

My jaw dropped.

Across the hall, Cass opened his front door and gave me an amused look—as much as he was capable of.

"Forgot to mention, he seems to be drunk." His gravelly voice sounded surprised. That was nothing on my shock, though.

"Seems to be?" I repeated, squinting at Cass in disbelief.

Cass just gave a one-shouldered shrug. "Never seen Arch properly drunk before. Maybe it's a stroke. You want me to get rid of him?"

I looked over my shoulder. Archer leaned against my kitchen island, chugging the bottle of pinot gris that Bree had left in my fridge. For fuck's sake.

I blew out a heavy sigh. "No, it's fine. I can handle him."

Cass jerked a nod. "Call me if you change your mind."

"I will," I replied, grateful for the backup. I started to close my door, and he spoke again.

"Don't forget to reset your alarm," he told me with a stern glare, "and, kid?"

I rolled my eyes with a smile. "Make good choices?"

Cass huffed something way too close to a laugh to be legit. Probably a tickle in his throat. "I was gonna say, 'Use protection.' But that works just the same." With a pointed look, he retreated into his apartment and slammed the door shut.

I closed mine too, locking it and making sure to reactivate the alarm. Then I turned to my unwanted visitor with a scowl.

"What are you doing here, D'Ath?" I demanded, folding my arms over my chest.

He just leveled a glassy-eyed glare back at me. "We need to talk, Wifey."

No shit.

CHAPTER 30

Archer *Infuriating* D'Ath made his way over to my sofa and sat down heavily, then took another gulp of wine.

"You just going to stand there all night, Princess? Or are you gonna grow some of those famous Madison Kate balls and have a conversation with me?" His eyes were glazed, and his words held a slight slur, but his focus was laser sharp on me.

Every instinct screamed at me to throw him out on his ass. He didn't fucking *deserve* my time or my attention. He'd made his bed of lies; now let him sleep in it.

And yet…I found myself glaring back at him as I made my way over to the armchair perpendicular to the sofa he'd selected. If he thought I was going to cuddle up and rub his feet, he was fucking delusional.

For a long time, way past the point of awkward, we just sat there in silence, staring at each other. Except he didn't seem the slightest bit uncomfortable. Not like I was, anyway. I was basically crawling out of my own skin with nervousness.

"You've been avoiding me," Archer said, finally breaking the silence.

I rolled my eyes. "I'm glad you noticed. You're not as brain-dead as I gave you credit for."

"Why?" he demanded with a small frown line forming between his brows. Fuck me, he was *drunk*.

I let out a short, bitter laugh. "Are you joking? Why do you fucking think, *Husband*? Maybe it was the bullshit on Riot Night, which I *still* think you had a hand in, even if Kody and Steele don't believe it. Or gee, maybe it was just the fact that you purchased me like a fucking broodmare and married me without my knowledge or consent. Maybe, just maybe, it was the secrets on lies on more secrets. Maybe I just think you're a despicable human being who isn't worth my time or energy. Take your fucking pick, *Sunshine*."

He didn't immediately respond but sipped another mouthful of pinot gris while seeming to consider what I'd said.

"All right," he eventually said, leaning forward and placing the half-empty bottle of wine on the coffee table. "That's fair. Let's talk some of this shit through, shall we?"

I blinked at him in confusion. "Sorry, what? You want to… No. This is a joke or something. I'm not fucking *talking it through* with you. If you need therapy, go and pay a professional. You've burned this bridge so hard there's not even any ash left. Go to hell, Archer."

Deciding to take Cass up on his offer after all, I started to stand up from my armchair. Archer moved shockingly fast for such a drunk bastard, though, grabbing my wrist and yanking me onto the sofa beside him.

"Running scared, Princess?" he mocked with a sneer. "I'm so shocked. It's not like that's your signature move or anything. Oh wait. Yes, it is."

Outrage heated my cheeks. "Excuse me? What the fuck would you know?"

Archer just shrugged. "Get some bad publicity, run to Cambodia for a year. Find out you're wrong about your hate campaign, run away to a hotel. Finally get the answers you want, run off to Aspen. You run so much, you should invest in some proper sneakers or something. You'll break a damn ankle running in those high heels you wear."

He was rambling. Totally rambling. But it was hard to focus on his words when his hand still gripped my arm, his thumb stroking little lines over my inner wrist.

I let out a shaky laugh but couldn't seem to pull my hand away. "You're a piece of work, D'Ath. You know that? I didn't get *bad publicity*. I was accused of violent crimes I didn't commit, then got *sent* away. That was not my choice. In fact, it was probably yours, considering how you're pulling Dad's strings now." I leveled an accusing glare at him, but he just shook his head.

"Nope, nothing to do with me," he murmured. His gaze dropped away from mine, his eyes falling to where his fingers still circled my wrist. "I did know those cops would pick you up on Riot Night," he admitted in a quiet voice. "But I didn't plant that key on you."

Drawing a deep breath, I extracted my wrist from his grip and counted to five in my head to keep from punching him in the teeth—only because I knew it'd hurt me more than it'd hurt him.

"You planned to have me arrested? *Why?*" It was taking all my self-control to keep my cool. But I was smart enough to recognize alcohol had loosened Archer's tongue, and this might be my only opportunity for real answers.

He dropped his head against the back of the couch, exhaustion leaking from his pores as his eyelids drooped. "Because it would have kept you safe. If you were trapped in the back of a squad car or in a holding cell, you wouldn't be on the streets that night." His voice was rough and...sincere. What the hell?

"You knew what was going to happen that night?" I bit my lip, running through it all in my mind. Violence and death at the Laughing Clown when the Reapers and Wraiths clashed were just the tip of the iceberg. All across Shadow Grove, damage had been done. Arson, vandalism, assaults... It'd been a total mess.

Archer just yawned and nodded. "Bullshit between Zane and Charon, sorting out some border disputes and balancing the power. Your dad took advantage, though, and cashed a few insurance claims out of it."

I drew a deep breath. Of course my father was neck deep in that whole mess. And yet Archer had tried to keep me *safe*?

Reaching out, I snagged the bottle of wine and quickly drank the remainder of it. I was way too sober for this kind of conversation. When it was empty, I got up from the sofa and went back to the fridge to find something else. There were a couple of pear ciders tucked into the back, so they'd have to do.

Returning to the sofa, I pulled my phone out and shot off a text to both Steele and Kody, letting them know Archer was at my place. Drunk.

"You need to drop this shit with Demi Timber," Archer announced after I sat back down. For some inexplicable reason, I'd sat back on the sofa beside him, rather than returning to the armchair where I'd have some physical distance to buffer the attraction between us. Idiot.

I unscrewed the top of my cider and shook my head. "Hell no."

Archer blew out a breath, like I was testing his patience or something. Poor dear, he'd learn sooner or later that I didn't play games. When I consulted a divorce lawyer, I fully intended to divorce his sorry ass.

"You can't divorce me, Madison Kate," he said, sipping his own cider, then screwing his face up in disgust. "What the fuck is this shit?"

"Pear cider," I informed him, my expression flat. "Bree loves them, and you are an uninvited and unwanted houseguest. So you'll drink it and you'll fucking love it, or your next beverage will be drain cleaner. Clear?"

One of his black brows raised at me, and his bloodshot eyes turned wary. "Yeah, all right then." He took another sip and this time only cringed a little bit.

Oh look, he can be trained after all.

"As for divorcing you, I'm absolutely making that happen. Unless you'd like to give me a *seriously* good reason why that wouldn't be in my best interests?" *Like…a prenup?*

He sighed heavily and ran a hand over his short beard. Once again, I found myself reconsidering my general distaste for beards… On the right face, they weren't so bad.

"If you divorce me, Princess, then you'll lose everything. Your entire inheritance from your father—paltry as it is now that he's nearly broke—but more importantly, your mother's trust will be transferred to me. You'll have nothing left." He delivered this news without emotion, like it was just a fact that was due no remorse or regret.

"What the *fuck*?" I hissed at him, my fury spiking to nuclear levels as I leapt to my feet. "Are you kidding me right now? Why would you do that? What the fuck did I ever do to you to deserve this?"

My breathing was heavy and hot and angry tears pricked at the corners of my eyes, but Archer just looked up at me, impassive and unapologetic.

"Because I forked over a shitload of money to free your father from his bad debts, Princess. No one in their right mind does something like that without an iron-clad contract. Spare me the theatrics too. It was a smart business move and you know it." He let out a harsh laugh, colored by his intoxication. "Hell, you'd have done the exact same thing in my shoes; that's what pisses you off more than anything. You *understand* the why of it, but you just hate that it was done to you."

My fists curled at my sides, my fingernails digging painfully into my palms. I couldn't argue with him, though, because he was right. From a purely business point of view, *of course* he'd safe-guarded his investment. From a personal point of view, though? I wanted to make him fucking bleed.

I worked through those thoughts, and he just stared up at me, his cool blue eyes assessing and curious. For the first time in as long as I'd known him, his mask was gone. He wasn't trying to guard his thoughts and feelings; he wasn't hiding his reactions. It was unnerving as hell.

"You want to hurt me, don't you?" he asked after a moment, a grin curling the corners of his lips. "You've got murder in your pretty eyes, Princess. It's such a turn-on."

Fuck me.

Turning away from Archer's all too intense stare, I checked my phone and found messages from both Kody and Steele. One of them had asked if I needed him to come pick up Archer's drunk ass. The other asked if I needed a body cleanup. Both made me smile.

"Calling in your guard dogs, Princess?" Archer asked with a mocking laugh. "Running scared again. Typical."

I rolled my eyes and tapped out a quick reply to both boys, assuring them we were *just fine*. I didn't need my so-called guard dogs to tear Archer a new asshole, thanks.

Spinning back around, I planted my hands on my hips and speared my asshole husband and owner with a glare that could boil acid. "Why did you do it in the first place?" I demanded. "Why buy me at all? It sure as fuck wasn't for the sex. And I seriously doubt it was for my mediocre trust fund. So why do it?"

He stared up at me a moment, his gaze locked with mine and an odd, almost wistful smile touching his lips. Instead of answering, he dropped his empty cider bottle on the coffee table and stood up, towering over me. Fucker.

Two steps saw him eliminate the space between us, and he dipped his head until his lips were right beside my ear.

"Because if I didn't, someone else would have. I saved your life, Princess. A little gratitude wouldn't go astray." His whispered words were harsh, full of pain for something I couldn't even remotely identify. It wasn't just that I hadn't thanked him, that was for sure.

It was something a hell of a lot deeper and more fucked up than I was fully grasping. Yet.

"Where are you going?" I demanded as he pushed past me. "We're not done here."

He barked a laugh. "You've got that right. I'm taking a piss. Is that okay with you, Darling Wife? That pear bullshit just went straight through me."

Oh.

Biting the inside of my cheek, I indicated he go ahead. The last thing I needed was a drunk Archer D'Ath to pass out on my couch and piss himself. Then again, maybe that would cure me of the potent sexual chemistry between us...

Too late. The bathroom door slammed, and I heaved a sigh.

I could safely say this wasn't how I had imagined my Friday night was going to play out. In an attempt to calm my nerves, I collected up our empty bottles and took them to the kitchen, disposing of them in the recycling bin.

The whoosh of water from my bathroom indicated that he'd flushed, but then the shower started up. What the hell? Was he taking a shower in my apartment? Since when had I agreed to that?

Enraged—and just a fraction tipsy from the wine and cider—I marched through to tell him he'd broken the damn rules of hospitality. I flung the bathroom door open dramatically, then almost swallowed my tongue.

"Do you mind?" my husband—my *very naked* husband—asked from beneath the shower spray. "Ever heard of knocking?"

Speechless, I clapped a hand over my eyes, but *come on*. I'd totally already seen *everything*. So had my libido, if the dramatic tightening of my nipples and pulsing of my cunt were any indication. Fuck, fuck, *fuck*.

"Why are you in my shower?" I demanded with shrill panic in my voice.

"Why not?" he replied, his voice carrying way too much

amusement for the current situation. "Wanna join me, Princess? I could scrub your back for you."

It was legitimately embarrassing how tempted I was by that offer.

Thank *god* I hadn't drunk anything more, or I'd be wet and soaped up right now. As it was, I was only one of those things.

Groan. Archer was slowly killing me.

"Just...get the fuck out," I growled, keeping my hand tight over my eyes. "I thought you wanted to talk, not shave your balls."

The water shut off and Archer's chuckle grew closer. Way too close. Enough that water dripped on my bare toes.

"Why not both?" he teased, his arm brushing me as he reached for a towel. "Relax, Princess. My dick isn't going to hypnotize you like some kind of snake charmer." He paused, and I just *knew* he had something to add. "Unless you want it to, of course."

Yep. Typical predictable Archer.

Growling insults at him, I kept my eyes averted—because holy crap, I was only human—and retreated back into my bedroom. I needed a hoodie or something to put an extra layer of protection between us. All of a sudden, my oversized T-shirt and short shorts were feeling way too see-through.

I heard Archer moving around behind me, but I kept my eyes firmly forward as I hunted through my dresser for the biggest sweatshirt I owned. Bingo. One of Kody's would be perfect.

Yanking it on, I finally turned around and did a sharp double take when I found Archer *in my freaking bed*.

"What the hell do you think you're doing?" I exclaimed, my eyes bugging out as he made himself comfortable, then threw an arm over his head with a yawn.

"I'm sleepy," he replied, like a petulant child. "You don't mind if I stay here, do you?" The clear implication of his tone was that he didn't particularly care if I minded. I wasn't getting a damn choice.

Still, I ground my teeth together, seething. "Yes, I fucking *mind*. Get out. Go home. You've got that big old mansion that you were passing off as my father's. Go sleep there if you're so tired."

He blinked at me from heavy-lidded eyes, shrugging one of those huge, muscular shoulders covered in ink. Goddamn he'd spent a bit of time under the needle for that many tattoos.

"Can't," he replied in a slurred drawl. "You're stuck with me, Wifey."

Frustration was spiking my temper to violent levels. I wanted to stab him with that pretty purple knife he'd given me. It was right there on my dresser, within reach...

But my curiosity won out, as it always did.

"What does that even mean, Archer? Why can't you go home? Don't you mean you *won't*?" I narrowed my eyes at him. His chest was bare, my rumpled blankets tossed over his waist. Had he put any pants on before climbing in there? Or was he totally naked? Why the fuck did I care?

He yawned again. "Can't," he repeated. "Kody and Steele threw me out and told me not to come back until I'd *resolved my issues*, so here I am." He spread his hands wide, indicating that all his issues centered on me. "Resolving."

Irritation pricked at my skin, and I mentally cursed out those two fuckers. Had their excuses for not being here tonight just been bullshit? No, they'd promised not to lie to me anymore. I doubt they could have known this was how Archer planned to deal with his baggage.

I folded my arms, glaring at the intoxicated bastard in my bed. "So, consider it done. Issues resolved. Now fuck off."

A smile curled his lips, and he shook his head. "Not even close. Why don't you come over here, and we can finish our conversation?" He patted the vacant space of bed beside him like he wasn't inviting me to lie with a viper.

It was on the tip of my tongue to refuse and tell him where to shove his conversation. But his pale eyes glittered with cunning.

"Unless you're so scared of your own body betraying you that you can't handle being so close. Understandable, I guess. You do have a history of throwing yourself at me." His smile was taunting me, and I rose to the bait. Dammit.

Seething with anger and indignation, I walked around to the other side of my bed and perched on the very edge of the mattress, facing him with a sour look. "Happy?"

Archer snorted a laugh. "Ecstatic."

I released a slow breath, mentally counting to five. If I wanted more answers, I needed to keep my cool and ignore the tattooed Adonis making himself at home between my sheets. Easy, right? Yeah, and Mount Everest was just a hill.

"So, what other pearls of wisdom do you plan on dropping in your attempts to *reconcile* our differences, Sunshine?" I asked in a dry tone when he made no signs of speaking first. For some, probably alcohol-impacted reason, he seemed perfectly comfortable just staring at me like a creeper.

He gave another heavy yawn, rubbing his eyes with the back of his hand. "I hardly ever drink this much, you know? Can't even remember the last time I was drunk enough to make the whole room spin."

I rolled my eyes. "If you vomit in my bed, I'll leave you to drown in it."

He just laughed. It was jarring to hear from him, like he'd been body-snatched by a jovial and friendly alien who just wanted to hang out and chat all night.

"Okay, how about this one," he drawled, tucking his forearms behind his head. "I think I know who is trying to kill you. Why, at least."

My brows shot up. "Excuse me?"

He rolled onto his side, grinning drunkenly. "You can tell Zane to stop sniffing around; he won't unravel the paper trail. I cleaned it up myself to stop anyone from tracking you down before Riot Night even happened."

I was speechless. Utterly speechless. Here I was with Zane and Demi both trying to uncover why my mother's family seemed to have been erased from documentation, and the culprit had been under my nose the whole time.

"Except," Archer continued, oblivious to or uncaring of my state of shock, "obviously, they'd already found you and placed the hit on the dark web. So all that work was fucking pointless."

Closing my eyes for a second, I tried to scrape together coherent thoughts. "Okay, start again. You know who is trying to kill me, and you're only *now* telling me?"

It was his turn to roll his eyes. "There's no pleasing you, Princess. Keep secrets, get kicked in the balls. Tell you the truth, get blamed for not doing it sooner."

"Wow," I replied, deadpan. "You're a real piece of work, you know that?"

He grunted a noise of agreement. "Yep. I am. But even with all my many, many failings, you still fantasize about what it'd be like to add me to your harem. What does *that* say about *you*, Madison Kate?"

Motherfucker had a point. Not that I'd ever admit it, though.

"No, I don't," I lied. "Get back on topic. Who is trying to kill me?"

Archer squinted at me, already seeming to be half-asleep. "Your uncle. I think. Or maybe your cousin... It's hard to know who's pulling the strings over there without an in-person visit."

I shook my head, even more confused than ever. "What are you even babbling about? I don't have an unc—" I broke off, comprehension dawning. "You motherfuckers. I have other family that I don't know about?"

He just shrugged one shoulder. "Don't blame me for that one. Besides, when you consider that one of them is trying to have you killed, do they really sound like the kind of people you want to know?" He twitched a brow at me, and I had to concede his point.

"So why do they want me dead? Let me guess. My inheritance is a shitload more than I think it is?" My voice was flat and resigned, and I wasn't even remotely shocked by the knowing smile on Archer's lips.

He nodded. "Bingo."

"How much?"

He shrugged. "Don't know. Billions, probably."

Outrage bubbled up in my throat. "You *don't know*? You fucking *purchased* me on the caveat of my trust fund passing to you when I turn twenty-one. You seriously want to tell me you *don't know* how much it's worth?"

He gave me a bored look. "Let's get something straight here and now, Princess. I didn't marry you for your trust fund. In case you didn't notice, I'm not exactly hurting for a dollar myself." His tone was harsh, somewhat less slurred than it had been a moment ago. "I married you because it was the only thing I could think of on short notice. If it wasn't me, you'd have gone to auction and probably wound up as a sex slave for some Venezuelan drug baron."

Shock rippled through me. When he put it like that...

"Trust me, Kate," he added in a grumble, "you're better off right now. By a long fucking shot. Those fucks that buy people at auction are disgusting, depraved, sadistic bastards, and a girl like you would have attracted the kind of buyer who likes to break and degrade his pets."

What was it Steele had told me? There was always someone worse out there. And yeah, Archer had a point. As furious as I was at the whole situation, it could have been a whole lot worse.

"Is that why you refused to sleep with me?" I asked before I could stop myself. The second the question left my lips, I cringed.

Archer just eyed me curiously. "Yep," he replied without even a hint of deceit. "Puts the whole thing into perspective now, doesn't it? Yes, I paid your father a crapload of money to clear his bad debts, and in exchange he signed over ownership of you and your trust fund. But I haven't hurt you; I haven't raped you or kept you caged. So why am I this big bad villain in your eyes, huh?"

His jaw pulled with another heavy yawn, and his lids drooped heavier. If I wanted any more answers out of him, I needed to be quick, before he passed out.

But the way he'd just summarized my whole problem had left me stunned and seriously questioning everything I thought I knew. Why was I so furious? Like he'd said, my situation right now could have been a million times worse if he *hadn't* acted to save me. That was what was knocking me around.

Archer D'Ath hadn't imprisoned me or taken away my freedom. Quite the opposite. He'd *saved* me.

Well fuck. Now where did that leave us?

"I can see I just exploded your brain," Archer mumbled, his eyes just cool blue slits framed by long black lashes. "I'll nap until you scrape all that scrambled gray matter together and come up with a new unfounded reason to hate me." He closed his eyes fully and shifted until he was comfortably wrapped in my blankets.

I still had nothing to say back to him. What the fuck was there *to* say?

For the longest moment, I just sat there on the edge of my bed, staring down at him as his chest rose and fell with his even breathing.

"Stop staring at me," he said, startling me enough that I jumped and almost fell off the fucking mattress. I actually would have if his hand hadn't shot out of the blankets and grabbed my wrist.

Embarrassment flooded my cheeks. "I thought you were asleep," I grumbled, like that was any excuse for staring at him. Come to think of it, that made it worse.

His fingers flexed on my wrist, and he pulled me closer to where he lay on the other side of my bed. "Lie down, Princess. Rest that paranoia for a couple of minutes. You can finish bitching me out in the morning, when I've got a hangover. Won't that be fun?"

I laughed, lacking the energy to pull away from him. Instead, I did exactly what he said and lay down in the vacant space beside him, pulling one of the spare pillows over to tuck under my head.

His eyes were closed, but I suspected he was still awake, even if it was only a fraction. So I pushed a bit more.

"Why do you care?" I murmured, half expecting to get no response at all. "Why do you care if I talk to Demi about divorcing you? Wouldn't that just be easier than keeping me alive until I turn twenty-one? Seems like a no-brainer." Because it was *just* money. If it meant regaining my name and my freedom, would I be willing to walk away with nothing?

Archer drew a deep breath, not even opening his eyes as he replied. "But then you would have no reason to stay in Shadow Grove," he told me on a sleepy mumble, "and I might never see you again."

My heart stopped beating for a second. "Would that be so bad?" I asked on a whisper, my stomach in knots and my skin prickling with anxiety.

"Yes."

I didn't reply to that confession. Words couldn't form, even if I did know what to say; the lump in my throat was too thick.

Some moments of silence later, Archer's breathing slowed and deepened, indicating he'd fallen asleep, and I tentatively shifted closer to him. When he didn't react, I slipped under the blankets and tucked my pillow farther under my head as I lay facing him.

So many romance novels described the way an alpha asshole male would soften in sleep, how they'd lose all that dickish anger and combative bullshit and reveal their true face. Archer wasn't like that. Even in sleep, his brow held a line of a scowl and his lips sat tight and tilted down at the corners, like he'd been frozen in mid-scowl.

Unable to help myself, I reached out and traced the line between his brows, like I could smooth the frown away. At my touch, he drew a deeper breath but didn't react beyond that. His forehead *did* seem to relax a touch, though.

I released a small sigh, letting my fingertip trail down the side of his face like an adrenaline junkie sticking her finger into a mousetrap.

"Why do you hate me so much, Archer D'Ath?" I whispered aloud, unable to keep that one overriding thought inside my head any longer.

He drew another, deeper breath, his lashes flickering open a fraction.

"I don't hate you, Kate," he mumbled, his voice so thick with sleep I could barely make out the words. "I hate myself…for loving you when I have no right to."

With those words, my heart exploded into a million bloody chunks. His eyes closed again almost immediately, though, and his breathing returned to the deep, even rhythm of sleep.

My stomach ached like it was wrapped in barbed wire, and the pain in my chest was enough to make tears prick at my eyes, but I said nothing. I *had* nothing to say. Instead, I rolled onto my other side, facing away from Archer.

I seriously doubted I'd be able to sleep, but he'd given me a hell of a lot to think about. And for some inexplicable reason, I didn't want to move any farther away.

Archer D'Ath wasn't the big bad villain I'd always painted him as. He was more of a dark knight. *My* dark knight.

CHAPTER 31

When I woke, it was to the feeling of being secure and loved.

What the fuck?

I blinked the haze of sleep away quickly, trying to work out what the hell was going on.

The heavily muscled and ink-covered arm tucked around my middle was my first clue. The sizable hardness pressed against my ass was my next clue. Thank fuck I still wore my sleep shorts, or it'd be all too tempting to arch back into that solid warmth.

Make smart choices, MK.

Well, thanks to Cass, that was going to become my new mantra. I needed to make smart choices if I wanted to stay alive. Fortunately, Archer's alcohol-fueled confessional had eased that process.

But first, I needed to establish some boundaries and draw clearer lines. I couldn't go into another day with Archer holding the balance of power and me just clinging on for the ride.

I shifted slightly, testing how asleep he was, and he didn't react. Soft, barely audible snores rumbled from his throat, and his face was buried in the mess of my hair. How the hell we'd ended up sleeping like that, I'd never know. Blame it on our magnetic connection pulling us together in sleep.

As carefully and gently as I could, I lifted his arm from around my waist and slithered out of the bed. Holding my breath for fear of waking him up, I quickly padded out to the living room. My phone was where I'd left it on the sofa, and I had a dozen or so messages from Steele and Kody each, along with a couple from Bree and Scott.

I sent a quick message to both the guys, reassuring them that we were both still alive. Kody immediately replied, asking if he should come over, but I told him not to bother. We'd be back at the mansion soon enough.

Because after all, I was making smart choices. And the top of that list was moving back under Archer's roof, where my security wasn't endangering any more of Zane's guys.

Tucking my phone into the back pocket of my shorts, I headed into my kitchen and pulled the jug of filtered ice water from my fridge. Grinning like a maniac, I carried the jug back through to the bedroom and stood beside the bed for a moment, admiring the sight of Archer in deep slumber.

He was gorgeous, but he had this coming.

I popped the lid off the jug, then upended the whole thing over his handsome face.

"What the *fuck*?" he roared, spluttering and choking as he exploded into wakefulness, and I took a swift step away from the bed. Not that I was scared of Archer's wrath, but because if the roles were reversed, I'd be swinging punches before assessing the situation too.

It only took him a second to get his bearings, though.

"Princess. I take it you're not a morning person, then?" Water dripped from his hair, face, and beard, running down his tattooed chest and across his washboard abs. Small mercies, the blankets were still bunched at his hips, hiding anything more.

I gave him a tight, sarcastic smile. "Quite the opposite, Sunshine. It's time to finish our conversation from last night, don't you think?"

His eyes narrowed at me, a flicker of doubt and concern in his eyes. Was he regretting being so honest? Or was that just worry about how I'd processed his truths?

"Get dressed," I snapped at him. "I'm taking a shower; then you can buy me breakfast. Trust me when I say I'm much less likely to jam my foot up your ass if I've been properly caffeinated."

I didn't wait for his reply, spinning on my heel and retreating to my bathroom. I slammed the door after me, then cranked the water and stripped out of my sleeping clothes. I'd need to come back and pack up my meager belongings at some point, but that could wait until Archer and I found some sort of truce.

Not two minutes into my shower, the bathroom door flew open, and suddenly the room was way too freaking small.

"What the hell are you doing, D'Ath?" I drawled, rinsing the soap from my body.

He just shrugged, opening the fogged glass shower door and stepping into the cubical with me. Naked. Both of us, totally naked and wet in more ways than one. Goddamn it, I wasn't strong enough for this shit.

"Showering," he replied with a smug grin. "I feel like I was run over by a truck last night."

I rolled my eyes, careful to keep them *above* the waist. There was no point in feigning modesty; he'd seen me naked several times before. But this was so much more intense. So much more tempting. Because we were *both* naked, and it'd be so, so easy to just…

"Well, luckily I was done. All yours, Sunshine." Because holy hell, I needed to abort mission before I made a fool of myself. Again.

I tried to exit the shower, but he stopped me with a firm hand on the back of my neck. A surprised squeak escaped me as he yanked me backward, spinning me around under the shower spray and crushing his lips to mine.

Shock prevented me from kneeing him in the balls; then lust

stopped me from pulling away. He kissed exactly the way I remembered. Full of dominance, passion, and desperate desire. It was the sort of kiss that simultaneously turned me to jelly and filled me with fire.

Eventually, I shoved him away, losing a few strands of hair in the process. My breathing was harsh and my lips burned with the heat of his kiss in the best possible way, but I glared death at him nonetheless.

"You can drop the act, Kate," he told me on a mocking laugh. "I know you want me. I think it's pretty fucking *hard* to deny how much I want you too." He quirked a brow, and I bit my lip to avoid taking the bait.

Pulling in a lungful of air, I let it out with a low chuckle, stepping closer to him. My hard nipples brushed against his chest, and my fingers curled around the hard evidence in question, drawing a sharp inhale from Archer.

"Sunshine," I all but purred, letting all the lust and wanting he'd stirred up in me show in my eyes, "you want to fuck me now? After all those chances you've had, now you want to fuck me?" My fingers tightened around his shaft, and I gave him a slow stroke.

His breath hitched. "You know you want it too."

"That easy, huh? I know your dirty secret, and now there's nothing stopping you from going balls deep in my cunt." I leaned in closer still, rising up on my toes so my lips could brush against his. Teasing. "You forgot one thing, though."

A pained groan escaped his throat as I gave his cock another firm stroke. He was huge, no point in denying that, and my pussy was throbbing with heat just imagining how he'd feel filling me up.

"Oh yeah?" he replied, his tongue running over his lower lip. "What's that?"

I pressed forward, kissing him properly this time and feeling his dick swell in my hand. Sucker.

Breaking away, I brought my lips as close to his ear as I could reach.

"I don't fuck desperate, D'Ath. Finish yourself off." Releasing him, I gave him a small shove against the tiled wall and stepped out of the shower for real this time.

He must have been in shock because I managed to snag a towel and retreat all the way to my bedroom before the sound of his laughter echoed through my apartment. Fucking psychopath.

By the time he emerged, dressed in his clothes from the night before, I was already changed and ready to go, thanks to the drawer full of new underwear that Steele must have provided. I was also stepping up my asshole game just a little bit.

"What exactly are you doing?" Archer demanded, squinting at me like he was in physical pain. He had to raise his voice to be heard, so I just smiled back at him a moment longer before turning the blender off.

"Sorry, what was that? I couldn't hear you over the blender."

He glared daggers. That hangover must really be kicking his ass. Or maybe he was sour about those blue balls.

"What the fuck are you making?" he asked, his voice under-scored with a growl.

I looked at the blender that I'd just been cranking at high power. "Oh this? Absolutely nothing." I popped the lid off and dumped the crushed ice into my sink. "Ready to go?"

His glower said it all, and I didn't even bother hiding my smug smile. It wasn't my fault he was hungover, but I'd damn well make it more painful if I could. Because taking shots at each other, trading insults and cutting remarks, that was our safe place. Without that, I was terrified of where it left the two of us. After all the things he'd confessed...

Hell, he may not even remember half of those. Maybe they weren't even true.

I knew they were, though. Undeniably.

Throwing on my coat, I grabbed my phone, keys, and wallet, then sat on the edge of my sofa to pull my calf-length boots on.

I'd opted for a pair with a higher heel, knowing full fucking well I needed the height advantage today. Yet at the same time, I'd opted for a short woolen skirt with a flared hem. The weather had warmed up a bit, but not *that* much. My only reasoning was that it'd drive Archer nuts, and I was all for that.

Neither of us spoke on the way down to the lobby, but I shot off a text to Cass, letting him know I was leaving with Archer.

Stepping out into the street, I frowned as I looked around. "Where's your car?"

He cocked his head to the side, giving me an amused stare. "You thought I drove here with that much alcohol in my system, Princess? I'm reckless, not stupid." He started along the sidewalk. "Come on."

Thunder rumbled across the gray sky above us as I hurried to catch up with his long strides. Motherfucker was doing it deliberately, forcing me to take two steps to every one of his. Apparently I wasn't the only petty asshole this morning.

"Where are we going?" I asked, gritting my teeth to keep from cursing him out in the middle of the street. I was hungry and I needed coffee, and goddamn, I had a serious case of blue ovaries. Maybe I shouldn't have pushed things so far with him in the shower, because as a result, I was all achy and needy, which made me an even bigger bitch than normal.

Archer just shot me a quick grin. That was going to take some getting used to, even when it was an evil sort of grin.

"You wanted breakfast, right? Well, then hurry up and quit your crying. We probably want to get there before this rain starts." He peered up at the sky without slowing his pace for even a moment, and I huffed my anger.

Two blocks later, he stopped abruptly in front of a nondescript diner and tugged the door open.

"After you, Darling Wife," he said, gesturing for me to enter ahead of him. I scowled but did so anyway. My stomach was rumbling hard enough to hurt, so I'd probably have happily dined with the devil.

Maybe I was about to anyway.

We took a seat in one of the window booths, and I eagerly scanned the menu. When I got this hungry, I wanted one of everything and could never make up my mind. It was a serious affliction.

Archer took the decision out of my hands, though, ordering me a tall stack of pancakes with syrup, ice cream, and caramelized bananas when the waitress came over to see us. He also ordered us coffee, which I knew would probably be his usual brand of swamp water.

"What the fuck was that?" I snapped when the waitress disappeared back into the kitchen. The diner was decently busy, being a Saturday morning, and I hated when people dragged waitstaff into their domestic disputes. So I'd smiled politely when he ordered, but now I was going to poke his eye out with my fork.

Archer didn't look concerned, though. "You're a sugar addict," he informed me, like this was some big secret. "You would have ordered eggs or something dumb, then you'd sulk about it when *my* pancakes arrived. Quit acting so outraged, Sweetheart; you secretly love that I pay enough attention to order for you."

I had nothing to say to that, so I just gritted my teeth and stared out the window at the storm rolling in. I loved storms, especially when the rain turned into torrential downpours. They calmed me, easing tension with every droplet on the ground or flash of lightning across the sky.

Archer seemed in no hurry to fill the silence with conversation, so we just chilled while waiting for our food. I watched the storm, and he…watched me. Yet it didn't make me uncomfortable. It just allowed me some breathing room to assess the shift in his personality and in our dynamic.

I'd pinpointed it perfectly in the shower. Archer's whole mood shift had occurred after I'd found out about the marriage contract.

It was like a weight had been lifted from his shoulders, and he was no longer punishing me for the secrets he kept.

"Steele has probably already told you this story," Archer commented shortly after our massive plates of pancakes arrived, "but I knew you before all of this...mess."

My mouth was full, so I took the time to chew and swallow before responding. "He mentioned it, yes. I don't remember, though."

Archer just nodded, his gaze dropping to his plate. For a while, we ate in silence, and I grudgingly admitted he'd chosen well. It was exactly what I wanted for breakfast, even though I hadn't known it in my hangry state.

"Try the coffee, Princess," Archer muttered at some stage, hiding a smile with his own mug.

I peered at the pitch-black liquid and wrinkled my nose. "No thanks. I enjoy the full use of my taste buds."

"You're such a snob," he commented with an edge of laughter. "Here, Your Highness, let me fix it for you." He added a heavy splash of cream to my coffee, then gave it a quick stir before pushing it toward me. "Just try it. I promise it's not laced with rat poison."

Rolling my eyes, I picked up the mug and took a cautious sip.

Shockingly, it didn't make my taste buds all howl like they'd been doused in battery acid. It was actually...not that bad. Still a long shot off the coffee at Nadia's Cakes, but it was drinkable. I'd give it that much credit.

"See, sometimes you just have to trust me, Princess." Archer's eyes flashed with a deeper meaning, and I shifted my gaze back to the rain that was now lashing at the window. For all my plans of pumping him for more information over breakfast, I found myself shying away from that conversation.

Weirdly, I just wanted to enjoy my breakfast...with him.

Archer had smashed my walls to dust with his drunken honesty, and now all I had left was a cardboard facade. He'd see through it in no time, if he hadn't already. But if he thought this new phase of our relationship would be nothing but rainbows and roses, he was severely mistaken.

After all, it was a fine line between love and hate, and our line was officially all tangled up in barbed wire.

CHAPTER 32

After our surprisingly pleasant meal, Archer led me to where he'd left his car the night before. It was just around the corner from where we'd had breakfast, directly in front of a seedy-looking underground pub, but I had to use my coat as an umbrella as we dashed through the pouring rain.

I chose not to comment on his choice of drinking establishments and slipped into the passenger seat when he popped the door open for me.

"Seeing as you're in such a sharing mood this weekend," I said, tossing my wet coat behind my seat and buckling my seat belt, "why don't you tell me what Kody and Steele were *really* doing last night."

Archer shot me a quick glance, turning his engine on and pulling out into the street before answering.

"What did they *tell* you they were doing?" he asked, sounding cagey as fuck. Goddamn it, maybe he needed that coffee spiked with whiskey to maintain the honesty.

I blew out a sigh. "Kody had some urgent meeting with Jase, and Steele was supposedly working on security."

"What makes you think that's *not* what they were doing?"

Archer pushed, and my temper sparked to life. He was deliberately making me question the guys' word…even though I was already. Gritting my teeth, I played his game. "Kody knew he would have gotten laid last night if he came over, so I find it hard to believe he took a meeting with Jase instead of telling him to get fucked." Archer snorted a laugh. "Maybe you're shit in bed, Princess." I glared at the side of his head. "You know that's not true, Sunshine."

The lightning-fast glance he shot at me was full of heat and lust, and it made my thighs tense. "Fine. Jase needed me to sign off on some samples as a matter of urgency. If it hadn't been done last night, we'd have missed the production deadline from the manufacturers."

I frowned, not making the connection. "So why'd Kody have to go?"

He shrugged, driving at his normal speed through Shadow Grove, despite the bucketing rain that his windshield wipers could barely keep up with. "Because I was doing shots of whiskey at the Wreck and Ruin and not answering my phone. I imagine Jase called Kody to get the papers signed instead."

Huh. Okay. Kody had been telling the truth, then. I was relieved, even though I hadn't truly thought he'd be throwing lies around again so soon. Not when he and Steele were working so hard to gain my trust back.

"What about Steele?" I asked, still curious about what security measures he'd been working on that had taken so much time.

Archer shot me another glance, this time pensive. "He was working on security, like he said." There was a cagey, secretive edge to his tone, though.

Dread pooled in my belly. "Elaborate on that."

"Ask him. I thought you guys were all anti-secrets these days anyway. I'm sure he'll tell you if you just ask." There was a note of bitterness or contempt in his tone that made my temper flare.

Come to think of it, that raised another question I had. "Tell me something, Husband Dearest," I drawled, propping my elbow on the door and leaning my head on my palm. "If you went to all these difficult, dangerous, and expensive lengths to keep me *safe*..."

He grunted a sound of annoyance. "I did," he snapped. "I thought we'd cleared that up already."

I gave a small shrug, like I didn't totally buy his reasons. I mean, yes, I did. But I also knew it would drive him nuts if he thought I was still doubting him.

"Well, okay, for argument's sake, you *did* do it all for my benefit—"

"It *was*," he cut me off, shooting a scowl at me. Whatever he saw on my face must have clued him in to the fact that I was just antagonizing him, though, because the tension visibly dropped from his shoulders as his gaze returned to the road.

"Uh-huh," I continued, enjoying how easy he was to provoke when he was hungover. It made me think I wanted to get him drunk more often. Did that make me a bad person? I mean, at least I wasn't thinking about stabbing him in the eye with a fork, so we'd made some definite progress in the past twenty-four hours.

"So *if* you went to all these lengths to *help* me...and *if* what you told me last night was the truth and not some fucked up D'Ath manipulation technique"—yeah, I was pushing all his buttons now if the rumble of a growl in his throat was any indication—"then I have one very important question."

I paused for dramatic effect—and also to work up the nerve to ask what was on my mind. But fuck it. I'd recently killed a man; I could suck up enough courage to ask a pretty boy a personal question.

"Spit it out, Madison Kate," Archer ordered, clearly dreading whatever I might be about to ask. His knuckles paled on the steering wheel as he gripped it tighter, and I smiled.

"If you care so much, why did you stand back and let both your best friends fuck me? You don't strike me as the kind of guy who likes to share his possessions, and yet…" I waved a hand, and he knew what I meant.

He drew a deep breath, his chest swelling as he seemed to debate his response to my question. I had to hand it to him; I'd expected that to be a sore spot, a reflexive snap back. But instead, he took his time to consider his answer.

"Because," he finally said, his voice calm but threaded with tension, "Kody and Steele mean more to me than any family could. I owe them everything, and I'd never stand in the way of something they wanted. Even if…"

"Even if what they want is your wife, who doesn't know she's your wife? The same girl you're secretly in love with but can't find the balls to make a move for yourself? That's some real tight fucking friendship, Sunshine." My tone was scathing and hurt, and I had no idea why. I felt *very* strongly for both Kody and Steele, and I was *glad* Archer hadn't stood in the way of them making a move. So why the fuck was I suddenly feeling stabby?

Archer shot me a perplexed look. "I never said I was in love with you, Princess." He all but spat the words like they tasted bad, and it only fanned the flames of my irrational anger.

"Oh no? I seem to remember you telling me that you didn't hate me, but you hated yourself for *loving* me. Your words, not mine." I folded my arms under my breasts, giving him an indignant glare, despite the fact that his eyes were still on the road.

He scoffed. He legitimately scoffed. "You must have been dreaming, Princess. I never said that. But it's cute to know that's what you were hoping to hear from me. Sorry to disappoint."

Stunned outrage rippled through me. It was my own fucking fault for bringing up our conversation from the night before, but for him to just straight up *deny* he said it? That one single confession from him had been the turning point for me. The straw that crumbled my defenses to dust. And he was going to sit there and *deny* he ever said it?

"Stop the car," I said, my voice cold and hard.

Archer did a double take, like he thought he'd misheard me.

My fists balled in my lap, and my whole fucking body vibrated with ice-cold fury. "Archer. Stop the fucking car *now!*"

I thought he would argue with me, maybe just flat refuse, but he didn't. His jaw flexed and the vein over his temple throbbed, but he pulled sharply into the grassy strip beside the road. We were on a deserted stretch of road on the outskirts of Shadow Grove, in the total opposite direction of where we were meant to be going. But on the upside, it meant there were no bystanders around to witness when I cut Archer's lying fucking tongue from his mouth with his own damn knife.

The second his car slowed, I unbuckled my seat belt and threw my door open.

"Kate, what the fuck?" Archer exclaimed as I stepped out before the car had even fully stopped. Whatever, it was slow enough.

The rain was utterly pouring down, and within seconds I was soaked straight to the core. But I barely even noticed. I was too mad. Too hurt. I just folded my arms around myself and started walking away from Archer's car.

"Madison Kate!" he bellowed after me, his voice dulled by the sound of the pouring rain. "Where are you going?"

I didn't answer other than to flip him off. Fuck that. Fuck him. Fuck this bullshit, paper-thin truce we'd been building. Seriously. Fuck it all straight to hell and then fuck it some more with a cactus up the ass.

Let him go back to his big, old, empty mansion alone and explain to Kody and Steele that he couldn't put his pigheaded pride aside for five minutes to repair things between us. If they truly had kicked him out until he could sort his shit out, they wouldn't be happy with *that* result.

The rush of falling rain dampened Archer's footsteps until he was too close to dodge. His huge hand locked around my upper arm and spun me around so fast my heels wobbled in the mud. I kept my balance, partly due to the iron grip he held me in, and raised my chin in stubborn anger.

"Take your hands off me, D'Ath," I hissed, my voice full of venom and hate.

"Get back in the car, Madison Kate," he ordered in a low, threatening growl.

It only made me want to fight back harder. "Or what?" I sneered. "You plan on spanking me for my disobedience?" It was simply a figure of speech, a taunt at best, yet with the way Archer's eyes flared with interest, I knew I'd just given him ideas.

Goddamn it all to hell. Again.

"You'd like that, wouldn't you?" he replied in a dark murmur, his eyes heating. "I've heard the way you scream and moan when Steele slaps your ass during sex. Damaged little girls like you always love it rough."

Fury and indignation spiked in my chest, and I shoved him away from me, able to detach his grip on my arm purely because he hadn't expected me to do that.

"You sound like an expert on the matter," I countered, my disgust carrying on every word. "Don't tell me, I'm not the only girl you've *purchased* before. Just like your great-grandfather, huh?"

His face twisted in rage, but I wasn't afraid of him. Only a truly weak man fought his battles against women with brute strength. For all Archer's failings, he was not weak. Not even close.

"You have no fucking clue what you're talking about, Madison Kate," he told me with a harsh hand gesture, like he was swiping those ugly accusations from the record. "Get back in the damn car."

I planted my hands on my hips, clenching my jaw to prevent my teeth from chattering. "No."

Archer's eyes narrowed to slits like he hadn't actually expected me to argue with him. "Get in the car, or I will *make* you get in the car." He took a threatening step toward me, and I backed up on reflex.

"Touch me again and I'll punch you straight in the balls, Archer. How many hits can a guy's testicles take before they're considered defective anyway?" I had no idea if that was a real thing or not, but Dallas once told me that if you took enough knocks to the balls, it'd damage sperm production or some shit. I didn't know the hard science behind my insults; I just threw them out and hoped one might stick.

Archer just laughed at my threat, and I got the distinct impression I might be in some real trouble.

His hand shot out quicker than I could even track, his arm banding around my waist and jerking me hard against his body. In seconds, he'd pinned me in such a way that not only was I totally incapable of freeing myself, I also couldn't follow through on my threat to reintroduce his junk to my kneecap.

"Let me go," I demanded, frustration coloring my voice with a small scream. "Archer, let me *fucking go!*"

He lowered his face until our lips were just an inch apart. Water poured down his face and dripped to mine, like we were a Renaissance-era fountain. The tragic, star-crossed lovers, doomed to kill each other before ever admitting their true feelings.

We were pathetic.

"Never," he replied with dark promise. "I'm never letting you go, Kate. No matter what you do, how hard you push, kick, scream, and fight, I'm never *ever* letting you go."

His mouth came down on mine in a hard crush, but I wasn't having a bar of it. Not now. Not after those cutting barbs he's just so casually tossed in my direction.

A moment later he pulled back with a snarl of frustration. "Kiss me back, you stubborn bitch."

Somehow his grip on my arm had loosened, and I yanked it free, bringing it up to crack my hand across his face. As wet as his face and my hand both were, the smack landed harder than even I'd intended, making my palm tingle and bringing a pink flush to his flesh.

"Call me a bitch one more time, D'Ath. I'll make you regret the day you ever laid eyes on me." I meant every damn word, and he knew it.

His lip curled in a sneer. "Maybe I already do."

I gave him a bitter laugh in return, rolling my eyes. "Cut the pity-party bullshit, Sunshine. You break everything you touch, then punish everyone around you for your own self-loathing and loneliness. It's no one's fault but your own, so how about you start accepting a little culpability for your fucked-up actions?" My words were backed up by a shove to his chest, which gave me enough space to maneuver away from his grip.

Or so I'd thought. He let me go just far enough that I thought I'd escaped, then reeled me back in, tighter than ever, like a spider wrapping its prey.

"What do you think I'm *doing*?" he demanded in a frustrated growl. "I'm trying to fix things. I'm trying to open up and show my hand. But you...you don't make it easy."

My back was to his chest now, and his fingers banded around my wrists, locking my arms across my chest like a straightjacket. We were both soaked from the rain to the point of dripping, but neither one of us paid it any mind. It was the perfect setting for this explosion of hurt.

"It's easier than you think, you caveman son of a bitch," I snapped back, breathing heavily as I struggled in his grip. "Admit you lied. Apologize. And *mean it*."

He released me abruptly, almost letting me fall face-first into the mud.

"It's that easy, huh?" he scoffed, bitter as a lemon.

I spun around to face him, my arms spread wide. "It's that easy."

My hair was pasted to my face, my arms, and my back like a

251

wetsuit and my makeup was probably halfway down my face, but I felt weirdly *free* standing there screaming insults at my husband.

He glowered at me like he was seriously cursing the day our life lines had touched. Then he sighed, his shoulders deflating some of that big-dick energy away.

"You're right," he finally said, lifting his face back to lock eyes with me once more. "You're right. I lied. I did say *that* last night, and I meant it. I…" He trailed off like he'd just hit his word quota for the month.

I folded my arms, shivering against the bone-deep chill of soaking wet clothes. "You…what? I'm not a damn psychic, Archer. If you have something to say, it needs to be said out loud."

His blue eyes blazed with determination. "I push people away because being close to me means painting a target on your back. I never want my loved ones to be used as bargaining chips, to be kidnapped and ransomed or beaten and raped as punishment for gang world bullshit. I want *better* than that for you, Kate. I want you to have a normal fucking life away from all of this." He paused, breathing heavily. I could hear my own pulse racing in my ears, and suddenly the rain and cold may as well have been a million miles away.

Archer didn't take his eyes from mine for even a second, but something shifted in his expression. It became harder, more resolute. "But I'm fast coming to the realization that if anyone can handle themselves in my world, it's you." His lips tightened, and his brow furrowed. "Which is a relief. Because as hard as I try to push you away, I keep drawing you back again. You're an addiction that I never want to quit, Kate. I'm tired of denying my own heart. Aren't you?"

My chest was tight to the point of physical pain, and I needed to force myself to breathe. He was staring at me, waiting for my response, and I wasn't capable of forming the words he so desperately needed to hear. Instead, I just jerked a nod. That was the best he was getting from me, so it'd have to do.

Archer let out a long breath, swiping his hand over his hair and sending a spray of water flying.

"Kate, I'm not sorry." He spoke the words with total sincerity, stopping my heart completely. "I'm not sorry for marrying you behind your back. If I was given the same option tomorrow, I'd do it again, even knowing how much it hurt you to find out."

My heart cracked in two. "You're a piece of shit, Archer D'Ath." The insult came out weak and broken, full of pain and desperation, and that prick just smiled.

"I'm not sorry for saving you, Kate. But I'm sorry for everything past that point. I treated you badly, worse than badly, because you manifested my worst fears for my poisoned soul. Every day that I looked at you, I saw Ana. I saw my unforgivable sins, and I *wasn't sorry*. For *that*, I'm truly sorry." His eyes had lost all traces of arrogant pride, and all I could find in his searching gaze was a desperate plea for forgiveness.

It was something I couldn't give him. Not yet. Not unconditionally.

I took a step backward, ducking my gaze away from his. "Thank you for being honest," I replied. It was all I had to offer. "Your apology is accepted, but I'm not even remotely ready to forgive the bad blood between us."

From my lowered line of sight, I saw his fists tighten at his sides.

"Fair enough, then," he said in a voice woven with disappointment and hurt. "Just get in the car. I'll take you home."

Panic swept through me. I wasn't ready to forgive and forget *yet*, but that didn't mean it wasn't an option in the future. But I could see how he'd just taken my words as a blank rejection, and I needed to rectify that before this fragile bond was broken for good.

"And if I refuse?" I taunted him, raising my chin back up with stubborn defiance. "What will you do about it?" Rain lashed against my face, blurring my vision, but I still caught the flicker of an evil smile tugging at Archer's lips.

He closed the gap between us, his formidable height and stature towering over me. "If you refuse, I'll be forced to bend you over the hood of my car and spank that luscious ass until it glows. Your choice, Princess."

Hope bloomed in my chest once more, mingling with a healthy dose of victory. All wasn't lost after all.

"You've got to the count of three to get back in the car," Archer growled, and my lips curved in a sly grin.

"One…"

I folded my arms under my soaked breasts.

"Two…"

I batted my water-logged lashes at him.

"Three."

I accepted my fate.

CHAPTER 33

Excited anticipation rippled through me as Archer grabbed me around the waist to throw me over his shoulder and storm back to his car. My wet hair hung in heavy ropes, almost dragging in the mud under his feet, and I gave zero shits. That was what shampoo was for.

Except instead of bending me over his hood and smacking my ass like he'd promised—uh, I mean *threatened*—he set me back on my feet and clasped my face between his palms.

"What are you doing?" I demanded, confused and turned on and conflicted as hell.

Archer smirked. "You really think it's that easy? Stand there and listen to me bare my soul, say *nothing* in return, then expect to just move past it all with the best sex of your life?"

I glowered, seeing no issue with this sequence of events.

"Best sex of my life?" I taunted. "That's an awfully big claim, Sunshine. The things Kody and Steele do to me in the bedroom…" I broke off with a moan, torturing myself with the memory of them both together inside me.

Archer just scoffed. "I guess you'll never find out for sure." He paused, giving me a shrewd look. "Unless…"

My eyes narrowed. "Unless what?" Yes, I was taking the bait. I didn't even care at this point.

The corner of his mouth pulled up in a grin of victory. "Unless you can give me something back. Meet me halfway, Kate, and I'll blow your fucking mind."

My excitement soured, and the warm feeling in my belly turned cold. "I'm not telling you that I love you, Archer D'Ath. If that's what you're waiting for—"

"I'm not," he cut me off. "Not today, anyway. I've treated you like shit, and all of our damage doesn't just evaporate overnight."

Well, now I was suspicious. "So what, then?"

He wanted me to meet him halfway? I was barely past the desire to murder him in his sleep. Love was a long-ass way away. So what did he want from me?

His eyes locked on mine, studying me and seeming to peer straight through to my soul. "Kiss me, Princess."

My brow furrowed. Kiss him? It wasn't as simple as he made it sound. He wanted my confession through my actions, even if he was miles away from it verbally. He wanted me to show that I cared for more than just a hot, dirty fuck in the rain. He wanted... an emotional connection.

What. The. Fuck?

"I'm not interested in *making love* to you, Archer," I told him in a scathing tone, pulling away from his grip on my face. I expected his temper to flare at that clear refusal, but he just barked a laugh.

"Good," he replied. "I doubt I'm even capable of that. Believe me, Kate, I'll give you *exactly* what you crave so badly right now... but only if you kiss me first." His eyes glittered with challenge, and it whipped up the hot determination inside me once again.

Archer thought he was still in control. Apparently that's how our whole dynamic was going to work—him thinking he controlled every situation and me proving him wrong.

Bring it on, bitch.

Snaking my hand around the back of his neck, I pulled him closer to my height so I could reach without killing my neck. Even though I was in heeled boots, he still had way too much height on me.

"You're playing a dangerous game, Sunshine," I advised him, quietly stalling while I drummed up the courage to give him what he wanted. My fingers threaded into the short hair at the base of his skull, gripping tight.

His eyes searched my face, taking in every tiny speck of my features. "Story of my life, Princess."

I released the breath I was holding, then tossed my insecurities out the window and closed the gap between us. My intention had been to kiss him quickly, just enough to fulfill his request, but the second our lips touched *this time*, it was like completing an electrical circuit. Sparks flew and a ripple of desire tore through me hard enough to make me shudder.

All my posturing crap evaporated, and I kissed him with all the pent-up frustration, anger, and heartbreak I'd been holding on to for far too long. His arms banded around me, his strong hands crushing my body to his as he kissed me back like I was his very breath. His kiss confirmed every truth he'd bared to me and begged my forgiveness.

It took far more effort than I ever could have anticipated to break free, but when I did, Archer let out a groan of frustration.

"Happy?" I asked with my chest heaving and my heart on fire.

He swiped his tongue across his lower lip like he was savoring the taste of my kiss. "Deliriously," he replied, his voice husky and dripping in lust.

I bit my own lip, knowing I was playing with fire in the best possible way. "Well then, what are you waiting for?" His brows hitched, and I decided I needed to spell it the fuck out. "Fuck me like you *own* me, Archer D'Ath."

He huffed a sharp laugh, like he could hardly believe I'd just said that; then a darkly dangerous look descended over his face. With a strong grip on my waist, he spun me around. His arm crushed me tight against his front, and his lips brushed against my earlobe. "I'm so glad that's what you want, Madison Kate," he murmured in a voice that promised my destruction. His other hand slid over my hip, down my thigh, then under my short skirt. "Because I *do* own you. It's about damn time you recognized that fact."

My snappy comeback turned into nothing more than a moan as his fingers slipped beneath my panties and sunk directly inside my pussy. There was no need to work up to it; I was already soaking. Had been since well before the rain had even started.

Archer let out a heavy breath, making shivers chase across my skin, which he then dissolved with a hot kiss on my neck. His hard length crushed against my lower back, promising more, but for now he seemed content to fuck me with his thick, tattooed fingers instead. Like an appetizer.

I bucked against his hand, desperate for more, but I was no longer calling the shots. He scraped his teeth over the bend of my neck in warning, and it only drove me wilder. My head pressed back against his chest, my neck exposed in silent offering.

For a moment, he just kissed my skin—hot, open-mouthed kisses that pulled at my flesh and probably left marks all over. His fingers toyed with my cunt, thrusting deeply, then teasing, then finding my clit and dodging just around the edges. It was infuriating and intoxicating; I was quickly losing my damn mind.

"Archer," I pleaded on a breathy moan, "don't be such a damn cunt tease and fuck me already." I reached behind me, rubbing at his cock through his jeans.

His teeth sank into my neck, making me scream. "So impatient, Princess."

I gave a shaking laugh. "Or maybe I'm just getting cold. Hurry up and fuck me till I see stars, and I'll blow you in the shower when we get home."

His fingers withdrew from my cunt, but only so he could strip my underwear off from under my skirt. They dropped to my ankles, and I kicked the cloth aside in the mud. Steele was right; underwear was overrated.

"Home?" Archer repeated, and I realized what I'd just said.

I craned my neck to look at him. "Yeah. Home. Unless you *like* Zane using me as a human shield?"

He made a sound of anger as he pushed me forward until my shins touched the front bumper of his car. "Put your hands on the hood, Princess," he told me in a low voice, "and don't fucking move them."

Excitement thrilled though me, and I did as I was told. The Stingray was a low-slung sports car, and by placing my hands on the hood, I found my ass in the air—exactly what he intended, no doubt.

He kicked my legs wider apart, then flipped my skirt up. I was totally exposed to the wind and rain—and to him. My husband. If anyone happened to drive past…well, too damn bad. I'd already been photographed having sex with Kody and Steele; what difference would it make to round out the trifecta?

Archer's hands smoothed over my ass cheeks, making my legs quiver, but that was nothing on the way my whole body shook when his mouth closed over my pussy.

Holy shit.

The sharp contrast of his hot mouth and the cold rain tormenting my nerves, and I already knew I was going to come before he even opened his belt. He was on his knees in the muddy grass behind me, tongue fucking me like my cunt was his favorite god-damn food on earth. In mere seconds, I was screaming.

He didn't let up, though. Even while my orgasm pulsed, he shifted his mouth to my clit, sucking that sensitive flesh while his fingers slid into my throbbing pussy, fucking me rough and hard through the bone-shaking waves of climax. It was intense and incredible, and my hands almost slipped on the rain-covered hood of the car as he brought me to the edge of another immediate orgasm. There was no warning, no time to prepare. He just dragged me to that cliff edge, then shoved me straight off.

This time, my vision darkened and my ears rang. By the time I came back to earth, it was to the unmistakable sound of Archer's infuriating chuckle.

"What the fuck?" I panted as he kissed my inner thighs and squeezed a handful of my ass cheek.

"Just giving you what you asked for, Princess," he replied with a heavy dose of satisfaction. "Fucking you like I own you."

I felt him rise to his feet once more but lacked the energy to turn my head. My chest was still heaving, my breath coming in rough, burning drags, and my pussy was on fire. Glorious, orgasmic fire.

The white noise from the rain, which continued to pour, drowned out all the subtle sound cues, so I didn't even realize Archer had undone his pants until the hot, hard length of his cock stroked down the ultra-sensitive flesh of my cunt.

A pleading whimper escaped me. I arched my back, pushing against him, but it only made him snicker.

"Hold on, baby girl," he told me in a husky voice as his huge palm gripped my ass cheek. "I've got you."

With that promise, he filled me in one forceful thrust, making me howl. He gave me no time to adjust to his size or even catch my breath, he just grabbed my hips and started fucking me with the ferocity of a wild animal.

Groaning curses fell from my mouth as he slammed into me, again and again, his massive cock stretching me and pushing me to my very limits, but still he didn't let up. By the time his hand cracked across my ass cheek, I was already on the precipice of another orgasm. The rain and his strength saw my flesh burn with warmth almost immediately, and when he smacked me again, I cracked into a million pieces.

This time when I came, he gave me a moment's respite. He drove fully inside me, his thighs against mine as he waited out my orgasm. His hands stroked and massaged the flesh of my rear end, though, and when his thumb brushed over my asshole I jerked in surprise.

"Tell me something true, Kate," he demanded, his thumb circling my asshole again as his other hand held me firm on his cock. "Did you take Kody and Steele at the same time?"

I moaned, way too shredded from pleasure to even attempt a lie. "Yes," I replied, my voice hoarse. "And I fucking loved it."

He let out a pained grunt, then pushed his thumb inside me. *Oh, for the love of orgasms...*

"Would you take all three of us, Princess?"

Was rain fucking wet, dipshit?

"Yes," I replied instead, rocking against him, begging for more. "Fuck yes, I would."

His thumb withdrew and he slapped an even harder smack on my other butt cheek. "Good to know, baby girl. I'll keep that in mind for another day when I'm more inclined to share."

He pulled his cock out of me in an abrupt movement, and I actually cried out in protest. It wasn't for long, though, just long enough for him to haul me up in his arms, linking my legs around his waist.

Two long strides carried us to the side of the car where he slammed my back into the door at the same time as his dick slammed back into my cunt.

"Oh shit, Arch..." My breathy moan dissolved into a long groan as he started to move once more, fucking me with such force I knew I'd be walking funny tomorrow. Hell yeah, sign me up.

I looped my arms around his neck, my fingers sliding into his wet black hair and gripping tight while he punished my cunt. His lips were against my neck, sucking, biting, kissing...*marking* me, and I loved it. I loved everything about it, including the inevitable conversations it would force when Kody and Steele saw.

Archer held me up with one hand, the other snaking between us and tweaking my clit in exactly the right way to spark yet *another* intense climax. This time, his control snapped, and he came with me. His hot seed filled me as he thrust deep, then stilled with a grunt.

For a long moment, neither one of us moved. Neither one of us spoke. The only sound over the pouring rain was our ragged, heavy breathing. My legs remained tight around his waist, and some part of me was loath to let him go, as if the second we parted, things would go straight back to the way they'd been.

But then he kissed me.

It wasn't the angsty clash of power we'd kissed each other with earlier; this kiss was pure, unfiltered affection. Love.

I kissed him back, gently and unhurried, even though I knew I was signing my life away. But so be it. Archer *was* the missing piece to my puzzle, and now that I'd felt him slot into place, I would do anything to keep him.

Anything.

"Come on," he murmured, ending our way too emotional kiss with a lingering touch of lips. "Let's get out of here before you catch hypothermia."

Now that the high of our fuck session had eased, he was right. My whole body was trembling, and this time it was purely due to the bone-deep cold of rain and wind.

My legs shook as he helped me stand again, and I quirked a grin at the state we were both in. Our clothes were saturated, Archer's jeans coated from the knees down in mud, and my panties were nowhere to be seen.

Still, he didn't even bat an eyelid as he opened the passenger door for me to get into the car. Apparently, he wasn't bothered about the damage to his interior, and I appreciated that.

He didn't even bother doing up his pants before getting into the driver's seat, just tucked his dick away and left the fly open. It shouldn't have been sexy, but I found myself drooling a little. Yep, I was officially addicted.

"Where are we going?" I asked as he cranked the heat on his dashboard and turned on the seat warmers. We were nowhere near his house, so...

He shot me a quick smile. "Somewhere private."

Excited anticipation made my pulse race, and my pussy tightened. Wow. That had to be a new record for me that I was already craving more. Or maybe it'd just been too long since my reconciliation with Kody.

"We're not going home?"

His gaze turned dark and hungry. "I'm not ready to share you, baby girl."

I bit my lip, my heart thudding heavily as desire flooded my bloodstream again. "Then I suggest you do some deep soul-searching while we fuck, Sunshine. Because by the time we return to Shadow Grove, you'll have either learned to share or you'll file this away as a fun memory never to be repeated."

He quirked a brow at me, challenging, but I shook my head.

"Save the alpha-male, big-dick energy for someone who cares, Archer D'Ath. You fucked up, and I fell for your two best friends while you sulked in the shadows. I won't give them up to appease your dominant nature, so wipe that thought from your mind entirely."

He just stared at me, his car idling but the emergency brake still on.

"You've fallen for them both, huh?" His tone wasn't bitter or accusatory, just curious.

I blinked at him, realizing what I'd said. Then I jerked a nod of confirmation because I had.

He blew out a long breath, swiping a hand over his short beard. "I'm glad. We heard Steele say it to you on the phone the other night, and...they deserve happiness."

"We all do," I corrected, my voice firm and uncompromising.

He met my eyes again, staring back at me a long time before giving a slow nod. "Just give me the weekend," he suggested, his tone hopeful. "Give me the weekend alone, just us. Let me have you all to myself for two days, and then..." He trailed off and my chest tightened, fearing what he might say next.

He surprised me, though. In a good way.

"And then I'll get on board with this dynamic. If it were anyone else, I'd kill them both to eliminate the competition. But seeing as it's them..." He exhaled heavily. "Fine."

My heart soared. No shit. It was like some anime crap erupting from my chest in an explosion of cartoon hearts and pastel colors. Not that I told Archer any of that, though. To him, I just grinned.

He rolled his eyes and shifted the car into drive, pulling out into the deserted road once more.

"How far is it to where we're going?" I asked, struck by a totally inappropriate yet totally intriguing idea.

Archer shrugged. "Around ten minutes or so. Why?"

I smiled, this time with a healthy dose of evil. "How good of a driver are you, really?"

His eyes narrowed in suspicion. "I'm incredible. *Why?*"

I didn't reply. I didn't need to when my actions answered for me. His pants were already undone, so it was no effort at all to tug his boxers down and free his dick. He was already hard again, and I licked my lips with satisfaction.

A sharp jolt of fear flooded through me, fear of car crashes souring my mood for a second. But I needed to start taking control of my own fears and not letting them rule me. I also needed to start taking some major steps to trusting the guys, and I couldn't think of a better way to do both. Or hell, maybe I was just crazy horny still.

"Princess..." Archer's warning growl dissolved into a gasp as I leaned over and took his cock in my mouth. His leg jerked as he stomped on the brakes, stopping the car dead in the middle of the road.

I ran my tongue around the tip of his erection, then looked up at him with a smirk. "I thought you could drive well, Sunshine. So prove it." My fingers curled around his base, stroking, and my mouth returned to his tip.

Archer let out a hiss of curses but did as he was told and started the car once more. I rewarded him for following directions like a good dog by taking him deep into my throat.

Ten minutes passed in no time as I toyed with him, bringing him to the brink, then backing off again. But by the time he pulled into the driveway of a pretty, English-style cottage, I was feeling generous. I let him come, filling my mouth as I swallowed greedily, then licked my lips as I sat back up.

The look he gave me when I grinned at him was equal parts awe and shock, and the fact that I could stun him like that gave me an exhilarating sense of satisfaction.

"Oh, Princess," he murmured, licking his lips as he caught his breath. "You'd better hold the fuck on. This weekend is gonna get wild."

Luckily for me, Archer D'Ath was the kind of man who kept his word.

CHAPTER 34

The house Archer had taken me to turned out to be one of *many* in his property portfolio. This one had been a recent purchase, fully furnished. It was a good thing he did own it because we legitimately fucked on every possible surface over the course of the weekend. As it was, I insisted on stripping all the bed linens and running them through the wash before we left on Sunday night. Which, of course, then resulted in Archer fucking me on top of the washing machine during spin cycle.

Our mood was subdued as we returned to Shadow Grove, though, with neither one of us speaking much on the drive. He did grip my hand the whole way, though, and as we turned into the familiar streets surrounding our home, he seemed to have something on his mind.

"Spit it out, D'Ath," I finally demanded when the tension became uncomfortable. "Have you changed your mind, then?"

Because we were about to arrive home and that meant he was either on board with sharing my time and affections or we were done. I desperately hoped we weren't done.

He frowned, shooting me a startled look. "What? No. I was just going to ask you something…" He trailed off, and I waited patiently. Okay, not so patiently, but I waited, and that was the main point. "I've got a fight next weekend. Nothing official, just a charity event, but I want you to be there. Will you come?"

I gave him a perplexed look. "Why wouldn't I?"

He shrugged, seeming awkward as fuck all of a sudden. "I don't know. I planned to ask you before…you know. Before this weekend happened. I just know if you're watching, I'll have the appropriate motivation to win."

His cheeks pinked just a touch, and my grin spread wide. He was embarrassed, and that was a new side to Archer D'Ath. I also remembered the last time I'd watched him fight and how I'd motivated him.

I let out a low chuckle. "All right, how's this then? I'll come to the fight, obviously. If you win, you can have me for the whole night in *any* way you want."

He gave me a narrow-eyed stare. "Can't I do that anyway?"

"Not anymore," I replied with a wide smile. "You had your weekend; now I'm barring your access until you win that fight."

He slammed his foot down on the brake. "What?"

"You heard me, Sunshine; don't pretend you didn't. You've got plenty of material stored in your mental spank bank to last the week, I'm sure." It was cruel of me, especially when I had no intention of applying the same restrictions to Kody or Steele. But *they* didn't have an MMA fight to win.

Archer glowered, but he was smart enough not to push the issue. "Fine. And if I lose?"

I bit my lip, dragging it through my teeth the way he liked to do to my nipples. "If you lose, I'm making you sit and watch while Steele fucks my ass and Kody chokes me with his cock." Archer's eyes widened, and I bit back a laugh. "Deal?"

His glare darkened. "Deal. But you know I won't lose."

I just shrugged. "It all sounds like a win to me."

He snorted a laugh and rolled his eyes, but he started the car again and drove the rest of the way back to the mansion.

We paused briefly outside the gates, and I huffed a sigh.

"D for D'Ath, isn't it?" I pointed to the ornate monogram on the gate as it swung slowly open. There was a black-uniformed security officer stationed to the side, and he quickly swept his flashlight over our car before waving us through.

Archer gave me a smirk. "Took you long enough to figure out, Princess."

I glowered back at him but didn't comment. If the D was for D'Ath, then it meant *Archer*, and not my dad, had set the gate code to spell out KATE.

We parked in the garage, and Archer grabbed my hand as we made our way past all the other cars. Before we reached the door, he pinned me to the side of a Range Rover and kissed me until my knees were weak and my head was spinning.

"Topping up that mental spank bank," he told me with a short laugh, letting me go with a lust-filled stare.

I just licked my lips and mentally scolded my pussy for reacting so easily to his touch.

"Anyone home?" Archer called out as we left the garage behind and made our way into the house. I was still in the same clothes I'd left my apartment in on Saturday morning, but they'd been washed and dried. It wasn't like I'd really had a lot of need for clothing in the meantime.

Of course, I still had no panties.

"Finally," Steele grumbled, eyeing us both as we entered the kitchen. He was leaning against the island, a half-full beer in his hand and black smears of grease decorating his forearms and T-shirt.

Kody just dropped his own beer onto the counter and stormed over to us, lashing out with impressive speed and punching Archer straight in the face.

"Kody, what the *fuck*?" Archer roared, clapping his hand to his cheek where Kody's fist had connected.

I'd apparently grown accustomed to violence because I hardly even reacted. Something about Kody's vibe told me he wasn't planning on killing anyone tonight.

"That," Kody barked back at Archer, "was for what you said to MK."

Archer scowled, but he didn't argue, just jerked a nod and grabbed Kody's abandoned beer from the counter. "I'm going to bed. I'm wrecked."

Steele scoffed a laugh. "It's seven in the evening. Arch, don't be a baby."

Archer just flipped him off and stomped out of the kitchen while pounding Kody's beer.

After he was gone, I tilted my head curiously at Kody. "What did Archer say to me that deserved a punch in the face, Kodiak Jones?" Because I hadn't exactly given him or Steele a play-by-play. Beyond assuring them that we were alive, I'd all but ignored my phone all weekend.

Kody just shrugged, giving me a smirk. "You tell me. I'm sure there was something said that deserved that punch."

I laughed and shook my head. "Yeah, that was a fair assumption. Come to think of it, you probably could have hit him a couple more times."

Kody stepped closer, catching my chin in his fingers and tilting my face up to meet his gaze. "Are you okay, babe?" His question was dead serious, and it filled me with a heady sense of security. He genuinely cared about me, and that was awesome.

"I'm fine," I replied honestly as he tilted my face to the side and inspected the mess of marks Archer had left on my neck. "Thanks for the heads-up, by the way. You two couldn't have warned me that you'd thrown him out until he fixed shit?"

Kody just grinned and shrugged, releasing my chin. "Nah, it was more fun this way."

"He means we had no way to know he'd *actually* go see you. We tried to make him deal with his issues once before, and it didn't work out even remotely as well." Steele came over to me and nudged Kody out of his way. "But we're glad things seem better between you two."

I shifted uncomfortably, not quite ready to discuss my multiple-partner sex life so soon. "Yup. We've reached a truce, and you don't need to worry about either of us accidentally shooting each other during target practice."

"Was that a concern before?" Kody asked, seeming legitimately curious.

I shrugged. "If it wasn't, it should have been. I pictured his face way more often than I probably should have while learning to shoot last week."

Steele just laughed, shaking his head.

"Brutal," Kody murmured, grinning broadly. "I love that about you, babe. Steele and I were about to go play a couple rounds of *Gran Turismo*. You wanna play?"

I raised my brows, giving Steele a hard look. "Playing video games, Max Steele? What would Jase say?"

He just scowled. "Fuck Jase. I'm going to wash up; meet you guys in the den." Before leaving the kitchen, he snaked a hand around my waist, pulling me close for a hard kiss. "I'm glad you're home, Hellcat."

Kody gabbed drinks out of the fridge, handed me one, and carried an extra for Steele as we headed through to the den to get comfy.

He flicked on the massive TV, and I looked around the room with new eyes. Now that I *knew*, it made so much more sense that this wasn't my father's house at all. Despite the fact that it was still an ostentatious mansion, it had warmth. Personality. This was their home...Archer, Kody, and Steele's. It was all set up to suit their needs, from the massive TV with every game console imaginable to the oversized garage for all their cars and a work-shop for Steele.

"Truth or dare, Kody?" I asked suddenly, drawing his attention away from the game screen where he was selecting settings.

He gave me a curious look. "Dare."

"Too bad, I want to hear a truth." I smiled so he knew I was just playing. "Who really painted my room pink before I arrived? Was it *actually* Cherry?"

He winced. I'd guessed correctly.

"You bastards," I muttered, sipping my drink and shaking my head at him. I could only imagine it was done purely for their own amusement, making fun of the Princess of Shadow Grove with a princess-pink room.

"I'm sorry, babe. We were unmitigated bastards when you got here. Can you forgive us?" He swept his arms around me, lifting me into his lap and burrowing his face into my hair.

I huffed, acting like I was actually mad about the sparkly pink bedroom. Which I wasn't particularly, especially since one or all of them had fixed and repainted it after I'd been stabbed. "I'll consider it."

He grabbed the console controller again, finishing his selections for the game without moving me out of his lap. I wasn't complaining either. Somehow, my weekend with Archer had served to solidify my feelings for Kody and Steele as well.

So I was more than happy to snuggle on Kody's lap while he and Steele played video games for the evening.

When Kody had the game screen loaded and ready, he tossed his controller aside and wrapped his arms back around me in a tight hug.

I let out a small groan at the number of aches in my body, and he gave a little growl of annoyance.

"You have no idea how jealous I was of Arch this weekend, babe," he confessed in a whisper, and I shifted in his lap so that I could see his face. "He's lucky all I did was punch him."

I bit my lip, studying his face. "Are we okay?"

His hand shifted from my waist to my thigh and he gave me a gentle squeeze. "We're perfect, babe. A little jealousy is good for our blood pressures, and it only shows how totally taken with you we all are."

I appreciated that sentiment, but an uneasy feeling still gnawed at me. "Are you *sure*? I don't know what the rules are with something like this thing we've got. Should I have talked to you and Steele first?" I wrinkled my nose at that thought. I hated talking about feelings at the best of times, and I definitely hadn't planned the way things had escalated with Archer.

Kody just shook his head. "There are no rules, babe. Just do whatever feels right, and we can figure the rest out as we go. But I need to make something totally clear before Steele comes back and crashes the moment."

I held my breath, nervous to hear what he wanted to say.

"I heard what Steele said to you the other day"—*when he said he loved me*—"and I have no doubt Arch threw out some soul-destroying truths to turn shit around with you this weekend." *Yes, that about summed it up.* "So, I guess what I want to tell you, MK, is that I—"

"Hey, guys, do we want to order in? Anna left a pot roast in the oven, but I'm more in the mood for pizza." Steele sat down heavily on the sofa beside us, cutting off whatever Kody had been about to confess.

Seriously?

"Max, babe?" I said sweetly, giving him a sharp glare.

He lowered one brow at me. "What's up?"

"Fuck off for like, two minutes? Kody was in the middle of telling me something." I kept my tone light and teasing but also *seriously, fuck off*.

Steele shot a look between Kody and me, then nodded his understanding. "I'll just…go order the pizzas, shall I?"

I smiled as he stood up. "What a good idea. Get me a supreme, okay?"

Steele's gaze turned wicked. "Of course. Who am I to deny my girl when she's in the mood for *all* the toppings?" He snickered under his breath as he left the den again, and I refocused on Kody.

"Talk," I prodded him.

He groaned and swept a hand through his hair before returning it to my thigh. "I'm in love with you, MK. This whole thing started so fucking badly, but I knew from that first kiss that you were my penguin. I just need you to know that—"

I cut him off with a kiss, sealing my lips to his and meeting his tongue with a desperate need to soothe his fears.

"Kody," I whispered when our kiss ended some moments later. "don't feel pressured to say things just because they did. We're good, I promise."

His brow creased, and he pulled back an inch. "I'm not... I mean, yes, that might have given me a push. But it doesn't make it any less true. I'm totally in love with you, MK."

The clear sincerity in his gaze made my chest tighten, and in my heart I knew beyond a shadow of doubt that I felt the same way for him. Yet I still couldn't voice it out loud. Instead, I just kissed him again and prayed he'd be patient with me while I sorted through all my emotional damage enough to verbally reciprocate.

Steele came back into the room a few minutes later, while Kody and I were still locked together at the mouth and one of his hands was inside my shirt, fondling my breast.

"I would say get a room," Steele commented, coming to sit directly beside us on the couch, "but I'm kinda into this scene. So please, continue."

I grinned but broke away from Kody's kiss anyway. "Shut up and play your video games," I scolded them, then brushed my lips over Kody's ear to whisper one more thing. "I love penguins." I smacked a kiss on his cheek, then snuggled into his chest while he and Steele kicked off their game.

Kody's arms tightened around me in response to my comment,

but he said nothing. He didn't need to; we understood each other perfectly well as it was.

Steele predictably won the first couple of games, then went to answer the door when our pizzas arrived. Kody took advantage of the break in game play to make out with me but froze when his palm slid up my outer thigh, under my skirt.

"Babe," he murmured, his lips hovering just over mine, "where are your panties?"

I grinned, pecking at his lips. "Lost them on the side of the road somewhere yesterday." And I hadn't wanted to waste time going up to my old room to put a fresh pair on when we got home.

Kody groaned, his fingers flexing on my bare ass and making me hiss with pain. He pulled away immediately, giving me a startled frown.

"Stop it," I scolded him, reaching up to smooth the line out of his forehead. "I'm just a bit…tender. I think I need a night or two to recover." Despite how casual I was trying to make it, my cheeks still heated with embarrassment.

Kody just blinked at me a couple of times, then let out a string of curses and lifted me off his lap. He placed me back on the sofa and stood up just as Steele came back into the room carrying a stack of pizza boxes.

"Whoa, what did I miss?" Steele asked, flicking his gaze between Kody and me.

Kody started to storm out, ignoring Steele's question, but then paused and turned back to me.

"Babe, I love you, but I need to drag Archer's ass out of bed and kick it around the gym a bit. Are we good?" He gave me a worried look, like he thought I might be offended by his reaction.

"We're good, Kodiak," I replied, trying *really* hard not to laugh. "Go kick his ass."

He gave me a relieved nod, then took off to drag Archer into the gym, probably under the guise of "training" for his upcoming fight.

"What was that all about?" Steele asked, sitting down in Kody's vacant spot and dropping the pizzas onto the table.

I grabbed the box labeled "supreme" and took a slice before replying. "Just Kody coming to grips with the whole Archer situation." I took a big bite and met Steele's curious stare.

"How so?" he asked, suspicious.

I shrugged, not really wanting to tell him how my ass was currently wearing the imprint of Archer's hand like it was tattooed on. If this dynamic was really going to work, he'd find out for himself soon enough.

"How *is* this going to work?" I asked aloud, wiping pizza grease from the corner of my mouth. "You three all kinda have that alpha-male, big-dick energy going on. It's not super-conducive to sharing one girl, is it?"

Steele just arched a brow at me as he finished his own mouthful of pizza—some spicy, Mexican-style one. "Isn't it?"

"Uh, I wouldn't have thought so." But then, what the hell would I know?

He shot me a lopsided smirk. "Anything is possible for the right girl, Hellcat. And trust me when I say this…*you're* the right girl. For all of us, as much as I wish that weren't true. Can I ask you a favor?"

I hadn't been expecting that, so I jerked a nod, seeing as my mouth was full.

"Leave the posturing, jealous, possessive bullshit to us to deal with. We've been friends a long time; we've got our own ways to work shit out. It doesn't need to stress you out." His tone was gentle, not at all dismissive. Just…reassuring.

I rolled my eyes, tilting my head in the direction of the gym. "Like beating the crap out of each other and calling it a workout?"

Steele grinned. "Exactly."

I supposed when he put it like that, it was kinda hot.

"Now, come on. Kody left me high and dry here, so you've got to race me." He wiped his greasy fingers on a napkin and handed

275

me Kody's game controller. "Then later, you can tell me where your panties went, 'cause I *know* you're not wearing any right now." The look he gave me was pure sex, and I squirmed.

Maybe I didn't need a night off after all.

Who was I kidding? I definitely did. But that didn't mean I couldn't play with *him* a bit.

CHAPTER 35

Apparently I needed that night off more than I'd realized because I fell asleep on the couch with a half-eaten slice of pizza in my hand. When I woke up the next morning, I was tucked up in my own bed in a pair of comfy sweatpants and a guy's T-shirt.

I cuddled into the warmth of my blankets for a few minutes, reluctant to get up but also well aware I couldn't miss any more classes if I wanted to actually pass.

Groaning, I clawed my way out of the blankets and staggered through to my bathroom. A quick glance in the mirror clued me in to who had changed me out of my clothes after I passed out. I was wearing Steele's favorite band T-shirt—Seventeen Daggers— and I could already tell he hadn't bothered giving me any panties.

I hurried through my morning routines, braiding my hair into two long ropes and going a little heavier on the eyeliner than usual. It worked, though, when I put Steele's T-shirt back on and paired it with black skinny jeans and chunky heeled boots. He and Kody had stopped by my apartment over the weekend and packed up all my stuff for me, which was all kinds of considerate of them.

"Fuck me," Kody groaned when I walked into the kitchen. "It

should be illegal to look that good in another guy's clothes." He slid out of his seat at the table and grabbed me around the waist.

Faster than I could even utter a "good morning," he had me pinned against the fridge while he showed me exactly how hot he thought I looked in Steele's shirt.

He only stopped kissing me when Archer whacked him in the back of the head with a rolled-up magazine.

"Ow, what the shit, bro?" Kody protested, scowling at his friend while I caught my breath and slipped away to make my coffee.

"Hands off my girl," Archer snapped back like a bear with a sore head. "It's too early for that shit."

I laughed, shaking my head. "Don't be salty just because you're on ice for a week, Sunshine."

The glare he shot me when I met his eyes was equal parts annoyance and sex. He wanted to strangle me, but he also wanted to fuck me raw. Nothing wrong with both, in my opinion.

"Whoa, what?" Steele asked, coming into the kitchen on the tail end of my comment. "Arch is on ice?"

Archer glowered, saying nothing.

"Until he wins this charity fight, yep." I efficiently went about making my coffee, grinding fresh beans and steaming the milk. I hesitated only a moment before using the larger milk jug to make coffee for everyone.

Kody let out a low whistle at my announcement, clapping Archer on the shoulder. "Guess I better put my money on you to win, then. With incentive like that, it's a sure thing."

Archer looked offended. "You wanna tell me you were betting on the other guy? Fuck you, dickhead."

Steele's arms snaked around my waist as I worked my machine to extract beautiful, dark espresso with perfect, golden crema. "You look gorgeous this morning, Hellcat." His lips pressed to my neck, and I leaned back into his embrace. I could definitely get used to this newfound peace between the four of us.

"I love this T-shirt," I replied, craning my neck to kiss him on the lips. "Thanks for tucking me in last night."

"It was purely selfish," he told me with a smirk. "I totally felt you up while I was changing your clothes. Then I needed to force myself not to wake you up."

I chuckled, turning back to finish our coffee off with silky steamed milk. "Well, I doubt I would have complained if you had." I handed him one of the mugs, and our fingers interlinked on the cup.

"Thanks," he said softly, pressing another gentle kiss to my lips. "As for the T-shirt, maybe we could go see them in concert sometime. I've met Zeth Briggs a couple of times; he's a cool guy."

My internal fangirl squealed, but I kept it calm on the outside. "Cool." I nodded, mentally high-fiving myself for that composure. "It's a date."

"Damn right it is," Steele murmured, letting me slip out of his embrace to deliver coffee to Kody and Archer.

Kody thanked me with a way too intense kiss, which ended in Archer elbowing him in the ribs. Archer just eyed the coffee like I'd handed him a cup of spit.

"Don't be such a snob, Sunshine," I teased him. "Drink the damn coffee. It might improve that surly temperament this morning."

Kody scoffed. "Unlikely."

Archer grabbed my wrist before I could walk away, though, hauling me into his lap and kissing me like I was all the stimulant he needed to start the day right.

"There's only one thing that's going to improve my temperament, Princess," he muttered in my ear, nipping my lobe with his teeth and making me moan. His hips pressed up, showing me exactly what he meant, as if there could be any misunderstanding there.

I clasped his face with both my hands, kissing him back just as hard as he'd claimed my lips. When I released him, we were both breathing heavily and his cock was rock-hard beneath me.

"Well then, I guess you'd better win that fight this weekend, huh?" With a grin, I hopped off his lap and circled around the island, away from his reach. "Until then, I recommend lots of cold showers, okay?"

Kody and Steele snickered and tossed teasing insults at Archer, but the man himself just locked eyes with me across the kitchen, silently promising retribution.

Good. That was what I was banking on.

"Actually, babe," Kody said after a moment, "there is something we need to discuss with you, on the subject of your many admirers."

A chill of dread ran through me. That couldn't be a good subject…could it? Then again, the three of them *seemed* okay with the new reality this morning.

"Okay…" I kept my expression carefully neutral, letting them take the lead. "What's up?"

Kody shot a pointed look at Steele, who sighed and scrubbed a hand over his buzzed hair.

"Scott," Steele said, grimacing.

I sighed. "Look, I know he's been a bit clingy and shit, but he met me when I was in a really negative headspace. I'd just had my heart broken"—all three of them winced at that—"and I was pretty upset. So, can you really blame him for being an asshole around you guys?"

Steele nodded, always the peacemaker. "That's all understandable, and I'm glad you had someone to support you aside from Bree. But this can't be ignored." He paused, his brow furrowed. "Obviously, you know I swept your apartment on Friday while you guys were in class."

I nodded because I'd assumed that when he'd given me new keys and a new alarm system.

"Well, I found a partial fingerprint. It looked like someone had done a pretty hasty wipe down and just missed one. A friend of ours ran it through some databases and found it matched Scott's." He kept his tone calm and even, but his eyes watched me intently. He was trying to read my reactions.

I frowned. "Well...that doesn't mean anything. Scott's been to my apartment a bunch of times. Of course his fingerprints would be there."

Kody made a sound of disagreement. "On your underwear drawer?"

My brows shot up, my mouth parting with surprise. I shifted my gaze to Steele, who nodded confirmation.

I wracked my brain for any reason why Scott's prints would be on my underwear drawer...or *anywhere* in my bedroom for that matter. I came up blank. Or rather, not *blank* but certainly envisioning the same conclusion they'd already drawn.

"How?" I asked in a small voice. "When would he have even had time? He was in the basement with us. Then you guys made him help clean up the bodies, right?" I directed this question to Archer, who nodded.

"We assumed your stalker entered the apartment while we were in the basement," Steele explained, "but what if that really was us who left the door open? Scott came back up when Zane arrived. He used the bathroom to wash his hands and could have done the mirror message then."

"And you were fast asleep," Kody added. "How easy would it have been for him to duck from the bathroom into your bedroom without anyone noticing? He could have raided your drawer then."

I came back over to the island with the bowl of Bircher muesli and Greek yogurt that Anna had left in the fridge for me. Sitting down on one of the vacant seats, I turned over this scenario in my mind.

They were right. My bathroom at the apartment had been right outside my bedroom and out of sight from the living room. If no one had been specifically watching Scott come and go from the bathroom, he *could* had slipped into my room unnoticed.

Fuck.

But it didn't add up. "Scott's not my stalker," I said, shaking my head. "It doesn't make sense. He wasn't even *in* Shadow Grove until I met him this Christmas. Not to mention he's *way* too young to have stalked my mom. The timeline doesn't match up."

It was Archer who answered me, his tone cynical but not unkind. For once. Shocker. "So he says. No offense, baby girl, you kinda walk around with blinders on most of the time. Could you even identify ten other students at SGU if you saw them on the street?"

My initial reaction was to be offended, obviously, but then… yeah, he had a point. I had become so used to all the negative attention my court case had caused that I'd gotten used to just blocking out everyone around me as white noise.

"Look, it's not definitive proof that Scott's somehow involved," Steele offered when I said nothing, "but we want you to be careful. I ran surveillance on him most of the weekend, and to be honest, he did nothing. Literally nothing. Barely even left his house. But he lives with two SGPD cops on Ferryman's payroll, so…" He trailed off with a shrug.

I rubbed my forehead, feeling a headache building. "Yeah, his older brother Shane or something. Zane warned me about him too—just that he was in league with the Wraiths, though. I figured it was a territorial thing."

Steele nodded. "We'll keep looking into it. Just stay alert around Scott at school, okay?"

"What he said," Kody agreed, carrying his dirty plates over to the sink. "We'll work it out, but probably best if Scott just fucks off back to wherever the hell he transferred from anyway. Just in case my fist finds his nose again."

I glared. "It could be a coincidence," I said, even though I didn't fully believe that myself. "Let's just not go killing people until we're sure, okay?"

Kody grinned broadly. "So you agree we should kill him when the evidence supports it? Excellent."

"Whoever the fuck almost killed me with a drug overdose, then slit Drew's throat and delivered a human heart to the doorstep? Yeah. I'm okay killing that guy." My tone was flat and uncaring, but that was what extended periods of fear and paranoia did to a person, wasn't it? Dampened the shock factor and blurred the line of morality.

"I'm so turned on right now," Kody informed us, and Steele threw a spoon at him. "Hey!" he protested, catching the spoon before it hit his face. "As if you're not."

Steele just laughed and shook his head. "Go and get dressed. Hellcat can't miss any more classes, so if you're late, we're going without you."

Kody rolled his eyes but left the kitchen to change out of his sweaty workout clothes anyway.

"I'll pull the car around," Steele told me, then left the kitchen as well.

Just like that, Archer and I were alone again.

Neither one of us made any attempts at conversation, finishing our breakfast and coffee in silence. When I was done, he got up and carried both our plates and mugs to the sink.

I started to move past him to leave the kitchen as well, but he stopped me with a firm hand on my waist, reeling me in and crushing me against his hard body.

"Archer..." I warned him, but he wasn't listening. His strong grip on my waist boosted me onto the counter, and his mouth claimed mine in a kiss that promised so, *so* much more than I was currently offering. Bastard was going to test my resolve on the ice-out, that was for sure.

When he bit my lower lip, I almost caved. It was scary how fast he'd learned all my weaknesses.

"Kate…" he replied in a low groan, mocking me as my hips rocked forward, grinding my denim-covered crotch against his hard length.

"Dammit," I hissed, breaking away from his lips with monumental effort. "You're gonna be the death of me, Archer D'Ath."

The laugh he gave me in response was a sound I could easily become addicted to. It was totally relaxed and…dare I say, happy? It was scary and intoxicating. I wanted more.

"Finally," he muttered, stepping back and letting me down from the countertop. "You're finally getting an idea of how you've been slowly killing me these last five months." He ruffled his hair with his fingers, messing it up in the most delicious way. "I've got to hit the gym this morning, but I've got a class this afternoon. Can I drive you home?"

I smirked at him and shook my head. "And convince me to suck your dick while you drive again? Keep dreaming, Sunshine. I'll see you on campus, though." I smacked a kiss against his lips and hurried out of the kitchen before he could break my resolve any more.

The second I was alone with my thoughts, though, worry and paranoia started creeping in again. Was Scott somehow involved with my stalker? Had it been him all along? I just didn't believe it. Even when the evidence suggested otherwise.

Time would tell, though, so long as I managed to stay alive long enough…

CHAPTER 36

Bree slammed her drink down on the table, coughing as she choked a bit. She flapped a hand at me to indicate she wasn't dying, then took a few deep breaths.

"Say that again," she demanded, staring at me like I'd grown three heads. We were having a quick catch-up in the dining hall between classes, knowing full well we couldn't really gossip with Kody and Steele breathing down our necks at lunchtime.

I sighed, tugging on one of my Dutch braids. "I know. It's looking pretty suspicious, huh?"

Bree frowned, shaking her head. "What? No, not that shit about Scott. I've been thinking he was up to something ever since that whole phone-tracker bullshit. Repeat what you just said about Archer!"

My cheeks heated. I'd glossed over that section of events. During the weekend I'd just told Bree that I was caught up doing shit with the boys, and she hadn't questioned it further. But just now, in getting her up to speed on Scott, I'd let slip that I'd, uh, made amends with my husband.

"Well, there goes one solid reason you could have annulled the marriage," she commented with a concerned frown. "Now that you've fucked him *and* moved in with him. Like, it's archaic and total bullshit, but not consummating a marriage is, like, a legit reason for annulment. But…it kinda sounds like that ship has sailed now, huh?" Her frown shifted into a wicked grin. "I'm gonna need *all* the juicy details, clear?"

I sighed, shaking my head. "Annulment was never going to work anyway. Neither is divorce, apparently." I groaned, rubbing my face with both hands. "This whole *everything* is such a mess, Bree. When is it going to get easier?"

She shrugged. "I would have said when you work out who is trying to kill you, then kill *them* and also get rid of your stalker. But then even after that, you'll still be in love with three pigheaded, dominant assholes who couldn't share a bowl of popcorn, let alone a woman they all claim to care for."

I glared at her. "Thanks, babe. Real helpful."

She beamed. "I try."

"And I'm not *in love* with all of them," I added in a grumble. "Maybe two of them…the third is barely more than tolerated."

Bree snorted a laugh. "Okay, cool. We're lying to ourselves. Just so I know where we're at." She checked her watch and cursed. "I've got to go. I need to hear the rest of this, though. Can we hang out this afternoon?"

I nodded. "For sure. Come by the house? Kody will be training Arch until dinnertime, so we can—"

"Perv over their insanely hot bodies while they wrestle around on the ground, all sweaty and delicious?" Bree beamed at me like a damn shithead. I glared, and she nodded enthusiastically. "I'll take that look as agreement. Catch you later, babe." She hurried out of the dining hall, snickering to herself, and I rolled my eyes.

I knew she was just teasing, but apparently, I was also turning into a jealous psychopath because I wanted to threaten her with permanent blindness.

Standing up and picking up my own bag, I started at the sound of a voice behind me.

"Shouldn't you be in class, Miss Danvers?"

My bag almost knocked my can of Coke flying, but Professor Barker's hand shot out and grabbed it just in time.

"Uh, I had a fifteen-minute gap in my schedule," I told him, carefully taking the can from his outstretched hand. "Thanks."

He just smiled at me, but it wasn't a professional sort of smile. It was too intense, too interested, too...*creepy*.

"Well, that works out well. I wondered if I might speak with you in my office?" He held his arm out, indicating that I should walk with him out of the dining hall, but my mental danger-meter was beeping like crazy.

Giving him a tight smile, I shouldered my bag properly and ducked away from his reach. "Sorry, my next class starts now. I need to get going."

My professor's eyes narrowed slightly, and then his expression faded into a watery smile. "Of course. I'll be sure to catch you again another time."

Something about the way he emphasized *catch* made my heart pound with nervousness. Surely he didn't mean... No, not Professor Barker. He was just a run-of-the-mill predator professor. Nothing more than that.

I nodded with a noncommittal smile and hurried out of the dining hall, tossing my Coke in the recycling on my way out. Call me crazy, but I was more than a little suspicious of anyone even remotely touching my food or drinks.

"Good gossip session?"

I jumped so hard I almost screamed, then whirled around and punched Archer straight in the chest. And immediately regretted it because, holy crap, his chest was *hard*.

"What the fuck, you lurker?" I demanded, cradling my now injured hand.

He just fucking laughed at me while rubbing the spot I'd hit. "You don't have a terrible punch on you, Princess. Maybe you should let me show you a thing or two..." His brows dipped suggestively, and I backed up a couple of steps.

"Uh-huh, I just bet you'd love that. A little bit of ground and pound, huh?" I gave him a knowing smirk, and he answered it with his own.

He gave a pained groan. "Hearing you talk dirty with MMA terms is unfair, baby girl. You're lucky I'm not dragging you into a supply closet and fucking you stupid right now."

My pulse raced. "Why haven't you?"

His teasing smile evaporated, and the look he gave me in its wake was dead-set caring. "Because you're afraid of small spaces, Kate." He reached out, twisting one of my braids around his fist to pull me closer for a kiss that was shockingly tender. "Now, get to class and learn things."

Archer released me and sauntered down the hall to his own class like he hadn't just blown my fucking mind and left me with a damp patch in my pants. Fucker.

The next couple of days passed pretty smoothly, all things considered. Bree came over that first afternoon to catch up on my weekend with Archer, but we ended up doing exactly what she'd joked about. Except with cocktails.

I had to hand it to her—watching Kody and Archer punch, kick, and wrestle each other in their home version of an octagon was insanely great entertainment. Especially after Steele became our personal bartender.

Bree enjoyed it so much that the next day she turned up with Dallas in tow, offering him up as a new sparring partner for Archer.

Shockingly, the boys were fine with this arrangement—probably because they'd known Archer would hand Dallas his ass, but my old friend didn't make it an easy win for him.

Come Wednesday, I'd evidently avoided Scott as long as I possibly could. He was waiting for me outside my second-to-last lecture of the day and looked all kinds of pissed off.

"Oh good, you *are* alive," he sneered when I stopped dead in front of him.

"Don't be dramatic, Scott," I replied with a flat glare. "I need to get to my psychology lecture. Can we talk later?"

His nostrils flared, and he grabbed my arm in a bruising grip before I could take off. "No, Maddie, we can't talk later because you'll just avoid me *again*." His grip tightened as he tried to drag me along the hall, but I dug my heels in, resisting.

"Scott," I snapped in a harsh tone, "let me fucking go. This is not okay."

There were enough students around that my demand drew attention, and Scott's cheeks heated with embarrassment under their curious stares. Still, he didn't release my arm.

"Scott," I hissed, harder this time. "Let. Go."

His eyes darted around at our audience, and he reluctantly peeled his fingers from my upper arm, where he was sure to have left bruises. Great. Now I'd have to explain *that* to my three overprotective shadows.

Scott let out a long breath, but his whole body radiated anger as he glared at me. "Maddie, I want to talk to you in *private* for five fucking minutes. Is that seriously so much to ask for? I transferred schools for you."

Annoyance flared inside me. "I *never* asked you to do that, Scott. And I don't have five minutes to give you right now; I'm late for my psychology lecture, so just..." I shook my head, wanting to say *just leave me the hell alone.*

"Just what?" he snapped, his hands balling into fists at his sides. "Just stand back and watch my girl get *used* by three guys who

289

think they own this fucking city? They don't even care about you, Maddie. You're just the latest in their long line of desperate sluts, and the second they're done fucking you, they'll toss you aside for the next tight cunt to catch their attention."

Smack.

As it turned out, I would need to skip psychology anyway. My hand needed ice from punching Archer earlier and now from popping Scott in the face.

"What the fuck?" Scott roared, clapping his hand to his face where my punch had landed. I made a mental note to send Cass a text, thanking him. I doubted I could have hit half as hard a couple of weeks ago.

The other students who'd gathered around to witness our argument all cheered and whistled at my punch, but I was just *furious*.

"Next time you call me a desperate slut," I told Scott in a low voice, not even caring who overheard, "I'll cut your fucking dick off. Now leave me the fuck alone."

I spun on my heel, pushing past a couple of cheering jocks on my way to the exit. My step faltered, though, when I spotted Steele storming toward me with a face like an avenging angel.

"I took care of it," I told him quickly as he reached me. He clearly wanted to go past me and deliver some hard truths to Scott himself, but I blocked his way with my body, looping my arms around his neck. "Max, babe? I need ice for my hand. Help me out?"

He scowled but huffed a sigh and nodded. "I'll kill that fucker later, then. Come on, I'll take you home early."

With a possessive, protective arm around my waist, he walked me out to his car while I shot off texts to Kody, Archer, and Bree.

Bree's reply came almost immediately, informing me that she already knew. Someone had started filming the second our argument had gotten heated. So much for the no-phones rule on SGU campus. I didn't even know why they were still pretending when at least half the student body was flouting the rule.

"I take it you already know what he said to me, then?" I asked Steele when we were both inside his car.

He gave me a furious look. "It was livestreamed, so yeah. I heard what he said, and I saw that punch you threw. Not bad, Hellcat." He reached out and took my injured hand in his, smoothing his thumb across my tender knuckles. "I'm still going to kill him for what he said to you, though."

Steele raised my aching hand to his lips, kissing my knuckles before he reversed out of his parking space.

"That's if Kody or Arch doesn't get to him first," I muttered, checking my phone. Sure enough, there were replies from both of them.

Archer D'Ath: He'd better fucking hide.
Kodiak Jones: How fucking dumb is this asshole? He must know we're gonna beat the snot outta him for that.

I sighed and sent a reply to both of them in a group chat. I figured we were all involved romantically, so we were probably okay to share a chat thread.

Madison Kate: His brother is a cop on Wraith payroll. Maybe it's a trap.

There was a long pause, but I could see they'd both read my message.

"What's the decision?" Steele asked, unable to join the chat while he was driving. "Are we executing that little prick or what?"

I rolled my eyes at the melodrama of it all.

Madison Kate: Insulting me isn't a killable offense today, boys. Save the aggression for the octagon, yeah?

Kody just replied with a glaring emoji. Archer didn't reply at all.

Heaving a sigh, I tossed my phone back into my bag and gave Steele a wide smile. "Forget all that. What are we doing with our afternoon alone?"

His brows hitched, and he peered at me from the corner of his eye. "Well, for starters, we're icing your hand. Cass must be slacking in his old age if he couldn't teach you to throw a punch without the padding of gloves."

I snorted a laugh. "He's thirty-three, not fucking eighty."

Steele just shrugged like I'd confirmed his point. "And then...I might have an idea. It's hard to get you alone these days, you know? I think I might have had better luck when you still had your own apartment."

"I know...but you have me for at least an hour and a half now. Longer if Arch and Kody go straight to the gym when they get home." I gave him a suggestive look, and he clicked his tongue stud against his teeth.

Shooting me a quick look, he nodded. "I can work with that."

My phone started vibrating and chiming in my bag, and I fished it out, thinking it was the guys. It wasn't.

I sighed heavily. "Scott."

"Is he dense?" Steele asked, genuinely confused.

"Apparently." I rejected the call and changed my phone to silent. It didn't stop Scott trying to call again four more times before Steele pulled into our driveway.

"Come on, let's sort your hand out," Steele said, opening my door for me like a gentleman. "Then I was thinking we could go swimming?"

I gave him a curious look as we headed through to the kitchen to get an ice pack. "Swimming? I mean, it's not exactly a warm day." It wasn't freezing anymore, but it sure as hell wasn't bikini weather.

Steele just grinned, heading to the freezer to find the medical ice packs. "It's an indoor heated pool, beautiful. So, do you want to?" He found what he was looking for and came back over to place it on my knuckles.

Swimming with Steele? As if I'd say no. "Hell yeah, just give me five minutes to change."

He grinned. "I'll meet you in there. I just need to make sure the guys haven't committed murder in broad daylight, all right?"

It was a valid concern. I left him in the kitchen and hurried out with the ice pack clutched to my knuckles, almost running straight into Steinwick.

"Crap, sorry," I apologized, stepping aside at the last second so we didn't collide. "My head was a million miles away."

"Not a worry at all, miss," he replied with a wrinkled smile. He reached out and stopped me before I could dart around him, though. "My apologies for the intrusion, miss, but what happened to your hand?"

"Oh," I started, then paused as I searched for a plausible reason. For some reason I didn't want to tell this well-mannered, proper old man that I'd punched a boy for calling me a slut. "Just had a disagreement with a hard object," I mumbled, flushing with embarrassment.

Steinwick frowned at me a moment, his bushy, white eyebrows drawn low. Then he sighed and moved out of my way. "If it still hurts in the morning, I suggest you have James take a look. He's recently completed his EMT training, so I'm sure he would be happy to help."

It took me longer than it should have to remember who James even was. The groundskeeper. Archer was way too accurate in saying that I paid little to no attention to the people surrounding me. No wonder I was proving such an easy target to stalk.

"Thanks, Steinwick," I replied with a smile, then hurried

on up to my room to change into the sexiest swimsuit I owned. Steele and I were way overdue a one-on-one catch-up, and I didn't want to waste even a minute longer than necessary.

Only one problem. I had no idea where the pool was located within Archer's mansion.

CHAPTER 37

My logical guess was that the pool might be somewhere near the gym, and I was right. Just past the gym doors was a set of double doors that I'd never ventured through. I guess I'd just assumed they went to a storage room or maybe another entrance to the garage or something. Either way, I'd never bothered to open them, so I'd never realized there was an indoor pool around four times the size of my bedroom in there.

"*How* have I never known this was here?" I exclaimed, spotting Steele sitting on the edge of the pool, already in a pair of black swimming shorts and nothing else. Good god, he was a *snack*.

"You've been a bit preoccupied since getting back from Cambodia," he commented with an amused smile. His gray eyes tracked my movements as I padded around the pool with bare feet and dropped my towel and robe on a sun lounger.

I sat down on the lip of the pool beside him, shivering as the cool tiles touched my ass. "That's true. I'm glad I know now, though." I dipped my feet in the water and groaned at how warm it was. "Oh my god, that's so much better than I expected."

Steele grinned. "You thought it was going to be one of those lukewarm, tepid kind of pools? Gross."

I shuddered. "So gross. Warm or cold. Not in between."

He pushed off the edge, sliding down into the warm water and spinning around to face me, his hand extended. "Coming in?"

His eyes were full of mischief, and his grin was all sex. How could I even consider refusing an offer like that?

I followed him in, my skin shivering all over as the warm water encased me and Steele's arms wrapped around my waist. It was exactly what I needed, but I'd have to do catch-up work on psychology later.

Worth it.

Steele gently moved us through the warm water, and I snuggled into his chest, resting my chin on his shoulder as he glided. His fingers were tight on my skin, though, and I knew he had something on his mind.

"All right, spill," I ordered when we got to the deepest part of the pool. It meant we both needed to tread water to stay afloat, but there was something crazy intimate about being there together. The whole room was dead silent, so even while talking quietly, our voices echoed.

"Spill what?" he replied, swimming around me like a sexy shark.

I smiled at his attempt at coy. "You've got something on your mind, so spill. No one else is around to hear us... What's going on, Max Steele?"

"What makes you think there's something to tell, Madison Kate Danvers?" he countered, sweeping his arms around me from behind and kissing my wet neck.

I tipped my head to the side, offering him better access and letting my own buoyancy hold me up in the water for the most part. Benefits of having big boobs, right there.

"Because," I replied in a soft murmur. "I can just tell. I *know* you."

"Mmm," he murmured against my neck, then captured my

earlobe between his teeth. Such a simple act shouldn't have been so insanely hot, but it sent electric ripples right through me. "Maybe it's not something to tell you," he whispered, an edge of wickedness in his voice. "Maybe it's something to *show*."

My brows shot up. What could he need to show me?

His hands glided over my body under the water, cupping my breasts teasingly. "This bikini should be banned, Hellcat."

I let him change the subject, tilting my body to press into his hands more. "Oh yeah? What should I wear instead, then?"

His lips were back on my neck, and a second later I felt the unmistakable tug of my bikini top being untied. With his teeth. Now, if that wasn't a talent...

"Nothing," he replied, tossing my top out of the pool with a splat, then quickly loosening the bottoms to join it. I wasn't exactly complaining. That was exactly what I'd had in mind when he'd suggested swimming in the first place.

My breath hissed between my teeth as his hands drifted all over my naked body, teasing me with light caresses under the warm water while his lips and teeth paid homage to my neck in the most delicious way.

"Max..." I groaned his name as his fingertips stroked at my inner thigh but didn't go where I really badly wanted them to go. "We're on the clock, remember?"

He made a frustrated sound, nipping at my neck but moving his hand to where I wanted it. His long, pianist fingers explored my slick pussy with a confidence that left me moaning in his grip. My head rested on his shoulder as I made a grand total of zero effort to keep us afloat.

Spoiler alert—that's a surefire way to drown your lover.

Both of us went under, popped back up coughing and sputtering a second later, then silently agreed to move farther down the pool to where we could reach the bottom.

"So, you're doing a very good job of distracting me, Max Steele, but I haven't forgotten you need to *show* me something." With my toes back on the smooth tile of the pool bottom, I felt confident snaking my arms around his neck once more. My nipples were hard despite the warmth of the water, and Steele banded his arm around my waist, pulling me tight against his chest.

He grinned, pecking little kisses against my lips. "I'm not distracting you, Hellcat."

"Mm-hmm," I replied, kissing him properly and toying with that tongue stud. Fuck, I loved that thing. Or rather, I loved what he *did* with it. There was a lot to be said for boys with piercings, that was for sure.

I gasped, a thought popping into my head. He needed to *show* me something?

"You know, you're a bit overdressed for this party," I murmured, dropping my hands down to the waistband of his swim shorts.

He smiled against my kisses. "Oh, you think so?"

"Yup," I replied, kissing along the line of his jaw and down his neck. These boys had too much fun marking me up with their kisses and bites. I needed to even the score somewhat.

Meanwhile, I peeled his shorts open and pushed them down his legs. I had a sneaking suspicion that—

"Max!" I exclaimed when my hand wrapped around his hard cock. Or I should say, wrapped around his hard, *pierced* cock.

He grinned wide. "I told you I had something to *show* you, Hellcat."

I gaped at him, my mouth open and my eyes locked on his while my hand explored what he'd had done. "Nope, this won't work," I muttered, and his smile slipped. "I need a better look. Hop up on the edge." I nodded to the side of the pool, and his smile returned.

"Hellcat, I'm not a piece of meat for you to ogle," he chastised me in a mocking voice but hoisted himself up on the edge as directed nonetheless.

Now that we were in the shallow end, I could easily stand in front of him with his newly pierced dick right in front of my face. Ho-ly *shit*. It was a work of art. Steele leaned back on his hands, his erection standing up proudly as I studied it from just a few inches away.

"When did you do this?" I asked, running my fingertip slowly over the series of barbell piercings running the length of his cock, from above his balls to just under his tip. Eight. There were eight of them, each with a small silver ball on each end of the bar.

His cock moved under my touch, but it only made me more intrigued. It had to have hurt *so* much.

"The day after you left," he replied, his voice quiet. "I'd had the appointment booked for ages, but for something smaller and less painful. Then, well, everything happened. I wanted to punish myself, I guess."

My brows shot up. "So you got your dick pierced eight times? Steele, this must have been excruciating." I wrapped my hand around him, testing how it felt to stroke his length with all that metal.

He groaned.

"I've had worse pain before," he confessed. "Besides, I knew this would be worth it, if you ever forgave me." His gaze was pure evil, but he made no moves to stop my inspection. He just stayed there, leaning back on his hands with his dick in my hands.

There were worse places to be, I supposed.

"So, is it…" Words escaped me as I tried to ask the question on my mind. "How long do you…"

He smiled, understanding. "Hellcat, if you're asking whether I can fuck you right now, the answer is yes. It only needed four to six weeks to heal."

I licked my lips, pleased as all shit, and he let out a pained sound.

"Beautiful, you're killing me. Can you finish looking later and let me fuck you now? It feels like it's been forever…" The pouty face he gave me would have put a spaniel puppy to shame.

"No way," I laughed. "Suck it up, Max Steele. I intend to get well acquainted with this… What's this called, anyway?"

"Jacob's Ladder," he informed me, and I nodded. Seemed appropriate; the bars climbed his erect dick like the rungs of a ladder.

"Right. So just be patient. If the boys come home, they can go kick the shit out of each other in the gym and leave us be." I dragged my tongue around the silken head of his cock, tasting the saltiness of his precum as he sucked in a harsh breath.

He let out another small groan as I dragged my tongue down the underside of his shaft, inspecting each and every one of those ladder rungs. "More likely they'll want to join in. But I don't want to share you tonight, Hellcat. I want you all to myself."

I reached the bottom piercing, then returned to his tip, wrapping my hand around his base instead. "Fine by me. I missed you like crazy, Max." I closed my lips over his tip, sucking briefly then letting go. "So, here's the deal. If they come home and *happen* to find us in here, then they can either watch or leave but no touching until you say so."

I took him into my mouth again, sucking deeper and stroking gently with my hand, and his hips bucked up to meet my touch.

"Deal," he agreed on a groan. "But you have no idea how badly I want to sink my cock into you right now, beautiful girl."

Based on the way his hand had just clasped the back of my head, coaxing me to take him deeper as his hips bucked up, I'd say I had a pretty good idea.

I was gentle with his new hardware at first, not wanting to hurt him, but it quickly became clear that I wasn't hurting him at all. Or if I was, he was into it.

Pushing up on my toes out of the water, I braced my free hand on his hip, holding him still as I sucked him off. My tongue explored every curve of his piercings, marveling at the contrast between hard metal and soft flesh, until his breathing grew ragged and his fingers clutched at my shoulder.

"Hellcat, baby, please. If you keep going, I'm going to come down your throat, and I really, *really* want to come inside your incredible cunt."

Well, with a request like that, how was a girl to refuse?

I gave his cock one last stroke, then released him and retreated back into the warm water of the pool with an invitation painted all over my face.

Steele was no idiot; he slid back into the water like a merman chasing tail and closed the gap between us in just a few quick strides. An involuntary peal of laughter escaped me as he pounced.

My feet slipped from under me on the pool tiles, and for a moment we both went under—again—but this time I latched my legs around his waist. When we popped back up, he gave me barely a second to draw a breath before his lips were on mine, his mouth dominating and possessive as he kissed me like a starving man.

I moaned into his kiss, pressing my body closer as he walked us across the pool. By the time my back touched tiles, his cock was lined up and I was damn near begging for it.

"Yes," I breathed as he released my lips and shifted my legs higher around his waist. It gave him the perfect angle, and words failed me again as he started pushing inside, piercings and all.

Fuck me dead. Whoever had suggested the Jacob's Ladder needed a goddamn medal or something. Maybe a statue *erected* in his honor. Because fucking Steele with eight bar piercings studding his cock was like *nothing* I'd ever felt. In a really good way.

"Is that okay?" Steele asked me hesitantly as he fully seated his cock inside me. I made a pathetic little mewing sound—the kind of sound I'd probably mock a book heroine for, but *clearly* it was an acceptable reaction to fucking a guy with a heavily pierced cock. I'd remember that in the future.

I nodded frantically, not totally sure what noises would come out if I tried to speak. Instead, I conveyed my meaning of *fuck yes, it's more than okay* by biting his neck and bucking my hips to get him moving.

Steele chuckled one of those totally masculine laughs that I'd only ever heard mid-sex. The kind of laugh that said he knew exactly what kind of power he was holding over my orgasm, and he *loved* it.

"Well then," he murmured, bringing one of his hands up to clasp my face and bringing my lips back to his. "I love you, Hellcat." He said it in a husky whisper, then saved me the need to reply as he withdrew all the way to his tip and slammed back in a whole lot faster than the last time. Then he proceeded to set a pace that made my toes curl, my throat go hoarse, and my fingernails claw raw lines out of his back. His piercings acted like a ribbed condom on *crack*... then supersized. It was insane, and I was one hundred percent a fan.

Like, *really* a big fan. So much that I wasn't even remotely prepared when my orgasm hit. I came hard, clinging to Steele like a lifeline as my cunt tightened and pulsed around him, then my hips rolled, begging for more.

"Fuck, Hellcat," Steele groaned, kissing me long and hard and letting his tongue stud echo what his dick was doing inside me. "I can't... It's been so freaking long and—"

"Do it," I ordered him, my breathing ragged and my voice rough from screaming. "Come in me, Max. Then take me back to your room and show me what those piercings are like from *all* the other positions."

He groaned hard at that suggestion. His pace increased until a second later his cock slammed deep into me, his hot cum filling me as his tongue found mine once more.

For a long moment we just stayed like that, kissing each other like we had all the time in the world. The warm water of the pool mixed with my post-orgasm haze was all kinds of relaxing.

"Come on," he murmured after a while. "We should get upstairs before we're seen. I have so very many ways I want to fuck you tonight, Hellcat."

I gave a short laugh, pressing my forehead against his with my arms still around his neck. "Making up for lost time, Max Steele? Or marking your territory?"

His lopsided grin was unapologetic. "Both."

I shrugged. "Fine by me."

We waded over to the steps to get out, and I made my way over to the lounge chair where I'd dropped my towel and robe. Steele had other plans, though. Instead of drying off and putting my robe back on, I found myself flat on my back with his mouth between my legs as he showed me all the benefits of his tongue piercing as well.

Breathy strings of curses fell from my lips as he sucked and licked at my already swollen clit, teasing me to the edge of another orgasm. My hands clutched at his head, my nails digging into his scalp as I pulled him tighter against my cunt, desperate for more.

He delivered on my silent plea, slipping his fingers into my aching pussy, filling me and fucking me as his tongue stud worked over my clit.

My head fell back on the lounge chair as my orgasm raced up, my breath gasping and my hips bucking. From the corner of my eye I caught the door to the pool room open, but paid it no mind. Staff were usually gone by this time, and if it was one of the other guys…too bad.

"Steele," I moaned, "I'm so close."

Like that was what he was waiting to hear, he did this…*thing* with his tongue piercing that bordered on pain but sent me hurtling into an instant, mind-blowing, earth-shattering orgasm.

This time it took me twice as long to come back to earth, and Steele seemed in no hurry as he kissed every inch of my available skin, ending at my lips.

"I don't think I can walk," I complained against his lips, tasting myself and finding it was only turning me on again.

He kissed the tip of my nose. "I'll carry you, then."

I grinned and didn't complain as he scooped me up in his arms. He didn't bother covering either of us up with towels or robes, just carried me out of the pool room totally naked.

"Steele!" I hissed in shock as he passed through the double doors. "What if Steinwick is still here?"

Steele hesitated a moment, looking concerned. Then shook his head. "In that case, let's hurry."

He all but ran through the house with me in his arms, both of us totally naked, until we reached his room—thankfully, unseen. Not that it would have been so bad for me; all my bits were covered by the way he held me. They'd have had one hell of an eyeful of his studded cock, though.

"You're insane," I muttered with a smile as he dropped me down onto his bed, then covered me with his naked body. "But I think I like you anyway."

He arched a brow at me, running his hands down my bare sides possessively. "Like? Hmm, I think you more than *like* me, Hellcat." His eyes were pure mischief. "I just have to work harder to shake loose that mental filter."

I bit my lip, not disagreeing. Also, I really wanted to see what he considered *working harder*.

As Steele reached over to his bedside table for lube, then flipped me on my stomach, I made a mental note to thank Scott. If not for him, who knew when I'd have had this opportunity to *reconnect* with Steele.

And he was right. I did *more than like* him. But the trust wasn't fully rebuilt yet. We were getting there, though. Every day it was getting easier, and every interaction showed he was one hundred percent on my team.

No matter what.

CHAPTER 38

Archer's charity fight was on Saturday night, but the rest of the week disappeared quickly with the amount of training Kody put him through. The two of them left early Saturday morning to drive to the venue for weigh-in and press shit, so Steele and I planned to meet them at the fight.

It was a decent drive to the town where the event was being held. So, because the event was being held at a hotel, we had booked rooms for the night. I was all kinds of excited for it too.

Steele eyed my outfit with amusement as I skipped down the steps to where he waited beside his car and handed him my overnight bag.

"What?" I asked, propping my hands on my hips when he kept staring.

"That's what you're wearing?" He laughed, dragging his thumb across his lower lip like he couldn't decide if he was annoyed or turned right the hell on.

I beamed, smug as hell. "What, you don't like it?" I twirled to give him the full effect. It was a hoodie I'd actually ordered before the fight on Riot Night, but it hadn't arrived in time for me to wear it. When I'd gotten back from Cambodia, I'd found it tucked into the back of my closet and this felt like the perfect time for it.

"He's going to fucking die," Steele muttered, running his fingertip across the text emblazoned across my breasts. "Are you even wearing any pants under that?"

The hoodie had been way too big for me, reaching halfway down my thighs, so I'd made a last-minute decision to ditch the skirt I'd planned on wearing.

I shot him a wink. "Nope." Just a pair of deadly, knee-high stiletto boots, not dissimilar to the ones I'd worn on Riot Night.

"Fuck," Steele groaned, shaking his head. "All right, get in the car before I change my mind and drag you back into the house."

Leaning into him, I placed a teasing kiss on his jawline. "Archer won't mind if we're late..."

Steele barked a sharp laugh. "Are you kidding? He'll probably break my damn face if his good-luck charm isn't there in plenty of time. What's the threat if he loses, anyway?"

I smirked, sliding into my seat as he stepped aside, then waited until he came around the hood and took his own place behind the steering wheel.

"What makes you think there's a threat? You know I took sex off the table until he won." I gave Steele my best innocent eyes, but I wasn't fooling him for even a second.

He shot me a *bullshit* look. "He could have talked his way around that. There must be a threat on the line if he loses too."

My grin spread wider, and I repeated the *consequence* of Archer losing this fight, verbatim. Steele's brows shot up, and he cast an interested look at me as we passed through the front gates. He gave a quick wave to the evening security guard—Dave—then turned out into the street.

"Well shit, Hellcat," he muttered after a moment of silence. "Now I want Archer to lose."

I gave him a casual shrug. "No reason we can't do both."

He drew a deep breath, his nostrils flaring and his chest rising. "Shit yes," he breathed on his exhale. "One of the many things I love about you, Hellcat. You think outside the box of societal norm."

His compliment warmed me. For the next while we just drove in companionable silence while the stereo played an epic selection of In This Moment, Amatory Riot, Seventeen Daggers, Aviva, and Indecency.

"Killer playlist," I murmured to him as one of my favorite songs came on, and I cranked the volume.

About half an hour into our drive, my phone started ringing. I fished it out of my bag, then sighed heavily as I saw the caller ID.

"Scott again?" Steele asked, guessing correctly. "He really doesn't give up, does he?"

I grimaced, rejecting the call. I'd lost track of how many calls I'd rejected from him now. "Apparently not." My phone immediately lit up with another incoming call from Scott. "Maybe I should just answer and let him say whatever he needs to say."

Steele shrugged. "If you want. But put him on speakerphone so I'll know if he insults you again."

I licked my lips with a grin. "And then what?"

He shot me a deadly serious look. "And then I'll break one of his bones for every word of that insult."

I swiped my thumb across the screen of my phone. "Scott," I said, switching the call to speaker. "Didn't I make myself clear the other day at school? I don't want you calling."

"Maddie, thank god! I thought something had happened. Did they hurt you?" Scott's voice was panicked and a bit nasal, like maybe his nose was blocked. Or broken.

I frowned, shooting Steele a confused look. He just shrugged back at me, as confused as I was.

"What? Did *who* hurt me?"

"Those fucking bastards who think they control you," Scott

spat, enraged. "Do you know where I am right now? Do you know what they did to me?"

I rolled my eyes at his theatrics. He did seem to lean pretty hard on the drama of any situation.

"I'm in the *hospital*, Maddie," he answered his own question, not waiting for me to respond. "They broke my wrist, my nose, four ribs, and gave me a concussion. I look like I've been run over by a car!"

I wrinkled my nose, rubbing at the bridge and trying to give Scott the shocked reaction he was hoping for.

"Well, it sounds like you learned not to call anyone a desperate slut again, huh?" *Whoops, that wasn't supposed to come out my mouth. Oh well, too late now.*

A strangled sound came down the phone, and I got the impression that wasn't quite the level of sympathy Scott had been fishing for.

I sighed. "Look, Scott—"

"They're changing you, Maddie. This cold, bitchy attitude isn't you; it's *them*." His voice was filled with venom and loathing, and it hurt my brain just listening to him. As if I didn't have enough drama in my life without Scott whining about what I'm sure was a minor ass-kicking.

"Okay, sure," I agreed, not really giving a shit about his opinion. We simply weren't good enough friends for his words to hit home with any weight. "Actually, Scott, I have something I want to ask you."

"What?" he snapped back, apparently irate at my lack of fucks given.

"Did you steal all my underwear and leave a creepy message in the bottom of my drawer last week?" I met Steele's eyes as I asked this and didn't even tense up when he took way too long to return his gaze to the road. Maybe the guys were slowly curing my fear of car crashes. Slowly.

There was a pause on the line, long enough to make me

suspicious as all hell. More so than I'd already been after hearing about the partial fingerprint.

"What?" Scott finally responded, sounding...weird. "What? No, no way. Of course I wouldn't...I wouldn't do that, Maddie. That's next-level creepy. Who would even do that? What did the message say?"

I needed to swallow past a lump of dread and anxiety to answer him. "Forget it. We're about to drive through a tunnel, though, so the phone might cut out."

"Maddie, babe, tell me what's going on. I'm really worried about you..." Scott paused, then his voice hardened. "Did *they* accuse me of doing that? You can't seriously believe them! This is totally jealous, possessive behavior, babe. They can't handle you being friends with any straight guys, so they're eliminating the competition. Maddie, you know I—"

I ended the call, cutting his bullshit off midsentence.

Steele glanced at me as he slowed down and pulled over to the shoulder before stopping the car completely. We were way out of town on an open stretch of road with no one around for miles, and certainly no tunnels to interrupt reception.

Fuck it. Whatever.

"Are you okay?" Steele asked me in all seriousness.

I bit the inside of my lip, thinking. Was I okay? Scott hadn't exactly admitted to being involved with my stalker, but he sure as shit didn't sound innocent.

But part of me couldn't accept that he was actually a bad guy. It was the same part that didn't want to admit how bad my judgment had been in choosing a new friend.

"Yeah," I replied with a sigh. "Yeah, I guess I just didn't really want to believe he'd done anything...you know...creepy."

Steele grimaced. "Yeah, that boat sailed when he followed you to the shoot with Arch, then lied about using Bree's phone tracker."

I gave a bitter laugh. "Fair point. Can we just forget about Scott for tonight? We can deal with all of that when we get back tomorrow." I paused, giving him a suspicious look. "Although it sounds like someone already started dealing with it, hmm?"

Steele's eyes widened, and he held his hands up defensively. "Not me."

I squinted at him, not believing his innocent act for a second. Maybe he hadn't physically dealt any blows to Scott for what he'd said to me, but Steele was fully aware that it'd happened.

With an easy grin, he shifted the car back into gear and we glided back out into the road. "But if it'd been me—not that it was—but *if* it had been, I'd be teaching him a lesson about grabbing my girl's arm so hard she had bruises the next day. *As well* as teaching him some respect for women." He shot me a wink. "Hypothetically speaking."

Heaving another sigh, I turned my face to look out the window, letting my long, pink curls fall over my cheek. I shouldn't be encouraging that kind of Neanderthal behavior, but I'd be lying if I said it didn't make me all warm and fuzzy inside. The fact that they cared enough...

It was a new thing for me. But I loved it.

––––––––––

The crowd was in full party mode when Steele and I arrived at the event center. Tickets to see the fight were just shy of two hundred and fifty bucks a head, but the money was being donated to a prominent women's shelter in our area.

"Kind of on the nose to raise money for battered women by, you know, beating the shit out of another dude, isn't it?" I asked Steele quietly as we made our way through the well-heeled crowd. Tuxedos and cocktail dresses seemed to be the attire for the night, meaning we were woefully underdressed. Not that either of us really cared. We weren't guests; we were support crew.

Steele snagged two glasses of champagne from a passing waiter and handed me one. "Actually, Arch has been stepping up in his support of this charity lately, teaching people there is a huge difference between training in MMA to hone his skills in a highly disciplined sport…and spineless fucks who bash their women because they lack the balls to deal with their problems the right way." He tipped his glass up, drinking half of it in one sip. "Come on, let's go poke the angry bear and get him all worked up. I've got my money on a knockout in round one."

I grinned, taking a sip of my own champagne, and followed him through the crowd. "Nah, my bets are for a ground and pound TKO," I replied, already buzzing with excitement to see the fight. "Arch has a whole load of frustration to get out; a clean knockout is way too easy."

Steele laughed, his smile easy and his posture relaxed as he linked our fingers together. "You're just bloodthirsty, Hellcat. It's such a turn-on."

I couldn't even disagree with that. We made our way through the main hall and past the cage where the fighters would meet in just under twenty minutes. Steele led me through a service door, nodding to the security guard stationed there, then led me down a corridor bustling with waiters and other hotel staff.

The makeshift locker room they'd assigned Archer was really just a meeting room set up with a handful of chairs and a folding trestle table holding several bottles of water. Kody leaned against a wall, his arms folded over his chest as he gave Archer a pep talk. Archer himself was jogging in place and shadowboxing, warming up his muscles.

When the door closed behind Steele and me, though, their eyes locked on me, and Archer's brows raised.

"Fuck," he breathed, his eyes raking over my outfit. "Where the hell did you get that?"

I beamed, pleased at the reaction I'd gotten. "Oh, this old thing?" I smoothed my hands down the front of my pristine white hoodie dress. "I've had it for ages, just never found the right time to wear it."

Archer prowled closer, his eyes pure predator. "That design was canceled after Riot Night, Princess. You wanna tell me you were a fangirl before you knew who I was?" His smile was half disbelief, half smug satisfaction.

I shrugged. "What can I say? I sure as fuck wasn't at The Laughing Clown for the other guy."

He shook his head, his hands clasping my waist as he pushed me into the wall. "Kody, bro, have you got that marker pen?"

Archer reached his hand out, and Kody handed over a chunky black pen from his back pocket. With one hand pinning my chest against the wall, he made an amendment to my limited-edition, fangirl hoodie.

When he was done, he eyed his handiwork with total satisfaction and capped the pen once more.

"Much better," he commented, then grabbed the back of my head and tilted my face up for a bruising kiss.

"Caveman," I muttered when he released me, but he just brushed his thumb across my swollen lower lip and winked with a promise of *later*.

I sighed, peering down at my hoodie when Archer turned back to Kody. The black text across my chest had previously just read THE ARCHER, and on the back was a Sagittarius constellation, like a watered-down version of the intricate tattoo on Archer's back. Now, though? My chest read THE ARCHER'S GIRL. BACK OFF.

The bastard himself met my eye across the room as Kody finished taping his hands and scribbled a signature across the inner wrists with his marker.

"You ready to win, bro?" Kody asked as Archer flipped his hood up and took a quick sip from his water bottle.

Archer paused a moment before he replied, running his gaze over me and staring at his handwriting on my breasts.

"Now I am."

CHAPTER 39

The crowd was in a frenzy of excitement by the time the four of us—plus Jase, the slimy fuck—made our way back through to the main event space. The celebrity commentator was having a grand old time in the cage with his announcements, really channeling his inner Bruce Buffer.

We paid little attention to him, though, making our way across to the side of the cage where the referee and an official did their mandatory safety checks, making sure Archer's mouthguard was in and that his gloves had been properly secured and signed.

Steele slipped away to the side, taking one of the seats that were reserved for us, and I started to follow him, only to be yanked backward by a gloved hand on the back of my neck.

Archer tugged his mouthguard out; then his lips crushed to mine, his tongue sweeping inside in a harsh, possessive, demanding kiss. When he released me, our foreheads pressed together for a second and his gaze drilled into me with scorching heat.

"Better hydrate, baby girl. It's gonna be a long night after I win this shit." With a confident wink, he replaced his mouthguard, then shed his hoodie, tossed it to Kody, and entered the fight cage.

Touching my fingers to my swollen lips, I breathed a heavy sigh and retreated to the seat beside Steele. Ecstatic butterflies flapped around inside me like they were tripping on acid, and my heart was in my throat. I wanted Archer to win—of course I did—but I was also looking forward to seeing a good fight. Here was hoping his opponent didn't totally suck.

The way Archer greeted the other guy in the cage, it seemed like they knew each other to some degree. Maybe just through the fight scene?

"Have they fought each other before?" I asked Steele, my eyes on the other guy, searching and assessing his physique. He was leaner than Archer, more like Kody's body type, but his muscles rippled under tanned skin. He didn't have a whole lot of ink, just one huge piece depicting a howling wolf on his side that wrapped from his back all the way around to his abs.

"Nah," Steele answered, "but they've met. Alexi is a Timberwolf, in case the ink didn't give that away."

I nodded slowly, considering this information. "I'd thought they no longer existed after…you know." *After you three wiped out their entire gang in just one bloody night.* "But they're not at all, are they?"

Steele gave me a knowing smile. "They restructured and now stay out of the public eye. The new management is *very* good at maintaining a professional front to their operation, but no. They're nowhere near as extinct as people like to think they are."

I bit at my lip, worrying that this was yet another player on the board for us to keep an eye on.

"We're on good terms with them, Hellcat. No need to look so concerned." He reached out and wove our fingers together. "Trust me on this, the Timberwolves are much more likely to come to our aid than attack. You don't need to stress on that front."

The fighters tapped gloves in the center of the cage, and then it was on.

"I'll trust you on that one," I muttered to Steele, my eyes glued on the fight. "I don't need to go borrowing extra anxiety."

"Fifty bucks says this is over before the end of round one," he told me, changing the subject to the fight in front of us. Archer certainly seemed to have the upper hand so far, landing his few test kicks and blocking the strikes Alexi threw back. But I had a feeling the Timberwolf was just biding his time.

"I'll take that bet," I replied, feeling sure. "Round three, ground and pound."

Steele barked a laugh. "You just wanna see more violence, you bloodthirsty woman. But alright, you're on."

The first round flew by, both fighters delivering and receiving some solid hits but neither of them making any power moves to try to end it. By the time the bell rang, Steele was groaning.

"They're just fucking playing with each other," he complained, throwing his hands up in exasperation.

I snickered a knowing laugh. "Yeah, no shit. All these people paid a bucket of money to see a fight. They'd be pissed as hell if it was all over in round one."

He grumbled curses, but he knew I was right. A short distance from us, Archer sat on his little stool, taking a casual sip of his water and barely even looking winded as Kody talked at top speed in his face.

Almost like he knew I was watching, Archer turned his head and met my eyes. He jerked his head, indicating he wanted me to come over, so I let go of Steele's hand to stand up.

My walk across that short gap to the cage held way more swagger than it needed to, but the way Archer's eyes darkened made it well worth the effort.

"Princess," he growled when I reached the outside of the ring, "you're a fucking tease."

"And?" I gave him a deadpan stare through the wire fence, and he just sighed.

"What's the bet, babe?" Kody asked me with a knowing grin. "Steele looks like he already lost."

I nodded. "He has. He bet me the fight would be over in round one."

"You want me to drag it out, huh?" Archer asked, swiping a gloved hand through his hair, which was barely even damp from perspiration.

"Like you weren't going to anyway," I scoffed. "But yeah, a round three ground and pound would be great. Sort it out, Sunshine."

He tossed his head back, giving a sharp laugh, then shaking his head. "Apparently I can't refuse you much of anything these days, Wifey," he muttered, almost sounding like he was in disbelief at himself. "You've got it."

He stood up as the referee called out to him, indicating the break was over, and Kody slapped him on the back encouragingly. Both trainers left the cage, taking the chairs, water bottles, and towels with them, and then the fight was back on for round two.

Before I could return to my seat with Steele, Kody snaked an arm around my waist and pulled me in front of him, my back to his front as we stood right beside the cage.

"Stay here with me, babe," he murmured in my ear. "I feel like I've barely seen you this week."

I smiled at his words. "You've been busy training Archer's stubborn ass. Besides, shouldn't you be yelling encouragement and shit at him right now? Getting him fired up?"

Kody swept my hair over one shoulder and dropped his lips to the bare side. "What do you think I'm doing right now?" His arm around my waist drifted lower, finding my bare thigh, then creeping up underneath the long hoodie I wore.

"Kodiak Jones, we're in *full* view right now," I scolded him but made no move to swat his hand away.

He chuckled against my neck, kissing the sensitive spot behind my ear. "Nah, we're not. This area is badly lit. The only people who can clearly see are in the cage right now, and *they* should be otherwise occupied." His hand slipped higher, finding my already aching core. The fabric of my hoodie was long enough to hide the graphic details, but if anyone was looking, it'd be pretty obvious where his hand was.

"MK, babe," he groaned, his fingers stroking over my bare flesh, "Steele's becoming a bad influence on you."

"Or a great one," I replied with a hitch in my voice as he slipped a finger into my cunt. "Matter of perspective, right?"

Inside the cage, Archer took a solid right hook to the face, knocking him back a couple of steps before he found his balance again.

Kody snickered an evil sound. "That'll teach him to pay attention to the fight." A second finger joined the first, and I couldn't stop myself from grinding into his hand.

"We're going to be seen." I murmured my weak protest even as my pussy clenched around his fingers and my clit throbbed.

"That was the idea," he replied. "I might have made my own bet with Steele for a round two submission. Arch just needed a little push to end the fight as fast as possible."

An outraged noise squeaked out of me, and I shoved away from his grip with *monumental* effort. "Playing dirty, Kodiak Jones?"

He just grinned, raising his fingers to his mouth and sucking them. "Always, babe."

Oh, come on!

My pussy clenched hard, my eyes locked on his fingers in his mouth and my nipples hard as goddamn rocks. I wasn't strong enough for this kind of sexual warfare. What the shit had I been thinking, getting involved with all three of these pricks?

"I figure Archer has this handled without his trainer yelling from the sidelines," Kody continued, reaching out a hand to me once more and reeling me in like a fish on his hook. When I didn't resist, he cupped the back of my head, bringing my lips to his for a passionate kiss that instantly made me regret my choice to forgo

317

underwear. My thighs were slick by the time he released me, and it took a second to realize the crowd was going nuts.

With a gasp, I spun around to find Archer pinning Alexi in a rear naked choke, his eyes hard on Kody and me.

My shock quickly shifted to annoyance, and my glare hardened at him as I held three fingers up. I wasn't losing fifty bucks over Kody's dirty tricks. Hell no.

Archer knew exactly what I meant too. He glared back at me; then a second before Alexi probably would have tapped out, Archer loosened his grip and surged back to his feet in a defensive pose.

"Dammit," Kody hissed in my ear, his arms wrapping around my waist once more. "So close."

"Fucker," I grumbled but still leaned back into his solid body.

He gave a soft laugh. "So does that mean you won't meet me in the bathroom for a quick fuck while Arch does his victory shit?"

I bit my lip, trying to fight the lovesick grin that *constantly* wanted to sit on my face. "Shouldn't you do that stuff with him? You *are* his trainer."

"Nah," he replied, "it's a charity fight. No one cares about the trainers."

I gave a one-shoulder shrug. "Well then…" I paused for dramatic effect, making him sweat it out as Archer delivered a vicious elbow to Alexi's face. "I guess if we're *quick*…"

That was all Kody needed to hear. The bell chimed for the end of the round, but he wasn't even sticking around to do his one minute of coaching before round three. He just grabbed my hand, tossed Archer's water bottle and towel to Steele, and dragged me through the crowd so fast I needed to run a little to keep up.

He slammed the door to the ladies' room open, startling the middle-aged woman washing her hands and making her shriek.

"Out," he ordered her, his tone totally uncompromising. The woman was shocked enough she did exactly that, leaving us alone in the lavish hotel restroom. Instantly Kody's mouth was on mine, his hands tight around my waist as he lifted me onto the edge of the vanity.

"You have no idea how badly I've missed you this week, babe," he muttered with frustration as he shoved the hem of my hoodie up and yanked my knees wide. "I've never had to jerk off so many times in my goddamn life."

I grinned against his lips, quietly pleased at that idea. It'd only been two weeks since we'd reconciled, but two weeks felt like an eternity now that his hands were finally on me again.

"Five minutes, Kody," I reminded him, tugging at his belt and pushing his pants down just far enough to free his huge erection. "Make me come."

He pulled back just long enough to line himself up with my soaked core, then gave me an arrogant smirk. "Yes, ma'am."

It took a couple of hard thrusts to get his thick cock fully inside me, and there was no time to mess about, taking it easy. The second he was fully seated, he started moving and I held on for dear life.

Kody's fingers gripped my ass, holding me tight as he fucked me senseless, the mirror behind me rattling with every thrust and the sound of our ragged breathing and moans echoing around the restroom. My pussy was tight around him, on the brink of an orgasm just from the illicit nature of a public fuck. Anyone could walk through the door and catch us, but that just made it so much more exciting.

"Babe," Kody hissed as my hips rolled against him. His cock struck me at a new angle, and a strangled groan escaped my throat. "Holy shit."

One of his hands left my ass, coming up to grab the back of my head and bring my lips to his for another bruising kiss. I toyed with him, my tongue meeting his in a clash of power. My teeth grabbed his lower lip, biting just a touch harder than playful, and he growled.

In response, the hand on the back of my neck shifted to my throat, and he squeezed.

I came. Hard. But he didn't let up until he was done as well, pumping himself into me with several hard thrusts. Only then did he release my throat, and I sucked in a deep lungful of air.

These boys were seriously bringing out my kinky side, and I was one hundred percent on board.

Kody kissed me again, his tongue as harsh and demanding as his cock had just been, then pressed his forehead to mine and locked those gorgeous green eyes on me.

"Seriously, babe," he whispered, his voice rough and his dick still twitching inside me like it was already eager for round two. "I love you so much it hurts. I've never felt like this for anyone before, but I'll happily murder any bastard who tries to tear us apart."

He kissed me again, saving me the pressure of a response, then lifted me off the vanity. I snatched a couple of tissues to wipe up the worst of the mess between my legs, but I already knew that wasn't going to cut it if I'd be standing for any length of time.

"Give me a minute to clean up properly," I told him. "I don't have any panties, remember?"

Kody just gave me a hungry, possessive grin. "Good. Come on, we went over our time."

He gave me no time to argue, taking my hand and tugging me back out of the restroom with him. We dove straight back into the crowd, making our way back to our seats right as Archer and Alexi were clasping hands in the center of the cage while the Bruce Buffer wannabe was rattling off his closing announcements.

"I hate you," Steele told Kody as we reached him, his eyes running over my undoubtedly disheveled hair and swollen lips. Jase was lurking a few feet away with pure venom on his face as he glared at me.

Kody just gave a cocky grin back, flipping Steele off as he

leapt up into the cage to take his place by his fighter's side. Archer's eyes blazed at me; then he delivered a subtle, but *vicious*, elbow to Kody's stomach.

Their infighting should have worried me. It should have stressed me out that, at some point, they'd either make me choose or they'd kill each other. But it didn't.

I loved the violence, and I was done pretending otherwise.

CHAPTER 40

Our accommodations for the night were booked in the same hotel where the fight had been held, so there was no real discussion around whether to stay for the party or not.

Not.

Archer didn't even bother showering or changing in the rooms they'd set up for him and Alexi to use. He just removed his gloves, threw his hoodie and shoes on, then all but carried me to the central elevators.

Kody and Steele followed, both joking and laughing, riding the high of Archer's win. I couldn't focus on anything for long, though. I was too keyed up with anticipation, waiting to see what he wanted to do with that win. With me.

"Hey, guys," Jase called out as we stepped into the elevators, darting forward and stopping the doors from closing with his hand. "We partying upstairs, or..." He trailed off, and it became awkward as fuck when no one immediately responded.

Archer cleared his throat, his arm tight around me. "Sorry, man. Private celebration tonight."

Jase's smile slipped, and his face flashed with anger. "But I'm your manager." The glare he shot me said the rest. *I'm your manager, but* she *is invited over me?*

"Yep," Archer responded, clearly not giving a fuck. "Enjoy the party." He reached out and peeled Jase's fingers from the elevator door. Their manager stood in stunned disbelief long enough for the doors to slide closed, and I let out a small sigh of relief. Jase creeped me out. Big-time.

Steele had taken care of the booking, so when we reached our floor, he directed us all the way to the presidential suite and opened the doors with a magnetic key card.

"Nice," Kody commented, striding in and picking up a bottle of champagne from an ice bucket set up on the dining table. "Looks like we're celebrating tonight, huh?"

"Screw you," Archer growled, snatching the bottle from his hand and sinking down onto one of the white leather couches. His hand was still clasping mine, and he gave me a tug, pulling me into his lap as he popped the cork one-handed. Seriously, that was an impressive skill.

Kody wasn't deterred, grabbing a second bottle and taking the sofa opposite us while Steele made his way over to the floor-to-ceiling windows, which were covered by a thin blind.

"Don't be a hater, Arch. We all knew you'd steal MK away if you won; I was just being resourceful." Kody grinned, smug as fuck, and I needed to bite my lip to stop from grinning back.

Archer's arm around my waist tightened, and he took a sip of champagne straight from the bottle.

"True," he conceded. "But later. First…" He trailed off, pressing his cool, wet lips to the back of my neck and making me shiver. "We have something to show you, Princess."

My brows shot up, and I took the bottle of champagne from Archer's fingers when he offered it to me. "You do?"

Kody nodded his agreement, opening his bottle and pouring glasses for all of us. I still sipped from Archer's bottle anyway, though.

Steele pressed a little button on the side of the windows, and the blind *slowly* rose up to reveal an impressive view of the city below.

"This would have been more dramatic if the blinds weren't so slow," Steele commented, tapping his foot impatiently.

I glanced between Archer and Kody, seeking some kind of hint, but neither of them was giving anything away. They were both focused on *me*, not on the window, though.

"Finally," Steele muttered as the blind rose past the halfway mark.

He stepped aside, and I instantly spotted what they wanted to show me. My jaw dropped, and I rose out of Archer's lap in stunned disbelief.

"Are you kidding me?" I halfway shrieked. "That's…"

"So freaking sexy," Kody finished for me when my voice dried up into nothing.

I crossed over to the window, staring out at the electronic billboard on the building directly across the intersection. It was me. *Giant* me. In nothing but a skimpy black corset, thong, and heels, leaning on a bar and looking every inch the sex kitten. Beside me was a bottle of vodka that I didn't remember being there in the photo shoot.

The image pixelated out, only to be replaced by an even sexier one of both Archer and me. I was in his lap, our eyes locked and our lips just a fraction away from a kiss. On the table in front of us was that same vodka and a martini.

"Guys…" I shook my head, unable to look away from the billboard as it changed again. This time it was a shot of me lying on the bar top, my back arched and every curve of my body accentuated, and Archer's hungry, desperate eyes on my face. "Someone please explain?"

"Remember I told you the photo shoot was a favor to a friend?" Archer asked, still reclining on the couch like a king on his throne. The bottle of champagne was back in his hand, and he held it loosely. "Well, she shifted the concept of the bar away from sexy burlesque and more to sinful strippers. But she loved our images so much she decided to use them on a launch campaign for her own line of vodka." He paused, seeming uncertain for the first time. "Do you like them?"

I blinked at him several times, at a loss for words. Turning back around to the window, I watched the rotation of images again. There were five in total. One had Archer more prominent and me in the background; then there was the one of me alone and three of us together. In every one, we looked like the living embodiment of sex and desire. It was a goddamn mystery how we'd held out five months before giving in to that insane chemistry between us.

"I love them," I whispered, letting my truth come out. "But this seems like a really risky move, all things considered. Where else has this ad been shown?" I turned back around to face my guys, a worried frown creasing my brow.

"It's a global campaign," Archer replied, not sounding even a fraction as concerned as I was.

My eyes widened. Global. Fucking hell.

"Babe, you can't put your life on hold because of some mentally unstable, serial-killing fucker. He thrives off your fear, and by hiding away, you'd be letting him win." Kody was practical, his tone calm, but he had to know I was a bit pissed off.

"You should have asked me first," I replied, catching all three of them with my accusing glare. "You said it was advertising for a new bar in Shadow Grove, not...*this*. You should have consulted me."

"Why?" Archer demanded, his own jaw flexing with annoyance. "So you could let your fear rule the decision and hand your stalker another win?"

My temper flared. Guess who wasn't getting his dick wet after all?

"Fuck you, D'Ath," I snapped back. "This was a huge step to take without giving me a heads-up!" I indicated to the *huge* rolling billboard of us. "Don't act like this was out of your control either. We both know they would have checked with you first."

Steele shifted into my line of sight, his expression apologetic. "Hellcat, we never wanted to take the control away from you. This was a last-minute thing, and we thought it would be an awesome surprise for you. Something special, you know? It wasn't supposed to start fights."

I squeezed my eyes shut, mentally counting to five to try to get a lid on my anger. It was a hard pill to swallow that this was a simple misjudgment, not a targeted attempt to raise my blood pressure.

Then again, that'd be really fucking stupid if they had been trying to piss me off. Even as dick drunk as the three of them had me, I was more than capable of servicing myself and icing them out indefinitely.

"How long ago did the campaign launch?" I asked, trying to keep my anger in check. It wasn't their fault; they just hadn't been fucking thinking.

Or hell, maybe they had. They'd weighed the risks and decided it was worth it to try to surprise me. Which…yeah, it was kind of sweet they wanted to do something like that.

"About two hours ago," Steele replied. He snagged two of the glasses of bubbles from the table where Kody had poured them and handed me one. "What can we do to bring the mood of five minutes ago back?"

I squinted at him but took the wine and gulped half of it. Dutch courage for what I was about to suggest. My lips suddenly felt dry, so I licked them nervously, my eyes dancing across all three of my men. Holy shit, I'd struck the triple jackpot.

Archer seemed to catch the shift in my mood before anyone else, and his scowl deepened. "Kate, I won the fight. You're *mine* tonight, and I don't want to share."

I propped my free hand on my hip, giving him a healthy dose of sass with my answering glare. "Then you should have considered that before pissing me off, Archer. Now I'm calling the shots again, and I want—"

My declaration was cut off by a peal of sound from Archer's phone.

He didn't make any move to check it, just held my gaze, daring me to finish my sentence. But then it rang again immediately after stopping, and his brow furrowed.

"Check it," Steele said.

"No shit," Archer muttered, fishing in the pocket of his hoodie for his phone, then swiping his thumb over the screen to answer the call. He said nothing as he brought it to his ear, simply listening to whatever the other person needed to say so urgently.

Within seconds, his expression morphed to fury, and he shot out of his seat. "Switch me to video call," he snapped at whoever had called, then lowered his phone to peer at the screen. Unable to contain my curiosity, I crossed over to where he stood and looked over his arm at the video call.

Archer seemed to know exactly what he was looking at, his hand clutching the phone so hard I was amazed it didn't shatter in his grip. As it was, his whole body vibrated with fury. To me, though, it just looked like a huge bonfire.

A moment later, when whoever held the phone moved to a different location, I sucked in a gasp as I recognized the image. That was no bonfire—it was a house fire.

Our house. The one Archer and I had just spent a life-changing weekend at, fucking on every available surface. Before we'd left at the end of the weekend, he'd told me that it would forever be our sanctuary. That goddamn house meant more to me than I had even fully comprehended until that moment as I watched it burn to the ground.

"Mother*fucker!*" I screamed, throwing my champagne flute against the window and watching it rain down glittering shards of glass.

"Thank you for the call," Archer said to whoever was on the phone. "Any signs of the responsible party?"

"No, sir," the caller replied in a gruff voice. "Security feeds were looped; we only knew what had happened after being alerted by the attending fire department."

Security feeds looped, just like at the mansion, allowing my stalker to deliver gifts undetected. They were always looped or wiped or just plain angled the wrong way. How was my stalker *doing* this?

"We'll be there in just under two hours," Archer told the caller, who I guessed to be someone on his security team. "Don't let anyone leave the scene until we arrive. No one. Understood?"

"Got it, boss." The man ended the call, and Archer threw his phone down on the couch with a long exhale. Neither Kody nor Steele spoke, waiting for Archer to fill them in.

"Wisteria was set on fire," he eventually ground out, his teeth clenched hard. "Arson."

Both guys breathed curses, and I found I needed to swallow past a lump in my throat. Shit. It was just a house…right? Why was I getting so fucking upset about it?

"We need to get out there," Archer announced. "I want to personally interview anyone on the scene and check for messages. He is escalating, and sooner or later, he's going to slip up."

"And it's pretty common for arsonists to return to the scene to admire their handiwork," Steele agreed, nodding. "He could well be hiding in plain sight somewhere."

Kody stood up from the couch, all business. "I'll grab our bags and call the valet for the cars."

Steele was already on his phone texting someone while Kody hurried to grab our bags out of the bedrooms. I just stood there, frozen to the spot with the giant illuminated billboard of Archer and me at my back.

My mind wandered, lost in the storm of emotions caused by watching Archer's cottage, Wisteria, burn down. I only jerked free of that dark headspace when a pair of heavily tattooed, strongly muscled arms wrapped around me.

"I'm sorry, Kate," he whispered in a husky voice, pulling me tight into his chest. I looped my arms around his waist, holding on to him just as hard as he held me, soaking up the comfort in Archer's embrace.

I let out a short, bitter laugh. "I don't know why you're apologizing to me," I told him with my cheek against his chest and no desire to move. "It was your house that got burned down. First he explodes Steele's favorite car, then he sets fire to your cottage? It's becoming an expensive and dangerous activity to be close to me."

"Fuck the house," he growled back. "This prick can destroy my entire estate, and you'll still be worth it. I'm only sorry because I knew you liked that house, and the look on your face when you realized it was gone damn near broke me."

I tipped my head back, peering up at him from the tight circle of his arms. Before I could get any words out, though, Kody called out that we were ready to go.

Archer kissed me quickly but meaningfully, then linked our fingers together as we hurried out of the presidential suite again. All four of us piled into the elevator, the mood somber, until Kody—typical Kody—broke the tension with a question already on the back of my mind.

"So…" he said into the tense silence. "We're calling a rain check on tonight, right? 'Cause I have a feeling I know what MK was going to suggest and—" Archer whacked him around the head. "Ow, dude. Not cool."

I met Kody's eyes with a mischievous smile, though, and mouthed my answer at him.

Rain check.

CHAPTER 41

The drive back to Shadow Grove was tense and silent. I took the passenger seat of Archer's car, wanting to stay close to him, seeing as this attack was aimed at the two of us. He drove fast, way faster than I'd have normally been okay with. But the steady weight of his hand on my leg the whole way kept me grounded.

Steele and Kody in the other car kept pace with us the whole way, pulling into the crowded driveway of Wisteria just seconds after us.

The four of us climbed out, and Archer took the lead as a rough-looking, middle-aged guy with tattoos covering his throat approached us. They greeted each other like they were already acquainted, and I guessed this was the man from the video call.

I tuned them out, though, staring instead at the charred, smoking remains of the beautiful cottage. It'd been devastating to see it in flames on the video call, but seeing it in person as little more than a pile of ash and burned out framework? Utterly heartbreaking.

Warm arms wrapped around me from behind, and I leaned back into Kody's solid form, soaking up his comforting presence.

"Are you okay, babe?" he murmured, kissing my cheek gently.

I heaved a sigh, nodding despite the sadness filling me. "Yeah, fine. It's just such a senseless act of destruction. We need to deal with this fucker sooner rather than later."

Kody rested his chin on my shoulder, staring at the mess with me as a fire crew doused the remains with water from their hoses.

"Maybe it was just a coincidence," he offered. "Faulty wiring or something."

"Unlikely," Steele replied, coming to stand beside us. "The first responders found several gas cans."

Neither Kody nor I had anything to say to that. What could we say? It was pretty obvious what had happened. My stalker had seen that *global* campaign for Copper Wolf Vodka and burned our love nest down in retaliation. The question that scared me the most, though, was how he even found out about the cottage.

"How long do we need to be here?" I asked, feeling way too exposed all of a sudden—like I could feel a thousand eyes on me, watching my every move.

Archer and the tattooed guy were farther away from us, talking to a uniformed firefighter and a police officer. From what I could see, there were just two firetrucks and approximately eight firefighters. Just one cop car sat behind the trucks, and only one other officer aside from the guy speaking to Archer.

"Not long," Kody assured me, his arms tightening around my waist. "Arch just wants to personally speak to all the attending parties. Maybe one of their faces will be familiar and give us a clue."

"Makes sense," I replied in a murmur. Still, I wanted nothing more than to go *home*.

"Come on, let's go wait in the car," Steele suggested. "Arch can handle this, but I think it's better if we all stick together right now."

I nodded, totally agreeing with that sentiment. Strength in numbers and all that. The three of us headed over to Steele's car— seeing as Archer's only had two seats—and I climbed into the backseat. Archer called out to Kody for something before he could join me, so I found myself in Steele's embrace instead.

For a long time, we just sat there in silence while the colorful glow of the fire engine lights danced across the interior of Steele's car. Kody joined us some time later, sliding into the backseat on my other side and seriously testing the limits of space. The car hadn't been designed to fit two people in the back, let alone three, which was probably how I ended up in Kody's lap with my legs tucked up on Steele's lap.

It was comforting, being so close to them both, but I wouldn't feel totally secure until Archer was back with us too. It was incredible to think that a little over a week ago, I'd have cheerfully run that bastard over with a backhoe and now he was utterly vital to my completed feeling of safety and comfort.

Steele's fingers trailed soft patterns on my bare legs, Kody stroked my hair as I laid my head on his chest, and if we'd been there much longer, I could have happily fallen asleep just like that. But a moment later, Archer tapped on the window, then popped the door on Steele's side open.

"We're done here," he announced. "For tonight at least." He reached a hand out to me, and I took it without questioning, letting him pull me out of the backseat and onto my feet. "Let's get home. We can deal with the insurance paperwork on Monday."

He opened the passenger door of his Stingray for me, and a few moments later, we were back on the road with Steele's car following close behind us.

"Did you find anything useful?" I asked when Archer made no signs of offering up information.

He just shook his head.

"Damn," I whispered on a heavy sigh.

"You should know," he replied, sounding reluctant, "I have a guy looking into Scott. None of us trust him, and there are too many red flags to dismiss him as your stalker."

I pursed my lips, thinking that over, and found I didn't disagree.

"What about his age?" I pondered aloud. "He's too young to have stalked my mom. It doesn't match up."

Archer just shrugged. "He could easily be a copycat stalker. Perhaps he found some old documentation of Deb's stalking and developed a fixation from there. It happens more than you'd realize."

I rubbed at my gritty eyes, feeling the weight of the past few months resting on my shoulders like a lead blanket. "I guess."

"We're not trying to cast suspicion on him because we're jealous bastards," he told me carefully, then grinned when I shot him a suspicious look. "Okay, we are jealous bastards, but that's not the reason we're looking into Scott. He's simply the most likely suspect right now. And I would happily eliminate every suspect rather than leave the guilty party walking free."

I got the impression that he meant *eliminate* as in *kill*, not simply eliminate from our search. Somehow, I was okay with that.

After some time, Archer broke the silence again.

"I want you to train with Kody," he announced, flashing me a quick look. "For real."

I studied the side of his face a moment, the tightness to his jaw and the tension around his eyes. This wasn't a casual suggestion he was making, and he was prepared to fight me over it.

"Okay," I agreed, getting a surge of satisfaction when his face flickered with confusion. "But he's training *you*. And his other clients. I don't think he really has a bunch of spare time for me as well."

The look Archer gave me was just short of an eye roll. "Kody would happily cancel his entire client list—me included—to train you, and you know it. Besides, he's almost finished all the necessary credits to graduate SGU, so he can free up his schedule pretty soon."

I smiled to myself, knowing he was right. "All right then."

Archer's eyes narrowed with suspicion, even as he still watched the road. "You're making this really easy, Princess. Are you feeling okay?"

A chuckle escaped me at his comment. "Jesus, Sunshine, we

don't have to fight about *everything*. Sometimes—rarely—but sometimes I actually think you've got a good point."

He frowned. "Yeah. But fighting with you is one of my favorite parts of the day."

Now I really laughed. Then shrugged. "Okay, well, how about this. I'll agree to train with Kody because I think it's a smart move to be able to defend myself confidently." I paused, thinking. "And you're a lousy lay. I can get myself off ten times faster with a vibrator."

My seat belt jerked me back into my seat as he slammed the brakes on his car and turned the wheel to stop us on the shoulder.

"What did you just say?" he demanded, his voice edged with outrage.

I smirked. "You heard me. You're a shitty fuck."

Steele's car glided to a stop beside us, Kody's window rolling down so they could probably ask us what was going on. Archer shot me a warning glare, then rolled his own window down.

"Carry on," he snapped. "We'll catch up."

That was all the explanation he gave before sending his window back up. Steele didn't stick around to ask questions, accelerating away at the same time as Archer reached over and unbuckled my seat belt.

"What do you think you're doing, D'Ath?" I teased, like I seriously didn't know. Hah. Men were so predictable.

He gripped my waist, lifting me out of my seat and depositing me across his lap in the blink of an eye. Pays to be stupidly strong in situations like this one, that was for sure.

"You threw down a challenge, baby girl," he growled, tugging his shorts down and revealing his hard cock. "This is one argument you're not winning." He lined himself up and thrust inside me with one rough motion, making me moan like a damn succubus.

My fingernails dug viciously into the sides of his neck, giving as good as I got, but goddamn…this was the kind of argument I was happy to repeat. He gripped my hips, pushing my white *Archer's Girl* hoodie up as he forcefully coaxed me into riding his cock. Like I really needed the encouragement.

Bracing my feet against anything that would give me leverage, I bounced in his lap, fucking him like I would a sex toy, taking complete control of the pace. It didn't last long, though, before his fingers flexed on my ass and his hips bucked up to meet me. Typical fucking Archer. Couldn't resist dominating from the bottom.

Not that he'd get any complaints from me; I loved the way he took control.

His thumb slid down my front, finding my clit as he fucked me. Within moments, I was coming *way* harder than I ever managed to achieve with my battery-operated boyfriends. Yeah, I was a dirty liar, but that suited the company I was keeping.

Archer joined me before I was even finished climaxing, his lips finding mine as he came, kissing me like I was his entire goddamn universe.

"Fuck, I love your smart mouth, Kate," he muttered when our kiss ended. My hands were cupping his face, my fingertips threaded into the hair behind his ears, so our gazes were locked together intensely.

I gave him a small smirk. "Well then, I'll make more of an effort to piss you off if you promise it'll end like this every time."

His gaze flattened into a glare. "Next time you pull some bullshit like that, you'll come away with my handprints all over your ass."

I clicked my tongue mockingly. "Promises, promises, Sunshine."

Narrowing his eyes farther, he rolled his hips, making me gasp. He was still inside me, yet somehow he was already hard again. Was that even humanly possible? Fuck it, who cared? Archer could be a damn alien for all I cared, so long as he made me come again before we returned home.

This time when our lips met and our bodies started moving

together once more, it was slower, less rough and demanding and more…*tender*. It was scary close to lovemaking—in our book—and shockingly, I was okay with that.

Because deep down and buried under piles and piles of emotional baggage, I knew I was falling in love. Three times over.

By the time we made it home, Kody and Steele were already waiting for us in the kitchen. They were both perched on barstools with crystal tumblers of scotch in front of them. And a slim, gift-wrapped box.

Goddammit.

"You two took your time," Kody teased as we entered the kitchen. As if my ruffled hair and rosy lips didn't give it away enough, Archer also held my hand in a death grip, our fingers interlinked.

"Had to sort out a disagreement," Archer replied, casual as all hell. "That from our friend?" He nodded at the gift box, and Kody grimaced.

"Yup."

"What's in it?" I asked, my heart in my throat and shivers chasing across my skin.

Steele shrugged. "We haven't opened it. Thought it was better to wait for you two first." He slid off his stool and grabbed two extra tumblers from the glassware cabinet, then poured the same scotch for Archer and me.

"Thanks," I murmured, taking the offered drink, aware I'd need it no matter what was in the box. Shit's sake. Being stalked and almost killed all the time was going to turn me into an alcoholic before I even hit my birthday next month.

I untangled my hand from Archer's and took a gulp of the liquor before moving closer to the package. It looked innocent enough from the outside, but so had the box with a dead bird in it.

"All right, open it," I said with a sigh.

Kody slid the box closer and flipped the lid off in one quick motion.

I let out a heavy breath. As far as stalker mail went, this wasn't the worst. Not by a long shot. But it was *right* up there on the creep factor. A page torn out of a glossy magazine had clearly been the trigger for today's attack, as the full-page image showed Archer and me locked in a crazy intimate embrace while the vodka bottle sat on the low table beside us. Archer's face had been scribbled over so many times in black marker pen that it was entirely blotted out, and the paper had torn slightly.

There was a Barbie doll with the pink hair, but she didn't wear any little replica outfits this time. Instead, down the length of her body, down her arms, legs, and even across her forehead, the same word was scribbled over and over.

MINE.

Then, just in case we didn't get the message, there was a box of matches and a pair of mud-crusted, black lace panties. The same pair I'd been wearing that day with Archer before we went to Wisteria. The same ones I'd kicked off on the side of the road and left behind in the rain and mud.

No one spoke.

Then Archer slammed his crystal tumbler down on the countertop so hard the glass shattered, but he didn't even flinch.

"He's a fucking dead man," he announced in a voice as cold as the grave.

I bit the inside of my lip, holding back the scream of frustration, rage, and *fear* that wanted to tear free of my chest.

"Are you okay, babe?" Kody asked in a quiet voice, his arm resting around my waist in a gesture of comfort.

I nodded, even though I wasn't. Not by a long shot. But then I wouldn't ever really be *okay* until my stalker was caught and the hit out on me cancelled. So for now, I just needed to be satisfied with *surviving.*

"I'm going to take a shower," I told them, placing the lid back on the box to hide the contents once more. "Can you guys store this wherever all the rest of the creepy shit is stored?" I didn't know, and I didn't care to know. Probably in my dad's fake office.

Steele gave me a frown of concern. "Are you sure?"

I forced an amused smile to my lips. "About showering? Absolutely. I smell like smoke, and I'm in serious need of a cleanup. Remind me to wear panties next time I leave the house, all right?"

Kody and Archer shared a fucking smirk, the bastards, and Steele just pouted.

"No fair," he grumbled. "But do you mind if I just double-check your room before you shower? This package was found on the front doorstep, so that means whoever left it there got past the front-gate security."

Another ripple of fear passed through me, but I nodded.

Steele and I left the kitchen, passing through the foyer to the main staircase, but a knock on the door caused us both to freeze just two steps up.

"I've got it," Steele murmured, stepping back down. He pulled a gun from beneath the hall table, which appeared to only be there as decoration. It always held a huge arrangement of flowers—Steinwick's doing—but apparently it also hid a convenient weapon.

I clutched the stair rail in a white-knuckled grip as Steele checked the security camera, then gave me a small nod of reassurance. He opened the door, keeping his gun just behind his back, but it was only the front-gate guard.

"Sir, letting you know we've checked the cameras. No sign of whoever left the box," the guard—Dave—told Steele in a clipped, professional voice. "Our guess is that he jumped over the south fence, where there's a dead zone."

Steele gave a sharp nod and murmured something in reply, then closed and locked the front door.

"There's a dead zone on the south fence?" I asked as he replaced the gun in its hiding place.

He rejoined me, placing his hand lightly on the small of my back and kissing my cheek. "There is. But someone would need to have seen *all* our footage to work that out. Kody and I can sort it out tonight, though."

I shook my head. "Don't bother. The stalker won't be back again tonight, and you guys are just as wrecked as me. What time is it anyway?"

He checked his watch then cringed. "Almost four."

I groaned. No wonder we all looked like the walking dead. "Well, in that case, maybe after you check my room for bugs, you can scrub my back, then tuck me in? You know I always sleep better when one of you is around."

His smile split wide. "That's an offer I'll *never* refuse, Hellcat."

With that renewed sense of purpose, we hurried up to my room, and I silently reflected on the *upside* to my stalker constantly lurking in the shadows of my mind. He was making me appreciate every single moment of happiness and not put anything off until tomorrow.

Because I had no idea just how many tomorrows I had left.

CHAPTER 42

Despite spending almost all of Sunday in bed—with company—I still needed to give myself a mental pep talk about getting up and going to class on Monday morning. Mostly because I was a ball of anxiety thinking I might run into Scott again. Hopefully he'd taken my warning to heart.

Bree had called me several times throughout the weekend, and I'd given her a brief rundown of the fight, the fire, and the creepy stalker gift when I called her back to chat at dinnertime. She was suitably horrified but wanted to know why we hadn't called the cops.

Honestly? It hadn't even crossed my mind. The SGPD had so far proven to be entirely useless in the search for my stalker, so it just seemed like a pointless gesture to call them. Archer's resources were far more practical, and we'd moved past the point of law-abiding citizens around about the time I'd shot Hank in the head.

Kody drove me to class in his sexy blue Maserati, leaving Steele and Archer at home, as neither of them had any mandatory lectures to attend. Bree was waiting for us in the student parking lot when we arrived, holding a tray of takeaway coffees and a bag of donuts.

One of the many reasons I loved her. She recognized my need for caffeine and sugar and didn't make any stupid attempts to wean me off.

"You beautiful human," I gushed, taking her offerings with a huge smile. "If I were into chicks, I'd totally kiss you right now." Bree laughed, but her cheeks pinked. Apparently I'd embarrassed her. "Yeah well, I think you've got enough going on with your reverse harem right now," she mumbled, then handed Kody a coffee too. "Hey, Kody. I see you kept my bestie alive for another weekend. Congrats."

He just drank his coffee and flipped Bree off. They were developing a cute level of bickering, which entertained me to no end. Especially since I'd have been dead months ago if Bree were my primary defense.

"Can we get lunch off-campus today?" Bree asked with a hopeful smile as we made our way inside the main campus building. "I want to catch up properly from the weekend, seeing as you sounded somewhat distracted when we spoke last night." She narrowed her eyes at Kody accusingly.

He just smirked, kissed me, and headed off to his own class. I liked the fact that he wasn't insisting on physically shadowing me all day, even though he had asked me three times in the car if I had my knife—I did—and installed a GPS tracker on my phone that only the three guys could access.

Not so long ago, I might have bucked those protective measures. But I was making better choices now, like not being stubborn and prideful simply for the sake of it. A tracker on my phone wasn't inhibiting my freedom; it was safeguarding me.

"Sure," I replied to Bree, "what were you thinking?"

"I've got a crazy intense craving for burgers," she told me with a pained moan. "Can we go to Grill King?"

I grinned. "Girl, yes. I haven't been there in forever, and their chicken burgers are *amazing*. But you know Kody will have to come with? I'm doing this new thing where I don't do dumb shit, like make myself an easy target."

"Ooh," she replied, her tone teasing, "that sounds like a smart idea. And yeah, totally fine. I'm coming around to their usefulness in keeping you breathing, you know?"

I laughed, adjusting my bag on my shoulder. "All right, well then it's a date. Just don't tell Scott if you see him, okay? I'm steering clear of his crazy ass."

Bree wrinkled her nose, horrified. "Girl, no. Scott is *dead* to me. Not that he's reached out at all, but if he did, I wouldn't fucking answer."

"Miss Danvers," a voice called from farther down the corridor, and I turned to find Professor Barker striding toward us with his briefcase tucked under his arm. "What excellent timing. This way, please." He passed Bree and me by about twenty feet, then stopped to unlock his office door.

"Uh...I was actually on my way to—" I started to protest, but he didn't seem to be in the mood for my excuses.

"To my office," he snapped, cutting me off. "I've already cleared it with Professor Chang; you won't be missed in her economics lecture."

Bree shot me a look like she was asking if I needed help. I shook my head, though, sighing. I could handle Professor Barker alone. It just might result in me getting kicked out of the university if I needed to shed his blood.

"I'll catch you later, Bree," I told my friend, reluctantly entering Professor Barker's office and flinching when he slammed the door after us. On the plus side, he didn't lock it, so that had to be a good sign. Right?

"Take a seat, Miss Danvers," he told me, hovering way too close to my shoulder for comfort. I did as I was told, just to create some breathing room.

He took his time circling around to the other side of his desk, like he thought he could somehow intimidate me with his silence.

342

Clearly, he had no idea what level of scary I interacted with on a daily basis. In comparison, a lecherous professor who preyed on his female students? Pathetic.

Eventually he sat in his chair, leaning forward to rest his forearms on his desk with his fingers linked. His gaze did a slow track down my body, hovering way too long over my breasts and legs to be professional interest. It was almost comical.

"Look," I said, breaking the silence with a bored voice, "if this is the part where you ask me to suck your cock in exchange for a passing grade, you're barking way up the wrong tree." I paused, then smiled. "No pun intended."

An innocent man would have been horrified by my blunt accusation, but Professor Barker just narrowed his gaze at me, assessing.

"I have no idea what you're referring to, Miss Danvers," he lied, a slick smile on his face. "Despite your poor attendance, you're still maintaining a decent grade in my course."

I gave him a deadpan glare, folding my arms under my breasts. His gaze dropped, almost like a reflex. "Oh yeah? So why am I here, Professor Barker?"

That fake smile spread across his lips again. "I had some questions I wanted to ask you for a personal project. You'll earn extra credit for your participation, of course. Despite the fact that you're not failing my course yet, you could really use the help."

My curiosity sparked, even though I was still getting major creep vibes off him. "What's the project?"

"Just a personal study I'm putting together on the history of unsolved crimes in Shadow Grove. Did you know, Miss Danvers, that our city has one of the highest rates of unsolved crimes in the whole country? Why do you think that is?" He steepled his fingers and leaned forward, intent on my answer.

I raised my brows. "I didn't know that. Perhaps our police are understaffed?" *Or being paid off by the gangs to turn a blind eye. One or the other.*

Professor Barker blinked at me, like he could hardly believe I was giving that bullshit answer with a straight face. But that raised the question: What made him think I knew more than I was giving away?

"Really, Miss Danvers? Your own mother was murdered here in Shadow Grove, her killer never charged, yet you're not concerned?" His tone took a waspish edge, like he was pissed I wasn't just spilling my guts.

My glare hardened. "What do *you* know about my mother's murder, Professor Barker? You look like you'd have been around her age. Did you know her?" *Did you stalk her or kill her?*

Professor Barker's face tightened up at my thinly veiled accusation. "I don't know what you think you're implying, Miss Danvers, but—"

"Yeah...no, I don't buy that." I cut him off, my voice loaded with suspicion. "I think you know *exactly* what I'm implying. So either you know too much because you're somehow involved or because you're the guilty party. Which is it, Prof? Because if you keep this line of questioning up, you'll find yourself the center of an unsolved crime yourself. Clear?"

It was a bit of a risky move. If Professor Barker was my stalker, or one of them, or intended me harm...yeah, I might not make it out of his office without a struggle. But at least then the curtain would be ripped aside, right? At least then I'd know.

But of course, he said nothing as I pushed my chair back and exited his office. That didn't mean he was innocent, not at all. It just meant that I'd probably detonated my passing criminology grade.

I made it all the way down the corridor before ducking into a restroom and letting my nerves take over. For several minutes I just sat on the toilet seat, hugging my arms around my knees and trembling. I knew it was just adrenaline running its course, but I didn't like it. My skin felt clammy and hot, and my heart was racing too fast.

Unable to think of anything else to distract my mind, I pulled my phone out and opened the group chat with the guys.

Madison Kate: Prof Barker is sketchy as fuck. Do we know anything about him?

Kody was in class but both Steele and Archer were at home, so it didn't surprise me when I got a response just a moment later.

Archer D'Ath: I'll get someone to do a profile on him.

I appreciated that he didn't ask me to explain. He took me at my word and didn't make me walk him through my reasons for drawing that conclusion. I *thought* that meant he trusted my judgment.

Max Steele: Try not to kill him on campus, Hellcat. It's mostly Wraith territory over there.

Madison Kate: I thought you guys were bigger and badder than Uncle D'Ath.

Archer D'Ath: We are.

I snickered a laugh at that. Yeah, they probably were, but they also didn't need me borrowing gang trouble and sparking power struggles right now. Still, it was fun to tease.

Kodiak Jones: Babe, why aren't you in class? Where are you? I'm coming to find you.

Tempting. So, so tempting. But no... He was so close to graduating.

Madison Kate: No need, I'm heading to economics now. Bree wants to do lunch at Grill King. That cool?

I sent it in the group chat, knowing full well Steele and Archer would want to know if I was leaving campus with Bree for lunch. It didn't mean they needed to tag along, but at least I wasn't skipping off and not telling them where I'd gone.

Max Steele: Sweet, meet you there at 1.
Archer D'Ath: Stay out of trouble, Princess.
Kodiak Jones: Yum, I hope they still do the double beef, double bacon, double cheese.

Then he ended his message with about eight of the drool-face emojis.

Just before I put my phone away, it lit up with another message.

Bree BFF: Okay, your prof was giving off epic sleaze vibes. Do you need a rescue? Text back in five mins, or I'm pulling the fire alarm, k?

She ended it with a thumbs-up, and I laughed.

Madison Kate: All good, I escaped already. But thanks for having my back, girl.
Bree BFF: Anytime. Then three kiss-face emojis.

After I put my phone away, I felt a hundred times better than when I'd walked into the restroom. So I washed my hands—force of habit—then headed back out in the direction of my lecture, which I was already crazy late for.

I'd only just turned the corner when I almost bumped straight into a group of football jocks coming the opposite way.

"Sorry," I murmured, not really paying much attention, aside from getting out of their way, but a hand touched my elbow and I startled.

"Whoa, sorry," Bark said with a laugh. "I thought you saw me. Are you okay?"

I snatched my arm out of his touch, even though it wasn't tight. "I'm fine, Bark. Sorry, I was a million miles away."

He shook his head, his attention following his friends for a second as they kept walking down the hall. "Nah, I mean after that shit with your boyfriend last week. You cracked him pretty hard." He grinned like me punching Scott was some kind of turn-on.

"Scott's not my boyfriend," I said on reflex; then when Bark's eyes lit with interest, I shook my head firmly. "I'm seeing someone else." Several someone elses.

Bark just gave an easy shrug. "That's cool. Hit me up if it doesn't work out." He shot me a wink and started following his friends, then paused and turned back to face me. "Hey, sorry to hear about that fire. I hope they catch the shithead who lit it."

My jaw dropped, but Bark was gone around the corner with his friends before I could fully comprehend what he'd just said.

Sorry to hear about that fire? How the hell had he heard about it? How had he known it had anything to do with me?

Cold chills skated over my skin again, and I pulled my phone out, sending a mental middle finger to the SGU no-phones rule.

Madison Kate: add Bark to that profile list too. He knows something.
Archer D'Ath: Done.

I let out a long breath, letting his one-word answer calm me. I'd messaged him directly, not the group, because I knew he would already be working on Professor Barker. Archer didn't mess around on security shit.

As I stood there, my phone lit up again. It was another message from Archer, but it didn't contain any words. Just an emoji.

A love heart.

347

What the fuck was I meant to say to that? What was it even supposed to mean? Maybe it was an accidental emoji. I decided to wait and see if he said anything else and pocketed my phone once more.

With all the suspicious shit from Professor Barker and Bark combined, I was starting to think I needed to take a break from my studies. Either I was making myself an easy target by keeping a set schedule in a public area or I was becoming paranoid. Neither option seemed to fit with my decision to make good choices.

Maybe that was something to discuss with my harem over dinner. Like in a real relationship.

CHAPTER 43

The rest of my morning seemed to totally drag—something that was only made worse by the slimy sensation of being watched from all corners. In fact, that wasn't just my imagination. Everyone *was* staring at me again, just like when I'd first returned from Cambodia. Except this time, they were staring thanks to the video circulating of me decking Scott.

Both Bree and Kody were waiting for me when I rushed out to the parking lot and all but fell into Kody's arms.

"I'm so freaking ready to get off campus for an hour," I lamented, snuggling my face into Kody's T-shirt and inhaling the manly smell of *him*.

His hands stroked down my back, soothing me even as he laughed at my theatrics. "Well, are you girls going to wanna talk about sex?" He sounded cautious, and I frowned up at him, confused.

"Hell yes," Bree answered for us.

Kody rolled his eyes. "Then maybe you should ride with Bree and get that part done in private. I'll follow behind you."

My brows rose in surprise. "Really?"

He nodded firmly. "God yes. I don't ever want to hear about

how my cock compares to Arch's or Steele's, thanks. Leave me alone in my fantasy that they're total crap in bed and I'm the only one who rocks your world, 'kay?"

Bree snickered and headed over to her car, parked a couple of spaces over, as Kody kissed me. "Come on, girl. You gotta tell me all about how *huge* Archer's dick is again. And did you tell me Steele pierced his?" She raised her voice enough it couldn't be anything *but* an attempt to tease Kody.

He gave a pained groan, then kissed me again and swatted my ass. "Go, enjoy. I'll be right behind you, okay?"

I smiled, rising on my tiptoes to smack another quick kiss on his lips. "Thanks. And you *always* rock my world, Kodiak Jones."

He rolled his eyes, but there was an amused smile on his lips when I blew a kiss over my shoulder at him before sliding into Bree's passenger seat.

Once we were in the privacy of her car, pulling out of the student lot with Kody's car right on our tail, I turned to her with an accusing glare.

"How'd you know Steele had a pierced dick? I never told you that!"

Her mouth dropped open in shock, and she gave me a wide-eyed stare while waiting for the traffic to clear. "Are you *serious*?" she shrieked. "I was just *joking*, but oh my god, this is too good. Tell me everything. What is it? Prince Albert? Guiche? King's crown? Magic cross? Come on, give me the gossip, MK!"

My cheeks flamed, and I deliberately looked out my window. "You know way too much about dick piercings, Bree."

She cackled like an evil witch, and I couldn't help the amusement silently shaking my shoulders. I couldn't believe I'd just accidentally told her about something *that* private.

"Come on, girl." She poked me in the leg, teasing. "You've admitted that much; you might as well tell me *everything* now."

"Bree!" I protested with a groan, but in reality I was entertained

350

as hell. This was the Bree I'd been missing—fun-loving, teasing, and a bit crude.

At least while she was driving, she couldn't focus all her attention on harassing me for the intimate details of my *very* active sex life. I'd always been pretty open with her about my sexual partners, even telling her about the douchebag from Shadow Prep who'd convinced me to try anal for the first time. But now I found I didn't *want* to share those intimate moments. They were private between me and my guys.

I changed the subject, asking her about how things were going with Dallas and listening when she told me all about a run-in they'd recently had with a couple of Wraiths while they were on a date.

"I mean, can you believe that?" she asked me rhetorically when we paused behind a bus at a red light. "We're sitting there in this *nice* restaurant, about to order desserts, and these two punk-ass kids with their pants halfway around their knees come at Dallas like I'm just not even sitting there."

I tried not to laugh. She was clearly irritated that that'd interrupted her date, but it sounded like typical, lower-level gang bullshit to me. Not that I was the expert, but I'd seen enough in the weeks I'd stayed at Zane's apartment building.

"You should have sprayed them with your Mace," I teased her as the light turned green and the bus started rolling forward. "You know, really taught them a lesson in manners."

Bree shot me a deadpan glare. "Very funny. That actually sounds like something *you'd* do, you—"

Through her window, I saw a blacked-out Hummer barrel through the red light. I sucked in a breath to scream at her, but I was too slow.

It all happened at once. The Hummer didn't even attempt to slow as it plowed straight into the side of Bree's car and pushed us across three lanes of traffic. Our car spun, then dislodged from the front grill of the Hummer. We spiraled out of control for several gut-wrenching turns until finally we came to a screeching, crunching halt.

Everything hurt. My ears rang and my face stung from the airbag deploying. Pain throbbed through my skull, sharp agony slicing through my neck with every breath. But…I was still alive. I was still conscious. That had to be a good sign, right?

"Bree?" I croaked, then coughed at the tight ache in my chest. My seat belt had locked up, pinning me into my seat like a band of iron. It'd probably just saved my life.

"Bree?" I tried again. "Bree, babe, hey." I reached out a heavy hand, touching her shoulder but not shaking her. If she had a spine injury, that could make it worse. Her face was tilted away from me, her hair wet with blood, and she wasn't moving. She wasn't responding.

Fear choked me, filling my lungs and cutting off rational thought. Was she dead? That Hummer had hit her at speed. Her whole side of the car crumpled in, trapping her arm and left leg in a mangle of metal and blood.

"Bree, hun, talk to me. I'm gonna get help, okay?" My voice shook as I spoke, but Bree wasn't listening. The only hopes I had to cling to were the fractional rising and falling of her chest and the blood trickling from her forehead. That meant she had a pulse… didn't it?

"I'm getting help," I told her again, determined. Kody had been following right behind us; he'd already be calling an ambulance.

The ringing was quickly fading from my ears, only to be replaced by a much more fear-inducing sound.

Gunshots.

Fuck. I needed to get out of the car. I needed to get Bree to help. I needed to make sure Kody was okay.

Yanking on my seat belt got me nowhere; it was locked in place. I couldn't unbuckle it either—the clicker was stuck hard. Another round of shots rang out and terror surged through me.

Kody was out there. Either he was shooting at someone…or they were shooting at him. I couldn't just sit there waiting for help. I needed to save myself. *And* my friend.

Gritting my teeth against the pain in my head, I wiggled my hand into the pocket of my jeans and pulled out my butterfly knife. Thank *fuck* I'd taken to carrying it everywhere with me, because it was about to save my ass.

It only took a couple of tries to slice through the seat belt fabric, and I sent multiple mental thanks up to Archer's grandfather for crafting such an impressively sharp weapon.

My door miraculously popped open on the first try, but I cast another panicked look over at Bree. It fucking *killed* me to leave her, but I wasn't doing either of us any favors by staying in my seat. She needed urgent medical help, so I was going to make it happen.

"I'm coming back, Bree, I swear. Just hang in there, girl. I've got you, okay? I'm getting help." Tears choked at my throat, my voice cracking over those words as I accepted that she wasn't going to reply. She hadn't moved even an inch since we'd crashed.

"Hang in there, bitch," I whispered at her, my cheeks wet as tears overflowed. "I'm coming back for you." More gunshots popped, closer. Or maybe my hearing was just becoming clearer. Either way, I was right in the middle of a goddamn gunfight.

I slid out of the car, keeping low to the ground as I looked around. We were in the middle of an intersection with banged-up cars scattered all around. They must have all been clipped as Bree's car hurtled out of control, but none of the drivers were coming to our aid. I didn't blame them either, as another spray of gunshots peppered a delivery van less than thirty feet from me.

Where was Kody?

Flattening my body to the ground, I peered under the car and spotted the familiar blue Maserati, its side littered with bullet holes and its tires totally flat. That pretty much confirmed it in my dazed and possibly concussed mind. There was nothing accidental about this accident. It was a deliberate, planned attack…on *me*.

Heavy footsteps crunched on broken glass somewhere nearby, and I held my breath on reflex. I was already belly down on the pavement; all I needed to do was shimmy under the car for protection. But what if it caught fire or something? Then…fuck. It was already too late.

A pair of black combat boots rounded the smashed-up hood of Bree's car, and I looked up, locking eyes with the stranger. And his gun.

He gave me a cold stare, like killing me meant absolutely *nothing* to him. My mind whirled, searching for some way out. But my only weapon was my knife, and this was a gunfight. I was sorely outmatched in the ranged-weapon scale.

My stomach lurched. There was a click, then the deafening gunshot, and my eyes screwed tight on reflex. But the bullet never reached me.

I opened my eyes again just in time to see my would-be killer drop to his knees with a perfectly circular hole in the middle of his forehead. Just a small dribble of blood trailed from it as his huge body wobbled a moment, but three more shots to his chest and another to his head saw him hit the ground in a spray of blood and tissue.

"Babe, are you okay?" Kody barked, crouching beside me on one knee but keeping his gun raised and his gaze alert for anyone else who wanted to try us. "MK, answer me!"

"Yeah," I croaked. "Yes, I'm fine. But Bree isn't. She needs help, Kody!"

His gaze jerked away from our surroundings for just long enough to peer into the car, and then he cursed. "All right, an ambulance is already on its way. It's going to be okay, babe, I promise. We're okay, yeah? Can you stand up?"

I nodded, then hissed at the agony that movement sent through my head. "I can, I'm fine. Just help Bree."

Kody wrapped his arm around me, helping me stand without letting his gun arm relax even a second. "Shh, I've got you, babe. You're safe."

I hadn't even realized I was crying again until he crushed me into his chest and I felt the wetness of my own face. Fuck. *Fuck.* If Bree died because of me...

"The boys are here; it's all okay now," Kody told me in a low rumble, and his body lost some tension as he tucked his gun away.

Seconds later, Archer's heavy hand wrapped around my wrist like he was about to yank me out of Kody's grip, but I tensed up.

"Don't!" Kody ordered, making Archer's movement freeze. "She's got whiplash or something. Just stuff the caveman bullshit in a box for now and sort out this cleanup. You can beat your chest and wave your dick around later when MK's got clearance from the hospital."

On the far side of Bree's car, an ambulance had arrived with a firetruck right behind it. Already, the first responders were out and assessing the situation with Bree. They were helping her. She was going to be okay...wasn't she?

"Hellcat, we're here." Steele's smooth, low voice reached my ears, and I pulled away from Kody's chest gingerly to look at each of them. "What happened to Grill King?" Steele's joke fell flat, but I gave him a watery smile anyway, appreciating the attempt.

"I need to..." My words trailed off weakly, and I peeled myself out of Kody's grip. "I need to tell them what happened." I tried making my way around to where two firemen were already cutting through the metal of Bree's car door with what looked like giant bolt cutters.

"Babe." Kody gently held me back. "It's not necessary. There were a shitload of witnesses here. *You* need to get checked out."

A second ambulance pulled in with sirens blaring, and an EMT from the first one approached us.

"Ma'am, you were in this car?" she asked me, not unkindly but simply all business.

"Yes," Steele answered for me before I could refuse the EMT's help. "Yes, she was the passenger."

The woman nodded, coming closer and laying a gentle hand on my arm. "Please, come with me." She was indicating to her ambulance, but I wasn't going anywhere. Not yet. Not until I knew Bree was being helped. I couldn't...

I shook my head, then cried out in pain. Fucking hell, my head hurt. And my neck. And my chest, my neck, my waist...I was one giant ache, but nothing was broken. More importantly, I was alive. The same couldn't be said about Bree. Not yet, anyway. Not until they got her out and started treating her.

"I'm not going anywhere until Bree is okay," I told the woman in a hard voice. "I won't fall over dead in the meantime, but I'm not using valuable resources when *Bree* is the one who needs help. Help her. *Please.*"

"Kate—" Archer started to argue with me, but I shot him a blazing glare.

"Fucking fight me, D'Ath. I'm not leaving until I see Bree treated."

He stared back at me, his eyes searching; then he blew out an exasperated sigh and ran his hand through his hair, mussing it up. "Fine, Steele, you're on Kate. Kody, let's sort out this mess. You can fill me in while we wait for the cleaners to arrive."

I frowned in confusion, but the EMT blanched noticeably.

Kody kissed my forehead and stroked my hair. "Stay with Steele, okay? This might take us a bit of time to fix."

I must have hit my head too hard because I wasn't understanding. "Fix what? They crashed into us deliberately."

He gave me a small smile. "I know, babe. But now there're eight dead bodies lying in the middle of an intersection and first responders can only pretend not to see them for so long before it causes even bigger problems." With a reassuring smile, he left me in Steele's care and joined Archer as they walked to the closest body—the guy who'd damn near put a bullet in my brain.

"What the fuck is going on?" I breathed, pressing a hand to my face and staring as the firemen kept hacking through the metal of Bree's car, racing the clock to save her.

Steele took my arm carefully, leading me away from the car and over to one of the ambulances with its back open. "Hellcat, I'm not making you leave," he reassured me as he gently relocated us, "but Nancy here needs to do her job and check you over, okay?"

The medic, Nancy, gave me a smile that bordered on pleading, and a rush of guilt flooded me. There was so much going on here that I didn't understand. But one thing I knew for damn sure. She was scared—probably of what the boys might do to her if she let me walk away with an injury that turned serious later. I knew they wouldn't blame her for my stubborn bullshit, but she didn't know that.

I shrugged, then whimpered at the pain radiating through my skull.

"Will you sit?" Nancy asked, motioning to the step of her ambulance. "I promise my colleagues are doing everything they can for your friend."

I drew a deep breath, trying to make good choices. Slowly, with my eyes locked on Bree's crushed car, I sank down to the step Nancy was pointing at.

The moment I did, I caught a shift in her attitude, like a small wave of relief passed over her at my acceptance of her treatment.

"Good girl," Steele murmured, crouching beside me and linking our fingers together. "Bree's going to be okay, beautiful. She'll be just fine."

I appreciated his comforting words, but he couldn't know that. None of us could. Bree might well already be dead for all we knew. And if she was, then it was on me.

The section of car metal the firemen had been working on came free, and the EMTs rushed in to attend to my friend, now that they could access her.

From the crush of bodies all around, I couldn't see anything except her lifeless, blood-soaked hand hanging out of the car.

Oh fuck. She was dead.

My best friend was dead because of me.

CHAPTER 44

The next few hours passed in a blur. After they freed Bree from the wreckage of her car, she was rushed into the ambulance and carried away with sirens blaring. That gave me a small measure of hope because why would they bother unless there was some chance to save her?

Steele and Nancy convinced me to be transported too, something I probably needed, considering the sharp pain every time I turned my neck. Also, it meant that we were following Bree, and I needed to stay close to her.

We left Archer and Kody behind to clean up the mess of what was almost certainly another assassination attempt. How the hell they'd manage to do that, given the number of witnesses, property damage, and dead bodies, I had no idea. But I had faith they'd work it out. Their resources were, I was quickly learning, seemingly endless.

When we arrived at the hospital, Nancy told me that Bree had been taken into surgery, and it'd be some time before we'd know anything. She handed me off to an ER nurse, who checked me in and gave Steele a clipboard of paperwork to fill out on my behalf.

"This seems like overkill," I mumbled, sitting on the edge of a hospital bed and watching Steele fill out the forms confidently. How he knew all that personal information about me off the top of his head, I had no idea.

"It's a precaution, Hellcat," he murmured back, not stopping his pen for even a second, "and one I'm glad they're taking. We're not taking chances with your health."

I had nothing to say back to that. Besides, if Bree would be in surgery for some hours yet, I had nowhere else I needed to be.

"It's just a bit of bruising and a headache," I said anyway. It always made me feel anxious and guilty to use medical assistance unless I *really* needed it. I never wanted them prioritizing me and my non-life-threatening injuries over someone else.

Steele clicked his pen off and set the clipboard aside, giving me a pointed stare. "You're getting checked out. End of discussion." He reached out and tugged my shoes off, then pointed for me to sit farther back on the bed. "So just get comfy. I'm not leaving you."

Grumbling, I did as he wanted and shuffled back against the pillows. He sat on the edge of the mattress, resting his hand gently on my knee as he checked his phone. A deep frown creased his face, and he started tapping out a rapid, one-handed reply.

"Fill me in, Max," I ordered, my fingers fidgeting with the stiff blankets. "I'm a mess of nerves right now; I need the distraction."

He glanced up at me, worried, then gave an understanding nod. "Just touching base with our guys working on profiles for Scott, Bark, and your professor. They said they'll send a report through on Scott shortly."

"Okay, that's good, right? So why the frown?" I got the impression bad news was coming.

Steele sighed and shook his head, though. "No reason. I'm just worried about what they might have found. Believe it or not, we would rather Scott *not* be guilty in this shit."

Surprise widened my eyes. "Really?"

"Yeah, really. You trusted him when you were betrayed by the three of us. He offered you friendship when we hurt you, and if that all turned out to be fake?" He gave me a pained smile. "I never want to see you hurting, Hellcat. Not physically." He indicated the fact that we were currently in a hospital bed. "Or emotionally. Scott turning out to be a stalker? That'd be a tough blow."

I gave a faint nod, as much as my aching neck would allow, and swallowed heavily. He was right, as per usual. But the sick feeling of dread churning inside me said that result was inevitable. Scott *wasn't* the nice guy I'd met in Aspen. That version of him was quickly showing as totally and undeniably *fake*.

The doctor came to see me a few minutes later, and Steele moved aside to let them run their tests. He answered a call from Archer at some point, updating him in low tones about where we were and what my doctor had said so far.

Eventually I was given some heavy painkillers for my aches and released. The diagnosis was mild whiplash, a concussion, and some severe bruising across my neck, chest, and lower body from the seat belt. All in all, I was insanely lucky.

"You should stay the night here," Steele commented again as I filled in the discharge form and signed my name. "The doctor said your concussion needed observation for at least twelve hours."

I shot him a warning glare. "He *also* said that could be done from home. I'm not staying the night here, Max. Let it go."

He glowered back at me, not even remotely letting it go. "You're not going home, though. You're going to sit in the waiting room on uncomfortable plastic chairs for fuck knows how long until Bree gets out of surgery."

I gave a tiny shrug, then winced. My painkillers needed longer to kick in properly. "So what? Sitting on a plastic chair sure as fuck won't kill me. And it's an incentive not to fall asleep, right?"

Steele scowled, but I handed the discharge forms over to the nurse and slid off the bed gingerly. He was still frowning as he helped me tie my shoes back on, then wrapped a gentle arm around me to walk back out to the waiting room.

Dallas was already there, sitting with his head clasped in his hands, so I took the seat directly beside him. Neither of us spoke, but after a moment, he reached out and took my hand in his, squeezing comfortingly.

Steele—despite his protests about me staying in the waiting room—went over to the drink dispenser and cranked out a cup of coffee for each of us, then took the seat directly opposite me, his knees deliberately touching mine.

I released Dallas's hand so I could sip my coffee, then almost choked on it. "Damn, that's bad," I sputtered, wincing as the bitter taste assaulted my tongue. I still took another sip, though. Coffee was coffee when you'd been through a car crash and gunfight over lunchtime.

Dallas gave a small smile. "You're such a coffee snob, Katie."

I didn't argue with him on that. Steele just gave me a lopsided grin, then turned back to his phone again.

"Boys are on their way," he told us. "Cleanup is finished."

Dallas gave a small grunt of surprise. "That was quick for a scene that public. You guys must have some serious help on your books."

Steele's answering grin was smug. "Hades owed us a favor."

Dallas replied with an understanding sound, like that explained it all. I was totally lost as to *how* that mess could be taken care of without Kody being arrested for eight murder charges, but then again, I apparently had very little understanding of where the power truly sat in Shadow Grove.

Or maybe I did understand; I was just having a hard time wrapping my head around it all.

"Have you heard anything about Bree?" I asked Dallas in a small voice, desperate to hear *something*, but he shook his head.

"No," he replied, sounding mournful. "They won't tell me anything because I'm not family. Just that she's in surgery."

Steele frowned. "Give me a minute—I'll sort it out." He started to get up from his seat, then hesitated.

"I'm fine here," I assured him, knowing exactly what his pause was about. "I won't move from this seat, and Dallas has got my back, right?" I gave him a gentle tap with my elbow, and he nodded.

Steele still looked uncertain but sighed. "I'll be quick and right over there. Yell if you need me."

I assured him I would, then watched as he approached the nurse's station. His smile was polite as all hell, but there was a determined set to his shoulders, and his whole vibe screamed *danger*. No doubt he'd have both Dallas and me listed as Bree's family in a matter of minutes. It was scarily impressive.

Dallas gave a small chuckle, pulling my attention away from Steele.

"What?" I asked him with a dose of accusation.

He smirked at me. "You're so fucking in love. It's cute as hell."

My cheeks flushed with heat. "What the shit, Dallas? Where did that even come from?"

He shrugged, tilting his head in the direction of where Steele was working his magic on a stern-faced nurse. "The way you were just watching him, it's like the way you look at a really well-made coffee…but a hundred times more. It's adorable."

I sat back in my seat, trying to fold my arms, but my chest hurt too much for that. "Whatever," I grumbled, uncomfortable discussing my love life while his girlfriend—my best friend—was fighting for her life in surgery.

Dallas seemed to let the subject drop, sinking into silence for several minutes. But then he spoke again. "Do they treat you well?"

I frowned. "What does that mean?"

His lips curved up on one side, mocking me. "If you don't know, then the answer is clearly no."

I rolled my eyes. "Of course they *treat* me well. I meant why are you even asking that? I wouldn't be putting up with their bullshit if they didn't. You know I don't tolerate stupid fuckboys for long."

He barked a laugh. "True that." With a sigh, he ran a hand over his shaved head. "Well, I'm happy for you, Katie. But if you ever need to dispose of their bodies, you call me first. No questions asked, all right?"

I grinned. "Will do."

We fell back into comfortable silence, sipping our shitty vending-machine coffee and waiting.

Steele came back over to us some minutes later, announcing that Dallas had been added to Bree's file as her fiancé. So as soon as the doctor had any update to give, we would be told first. Given her parents were currently out of town on some lavish vacation somewhere, that was a relief to hear.

Kody and Archer arrived shortly thereafter, storming through the hospital doors like avenging angels, all streaked in blood. My jaw dropped slightly at the sight of them, and I drank in every inch of their bodies, checking that none of the blood was theirs.

Dallas let out a small snicker beside me, and I jabbed him with my elbow. But that motion made me wince, and a second later I had all three of my guys surrounding me with concern creasing their features.

"I'm fine," I groaned, fending off their attention. "I'm only a bit bruised."

"Those painkillers should be working by now," Steele muttered, scowling. "I'm going to talk to someone about something stronger."

He was gone before I could protest, heading over to chat with his new friend in the nurses' station. Archer took the seat directly beside me, gently placing his hand on the inside of my knee, and Kody sat opposite me.

"Steele gave you guys the update, right?" I asked, and Kody nodded.

Archer rattled off my list of injuries in their entirety, and Dallas winced.

"Fuck, Katie. Why are you even sitting here right now? You should be in bed." His face was drawn, though, and he knew exactly why—because my best friend was in life-or-death surgery thanks to *me*.

"I'm fine," I muttered unconvincingly, but when Steele returned with two white pills, I took them without complaint. My body was still aching, and it'd really be great if it could stop doing that for a little while.

The five of us sat there in silence for a long time, not even speaking when Archer got up and got more coffee for everyone. It was sometime later when my eyelids were officially drooping as the stronger painkillers did their work, that several phones beeped in unison.

Archer, Kody, and Steele all pulled their cell phones out, and Dallas exchanged a curious look with me.

"Did Charlie just call the angels in for a job?" Dallas joked, and I tried to force a weak smile in response. The three guys were reading something they'd all been sent, though, and Kody breathed a curse.

"Spit it out," I ordered, the suspense of waiting overwhelming me. "What's happened now?"

"Remember I told you our guys were forwarding the profile for Scott over?" Steele said, his voice grim and resigned.

Dread filled my gut. This couldn't be good. Not at all.

Archer handed me his phone by way of explanation. It took me a minute to work out what I was looking at; then I recognized it as an assortment of trash all laid out on a table. I flipped to the next image and found a close-up of a crumpled receipt. My eyes scanned the details; then I swallowed heavily.

"Is this…" My voice cracked, my fear getting the better of me. "Where was this found?"

"Analysis of Scott's trash," Kody replied, his green eyes laser focused on my face like he was scrutinizing my every reaction.

I let out a long breath as the prickling shivers of panic broke out all over my skin. I read the receipt again, but it didn't change the information there. It was a receipt from a toy store for six Barbie dolls. If that wasn't the proof we had been waiting for, I didn't know what would be.

"Fuck," I whispered.

Steele dialed someone, brought his phone to his ear, and waited for them to answer his call.

"Wait there," he told the person on the other end. "When Scott shows up again, detain him." He ended the call, then made another to someone else. "Scott Randall," he said. "He's somewhere in Shadow Grove. Find him and detain him. Double the usual rate."

"Just detain?" Dallas asked as Steele ended his call. "I'd have thought you'd be putting out a hit. That's proof he's been stalking Katie, isn't it? He needs to fucking die."

The look Steele gave Dallas was pure ice. "Detain only. We'll take care of the rest ourselves."

"Damn right we will," Archer agreed in a low voice, his fingers flexing against my inner knee. Now that my painkillers had kicked in nicely, it didn't hurt, but Kody snapped at him to be gentle nonetheless.

Steele was still on his phone, reading something else, then running a hand over his face. "I don't know if this helps or not, but I think we worked out why Bark was giving off the creep vibes."

I almost didn't want to ask. "Why?"

Steele passed his phone over to me. "He is apparently the major contributor to this blog site."

Scrolling the page, I found all kinds of Shadow Grove crimes documented, with heavy emphasis on the crap going on with me and my guys. There was the fire at Wisteria, an article about Steele's car exploding in the SGU parking lot, a ton of gossip and hearsay about Drew's murder...even the video of me punching Scott in the halls of school.

There were a hundred and one theories about my guys and me, ranging anywhere from human trafficking—which wasn't super far from the truth—all the way through to the most popular theory. One that several hundred people had commented their agreement or support on.

Aliens.

I let out a sharp laugh, relief washing over me. "Okay, so Bark isn't a stalker, he's just plain nuts. Good to know, I guess."

"Aliens?" Kody mumbled, sounding outraged as he browsed the comments on his own phone. I handed Steele's to Dallas for him to see too, and he chuckled.

"Aw, come on, this commenter has a valid point," my friend teased, pointing one out to me. The username was *@freemadisonkate* and the comment were all in shouty capitals.

MADISON KATE PUTS THE EXTRA IN EXTRATERRESTRIAL. SHE'S SO PRETTY, I HOPE ALL ALIENS LOOK LIKE HER! #BEAMMEUP #IWANNABEPROBED

It was absurd enough that I couldn't help but laugh as I handed Steele's phone back to him. "I guess we should have done a better job of hiding the spaceship. People are onto us."

"Fucking morons," Archer growled. "I'm not even remotely green *or* little."

The humor of the moment quickly extinguished as a doctor in full scrubs came hurrying through the doors of the surgical wing, unhooking his mask from his face. His eyes were on us, and I already knew he was coming to update us on Bree.

Dallas shot out of his seat the second he spotted the doctor, his fear rolling from his skin in palpable waves. "Is she...?" he started, licking his lips to wet them, then trying again. "Is Bree okay?"

The doctor's face was serious, but his small nod was enough. Dallas dropped back into his seat like a puppet with his strings cut, his breath whooshing out of him in relief.

"She's in serious condition still," the doctor advised, "but she's stable. We're optimistic."

My pulse thundered in my ears, and a small amount of the tightness in my chest loosened. Still, fresh tears rolled down my face from the sheer staggering emotions talking to Bree's doctor had resurfaced.

Archer scooped me up in gentle arms and lifted me into his lap. His arms linked around my waist as I cuddled into his huge frame, and he murmured soothing nothings in my ear as the doctor continued to outline Bree's injuries.

I only caught bits and pieces of what he was saying. Her leg was broken in three places and needed bolts to stabilize the bones. Her wrist had been crushed and would likely need several more surgeries in the months to come. Probably the most serious was her head injury, which had caused swelling in her brain. They'd done something to relieve the pressure and drain the fluid, the doctor said, and he seemed pleased with how it'd all gone.

The next thing he said saw me startle upright, though.

"What did you just say?" I exclaimed, positive I'd just heard him wrong.

The doctor shot me an uncertain look, then nervously cast his eyes over my guys. He seemed to know who they were and was breaking the rules of confidentiality on account of that.

"I said, the baby seems to be totally fine. It's a miracle, obviously, and she'll be required to remain in the hospital for the duration of the pregnancy so we can monitor the fetal growth closely. But all signs seem positive so far." He reached out and patted Dallas's shoulder in a comforting way, but my friend seemed totally shell-shocked. Stunned.

"She's recovering from the anesthesia now," the doctor continued when he realized Dallas wasn't going to say anything, "so it'll be some time before any of you can see her. Would you like us to call you when it's okay?"

This seemed to shake Dallas out of his trance. "What? No. No, we'll wait here. I mean—" He shot a quick look at me and the guys. "I mean I'll wait here. I'm not leaving."

"We'll all wait," I said firmly, meeting Dallas's panic-filled gaze. "Thank you, Doctor. Please let us know as soon as Dallas can go in."

The doctor nodded, assuring us that he would, then left.

"Did you know?" my friend asked me in a broken voice, his eyes accusing.

I shook my head firmly, grateful that my painkillers allowed me that gesture. "I had no clue. None. I can't believe—"

"I'm gonna be a dad," Dallas whispered in total shock.

My best friend's baby almost died today.

Guilt flooded every inch of my body, choking me and rolling my stomach sharply. I scrambled out of Archer's arms abruptly and raced in the direction of the ladies' room.

Bree had almost died.

Her baby had almost died.

I needed to find out who was behind that attack and make them pay.

CHAPTER 45

Kody followed me into the ladies' room not a minute later, sitting with me on the cold tiled floor as my body trembled and my stomach rolled. I never had been a big vomiter, even when I was *sure* I would. So eventually I had to accept the fact that I couldn't expel my guilt so easily.

I crawled into his lap as he leaned against the wall and let him wrap me in his comforting warmth for a while.

"We'll get them, babe," he whispered as he stroked his fingers through my tangled hair, gently working the knots out as he found them. "None of those bastards today walked away, but until we find the money behind the hit…"

"They'll keep coming," I finished, already knowing this. "Archer thinks it's one of my relatives on my mom's side." I sat up slightly, peering at him with a small frown. "Are we looking into that more?"

Kody jerked a nod. "Absolutely. And I agree with him…but they're not easy people to find. Even before Arch erased your mom's paper trail, they'd muddied the waters already. When we get home, I'll get Archer to run through all the info we have. There's not much, but maybe you'll spot something we've missed."

I sighed. He probably had a good point; sitting on the restroom floor wasn't the ideal place to start combing through all the clues on who might be trying to assassinate me.

Guilt was still clogging my arteries, but I knew that wouldn't change anytime soon. Not until we could hold someone responsible for what'd happened to Bree.

Someone in addition to me, that was. Because if not for me being in her car, this whole day would have ended differently. Maybe Bree and her baby would have been sitting at Grill King, Bree wondering why we'd never showed. And maybe Kody would be the one in a hospital bed.

Ugh. That just made me feel even worse.

I scrambled out of his lap and stood up with a small groan. The aching stiffness was returning to my limbs, and I peered in the mirror. Lifting my shirt, I saw what the doctor had been probing earlier. Mottled purple, black, and blue bruising colored my flesh in a thick line from hip to hip and in a diagonal from my right shoulder, between my breasts, and down to my left hip. No wonder I needed stronger painkillers.

Kody stepped up behind me, his gentle fingertips tracing the lines of my seat belt. "I almost lost you again today, babe." His whisper was rough, and his gaze met mine in the mirror, swimming with fear. Fear for *me*. "I thought it was bad last time, after you got stabbed. This was worse. So much freaking worse."

My smile was watery as I tried to reassure him. "It's just a bruise," I replied. "In a week, it'll be totally gone."

He shook his head. "MK, that was a well-coordinated attack. They had vans ready to intercept me, making sure I couldn't get to you. That guy had his gun pointed at your head, babe. If I'd been even a second slower—"

"But you *weren't*." I cut him off firmly, spinning around to face him and looping my arms around his neck, ignoring how it pulled on the bruises. "You were there exactly when I needed you, Kody.

The only reason I'm standing here right now and not on a tray in the morgue? You."

Holy crap. That hadn't fully sunk in until now. I'd very nearly died today.

He started to argue, and I cut his words short with my lips against his. He held me carefully, conscious of my bruising, but he didn't pull away. He kissed me back gently, his lips pouring adoration into me until a warm glow cracked through the stifling guilt inside me.

"You kicked ass today, Kody," I whispered when we broke apart. "You saved both me *and* Bree. Focus on the positives. We're alive."

He gave me a small nod. "You'd be wise to do the same, babe. Focus on the positives, okay?"

I swallowed heavily, feeling like a giant hypocrite, but nodded back. We started to leave the restroom, but just as he opened the door, I tugged him back for a second.

"What's up?" he asked, a worried set to his eyes.

I bit my lip, mentally kicking my own damaged ass. "Nothing. Just…"

Holy fuck, just say it, MK. Tell him you love him!

"Nothing," I mumbled again, chickening out. "Let's go."

He gave me a quizzical look but continued out of the restroom anyway while I mentally berated myself.

Epic feelings fail.

Archer was right outside the door, leaning against the wall opposite with his huge arms folded over his chest and a scowl set in his features.

"Everything okay?" he asked when we stepped out. His gaze ran over me, scrutinizing.

"Yep," Kody replied as he brought our linked hands to his lips and kissed my fingers. "I'm going to duck out to the coffee shop around the corner, grab us all some better coffees. You guys want anything else?"

Both Archer and I shook our heads, so Kody released my hand and left me there while he headed for the exit.

"Are you okay?" Archer asked, his question more pointed and deliberate this time. Caring.

I started to tell him *I'm fine*, but that was a straight up lie. I shook my head instead, feeling fresh tears well up and cursing myself for being such a weepy mess. Archer just reached out, folded me into his embrace, and held me tight as I sobbed into his chest.

"Come on," he murmured in my ear. "Let's get some fresh air, okay?" He kept one arm wrapped around me, and my arms stayed locked around his waist as we made our way outside and into the cool evening air. Archer took me past the parked ambulances and across to the grassy lawn facing the main entrance, where there was a park bench.

He sat down there, then pulled me gently into his lap before burying his face in my hair with a deep inhale.

"I think," he whispered in a husky voice, his lips brushing my ear, "that loving you is giving me wrinkles and gray hair."

I scoffed a laugh at that, then swallowed heavily as girly butterflies erupted in my stomach. It was a sickening sensation when I was already so full of guilt and fear.

Archer's lips found the sensitive patch of skin behind my ear, and he laid a soft kiss there, his breathing loud. Still, I made no move to pull away. In fact, I found it calming, so I just leaned into his touch farther.

He seemed to sense my inability to make words happen, and it didn't bother him. Apparently he had enough to say for both of us.

"Bree getting hurt was *not* your fault, Kate; you need to know that," he said in a soft, emphatic whisper. "You need to *accept* that, because if we're going to find whoever is responsible, then I need you full of that incredible fire, not drowning in guilt. You're so damn strong, Princess, and we *will* make someone pay. That I promise you." He pressed another kiss behind my ear, and I let out a sigh.

He was right. He was always fucking right.

"I know," I replied in a small voice. "But it's not so easy to let go of that feeling of responsibility. Bree's collateral damage here. She did nothing to deserve this, and what if—" Panic was starting to get the better of me again, and I swallowed my words, cutting them off. The world didn't turn on what-ifs. Quite the opposite. If I wallowed in fear of what might have been, we would get utterly nowhere.

"Bree is going to be okay," Archer reassured me in his low, calm voice as his hand stroked gently down my back. "Her baby is going to be okay. The best thing *you* can do for her now is to keep surviving. She loves you, Kate. She wouldn't want you blaming yourself for this, not when it's *not* your fault."

I nodded. Even if I didn't fully believe that statement, I knew he was right about Bree. She'd be horrified if she saw me crying and self-pitying.

I drew a deep breath, counting to five in my head and forcing the toxic guilt and fear out of my mind. Or as much as I could on my own.

"I need a distraction," I confessed to Archer in a small voice. "Help me take my mind off everything so I can refocus on what's important. I need to concentrate on the positives, right?"

He hummed a sound that might have been agreement, kissing my neck again…harder this time and with a teasing scrape of teeth. "Distraction, you say?"

I groaned. "Of course that's where your mind went."

His lips curved against my neck, and his breath fanned my skin as he gave a silent chuckle, even as his hand found the waistband of my jeans and popped the top button open. "Say no and walk away now, Kate. I won't be offended."

I rolled my eyes. "No? You'll just make me beg next time as punishment."

His fingers dragged my zipper down, opening the front of my jeans right there on the park bench in front of the hospital.

374

"You love to beg," he countered, nipping my neck with his teeth playfully. "You especially like it when I smack your ass in punishment or when I shove you to your knees and fill your throat with my hard cock."

His hand slipped into the front of my jeans, his fingers working their way underneath my panties when I made no move to stop him.

I groaned, my hips rolling against his touch before I remembered where we were. How public we were.

"Archer," I protested weakly. Really weakly. "Anyone could see us. If my stalker—"

"If Scott were watching right now, I think he'd probably snap and show his hand, don't you? We have guys out all over the city looking for him. They'll catch him, I have every confidence. It's just a matter of days, not weeks." His fingertip dipped inside my pussy, and I shuddered. "Besides, it's dark out here. No one is watching, Princess. Just let me take your mind off things for a moment."

He pushed his finger farther into me as his thumb found my clit and stroked a teasing circle around it. My hips rocked again, pushing my cunt into his hand. I was helpless to refuse an offer like that, and he knew it.

My response was to bring my lips to his in a gasping, heated kiss. My tongue danced with his, our lips moving in unison as his fingers sank into me fully. We didn't speak again as he got me off, our kiss not ending until my cunt clenched around his fingers and my whole body quaked with a silent orgasm. Even then, he just trailed gentle kisses across my jaw and down my throat as I sagged against him.

"You're my whole world, Kate," he whispered in my ear as he fastened my jeans again. "You're my reason for breathing, and I'll personally slit the throat of anyone who tries to take you away from me."

With that insanely heartwarming promise echoing in my head, we made our way back into the hospital. I had to hand it to him, though. The distraction had worked. When we stepped back through those doors, I felt stronger and more focused. Tears could wait until the threat was eliminated.

I could do this. *We* could do this. I wasn't in it alone. With Archer, Kody, and Steele beside me, I doubted I'd ever need to face a challenge totally alone again.

We only waited a couple more hours before Dallas was given the okay to visit Bree. The nurse gently told us that only one visitor was permitted for the night, though, so Dallas sent us all home. He intended to stay there with her as long as they'd let him, even though she was still unconscious from the heavy sedatives they'd put her on.

Kody's car had been shot to hell back at the accident site, so the four of us all rode together in Archer's Range Rover. We were just a few minutes away from home when Archer's phone, hooked up to the car's Bluetooth, rang. The display said *Steinwick*.

"Steinwick," Archer answered, putting the call on speaker for us all to hear. "What's happened?"

"Sir," the elderly butler replied. "There has been an incident here at the house. What time will you be returning home?"

I exchanged a worried look with Steele, who shared the backseat with me. An *incident*? I wasn't so sure I could handle another incident just yet.

"We're three minutes out," Archer replied. "Does this incident require additional firepower?"

"Not at all, sir," the butler responded, sounding almost amused. "We have the situation well under control here. No need to rush; we just wanted you aware."

"I appreciate it," Archer said, then ended the call without another word.

Kody was the first to comment. "What the hell could that be about?" he wondered aloud. "Old Stein-y didn't sound too annoyed, so it can't involve property damage."

Steele snickered a laugh. "Remember when we decided to practice throwing knives in the formal dining room? I thought the old goat was going to have a heart attack."

I eyed the three of them in fascination, and Archer met my eyes in his mirror, a sly smile curling his lips. "Nah, he's as tough as the hills. It'd take a hell of a lot more than that to make him croak." He shot me a wink, and I shook my head in disbelief. Apparently, Steinwick had worked for Archer and his boys longer than I'd thought.

When we pulled into the driveway, Archer paused a moment to speak with the gate guard. He was a uniformed man with a bushy mustache who I vaguely remembered was called Wayne.

"I heard there's been an incident?" Archer asked, and Wayne jerked a nod.

"Yes, sir. Dave and Sampson have been up at the house to keep an eye on things until you got home." Wayne looked uncomfortable as shit, and he quickly waved us through, closing the gates after us.

Steele blew out a long breath. "Anyone else dying of anticipation here? Or just me?"

Kody raised his hand, and I smiled. Whatever the "incident" was, I didn't think it was anything terrifying. Not by the calm way everyone was handling it.

Archer parked in front of the main steps, not bothering to take the car into the garage, and we all piled out.

Steele linked his hand with mine as we made our way into the house, Archer taking point and Kody the rear. It was subtle, how they did that, but I noticed it nonetheless. They'd put me in the most protected position of their formation...just in case.

"In here, sir," Steinwick called from the dining room.

We followed the sound of his voice and found him sitting on

one of the heavy dining chairs at the long table, opposite Jase. Jase...who had his hands bound in front of him on the tabletop and seemed to be totally naked.

"I take it this is the incident you spoke of?" Archer asked his butler in a dry voice. Two security guys in black uniforms stood against the wall behind Jase's chair, and a more casually dressed guy leaned on the windowsill with an ice pack to his face.

I wrinkled my nose in confusion, staring at the boys' manager, but Jase just glared daggers back at me like he totally loathed my mere presence in the room.

"Why is *she* here again?" he sneered, confirming my gut feeling. "Why is she *always* around? I thought she moved out weeks ago?"

"*She* moved back in," I snapped, not waiting for the guys to answer first. I fucking despised when people spoke about me as though I weren't in the room. "And while we're asking questions, Jase, *she* would really love to know why you have no shirt on right now."

His venomous glare darkened as his lip curled in disgust at me; then he turned his attention back to the guys. My guys. Or specifically, to Archer.

"You let her do all the talking now, Archer? I thought you were the leader here." His words fell flat when Archer said nothing in response.

Steinwick cleared his throat, drawing our attention. "Sir, your manager stopped by this evening with some business he wanted to discuss with you," he told us, the dry tone betraying what bullshit he thought that to be.

Jase huffed. "We need to discuss this Copper Wolf ad campaign, Arch. None of that was signed off by me, and you know all paperwork needs to come across my desk before you sign it. What if they slipped some kind of noncompete clause in the contract? That could ruin any prospective beverage sponsorships in the future."

It took me a moment to understand what he was talking about. Copper Wolf must be the brand of vodka Archer's friend owned.

Archer said nothing still, folding his arms over his chest and letting his silence make Jase sweat.

"None of that explains why you're sitting at our dining table with no shirt," Kody commented, also folding his arms and spearing Jase with a hard glare.

"No pants either," one of the black-clad security guys offered. "He's totally naked."

I squinted harder. What the fuck?

"We left him waiting in the den," Steinwick explained. "But when I came back a few minutes later to check if he'd like a beverage, he was gone."

"I found him upstairs," the guy leaning on the window ledge added. He pulled the ice pack away from his face as he spoke, showing off the start of a black eye. "He landed a lucky punch while I was detaining him."

I blinked a couple of times, trying to place this guy. His face seemed vaguely familiar...

"Getting slow in your old age, James?" Kody teased, and the man's familiarity clicked for me. James. Our groundskeeper.

The guy was probably only in his forties, but he flipped Kody off anyway. It was odd, but then again, just because I paid no attention, that didn't mean Kody hadn't become friendly with the staff.

Steinwick cleared his throat again. "Mr. Jase was found in your bedroom, sir," he said to Archer, and Jase's face and neck darkened with a deep flush.

Archer's brows twitched. "*My* bedroom? Doing what?"

The elderly, proper butler looked like he'd smelled something bad and seemed to really not want to explain further.

James the groundskeeper snorted a laugh. "Jerking off on your pillow, boss."

What...the...?

I couldn't help it. I really couldn't. I started laughing. Then I tried to stop laughing, and it only made me laugh harder.

Archer turned to me with an incredulous expression, and I laughed hard enough that tears leaked from my eyes. I shook my head, trying to draw calming breaths.

It wasn't working, though. The dam had broken, and in my defense, both Kody and Steele looked like they were on the verge of laughter too.

"Sorry," I gasped out, my shoulders still shaking with chuckles. "Sorry, it's not funny." *Snicker.* "It's just…I'm not the only one with a creepy, obsessed sexual stalker."

I dissolved into more totally inappropriate giggles and decided I needed to remove myself from the room. The security guys, James, and Steinwick were all staring at me like I'd grown tentacles, and I knew part of my amusement was due to the heavy painkillers. I'd just taken another dose in the car, and they were making me all floaty.

"I'm just gonna…go…" I waved my hand in the direction of anywhere else. I started to leave the room, then jerked to a halt and turned around to give Archer a stern look. A stern look that was only slightly ruined by the waves of giggles still bubbling out of me. "You're burning that bed, Archer D'Ath. And that chair." I pointed to the one that Jase's balls were all over, then left them to it. I didn't need to stick around while they fired their shitty manager.

Footsteps followed me, and Steele caught me in a careful embrace just as I reached the stairs. "Not so fast, giggles," he told me with a laugh of his own. "You're concussed, remember? You have to stay under observation for another few hours." He kissed my throat, walking with me up the stairs.

I groaned, tilting my face to give him my best pouting face. "But, Max…"

"Uh-uh, no negotiations. You can come to my room instead. I'll teach you how to play the piano." He grinned, like that was

380

something he was really excited to do but had just been waiting for the right opportunity.

I wrinkled my nose. "I already know how."

His grin spread wider. "I'll teach you how to play *properly*. Trust me, Hellcat. You'll like this lesson."

Well, how was I going to pass up an offer like that? Besides, after the day we'd just had, the absolute last thing I wanted to do was be alone.

CHAPTER 46

Steele eventually let me sleep after the fully allotted observation time was over for my concussion, but by then it was almost dawn. By the time I finally woke up, I'd long since missed my classes for the day.

So it was really no surprise when I opened my emails to find an official warning from Shadow Grove University advising that if my attendance and grades didn't improve dramatically and soon, then I'd be on academic probation.

I saved them the trouble and sent a response advising that I was withdrawing. Bree almost dying gave me a serious dose of perspective in that I had no idea how many days I might have left. I could walk out the front door in two hours and be killed by a sniper. Or mailed a time bomb. Or hit by a bus. Or any number of accidental or intentional ways my life could end.

Until I could look further into my future than *tomorrow*, my time at the university was a waste.

"Good morning, gorgeous," Kody greeted me, coming into the kitchen where I sat at the island with a bowl of cereal. I didn't care much what time of day it was; I just wanted Froot Loops.

I swallowed my mouthful, leaning into him as he kissed my

hair. "It's actually afternoon," I told him, eyeing his pajama pants and lack of shirt. His blond hair was all mussed up, like he'd also just rolled out of bed. "Almost evening, come to think of it."

Kody just shrugged and took a sip of my coffee. "Morning is whatever you want it to be." He gave me an eyebrow waggle like that was somehow a deep and meaningful statement, then smacked a kiss on my lips and went to find his own "breakfast" in the fridge.

"How'd everything turn out last night?" I asked his sexy, tattooed back while he hunted. "With Jase, I mean."

Kody pulled out a plate of pasta that Anna had left for our dinner last night and carried it over to the oven to reheat. "You mean after you started laughing hysterically about him jerking off on Archer's pillow?"

He said it so straight-faced, and I could already feel the laughter bubbling up in my chest again. I bit my lip, but I couldn't hide my wide grin. Kody just shook his head.

"You're the worst, babe. You know how hard it was to keep a straight face after that? We had to fire his ass and make damn sure he knew what terrible fate would befall him should he ever step foot back in Shadow Grove, and all I wanted to do was laugh at him." He planted his hands on his hips, giving me an accusing glare.

A small snicker escaped me. "It's not my fault," I protested. "These painkillers make me all loopy. Besides, how was that *not* hilarious? Given the stalker scale we're working with, Jase is totally on the funny end. Right?"

Kody closed up the oven with his dish of pasta inside, then came around to where I sat. He spun my chair around with me still on it, then braced his hands on the counter to either side of me.

"I fucking love this kitchen, you know that?" His tone was low and serious, all traces of teasing about Jase forgotten.

I tilted my head back, thankful the pain of those small movements had eased already. "Oh yeah? Why's that, Kodiak Jones?"

A sly smile lit his lips, and he leaned in closer, his mouth hovering just over mine. "Because every time I look at this marble countertop, I see you splayed out across it, gloriously naked with my cock buried deep inside you."

Oh yeah. That was a pretty good reason. My thighs tightened involuntarily, and my nipples hardened against Steele's band T-shirt that I'd borrowed.

Instead of kissing me—or the whole lot more I was picturing—he moved away again. "Did you want to go back to the hospital to see Bree? Our team hasn't found Scott yet, so I'd rather you didn't leave the house without one of us, okay?"

"Totally fine by me," I agreed, spinning back around on my seat to finish my bowl of sugary cereal. "But Dallas already sent me a message saying they wouldn't be letting nonfamily see her today."

Kody gave me a sympathetic look. "Did he say how she was? Has she woken up at all?"

I shook my head. "Didn't sound like it. He's been there all day, and the nurses will probably kick him out soon. So he'll go home and shower, then stop by here to update us."

He nodded. "Sounds normal. I'm sure she'll pull through okay. Brianna Graves is one tough chick, and you know it."

I sighed. Was she, though? Or was she just a normal girl who didn't deserve all this bad shit heaping on top of her?

"Do you guys have plans tonight? I just withdrew from SGU, so I'm officially homework free, I think." I finished the last spoonful of Froot Loops, then pushed my bowl aside to focus on coffee.

Kody slid onto the stool beside me, still waiting for his pasta to heat through. "You withdrew? How come?"

"Well, for one thing, they threatened academic probation. For another, my head's not in it. It seems completely insane to me, spending all that time, money, and effort on a degree that doesn't have your total dedication and passion. Right? So I figured that when this craziness is all over, when Scott is dealt with and my hit has been canceled…maybe then I can reevaluate my life goals and pick something that fits my new version of life." I shrugged and sighed heavily. "Maybe nothing at all. Who knows what tomorrow will bring? I might decide I just want to lurk around here and pick fights with Archer all day, every day."

I was teasing, but Kody groaned. "Please don't. I'm pretty sure he's just fucked up enough to think of that as the best kind of foreplay."

How right he was.

"Well, if we're not going back to the hospital, then I'm going to smack Arch around the gym a bit. I canceled my clients for the day so I can give him my full attention." He gave me a wicked grin, and I shook my head, smiling.

"You're a sadist, you know that?" My mind flickered back to that night we'd reconciled, how he'd bound my wrists with his belt as he fucked me hard. Yeah, come to think of it…there was a definite sadistic edge to all three of my boys.

Luckily, I didn't mind a little pain with my pleasure, or this all could have ended in tears.

Kody just snickered, not disagreeing with me. "Well, you're welcome to come hang out in the gym with us. I promise we won't wear anything except shorts and sweat."

I groaned. "Tempting. So freaking tempting. But these painkillers have me all fucked up. I might end up trying to drag you guys into a four-way right there on the gym floor and really do some damage."

He wrinkled his nose. "You're probably right. We can wait until you heal up properly." He winked, and I gave a short laugh.

"Well, anyway," I continued, "I think I'm just going to have a hot date with the couch and some Netflix. Maybe some Chinese takeout if I'm feeling crazy."

He leaned over and pressed a kiss to my shoulder where Steele's T-shirt had slipped down. "That…also sounds tempting. But I might go crazy if I miss another day in the gym. Can you just come get me for the Chinese and ice cream part of the night?"

I raised my brows at him. "Who said ice cream was invited to this party?"

"Babe, of course it is." He laughed. "Do we have a deal?"

I leaned over and kissed his cheek. "Deal." I hopped off my seat, carrying my dishes over to the sink, then blew Kody a kiss as I left the kitchen. I wanted to check in on Steele quickly, then run back to my room to put some sweats on. I'd stolen one of Steele's shirts off his floor, but I preferred my own sweatpants so I wasn't hauling them back up off the floor every three steps.

Slipping back into his room, where I'd spent the day, I found him in the exact same position as I'd left him when I woke up, fast asleep and so peaceful. I should have left him and crept out again, but my stupid heart took control and I found myself sliding back under the covers with him.

The second I was horizontal, though, he roused enough to snare me in a tight bear hug. He grumbled unintelligible things as he buried his face in my hair, then huffed a sigh as he slipped back into sleep once more.

I bit the inside of my cheek to keep from laughing. Instead, I pressed a kiss to his bicep, the only part of him I could reach without wriggling free.

We lay like that for long enough that I drifted off lightly, but then anxiety and guilt about Bree started creeping in again, making my lids snap open. I needed to get up in case Dallas came over earlier than planned.

As carefully as I could, I lifted Steele's arm off me and wiggled out of his warm nest. He didn't stir as I made my way to the door, and I didn't make any more noises to wake him up.

Back in my own room, I found my bed rumpled and my bathroom still steamy from recent use. Archer must have slept in my bed rather than risk a bit of Jase's jizz getting on his face. Snickering to myself, I hunted out my comfiest pair of sweatpants, then tucked my butterfly knife into the pocket. Archer had found it at the crash site and returned it to me while we were at the hospital. Call it paranoia or cautiousness, but I wasn't willing to be anywhere without my knife. The moment I put it in my pocket, it eased a small amount of my stress.

Music was booming from the gym as I made my way back downstairs, and I smiled when I heard Kody yelling at Archer over the thumping bass. Total fucking sadist.

The big, comfy couch in the den was calling my name, so I tucked in with blankets and pillows, creating a cozy nest before turning on Netflix. I was usually the first one to select action and adventure movies, but some part of me just badly craved sweet and normal.

Perfect. Utterly perfect. I hit play on *The Kissing Booth*.

I'd made it around halfway through the movie and was crazy into the angst between the adorable lead characters when Steele leaned over the back of the couch to kiss my hair.

"Hellcat," he murmured, still sounding half-asleep, "you look way too cute there right now."

I tipped my head back to look up at him. "You wanna join me?"

Steele glanced at my choice of movie and wrinkled his nose. "Maybe another time. I'm going to go join the boys and work out a training plan for when you're back to top health again."

I shot him an understanding smile. "Your loss..."

He cupped my cheek gently and kissed me softly from upside down. *Just* like Spider-Man. "I'll come back out when food arrives. What's on the menu tonight?"

"Chinese," I told him, already feeling hungry. "Don't worry, I'll overorder for you three."

He beamed. "You're the best."

I couldn't help watching him leave the room, his muscles shifting under tanned, tattooed skin. The huge battle angel in the middle of his back—the piece that represented Rachel—drew my eye like a magnet. The fact that my guys seemed to be allergic to shirts inside the house? Amazing. I never wanted that to change.

My phone buzzed with a message just as the closing credits on my movie started rolling, and I picked it up to see Dallas's name.

Dallas Moore: Katie, I'll be there in 5, okay?

It was sooner than I'd expected him, but that suited me fine. I was desperate to hear news on Bree and the baby. Fucking hell, Bree was pregnant. Did she even know yet? She hadn't mentioned it to me, and Dallas had been totally blindsided.

Madison Kate: Cool, see you soon.

I climbed out of my blanket nest and made my way to the gym to let the guys know. One of them would need to tell the gate guard to let Dallas in when he arrived because I hadn't saved the new security team's numbers yet.

"I'll order food now too," I told them. "So you've probably got another half an hour or so, all right?" I eyed their bare chests, slick with perspiration, and mentally high-fived myself. Fuck yeah, my guys were *gorgeous*.

Kody clapped his hands sharply. "You heard her! Half an hour and I want to see you *push it*." His voice was like the crack of a whip, but he shot me a cheeky wink as he turned the music back on.

Laughing to myself, I went back to the kitchen to take another painkiller. Just as I washed it down, a heavy knock sounded on the front door. Apparently Dallas's five minutes was really three.

Padding back to the foyer, I opened the heavy front door with a smile to greet my friend. Then froze.

"Maddie," Scott said, his bruised face tight with anger. "I heard your keepers have been looking for me. Well, here I am."

I stepped back, trying to slam the door shut in his face, but he jammed his foot in the gap. One heavy shove sent me staggering back a couple of steps, and Scott entered the foyer, closing the door behind him.

"Guys!" I shouted. "Guys! Scott's here!"

But the only response I got was the thumping sound of their music as Kody pushed them through a thirty-minute power session. *Fuck*.

I darted to the side, intending to run for help, but Scott moved faster than I'd realized he could, snatching a handful of my hair and wrenching me back to him.

"Maddie, stop it!" he snapped, giving me a rough shake like that would somehow make me more amenable to what he wanted. "Stop this! You're acting like I'm some crazy person. I'm not! All I've *ever* done is try to protect you, and this is the thanks I get? You put out a notice to detain me for your psychotic boyfriends to kill? What the fuck, Maddie?"

Fury rushed through me in waves, and my teeth clenched together hard. "Let me go, Scott," I ordered him, my voice a low growl. "Let me the fuck go. You don't wanna be labeled a crazy person? Don't fucking force your way into my house and hurt me!"

His grip loosened a fraction, and I thought I'd succeeded. But then it tightened again, and he gave a low, bitter laugh. "Oh yeah, I'm really going to let you go so you can run off to those *criminals* before I can explain things to you."

Frustration made my eyes burn, and I reached down to my pants to find my knife. Fuck this. Seriously.

"Scott, no offense, but I don't wanna hear your bullshit explanations," I told him. In a smooth, practiced motion, I pulled my knife out of my pocket, flicked it open, then sliced it across his wrist holding my hair.

He let out a shout, releasing my hair and giving me an opportunity to jerk free. But now I had my back to the wall and Scott was blocking the hallway to the gym. If I wanted to get help, I needed to get past him first.

My blade out in front of me, I eyed him carefully. His hand was clasped to his wrist where I'd cut him, bright blood staining his skin, but I knew it hadn't been a deep cut. He knew it too because a second later he started laughing.

"Seriously?" he challenged me, looking at my knife with a mocking smile. "You're going to threaten me with that pathetic little blade? It's so pretty; did it come as a bonus accessory in your Barbie Dreamhouse?" He was snickering at his own joke, but adrenaline, fear, and determination flooded my blood.

Two side steps took me to the hall table with the huge arrangement of flowers, and a second later, I had Steele's backup gun in my hand and pointed at Scott's head.

"How about now, Scott? Does this work for you?" My voice was cold and calm. I barely even recognized it as mine, but my hand remained steady too.

Scott's eyes narrowed, flashing with raw hatred and anger, and his mouth twisted in an ugly sneer. "You're not going to shoot me, Maddie. I bet you don't even know *how* to fire that thing. Girls like you, Maddie, are only good for one thing. Apparently your *three* keepers already worked that out for themselves, huh?"

My stomach clenched, but that cold calm was spreading over my whole body now. "Slut-shaming. Real original."

Scott just scoffed, his posture far too relaxed. "It's not slut-shaming, Maddie. It's just the fucking truth. You're so dumb, you know that? People out there are trying to kill you, and all it takes is a text from a trusted number to make you open the door. How *stupid* can you be? That's why, Maddie. That's why you'll only ever be good for fucking. God knows your brain isn't worth shit." With each insult he spat, he was inching closer. He thought I hadn't noticed, but really…

"I'm fucking done with this, Scott," I told him in a flat,

emotionless voice. "I'm done with you terrorizing me. I'm done with the packages and the phone calls and the photos. I'm *done*. Kiss my ass, motherfucker."

Bang.

The gun kicked in my hand, but my aim was true. Scott inching closer had made sure of that for me. The bullet hit him clean between the eyes and sent his body sprawling across the black-and-white tiles of the foyer.

For a moment, I stayed exactly where I was, my gun aimed at Scott's body. But when the puddle of blood began to spread, I decided he wasn't getting back up to grab me like in a horror movie. I gingerly stepped over his legs and hurried down the hallway to the gym, where the music had just shut off.

The door burst open as I arrived, and all three guys rushed into the corridor, probably having heard the gunshot.

"Um," I said, licking my lips and looking down at the gun still clenched in my hand. "Something happened."

CHAPTER 47

The guys cleaned up my crime scene with professional efficiency. There was no suggestion to call the police. Not only were almost all of them under the payroll of one of Shadow Grove's gangs but Scott's brother *was* a cop. Even with all the guys' connections and payoffs, it was unlikely Shane could be kept quiet.

Kody found Dallas's phone in Scott's pocket, and a quick call to the hospital confirmed he was still there by Bree's side, totally unaware anyone had stolen his phone. He hadn't planned to leave the hospital until visiting hours were over in another hour.

Archer called his security guys—the ones watching Scott's house—and told them what'd happened in a rather abridged version of events. He also told them to search the property fully and subdue anyone who interfered.

"Why bother?" I asked when he hung up the call. I sat on the bottom step of the stairs, watching with cold detachment as Kody and Steele wrapped Scott's body in plastic sheeting and scrubbed the blood and brain matter off the walls and marble floor. The Persian rug in the entryway was a lost cause, though, so they just rolled it up and stacked it beside the body.

Scott's body. My *stalker's* body.

Archer crouched down in front of me, his body blocking the sight of the plastic-wrapped dead man that I'd been staring at.

"He could have been a copycat stalker," he told me quietly, repeating his theory we'd discussed previously, "or he could have been working with someone. I want any scrap of evidence from inside his home to be sure."

Dread washed through me, and I felt my face drain of blood. Another stalker?

Archer was quick to reassure me, though. "I doubt that's the case. The tone of all his messages was possessive, obsessed. People like that don't share, and the terminology was all wrong. It was *mine* not *ours*." He stroked my hair back behind my ear. "Searching his place is just a precaution, okay?"

I nodded, still trapped in a weird halfway point between terrified and numb as fuck. He leaned in to kiss my forehead, and I let my eyelids close briefly. I was so damn tired, but this...this was the beginning of the end. Wasn't it? My stalker was gone. Dead. Now I just needed to get the hit on me canceled, and it was smooth sailing forever.

Right? That was how these things were meant to work out? The bad guys got caught, killed, dealt with in some way, and then the heroine gets to skip off into the sunset for her happily ever after?

I snickered out loud at that thought. Bree always defined her storybook happily ever after as the main character getting marriage and babies in the end. It was something we'd had many, many arguments about—because shouldn't a kickass woman who'd saved the world deserve more? But I was fast coming to terms with the fact that people's perceptions of happily ever after could vary dramatically.

For Bree, she was already getting hers in a way. She would have a hard road ahead with physical therapy and surgeries to mend her bones, but she had *love*. She had Dallas, who thought the absolute world of her, and she had her second chance at a baby.

393

"What's funny?" Archer asked, his thumb stroking over my cheek and coming away damp.

I met his gaze, searching his ice-blue eyes and remembering how cold and cruel I used to find them. "Just contemplating what our future might look like," I admitted.

His brow twitched. "*Our* future?"

I gave a one-shouldered shrug. "Yeah. Mine, *yours*...Kody's, and Steele's. Ours. Is that a problem, D'Ath?" A touch of sass lit my tone, and I found I was slowly wading out of the numb haze I'd fallen into the moment my fingers touched the handle of the gun.

Archer's gaze narrowed slightly; then a grin tugged at his lips. "I wouldn't have it any other way, Wifey." He cupped my face in his hands, kissing me tenderly, like an unspoken declaration of his *love*. Fucking hell, I thought shitty angry Archer was overwhelming? He had nothing on open, honest, and *in love* Archer.

I scoffed a laugh. "You're such a liar," I accused him with an eye roll. "You hate having to share me."

He kissed me again, possessive and demanding, as his teeth pulled on my lip, making me moan.

"True," he admitted. "But I'll do anything to see you happy, Princess. Fucking *anything*."

"Arch!" Kody called out, coming through from the garage with his phone in his hand. "You're going to wanna hear this." He sat on the step beside me. Steele joined us, wiping blood-tinted, soapy water from his hands with a rag.

Kody held his phone out in front of us, the speakerphone icon lit up. "All right, go ahead, Sampson, I've got you on speaker."

"Right then," the man on the other end said. "I'll send through documentation images shortly but wanted to give you a quick briefing. This guy was definitely the stalker you've been hunting. His bedroom held all kinds of incriminating evidence. Copies of your girl's schedule, printouts from security footage, codes for all our gates and surveillance systems. Boss, there's some creepy-ass dolls here, all with their hair dyed pink." He paused, exhaling heavily, and that creeping numbness froze me over again. "There's more. I'll package it all up anyway, but it looks like this kid has been obsessed for a long time. And I found different passports and licenses, all with different names and dates of birth. He could have been anything from eighteen right up to thirty-two."

The shocks weren't even hitting me anymore. It was all just noise because I'd heard what I needed to know. Scott was guilty. I hadn't just shot an innocent guy out of panic and paranoia.

Kody wrapped his arm around me, sensing I needed the comfort. Maybe because he was crazy intuitive.

"Thanks for that, Sampson," Kody said to the guy on the other end. "Box it all up and bring it back. We can have a more thorough look here."

"You got it, boss," the man replied.

Archer spoke before the call could end, asking the other pressing question. "Sampson, any signs pointing at a coconspirator?"

"None," Sampson replied. "Nah, this is a solo job for sure. Everything here screams sexual obsession, and those freaks don't play nice with others."

"Thanks," Archer replied, his tone edged with relief.

Sampson drew a breath, then hesitated like he had something else he wanted to say but second-guessed it.

"Something else?" Archer asked, frowning at the phone.

The call rustled slightly, maybe from Sampson releasing that breath in a sigh. "Yeah, boss. Just…this is some fucked-up shit. If it were my girl…" He broke off, making a sound of disgust. "I understand this is crossing the professional line here, but you three better treat that woman like a goddamn queen the rest of her life. No one should have this crap happen. The fucked-up psychological shit that this whack job has been cultivating? That's way worse than physical pain."

There was a pause, and my eyes burned hot with unshed tears.

It was Steele who answered, though. "That's exactly what we intend to do, Sampson." His eyes were locked on me, though, not the phone.

I didn't hear what their security guy replied before Kody ended the call, my gaze captured by the deep sincerity in Steele's eyes. He meant every word of that promise, and it warmed my cold heart.

"All right, let's get this dealt with," Kody said, giving my waist a gentle squeeze before standing up. "Steele and I can handle the body if you want to stay with MK?" he asked Archer.

I shook my head, though. "No, I need to come with you. I need to see this right through to the end."

All three of them gave me worried frowns, but I shrugged off their concern. "Just give me five minutes to put jeans on."

"Hellcat, you don't have to—" Steele started to protest, but I cut him off with a sharp gesture as I stood up from my step.

"I do," I insisted, firm. "We're a team, right? The four of us? We're in this together, no matter what?" He nodded, and I flickered my gaze over the other two for their affirmations. "Then yes, I need to come with you."

I left it at that, hurrying up the stairs to my bedroom to get changed into more disposing-of-a-body appropriate attire. What the fuck that looked like, I had no idea. I just went clichéd and put on black skinny jeans, flat boots, and a black hoodie that I'd stolen from one of the guys. Boys' hoodies were so damn comfy.

My knife went into the pocket of my jeans. Now that it'd saved my life three times over, I wasn't ever leaving the house without it again.

When I made my way back downstairs, I found the boys had changed too, throwing T-shirts, hoodies, and jeans on, seeing as they'd all been in just gym shorts before. The rolled-up carpet was nowhere to be seen, and the plastic-wrapped body was gone too.

To the unsuspecting eye, there were absolutely no signs that a man had died in the foyer less than an hour ago.

Steinwick totally knew, though. He was standing in the doorway with his hands on his hips and a deep frown across his wrinkled face as he glared down at the tiles.

"Miss Danvers." He greeted me, looking up as I reached the bottom step. "I hope you're feeling better today."

I lifted my brow; then I remembered the bruised-up, giggling mess I'd come home as yesterday and jerked a short nod.

He gave me a tight smile. "Good. I'll ensure this mess is cleaned up before you get back, sir," he said to Archer, waving a hand at the spotless floor, which was missing its rug.

Kody snickered and rolled his eyes, but Steele scowled like Steinwick had deliberately insulted his cleaning skills.

Archer just headed through to the garage, and we followed behind him. He passed all the fancy sports cars and expensive SUVs, then popped the driver's door open on a midrange silver sedan. Oh yeah, this was their "transporting dead people" car *for sure*.

"Let's go," he said, clicking the garage door open and sliding behind the wheel. Kody and Steele jumped into the backseat, leaving the passenger seat open for me. It took me a couple of seconds to force myself inside, though.

Gritting my teeth against my welling anxiety, I pulled the door closed but flinched at the sound of my seat belt buckling. Yeah, the crash with Bree hadn't done wonders for my car anxiety, that was for sure.

"Are you okay?" Archer murmured quietly as we drove out of the garage and down the main driveway.

I jerked a sharp nod, my fingers gripping the strap of my seat belt in a white-knuckled grip. Mainly because I was badly fighting the urge to cry from pure stress and fear. Also because I couldn't handle the sensation of the diagonal belt across my tender bruising.

"I'm fine," I croaked, feeling cold sweat beading on my chest.

Archer raised a brow at me, clearly not buying my shit, but he didn't call me on the lie. He just reached out, his hand finding its favorite place on the inside of my knee as he drove. Somehow, that worked. A small amount of my fear eased with every moment his heavy, warm hand rested on my leg. It was grounding me, reminding me that I was in good hands.

––––––––––

We drove for a little over an hour in near silence, everyone lost in their own thoughts and no one even turning the stereo on. Eventually, though, Archer turned off the rural road we'd been following for miles and onto a dirt driveway.

"Where are we?" I asked, trying to peer at a sign as we passed it. It was dark outside, though, and we were going too fast for me to make out the details.

"Benny's Pig Farm," Steele answered, drumming his fingers on the door handle as we approached a farmhouse. "We've got an arrangement with the owner."

I wanted to ask more, but I also totally lacked the energy to make my thoughts into words. So I just waited and watched. When we stopped, Steele hopped out of the car, approaching the middle-aged man who came out of the house to greet us. No one else made any moves to leave the car, though, so I stayed put as well.

Steele and the man—Benny, I supposed—exchanged a few words; then Steele handed him an envelope. Benny then went back inside the house while Steele returned to us in the car.

"All clear," he advised Archer as he slipped back into his seat.

Archer started the car again, driving past the farmhouse and farther into the property, then pulling up outside some fenced-off pens.

"You can stay here if you want," Archer told me as he, Kody, and Steele climbed out. Arch reached down to pop the trunk open, and I shook my head in refusal. I needed to see it through to the end.

I climbed out of my seat, tucking my arms tight around me as

I watched the guys unload Scott's body from the trunk. Kody used his own butterfly knife—an emerald green one that I'd never seen before—to slice through all the plastic sheeting they'd packaged Scott up in. Then he and Steele hoisted the body up between them and tossed it straight into the middle of the pig pen. Clothes and all.

"You're not serious, are you?" I whispered, aghast. "That's... guys, that's not going to work. This isn't a movie. Pigs don't just chow down on a human body and leave no evidence after the fact."

As if perfectly on cue, there was a sickening sound of crunching bone. Shocked, I moved across to the fence just in time to see a huge, hairy pig rip Scott's hand off his body, then trot away to eat it in peace.

What. The. Fuck?

"Trust us, Hellcat. This one is pretty damn foolproof." Steele gently moved me away from the pigpen as the rest of the animals swarmed the corpse and the gut-churning sound of tearing flesh filled the air.

I shook my head in stunned disbelief. "I don't know if I'm horrified or impressed. Which one of you twisted fucks even thought of this?"

The three of them exchanged smug smiles, knowing full well I wasn't actually horrified.

"We can't claim credit for this one," Steele told me with a laugh. "A friend of a friend suggested it some time ago, and it's worked out well ever since. So much more reliable than dumping weighted bodies off the coast."

"And quicker," Kody added. "Remember how long those boat trips used to take?" He grimaced, and I just shook my head again. These guys were a whole other breed. Maybe Bark was onto something with his alien theory after all.

"So now what happens?" I asked, snuggling closer into Steele's warmth.

Archer shrugged, leaning against the side of the car. "We wait until the pigs do their thing so we can see with our own eyes that it's all gone. Then we dispose of the plastic wrapping at a recycling facility a few miles from here and head home again."

I couldn't fight my grin. "You guys recycle the plastic you use to transport bodies?"

Archer gave me a serious look. "If we don't take active steps toward a greener planet, we'll fuck it right up."

"Worse than it already is," Kody added, peering over the fence to check the pigs' progress. "I think we're good to go." He pulled out his phone, using the flashlight app to check the pen more thoroughly. "Yep, all done."

"That was fast," I murmured, following as they all piled back into the car.

Archer shot me a smirk. "Hungry pigs today."

He drove us out of Benny's Pig Farm without stopping at the main house again, and a few minutes later, we pulled into the parking lot of the recycling plant. It was deserted, closed for the day already, but there was a self-service drop-off zone where you could dispose of recyclables through segregated chutes.

Steele climbed out, grabbed the plastic sheeting from the trunk, and strode across the gravel to drop it in the plastics area.

I watched him go, but my attention caught on something red that kept flickering on the side of the building. The facility was totally closed up, though. We were the only car in the lot. So what was making that red light flicker?

"Guys," I murmured when my curiosity burned. "What's making that red light?"

Kody leaned forward from the backseat, trying to see what I was pointing at. "I don't see it," he replied.

I frowned, no longer seeing it myself. Maybe it'd been a trick of my imagination or something. But then it flickered again.

"There!" I said, pointing. When neither Kody nor Archer seemed to follow my line of sight, I let out a frustrated sound and pushed my door open, climbing out to get a better look. They both followed me, and Steele gave us a curious look as we headed in his direction.

"What's going on?" he asked, meeting us halfway across the parking lot after discarding of the plastic responsibly.

I frowned in the direction of the light…which was now gone again. Was I going crazy?

"MK saw something that worried her," Kody answered. "We couldn't see what it was, so we're taking a closer look…right, babe?" He tilted his head as he looked to me for confirmation.

I nodded slowly.

"Okay, well—" Steele paused what he was about to say, pulling his phone from his pocket to check a message. Then his brow furrowed in a deep frown. "This can't be good," he muttered, then held the phone out for us to see.

It was a text message from a private number with just three words and a video link.

I swallowed heavily, staring down at the screen.

For Madison Kate.

Someone knew I didn't have my phone on me…so they'd messaged Steele instead. Archer reached out and hit play on the video link, and instantly my skin prickled. Cold sweat broke out all over my body and my heart raced so hard I thought it might stop beating.

The video was shaky and a bit blurred, seemingly taken on someone's phone through the window at our front door. But the content was clear enough. It showed me shooting Scott in the head, then standing over his body totally expressionless and cold. Then I just…walked away with the gun in my hand.

My stomach churned with icy terror, but the message wasn't over.

Once I was gone from the camera, the video faded into blackness and words appeared on the screen, letter by letter, in a bloodred font.

WHOOPS, WRONG PERSON. YOU MISSED.

My chest tightened and my pulse thundered in my ears as that message faded and a new one appeared.

I NEVER MISS.

Understanding flashed across my mind in a split second as the red light appeared again, but this time in the middle of Steele's chest. It was a dot. A red dot…like a laser sight might make.

A panicked scream tore out of me at the same time as the shot echoed through the silent night air.

Something hard and heavy slammed into me, and my face scraped against the gravel of the parking lot. Pain ricocheted through my chest and I cried out, but it was no use.

Blood coated the ground in front of my face and an anguished scream tore out of me. I stared into a beautiful, heartbreakingly familiar pair of gray eyes and watched as the light ebbed from them.

That last message repeated over and over in my mind.

I never miss.

BONUS SCENE
SET BETWEEN CHAPTER 1 & 2

Steele

Pain lanced through me, worse than any pain I'd ever experienced, and I barely swallowed back my shout of agony. Considering I'd been shot, stabbed, *and* burned in my lifetime, for me to admit this pain was worse...that was saying a lot. I'd been warned, of course, but arrogantly, I figured I was tough enough.

I was wrong. But that was a good thing. I *needed* the pain. I *needed* to hurt. The injuries inflicted on my flesh were nothing compared to how she must be feeling—Madison Kate, my Hellcat. The look on her face as she'd shut down, as she'd *shut us out*, hurt like a bullet through the chest.

"You good?" The middle-aged woman covered in tattoos named Betty raised a brow at me, her needle poised to enter my flesh for a second time.

I swallowed hard before nodding. "Yep," I confirmed, despite how tense my entire body was. "Keep going. Please."

She replied with a one shoulder shrug. "Tap out anytime, you don't have to be a hero and do them all at once."

It was the same thing she'd already warned me multiple times, but I was determined. I needed to punish myself. "I'm fine," I muttered. "Keep going."

"All right." She reached up to adjust her light slightly, then quickly punctured the soft skin of my dick with her needle for the second time. *Fuuuuuck.*

Every part of me wanted to jerk and protect my junk, but my piercer had been crystal-clear when she told me to stay *still*. Otherwise, the spacing wouldn't be perfect, and that would drive me nuts after it was all said and done. Part of me was clinging to the hope that one day Hellcat would forgive me for letting Archer's lies build and that she might like my new piercings. So they needed to be perfect.

With that in mind—but not so in mind that things grew awkward for my piercer—I closed my eyes and gritted my teeth against the pain. According to my expert, most guys only got three rungs on their ladder, but I'd asked for eight. A perfect octave.

After the next few, she stopped asking if I was okay and got on with the task while I tried to meditate, tried to distance myself from the physical pain—but my mind simply replaced it with the emotional pain of what we'd done to MK. I was fucked either way.

"You're all done," Betty told me after what felt like an eternity of pain. My dick throbbed and not in a good way, but when she presented me with a mirror and I inspected the eight perfectly spaced barbells decorating the underside of my shaft, it was worth it…hopefully Hellcat would agree. One day.

"Thanks," I grunted, gingerly sitting up.

Betty pulled off her gloves with a clinical snap as she rolled her chair away to give me space. "All right. I'll go over the aftercare instructions again, but I'm also giving you this printout so you don't forget." She pulled out a pamphlet from her drawer, then started rattling off the rules that I'd already heard before she began. No sex until the piercings healed—that wouldn't be an issue. I'd found my soul mate and my dick was hers. Until she came back to me—to *us*—I'd be celibate.

I listened to the rules, though, carefully putting my clothes back on and wincing when the fabric touched my swollen cock. I needed to ice it or something.

The drive home was a slow one with me sitting awkwardly in my seat to protect my dick, then I parked right at the front door and made a beeline for the kitchen freezer. I spotted a bag of frozen peas and grabbed them, since frozen peas made a much better ice pack than ice itself. They just molded better to the body.

A low groan rolled out of me as I cupped the vegetables to my dick.

"Uh, should I give you some privacy?"

I startled so hard I knocked my elbow on the countertop, spinning around to find our cook, Anna, watching me with bemusement.

"Um. No. Sorry this is…not what it looks like," I replied, feeling my face flame with embarrassment. I didn't exactly want to go telling her about my new jewelry but also didn't want her thinking I was developing some kind of frozen veggie kink.

She held her hands up. "I don't wanna know. You do you, hon." With a smirk, she left the kitchen before I could find any words to explain, and I groaned.

Alone, I leaned against the counter and let the cold peas do their work to numb my throbbing cock. I stared at the clock on the wall, lost in thought about MK. She was out there, without protection—without *us*—thanks to the stupid-ass secrets we'd been keeping. Sure, it had been Archer's shit to tell, but the second I started developing feelings for her, I should have said something.

I shifted the bag of peas to my other hand and pulled out my phone. No new calls. No new messages. Just a depressing list of my attempts to contact her, with no answer or response.

Footsteps coming down the main staircase saw me shifting the peas off my crotch to straighten up. I hadn't told anyone about my piercing appointment and wasn't keen to brag about it either. It was personal.

Archer stomped through the kitchen door with a scowl on his

face and a duffel bag slung over his shoulder, then hesitated when he saw me standing there. "You good?" He nodded to the bag of peas I'd shifted onto my hand. It wasn't unusual for us to ice our knuckles like this after punching the shit out of someone.

I jerked a nod. "Yeah, fine. You going somewhere?"

He didn't answer straightaway, his face impassive and guarded. Bastard was still hiding shit from us, and he wasn't even trying to act like he wasn't. "Yeah," he finally admitted with a small sigh. "Aspen."

My brows shot up and I clicked my tongue piercing against my teeth. "You found her." It wasn't a question; it was a statement. There was only one reason Archer would be leaving Shadow Grove right now and it sure as shit wasn't for a ski trip.

His small, tight nod was all I got. Then he continued out of the house and slammed the front door behind himself. I shifted the peas back where I needed them and listened for the rumble of his engine firing up. Stubborn, selfish asshole.

I discarded my bag of not-so-frozen peas. Now that I was being a little less dramatic, I had to admit the piercings didn't hurt quite as much as I'd been imagining. Some of my tattoos had been worse, come to think of it.

Sighing, I pulled up Kody's contact on my phone and hit dial. It rang only a couple of times before he picked up with a curt "*What?*"

"Arch found her in Aspen," I told him. Hellcat had disappeared after leaving our house with Cass and Zane, and we knew they'd covered her tracks. It was Bree's disappearance that tipped us off to her leaving Shadow Grove entirely.

"Aspen?" Kody exclaimed, then muttered something about Bree's family money. "When do we leave?"

I took a moment, weighing the options before I replied. "We don't." The words tasted like acid. "She wants space *away* from us, and I think we have to give it to her."

Kody cursed and it sounded like he'd just broken something, but I knew him well enough that he agreed with me. Now, more than ever, we had to respect her boundaries. She left for a *reason* and it sure as fuck wasn't just to make us follow.

"Her stalker—" Kody started to protest.

"Arch has just left," I cut him off. "He'll keep her safe, and she'll never even know he's there."

Kody grunted his agreement. We both knew Archer was such a stubborn prick, he'd rather drink hydrochloric acid than apologize to her. It'd take more than a few days to shake better sense into him, but I had total faith that he would ensure no one harmed her in the meantime. Her eternal shadow, protecting her from the darkness for much longer than she knew.

"Are you coming home?" I asked Kody after a moment of tense silence. We were all dealing with the fallout in our own ways, but I was worried about him.

"Maybe tomorrow," he replied, a heaviness in his voice that made my chest ache. He was hurting just as much as I was. We'd both fallen so hard for Madison Kate Danvers, it was almost laughable…if it hadn't been so painful right now.

He ended the call, and I stared down at my phone screen a long time. Then I opened my unanswered message thread.

She wouldn't read it. She hadn't read a single one of my messages since before the night she almost died of a fentanyl overdose. But that didn't stop me from trying…

Me: Whatever it takes, however long it takes, I'll earn your forgiveness. One day we'll be together again but in the meantime I hope Bree is being good to you. Tell her not to hold back on the insults, we all deserve it.

I sent that one, then sighed heavily as I typed out one more and sent it.

Me: Merry Christmas, Hellcat. I miss you.

AUTHOR'S NOTE

I don't even know if this is totally safe to chat with you right now.
Maybe I should give my Author's Note a skip this time?

Naaaaaaaaaahhhh, you're tough! You knew this was gonna be
a doozy from the moment you read the first chapter. YOU GOT
THIS! But just in case you're currently plotting MY death, I'm
gonna give you a quick sec.

...

We good? All forgiven? Sweet! Well then, let's move on to the
important shit for this part of the writing process. Acknowledgments
for the people and things that majorly helped me get through and
create a book that, quietly, I'm super proud to be sending out into
the great, wide world.

As always, I couldn't make my books what they are without the help of my awesome editors, Heather and Jax. They
seriously held my hand on this one. And by "held my hand,"
I do mean they kicked my ass relentlessly. I'm a sucker for the
paaaain.

Thank you, this time around, to the handful of seriously awesome, strong, hardworking women in the author community who
recognized when I was struggling and did everything they could

to build me up and support me. They're legit crown fixers and true friends. You badass bitches rock, you know that?

This book, this whole series, has been such a surreal experience. These characters have sucked me into their world like none other, and for the first time in forever, I'm wondering if I should really learn to type properly, just so I can get the words down faster! For those who've seen me type on Zoom lives, you'll know I use three fingers and look like a drunk T-rex.

Anyway, I'll keep this sucker short and sweet because I'm already neck deep in *Kate* and am just dying to see what happens next. How about you? Are you ready to see how MK's story concludes?

If the answer to that is a bittersweet kind of "I dunno, man, I really like these damaged fuckers," then you're in luck. I already have a new series in the works, which is also set in Shadow Grove. Book one is called *7th Circle*, and if you jump all over my ass in my readers group on Facebook, then I might be persuaded to share a bonus POV from one of the leads…Hades.

Thank you for reading! Thank you for reviewing (wink wink), and thank you for not pinning my picture to your wall and throwing darts in retaliation for this ending. Heh. Yeaaaaaah.

ABOUT THE AUTHOR

Tate James is a *USA Today* bestselling author of contemporary romance and romantic suspense, with occasional forays into fantasy, paranormal romance, and urban fantasy. She was born and raised in Aotearoa (New Zealand) but now lives in Australia with her husband and their adorable crotchfruit.

She is a lover of books, booze, cats, and coffee and is most definitely not a morning person. Tate is a bit too sarcastic, swears far too much for polite society, and definitely tells too many dirty jokes.